THE BOOK *of* BOOKS

BEYOND THE SACRED PAGE

A Novel

The Tyndale Translation

JACK CAVANAUGH

GRAND RAPIDS, MICHIGAN 49530 USA

We want to hear from you. Please send your comments about this book to us in care of the address below. Thank you.

ZONDERVAN™

Beyond the Sacred Page

Requests for information should be addressed to:
Zondervan, *Grand Rapids, Michigan 49530*

Library of Congress Cataloging-in-Publication Data

Cavanaugh, Jack.
Beyond the sacred page : the Tyndale translation / Jack Cavanaugh.
p. cm. — (Book of books ; bk. 2)
ISBN 0-310-21575-7
1. Tyndale, William, d. 1536 — Fiction. 2. Great Britain — History — Tudors, 1485–1603 — Fiction. 3. Foxe, John, 1516–1587 — Fiction. 4. Bible — Translating — Fiction. 5. Translators — Fiction. 6. Reformation — Fiction.
I. Title.
PS3553.A965 B49 2003
813'.54 — dc21 2002151905

Published in association with the literary agency of Alive Communications, Inc., 7680 Goddard Street, Suite 200, Colorado Springs, CO 80920.

Interior design by Tracy Moran

Printed in the United States of America

03 04 05 06 07 08 09 /❖ DC/ 10 9 8 7 6 5 4 3 2 1

To Joan Bocher

Through your sacrifice may we learn the value of God's Word.

Joan Bocher was charged with heresy during the reign of King Henry VIII for distributing among the ladies of the court copies of William Tyndale's forbidden English translation of the New Testament. Later, after an unsuccessful attempt to persuade her to recant, she was condemned to death. Joan was burned at the stake on May 2, 1550, in Smithfield, England.

Hebrews 4:12

For the worde off god is quycke & myghty in operacion and sharper then eny two edged swearde: and entreth through, even unto the dividynge asonder of the soule and the sprete and of the joyntes, and the mary: and judgeth the thoughtes and the intent off the herte.

TYNDALE'S NEW TESTAMENT, 1526

Forsothe the worde of god is quycke & spedy in wirchyng & more able for to peerse than al two eggide swerde & strecchyinge departide of soule & spirit & or joyntours & merowis & the departer (or demer) of thoughtis & intenciouns of hertis.

WYCLIFFE'S ENGLISH NEW TESTAMENT, 1380

For the word of God is liuely, and mightie in operation, and sharper then any two edged sword, and entreth through, even vnto the diuiding asunder of the soule and the spirit, and of the joynts, and the marow, and is a discerner of the thoughts, and the intents of the heart.

THE GENEVA BIBLE, 1560

For the word of God is living, and powerful, and sharper than any two-edged sword, piercing even to the dividing asunder of soul and spirit, and of joints and marrow, and is a discerner of the thoughts and intents of the heart.

THE KING JAMES VERSION, 1611

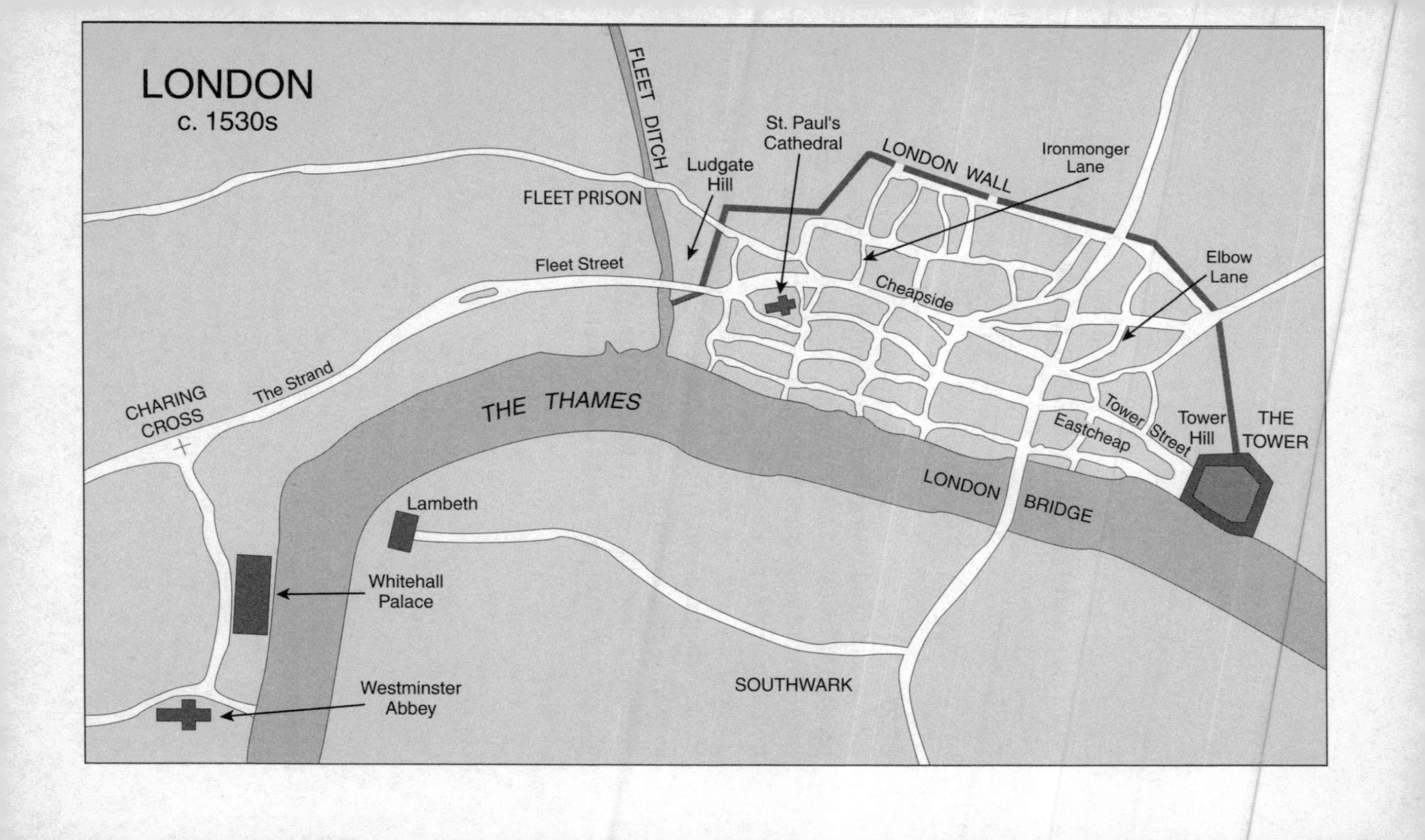
LONDON
c. 1530s
FLEET DITCH
St. Paul's Cathedral
LONDON WALL
Ironmonger Lane
Ludgate Hill
FLEET PRISON
Fleet Street
Elbow Lane
Cheapside
The Strand
CHARING CROSS
THE THAMES
Tower Street
Tower Hill
THE TOWER
Eastcheap
LONDON BRIDGE
Lambeth
Whitehall Palace
Westminster Abbey
SOUTHWARK

Acknowledgments

A special thank-you to Rebecca Farnbach for the gracious loan of her copy of Tyndale's New Testament and video documentary on the English translations of the Bible. Both were extremely helpful as historical references for this novel.

And my undying gratitude to Dave Lambert, Bob Hudson, Robin Schmitt, and the staff at Zondervan for their patience and support during the writing of this novel. Personal health-related problems delayed the project unduly. Through it all they were compassionate and supportive. I'm in your debt.

Prologue

April 1535

The door to the print shop banged open.

"Herr Löwe is coming for his order!"

The pressman froze, as did the three compositors and two apprentices. Anxious glances were exchanged.

"You heard him!" the pressman shouted.

The room sprang to life with a feverish intensity that hadn't been there before. The compositors dumped type from their trays as the herald slammed the door shut behind him and ran to assist an apprentice, who was pulling down sheets of drying text draped over a rope strung between presses. The two of them looked like washerwomen hauling in laundry beneath darkening skies.

Gunther, the younger apprentice, cleared a long table of stacked sheets of finished pages, replacing them with stacks of theater advertisements while the pressman, with speed that comes from years of experience, rammed a wooden bar into a hole that operated the press's worm screw. He pulled, removed the bar, sought the next hole, and pulled again, raising the press. His gaze alternated between the press and the front door.

"Gunther!" he yelled. "Make the river run!"

The thirteen-year-old boy shivered at the sound of his name. This would be his first river run. For a year he'd hounded his uncle to let him make the run, but the answer had always been one excuse after another. *"You're too young." "You're too puny." "Your legs are too short."*

"Schnell, Gunther! *Schnell!"*

Ripping off his apron, Gunther ran to the back of the shop, grabbing a canvas bag along the way.

A stack of twenty books sat on a counter. He thrust them into the bag hurriedly, one at a time, careful not to damage them. They were small, as books went. Compact. Six inches tall, four inches wide, one and a half inches thick. They fit comfortably in his hand.

The ink-stained fist of the pressman grabbed his arm, startling him, knocking the last book from his hand. It hit the floor hard, denting the top corner of the cover.

Gunther braced himself for the thunder that would most certainly follow. Instead concerned eyes locked onto him.

"Do you recall what I told you about the lion?"

"Ja, Onkel."

"Repeat it."

"'Be vigilant; because your adversary the devil, as a roaring lion, walketh about, seeking whom he may devour.'"

The door to the print shop slammed open a second time. Soldiers with lances stormed through the opening.

"Remember, Gunther, vigilant! Now go! Go!" the pressman whispered. "And God be with you."

Gunther dropped to his knees. Snatching up the damaged book, he tossed it into the bag. His uncle's legs provided him cover.

Opening a cabinet door, Gunther crawled inside and pulled the bag in after him. The cabinet door slammed shut with a kick of his uncle's heel.

The quarters in which Gunther found himself were dark and cramped. He lay on his side, his head bent at an awkward angle, his chin pressed against his chest. From the other side of the cabinet door he could hear shouts and curses. A tray of type clattered to the floor, scattering the alphabet across hardwood.

While his uncle's intent was to encourage the boy, in the darkness of the cabinet his words triggered an onslaught of nerves. Gunther had always fantasized the river run to be a great adventure, one in which he cleverly outwitted an army of soldiers. But just now, when his uncle spoke to him, Gunther had seen fear in the stout printer's eyes. And it scared him.

What if he couldn't outwit the soldiers? What if they caught him with the bag? Gunther bit his lower lip in an attempt to fight back a rising tide of tears.

Just then something heavy slammed to the floor in the print shop. Two voices erupted in a duet of shouts. One voice belonged to his uncle. He was buying time so Gunther could make good his escape.

Gunther wiped his nose with the back of his hand. *Dummkopf! No one will think you're a man if you cry like a boy.*

His hands moved across the back panel of the cabinet, feeling for latches that held it in place. There were two of them. Once they were turned, the panel opened outward. He found them. Sunlight burst into his darkness. Gunther squinted against the glare.

He shoved the panel to let himself out. It moved barely an inch, then hit something solid. Gunther's heart stopped cold. He pushed again, with the same result. Panic covered him like a cold sheet.

He pressed his cheek against the panel to see what was blocking it. Looking up, he saw the rim of a wooden barrel, arched against the blue sky like a rusty rainbow.

His uncle's voice came from beyond the cabinet door. "Search every shelf and cabinet in this shop," he shouted. "You'll not find any heretical literature here."

Any moment now the cabinet door would open and a soldier's face would appear. Gunther's time was running out.

He shoved the panel. As before, it didn't move.

So this was to be his legacy. For generations German fathers would tell their children the sad tale of the puny printer's apprentice who boasted he was big enough to make the river run. And how when his chance came, he failed. As a result his uncle, who believed his boasts, was sent to prison for many, many years. All because little Gunther wasn't as big as he claimed to be.

Well, Gunther wasn't going to let that happen to his uncle. He clenched his teeth, mustered his energy, and shoved the panel with a strength he didn't know he had. The barrel budged. Not much, but it budged.

Encouraged, he tried again. Bit by bit, with repeated effort, Gunther managed to move the barrel until finally the opening was large enough for him to wiggle through.

He reached back inside for the canvas bag and pulled it after him. It slid partway, then stopped. It was stuck.

Desperately he pulled again but the bag was wider than he was. The opening was still too small.

Jumping to his feet, Gunther grabbed the top of the wooden barrel and, planting his feet for leverage, leaned into it, spinning it inch by inch away from the panel opening. He reached for the canvas bag. This time he pulled it out.

Tossing the bag to one side, he knelt to replace the panel. Just then the cabinet door opened and Gunther could see his uncle's shoes and the boots of a soldier. He rammed the panel into place and slumped against it, holding it there with his back. For good measure, he braced his feet against the barrel.

Then he felt a thump. Whether it was a lance or a boot or a soldier's hand, he didn't know; all he knew was that someone was pushing on the panel from the shop side, hitting it, testing it. Each jab made the wood shudder against his back. Gunther held his breath.

After several more thumps there was nothing. Gunther waited. Afraid to move. Afraid to breathe.

"You! Boy!"

The voice came from the mouth of the alley.

"What are you doing there?"

Two soldiers appeared.

Their heads cocked, they attempted to see what he was leaning against. With long strides they came toward him.

Gunther grabbed the canvas bag and ran.

"Hold! Hold, I say!"

"Your adversary the devil, as a roaring lion, walketh about, seeking whom he may devour." Only his adversary wasn't walking; he was running after him.

Gunther's legs churned as he flew out the back end of the alley. He headed toward the river by way of the shopping district.

As he'd hoped, the streets of Worms were alive with morning business. He weaved in and out and around people and fruit stands and tables with clerics selling indulgences, the heavy bag on his back swaying from side to side, knocking people off balance as he passed them, adding to the commotion. Over the din of business he could hear the shouts of the guards ordering him to halt.

He slipped between two buildings, through a space barely wide enough for him and his load to pass. He had but a single thought. *Reach the wharf.* He had to make it to the wharf before the soldiers caught up with him. However, the weight on his back grew increasingly heavy and his legs were becoming wobbly. He was beginning to fear he wasn't strong enough and wouldn't make it all the way to the wharf.

Exiting the alley between the buildings, Gunther could smell the damp river air. He ran to the edge of a stone retaining wall situated high over the wharf.

"Herr Löwe is coming! Herr Löwe is coming!" he shouted.

Beyond the wharf the Rhine stretched serenely into a misty horizon, an unwitting accomplice in the religious war that was embroiling all Europe and England. It was a war that featured a new form of armament—the printed word. And Gunther had a bagful of weapons.

"Halt, boy!"

The first of the two guards emerged from the narrow alley.

Gunther tossed the canvas bag over the stone wall. With a dusty thud, it landed on the cobblestone street below just as the guard lunged for him.

Gunther ducked. Without the weight of the bag on his back, he fairly flew down the street as it paralleled the watery course, then zigzagged down to the river. Retrieving the bag at the base of the wall, he ran for the wharf.

He shouted as he ran. "Herr Löwe is coming! Herr Löwe is coming!"

Gunther saw the boat and yelled again.

A sailor's head snapped up. His eyes fell on Gunther, then on the guards close on his heels. The situation registered on his face. He leaped to the dock and began throwing off lines. Shoving the bow of the boat into the river, he scrambled aboard.

Gunther's legs grew heavy and his muscles burned. He managed to make it to the boat just as the current gripped its hull.

The pounding of the soldiers' boots on the wharf behind him told him they were close. Grabbing the canvas bag with both hands, Gunther twisted his body and flung the bag toward the deck of the boat with all his might.

The bag flew over the water and landed on the deck at the sailor's feet. A single book spilled out of the bag. The book with the dented corner.

Exhausted, Gunther collapsed onto the dock, greedily gulping down mouthfuls of sweet river air. The soldiers reached him. But there was little they could do except stand over an empty-handed boy and pant heavily and watch as the boat's sail luffed, then filled, as it propelled the craft downriver.

The sailor picked up the book from the deck. He held it over his head.

"Today you beat the lion!" he shouted.

Gunther smiled.

Chapter 1

"She's laying over!"

The captain cupped his hands around his mouth and shouted at the deck. "Larboard! Into the wind! Turn her into the wind!"

Somewhere beneath the groaning wooden planks, a helmsman fought to right the ship. His efforts had no effect. The vessel pitched onto its side as a wave the size of Goliath slammed a watery fist amidships.

Pernell Foxe released his salt beef and biscuit dinner to grab hold of the railing. His meal skidded across the tilting deck and tumbled overboard. It took every bit of Pernell's considerable strength to keep from following after it.

While he didn't mind the loss of his dinner, he wasn't about to lose sight of his prey as well. Pernell squinted against the slanting rain. The heretic Tyndale was clinging to the forward shrouds. Just then the bow of the ship rose dramatically, as though it were offering the apostate to God.

For two months Pernell had followed leads and rumors and hunches to Antwerp. While he could have arrested the heretic on the Antwerp docks, he chose instead to follow the man. God willing, the outlaw would lead him to his German printer. He envisioned not only bagging the heretic but smashing the press that printed his pernicious filth as well.

A deliberate man, Pernell Foxe had weighed the risk of delaying the arrest and determined it to be a moderate one. Once on board, where could the heretic elude him? For the length of the journey to Hamburg, the man would be confined within the ship's railings. He had given no indication that he was aware he was being followed, so all Pernell had to do was keep a discreet distance. And should the heretic recognize him aboard ship, Pernell could arrest him on the spot. He would lose only the printer. All things considered, the reward warranted the risk.

Then the weather had turned sour.

For half a day a black storm had paralleled the ship's course, looking them over. At dawn it sprang. Rain assaulted the decks above. Currents ripped at the hull beneath. Mariners scampered from the hold, their positions orchestrated by a litany of shouts from the captain, most of which Pernell didn't understand.

But a person didn't have to know the language of the sea to realize that their situation was grave. Muscled arms strained at the lines. Canvas-covered legs scurried up shrouds and masts. Furrowed brows and gaping mouths full of blackened teeth told a grim story.

Overhead, lines creaked and blocks moaned as sails were furled. Men shouted against the wind, sounding like a flock of agitated seagulls. For all their yelling, for all their effort, nothing they did countered the force of the storm. The ship was at the mercy of the horrendous wind and the mountainous swells.

Pernell examined the charred sky. A thought gave birth to a realization. *"Dixit et surrexit ventus tempestatis et elevavit gurgites eius. By His word He raised a storm wind that made the waves surge."*

Someone else was pursuing the heretic, the very One who in ancient times had tracked down a renegade prophet named Jonah. How many students at Oxford had copied these verses at Pernell's instruction?

"Dominus autem misit ventum magnum in mare; et facta est tempestas magna in mari, et navis periclitabatur conteri. Et timuerunt nautae, et clamaverunt viri ad deum suum. The L*ORD sent out a great wind into the sea, and there was a mighty tempest in the sea, so that the ship was like to be broken. Then the mariners were afraid, and cried every man unto his god."*

Like the biblical storm, this one had a divine purpose. Pernell firmly believed this. He was witnessing God's judgment on the heretic.

Because of this man's sin, a ship would perish along with everyone on board.

Clinging to the railing, Pernell pondered his fate with a theologian's template. This wasn't the first time he'd contemplated his own death. He felt a calmness that ran counter to his surroundings. This pleased him. Though he was not eager to die, neither was he afraid. He knew his life rested in the palm of God's hand. It was God who gave him life and if God were to require that life for the good of Christian England, Pernell was content to surrender it.

It didn't disturb him that his life was forfeit due to another man's sin. This too was God's economy. Better the loss of a single ship than the loss of a nation should this man's heresy reach England's shores and poison the minds of all who read it.

His only regret was that he and Meg had parted on bitter terms. Fumbling in his pocket, he withdrew a sprig of rosemary and sniffed it. The scent reminded him of Meg. His Meg. She was the only woman he'd ever loved.

He remembered the day he sailed. As always, he'd waited at the door to bid her good-bye with an embrace. She shunned him and went upstairs.

Even now her rebuke stung. At the time he was angry. Now the remembrance prompted a wry grin. Circumstances were proving her right.

She had been against his embarking on this journey. She sensed something terrible would happen. He dismissed her warnings as nothing more than female emotions. He had a duty to perform, he told her. She pleaded with him. He called her fears foolish.

"Meg."

For reasons known only to a man who is about to die, Pernell felt an all-consuming need to hear the sound of his wife's name, but the roar of the wind swept her name from his lips before it could be heard. He spoke her name again, this time louder.

"Meg!"

A cacophony of flapping canvas, shouting sailors, roaring waves, and howling winds conspired against him.

He shouted anyway. "Meg! Meg! Meg!"

The ship rose suddenly with a force that buckled his knees. He clung to the railing, his leather-soled shoes scrambling for a foothold upon the slippery deck. A monstrous wave loomed over the ship, hovering for the slightest moment like a cat eyeing a cornered mouse.

Pernell screamed at the wave as it rose.

"Meg! Meg! My wife's name is Meg!"

The heavy fist on the door downstairs brought Meg bolt upright in her bed. Confused and frightened, she clutched the sheets to her heaving chest. The sound of her breathing was exaggerated in the cavelike darkness. She waited, her ears straining against the silence.

Had it just been a dream?

Bam! Bam! Bam! Bam! Bam!

Her hand shot to her throat. *Pernell?* She reached beside her. The mattress was cold. She was alone.

The pounding started again, this time accompanied by a croak of a voice. "Open! Open, I say!"

Meg cowered in her bed, her legs pulled tightly against her chest. She was afraid to answer yet afraid not to, afraid to climb out of bed and afraid to stay where she was.

Just when she decided it was better to stay in bed and hope the intruder would grow weary in his efforts and leave, the darkness brought to life old, persistent fears. They became walls pressing in upon her, and for a moment she was back in the wedge-shaped closet beneath her parents' stairs, cramped, unable to move or make a sound, with cobwebs brushing her cheek . . .

Bam! Bam! Bam! "Open, I say! Open!"

The pounding brought her back to the present. As she scanned the darkness, her anger flared. Pernell should be here. Hadn't she warned him not to go? She spoke his name, half curse, half plea. Of course, there was no answer.

The pounding downstairs took on greater intensity.

With trembling hands she pulled the covers aside. The bed's rope webbing creaked as she swung her legs over the side. A cold wooden floor touched her feet.

In the bedroom she had no better weapon at hand than a hairbrush or candlestick, so she skittered downstairs, racing past the booming door and into the kitchen.

She found a carving knife and gripped its bone handle. The sensation of fear was immediate. The blade loosed even more memories—bloody, violent scenes that would torment her to her grave.

The knife dropped from her hand, clattering against the wooden floor. With the knife went the memories, but they'd taken their toll. Her knees turned to water. She had to steady herself with a forearm on the kitchen counter.

Bam! Bam! Bam! "Open, I say!"

Seeing no other recourse, Meg made her way to the door with empty hands. The closer she got to it, the more the pounding sounded like thunder. She knew she could never shout over it, so she waited for a pause in the assault. When it came, she was ready.

"Identify yourself!" she said. Her voice was that of a field mouse.

She heard the voice outside ask, "Did you hear something?"

A second voice answered. "Don't know. Thought I did. Could be wrong, though."

"Open up!" the first voice shouted uncertainly.

Meg swallowed. She took a deep breath and tried again.

"Identify yourselves!"

This time she was heard.

"Palace guards. We've come for Meg Foxe. I command you to open the door!"

The late-night intruders stood impatiently just inside the open door in their scarlet and gold uniforms while Meg dressed, their backs as rigid as the lances they carried. Behind them a third intruder, the night air, heavy and dank, rushed past them, invading Meg's sanctuary.

Feigning serenity, Meg adjusted her bodice as she descended the creaking wooden stairs under their watchful gaze. Her legs were uncertain and her heart was still shivering from the cold start it had received upon their rude arrival.

"You're coming with us" was all they'd said to her when she asked them where they were taking her and under whose authority.

Her fingers fumbled with two renegade strands of auburn hair, an act normally done without thought but one that now took concentrated effort. She shoved them beneath her gabled hood. That done, she fastened the hood with hairpins, glancing again at the uniformed guards.

She shivered at the thought forming in her mind. Pernell was dead. She was certain of it. Why else would palace guards come for her at this hour? Bishop Stokesley sent them to fetch her so he could tell her that her husband was dead.

A single tear ran down her cheek despite her attempt to hold it back. She had always feared this day, and now it was here.

She thought back to two months earlier, the day Pernell had set sail. His frame had filled the same doorway now blocked by the guards. His seabag slung over his shoulder, he had stood there waiting.

He was waiting for a kiss good-bye. But Meg wasn't about to give him one. She remembered turning her back on him and walking up the stairs. His feet had shuffled at the doorway and she'd risked a glance. Their gazes met. The hurt in his eyes was unmistakable. She remembered thinking that he deserved it.

And now she would never see him again.

Meg turned away from the guards at the door. She didn't want them to see her tears, so she brushed wrinkles from her skirt with angry hands.

A child. She'd acted like a child, and her childishness would forever mar her last moment on earth with her husband. To think that after all these years, after all they'd been through, after all Pernell meant to her, it would end like this . . .

She couldn't imagine life without his big feet clomping down the stairs, his eyebrows knit in concentration over a book as he read by candlelight, the way he would pull her roughly onto his lap whenever he was feeling . . .

"We don't have all night," the taller guard groused.

Meg wiped a tear from her cheek. Bracing herself, she grabbed her cloak and swept it over her shoulders with a show of self-confidence she did not feel. The guards parted to let her pass. Stepping between them, she left the house and crossed the courtyard onto the glistening stones of the wet London streets, mindful that she did so as a widow.

Chapter 2

A white-capped, curling wave rose over Pernell, breaking down on him with Herculean force, wrenching his grip on the ship's railing, washing him across the deck, slamming him against the railing on the other side. The watery blow knocked the wind from his lungs, which was probably a good thing—it kept him from inhaling as he tumbled beneath the water. The ship rolled to its side. Like a hobbyhorse, it rocked back for more.

Pernell's hands and feet flailed as the deck rose beneath him. Gasping, he managed to grab the railing again and pull himself up just in time to see another wave snatch the heretic from the forward shrouds. Just like that, he was gone! The hand of God had plucked the man off the ship and plunged him into the ocean depths.

Pernell nodded solemnly at the display of God's righteous judgment. "Thy will be done," he managed to say.

If God's right hand executed judgment against the heretic, his left hand did the same to the ship that transported him. A watery fist smashed the foremast, reducing it to splinters and sending a treeful of screaming sailors to their deaths.

At that same moment the deck Pernell was standing on reached its apex. The railing to which he clung shuddered. A death rattle, the kind that shakes a man's chest as he takes his last breath.

The deck disappeared beneath Pernell's feet. A watery cavern opened beneath them. His hands still gripping the railing, Pernell was pulled into the abyss with the ship. Down they plummeted, doing a slow pirouette.

Everything turned dark as the swirling cavern caved in on itself. The tumbling slowed. Pernell fought the urge to breathe. His arms and legs flailed silently in the water. He sought the surface. But which way? His eyes, stinging from the water, searched frantically. Everything was murky. He swam wildly in one direction, then another.

Then he saw a bubble. A mindless, insubstantial bubble. But it knew the way to the surface, and with desperate strokes he followed it. The water grew lighter and lighter.

His head broke the surface just as his lungs gave out. With deep, violent gulps he swallowed air and foam. He choked, coughed, and gasped for more air, keeping himself afloat in the rough seas only with constant effort.

The ocean swells toyed with him. When they peaked, he searched for something to which he could cling. Debris was everywhere, but most were mere splinters of what once was a ship.

His eyes caught some movement in the distance. Human forms, he was sure of it. Then walls of water rose around him, obstructing his view. Anxiously he awaited the next swell.

There! Two men in the distance on what looked like a raft, undoubtedly a large portion of the wreckage. They were pulling a third man from the water.

Again the waves cut off his view, but not before he saw something that disturbed him. He didn't want to believe it. His jaw set, he awaited the next swell.

Pernell rose again. His view cleared. With every ounce of concentration, he focused in the direction of the raft.

He was not mistaken! One of the men on the raft, the one they had pulled from the water, was Tyndale. He was alive!

Defeat and disillusionment are great consumers of physical energy, and suddenly Pernell felt drained. His wet clothes and shoes weighed heavily on him. His arms and legs had no strength. His spirit was tired and frustrated and confused. The heretic's survival flew in the face of his theology.

A wave swept over him. Pernell offered little resistance.

He was weary but his weariness was more than just lack of strength. He had dedicated his life to two things: serving a righteous God and preserving a godly England. Over the years, to his bitter disappointment, it had become clear to him that saving England from herself was a losing battle. England had forsaken God; she deserved his wrath, as a wayward child deserved discipline. But this went beyond discipline. Had God forsaken England? Had he handed her over to the heretics? If so, what good was it to go on living?

Pernell gave in to the waves. He let his legs and arms go limp and surrendered to the downward pull of the ocean. His face heavenward, he slipped beneath the ocean surface. He would soon be in God's presence. Then everything would be made clear.

Meg followed the guards down Ironmonger Lane. The moonlight cut a silver swath through the narrow alley. A thousand cobblestone crescents paved their way. Doors and window shutters cracked open as her neighbors, awakened by the commotion, peered at her from the darkness.

With each step, the thought of Pernell's death soaked deeper into her soul. She tried telling herself her fears were unfounded. But for a woman alone at night in a situation such as this, there is no rational thought. Fears dominate.

Her greatest fear was that she had no one now to care for her, to hold her when tormenting episodes of her past came a-haunting. She had no parents. No brothers or sisters. No friends. Since their wedding day it had been she and Pernell.

Meg blamed herself for her lack of friends. She'd always kept to herself at the market and the water conduit, preferring her own thoughts over the mindless chatter of the other women. What was not to prefer? If the other wives weren't complaining about their unruly, obnoxious children, they were swapping sordid stories about their husbands' filthy habits or coarse marital expectations. It was a daily dose of disagreeable verbiage Meg could do without.

As for husbands, Pernell was not like other men, which wasn't to say he was without his faults. Good Lord, no. The man's stubbornness was legendary. When he got an idea into his head, a mule's kick couldn't dislodge it. On the other hand, there was no more loyal man in the kingdom. He was faithful to a fault, equally stubborn in mind and will and devotion. In their fifteen years of marriage Meg never once doubted Pernell's love. In fact, he loved her so much, there were times when his love bordered on veneration.

How could she live without him? The thought tolled in her mind like a death knell.

Only one other time had the emotional ground been this slippery. The day of the red tulip.

Meg's throat constricted at the memory. She saw the lifeless eyes of her mother and father staring up at her from the kitchen floor. She could smell the odor of burning fowl. She could hear the wicked, henlike cackle stalking her. Mother. Father. To lose them both on the same day. And Robert, her first husband. All bloodied. All dead. Pernell had rescued her that day, and every day since. Who would keep her safe now?

Despite the night's chill, Meg began to perspire. It was a cold sweat. Fishing for a handkerchief, she wiped her brow. She could feel her icy fingers through the cloth.

"Come now! Don't dawdle!" a guard yelled at her.

Meg's eyes darted from side to side. It was as though London's shadows were stalking her. The river air, like a cad, stroked her cheek with a clammy hand, and the pungent gutter-breath of the garbage-strewn street sidled up to her in familiar fashion. Even the night sensed her vulnerability.

Her lower lip quivered. She tugged her cloak tightly around her shoulders and quickened her step as she followed the guards around the corner onto West Chepe. Taking deep breaths, she fought back the tide of panic rising within her.

On the far side of the street there were two ragged, dirt-encrusted men huddled over the lead-pipe conduit that carried water to the district. Startled, they glared defensively at the intimate procession. A gush of water swirled around their muddy boots. Water thieves, they were tapping the conduit illegally.

Their suspicious eyes glared at Meg and the guards. Meg drew closer to her escort. The guards showed no concern for the thieves.

Their boots maintained a steady rhythm that echoed across Cheapside's wide expanse. The spire of Saint Paul's Cathedral came into view.

The road bent as it paralleled the historic Thames River. The trio passed Charing Cross, the last of a series of twelve crosses that marked the stages of funeral processions leading to Westminster Abbey.

Like small, white, translucent serpents, wisps of fog from the river curled about Meg's feet. They reminded her of the maps she'd studied as a child, depicting the far reaches of the sea as the haunt of a variety of sea beasts and serpents. A warning to sailors—or husbands—not to venture too far from home.

Pernell's funeral procession would probably take this same route. It would be small. Bishop Stokesley and possibly a few of Pernell's associates from Oxford. His closest friend, Sir Thomas More, would be unable to attend, having just taken up residence in the Tower of London. He'd been imprisoned for refusing to recognize the king's divorce from Queen Catherine of Aragon. More and Pernell were cut from the same theological and ideological cloth, another reason why some people would be reluctant to attend Pernell's funeral.

These were uncertain times for both church and state, much more so for a woman who had no husband.

A sudden surge of panic gripped Meg's heart. Her breath caught in her chest. She gasped for air.

The lead guard glanced over his shoulder. He scowled. "Hurry along!"

Meg couldn't go on. The grief and tears she'd managed to hold at bay had returned with reinforcements.

"What's this now?" moaned the guard. Pivoting, he retraced his steps to Meg. The other guard held his ground and watched, neither his expression nor his posture showing evidence of sympathy.

Meg's legs were drained of strength. She grew light-headed.

"What's all this?" the guard bellowed. "You weren't sick a moment ago."

Meg drew a ragged breath.

"Come now," the guard moaned. "We're almost there!"

"Give me a minute," Meg said.

The guards exchanged exasperated glances.

"You should have told us you was sick before we set out," griped the guard beside her. "This is no good . . . no good at all!" He grabbed Meg's arm and yanked her forward.

Meg wrenched her arm free. With her anger came a measure of strength. "I'm not sick," she insisted. "Continue on."

The guard glared at her as if she were a stubborn child.

Meg didn't wait for him. She started walking.

The second guard, seeing her coming, didn't know what to do. Hesitantly he lowered his lance to keep her from passing him. Then as the other guard overtook them, he shouldered his lance and the two of them fell into step and proceeded as before.

In short order the twin octagonal towers of Whitehall Palace's northern gatehouse came into view. Night's darkness was not thick enough to mask its richly decorated flint chequerwork, its stone badges and arms, and its terra-cotta roundels. As expected for this time of night, the arched wooden center gate was closed. They entered through the guard's entrance to the right.

Glances were exchanged between the escorting guards and the guards at the gate. Moments later the procession of three emerged on the palace side and continued down King Street, where they approached a second gate. This one had circular turrets. The doorcase was flanked by pillars and busts. Recently built, the facade was adorned with a mix of coats of arms, heraldic beasts, and signs of the zodiac.

While this land of turrets and gates and chequered facades was familiar to Pernell, it was foreign territory to Meg. She had only heard descriptions of it until now, descriptions that were largely understated.

Silently one of the guards with her held open a door. When she stepped through, he fell in behind her. She found herself in a vast, golden, elegant cavern. Their footsteps echoed as they walked. The sound was intimidating.

They came to a long corridor that seemed to stretch into forever. The walls were lined with paintings of all sizes. Interspersed among the requisite portraits of kings and queens and royal families were paintings of royalty occupied in more leisurely activities—banquets with foreign kings and dignitaries, both secular and ecclesiastical, fox hunts, deer hunts, quail hunts, even dragon hunts. Occasionally there was a painting of women reading or sewing or simply engaged in casual conversation.

In the distance a trio of court maidens approached them. They leaned into each other, whispering and giggling. As they drew closer, they hid their merriment with dainty white hands. They had eyes for the guards—the kind of stare associated with brazen women. Barely had they passed by when all restraint gave way. Their laughter filled the hallway.

Hallway traffic increased, which seemed odd to Meg, considering the lateness of the hour. There were older women, young boys dressed in court attire, and just about everything in between. The only thing the people in the hallway had in common was the way they stared at Meg as she passed them. Their faces were a mixture of curiosity and fear, or was it sadness? Did they know who she was? Had they heard of Pernell's death?

Tears threatened to return. Meg fought them. She lifted her chin high, determined to greet the bishop with quiet dignity and to accept his condolences with as much grace as she could muster. There would be plenty of time to give in to her tears at home.

The guards stepped to a door and waited.

Meg took a deep breath. She straightened her dress and adjusted her cap. She wasn't familiar with the protocol of a bishop's court, but considering the circumstances, she figured all that would be expected of her would be to stand and receive the news, which she was prepared to do.

The doors remained closed. The guards offered no explanation. Pernell was forever telling her about hours he'd spent waiting for an audience with the bishop, though it seemed odd that the bishop would be busy so late at night. But who was she to make commentary on a bishop's working hours? She was grateful that he saw fit to relate the news to her personally rather than entrust it to one of the oafs who had escorted her here.

She shifted her weight from side to side as she waited.

The guards stood perfectly erect.

Meg took another deep breath and straightened her dress again. Her fingers brushed something—a loose thread? She looked down. Just as she did, the doors swung open.

The guards parted and bowed.

"Your Majesty," they said in unison.

Meg glanced up to find herself standing in the presence of the queen of England.

Chapter 3

The waters closed over Pernell's head like a cargo hatch, shutting out the roar of the rushing wind, the crash of the waves, and the cries of drowning men. He sank into the liquid world of muted sounds, where the light of the surface gradates into darker depths, and death.

Defeated. He resigned himself to death. Pernell sank without struggle, the ship's debris encircling him, his arms stretched out, crucified to his fleshly desire to hold on to this life, fully prepared to step into eternity, where righteousness reigned.

His only pain came from knowing that Meg would suffer because of his death. She was not a strong woman. Like most women, she needed someone to care for her. It was a task Pernell cherished. He had never considered her a burden in the way that some men viewed their wives and families. He loved caring for her. To his surprise, he had found it a pleasurable paradox. The more he cared for her, the more he wanted to care for her. She was his addiction.

Thoughts of Meg made his heart burn with anguish. In this too he had failed. With his death he had failed in his pledge to protect her for the rest of her life.

The physical act of dying was surprisingly peaceful. He'd always thought of drowning as a desperate struggle to breathe, but as the salt water filled his mouth and lungs, he felt no desperation, no pain. Maybe it was because he realized it was his time to die and chose not to fight it. Unlike those above him, who thrashed at the surface and fought death's downward pull, he relaxed in the sea's invisible hands as they lowered him to his ocean grave.

Meg. His only regret was leaving Meg.

Pernell's eyes grew weary. Through half-closed eyelids he saw the men on the surface. Between him and them there was an expanse of floating objects falling gracefully all around him—clothing, shoes, splintered planks, barrels, plates, and papers. A canvas sail waved with the current like some ghostly apparition. A printed page passed in front of him, looking like a white flatfish, its words barely legible in the dimming light. A single word at the top of the page came into focus. It struck him with the force of a physical blow.

Pernell's hand snatched the paper; his clenched fist shook with rage.

Infidel! Wretch! Servant of Satan and everything that is unholy! Would he flaunt this heresy in the face of God and the king?

Like flint striking steel, righteousness and justice ignited his passions. His life's work had been to root out heresy, which he considered a poison, an infection, a contagion attacking the very body of Christendom.

Pernell kicked for the surface with determination. He would not die today, not while there was a heretic to burn.

The ocean, however, wasn't about to relinquish its prize. The current tugged at his saturated clothing; it shoved objects in his way, which he batted aside. The watery bile inside his lungs flamed, burning them, ramming the fiery liquid up his throat.

Pernell fought back. Fueled by rage, he stroked and kicked and clawed his way upward. Twice he'd felt death's darkness cover his eyes; twice he'd shoved it aside in the battle for his senses. But the struggle was proving to be too much for him. He felt himself losing consciousness. Death had too firm a grip on him.

Just when he thought he was about to lose the battle, his face broke the surface. He gasped hungrily for air. It went down halfway, then returned with a watery vengeance. He coughed convulsively and gasped again. The intake of air fed his strength.

His arms thrashed the water, searching for something, anything, to cling to that might keep the ocean grave from regaining its grip on him. The wind and waves took turns slapping his face. Time and again his lungs purged themselves of water with a force that doubled him over. He slipped beneath the surface again and heard the now familiar muted sounds. Two frantic kicks and he was back on top. And so it went until his elbow bumped something. It was hard. Round. Long. Part of the mast? He couldn't tell but it didn't matter; it was floating better than he was.

Pernell threw a desperate arm over the debris; it dipped, then held. His head lurched back and forth as he alternately coughed and gasped. His throat was raw. His head hammered. Every muscle burned. For what seemed an hour but may have been mere minutes, he did nothing but cling to the debris and, between purgings, learn what it was to breathe again.

After a time his strength rallied and he began searching the watery surface for other survivors. All around him were shattered remnants of the ship, mingled with the bodies of those who had lost their struggle with the sea.

With a dogged stubbornness that would have put a Scotsman to shame, Pernell Foxe held on to life with one hand while fiercely clutching the soggy printed page of the English Bible in the other.

"Who is this?" the queen thundered.

Meg was stunned, acutely aware that she was not dressed for an audience with the queen of England. A bishop, yes, but not the queen.

"Has everyone been suddenly struck dumb?" the queen shouted. "Who is this?"

The entourage surrounding the queen, about the size of a small village, were all staring at Meg. The two guards flanking her exchanged dumbfounded glances.

One of them managed to sputter, "We were told to bring this woman to you."

Meg had heard of the queen's legendary eyes. It was said of them that they were her most attractive feature and that she knew how to use them to her advantage. At the moment they were black as crows.

"Curtsy," the guard hissed at Meg. He reached over and tugged on her kirtle.

Meg stared absently at him. His words failed to register. In her surprise she'd forgotten her courtly training, even such an elementary thing as—

"Curtsy!" The guard shouted this time.

"Oh! Forgive me, Your Majesty," she said in a voice that was barely audible.

Placing one foot behind the other, she executed her best curtsy. It brought a derisive laugh from somewhere among the attendants.

"What a cow," someone whispered loud enough for everyone to hear.

Meg's cheeks burned with color.

The queen addressed Meg's escort. "Who told you to bring this woman to the palace?"

"May it please Your Majesty, I did."

The firm yet feminine voice came from behind Meg.

Though she was curious as to the identity of the person who had summoned her, Meg's fear of making more of a fool of herself prevented her from looking up. She thought it best to keep her eyes downward until instructed to do otherwise. So, while she heard the conversation that followed, all she saw was the intricate red, blue, and gold pattern in the rug.

"For what purpose was this woman summoned?"

"Madam, she plays the virginals."

"Where's Philippe?"

"In France, Your Majesty."

Silence. Meg wanted to look up but she dared not.

"She won't do," said the queen. "Dismiss her."

"But if it please Your Majesty, you need your music."

Meg's knees began to ache. She felt ridiculous and wondered if she looked equally ridiculous. Was she the only one bowing? And even more perplexing, what did any of this have to do with the bishop and Pernell's death?

"Get out!" the queen shouted.

Meg shook at the force of the command. Was the queen addressing her or the person behind her? Or all of them? Meg's eyes searched from side to side for some form of movement. There was none. Everyone was out of her field of vision. She listened for the scraping of a shoe or the rustle of a dress. She heard nothing.

"Are you deaf?" shouted the queen. "I said get out!"

Meg dared raise her head. The queen's steely black eyes were leveled straight at her.

"Yes, Your Majesty," Meg said, her voice nearly failing her.

Meg backed away, her gaze still lowered. After a few steps she turned to flee and ran headlong into a young woman of medium height with a pale, nearly white complexion. Meg stepped to one side. The woman blocked her retreat.

"If it please Your Majesty . . . " said the pale woman.

The voice that had sent for her now had a face.

". . . why let Philippe's absence deprive you of a pleasant night's sleep? This woman is an accomplished musician. Let her play for you. If you don't like the way she plays, you can dismiss her."

Placing her hands on Meg's shoulders, the pale woman turned Meg around until she was once again facing the queen.

Should she curtsy again?

"Bring her here," said the queen.

A gentle but insistent hand shoved Meg forward. She moved only as far as she was pushed. When the pressure against her back stopped, Meg stopped.

"Look at me!" the queen commanded.

The command horrified Meg. She had been taught never to look royalty in the eyes. The lesson was always accompanied by an endless assortment of unspeakable punishments.

A hand gripped her chin none too gently. "I said look at me!" the queen hissed through clenched teeth.

Meg allowed her head to be raised. The instant her eyes met the queen's, Meg averted her gaze. The queen responded by tightening her grip. Reluctantly Meg raised her gaze until she was looking at the queen of England eye to eye.

She saw a dark-haired woman with a thin face, high cheekbones, and a pointed chin.

Releasing her, the queen stepped back to get a better look, which also allowed Meg a better look at the queen.

She was a not a pretty woman. While standards of ideal fashion favored voluptuous figures and pale complexions, the queen had small breasts and a sallow, even swarthy complexion. Meg found it hard to believe that this was the woman who had so captivated the popular and charismatic King Henry of England that he would choose excommunication from the church just to have her.

A high neckline concealed the queen's neck and, if street gossip was accurate, a number of unsightly moles and an Adam's apple as large as a man's. One hostile critic described the queen as having a large wren under her chin. Long-hanging oversleeves stretched over her hands to conceal what Meg had heard was a second nail upon one of her fingers.

But for all these physical shortcomings, the queen had an indefinable presence about her that was enhanced with strings of pearls, a black velvet gown with furred sleeves, a French hood edged with pearls, and a pendant bearing the initials *AB*.

The queen took her time assessing Meg. She stared at Meg's cheeks, her shoulders, her chest, her stomach, her waist, and so on down to the floor, her nose wrinkling as though Meg were soured milk. The queen's gaze reversed and traveled upward.

While Meg had received instruction in court etiquette as a young woman, she had never been in the presence of royalty. Her heritage was not of royal stock. Against great odds her father had risen to a position of wealth and status. The first in his family. His greatest desire was that one day his daughter would serve in the queen's court. Meg knew just enough about courtly customs to understand that every king and queen had peculiar idiosyncrasies. Such as—

"This won't do." The queen reached for Meg's hood and ripped it off her head, pulling pins and hair with it. She tossed the hood aside. "In my presence you will wear a gabled hood with stiffened frontlets. Do you understand?"

"Yes, Your Majesty."

The queen picked at Meg's dress. She lifted it to see what was underneath.

Meg fought the instinct to step back and slap the woman's hand. Instead she stood there and flushed until her cheeks burned, while everyone in the room joined in the queen's examination, including the two guards and at least ten ladies-in-waiting.

After a time the queen released the dress, letting it fall mercifully back into place. She said, "Purchase two good gowns, one of black velvet, the other of black satin. And replace that coarse linen undergarment with one of fine lawn. As for your girdle, there are no pearls stitched into it. Did you truly think you could appear in court without the proper clothes?"

Meg didn't know whether or not to respond. Her silence angered the queen.

"Are you mute as well as deaf? Get out! Get out! Get out!"

This time Meg felt no indecision. Her face burning with shame, she turned and fled the room, sidestepping the pale-faced woman who this time made no effort to block her retreat.

Chapter 4

Meg stumbled down the hallway until her humiliation caught up with her. She collapsed onto a padded bench beneath a painting of some pompous-looking nobleman whom the artist had depicted on a rearing white horse.

Her efforts to hold back her emotions snapped like harp strings. Her sobs consumed her. Her tears fell on a red velvet cushion.

A hand rested on her shoulder. Startled, Meg whirled around. It was the pale-skinned lady-in-waiting.

"Her Majesty is not herself tonight," the woman offered.

Meg stared at the girl through watery eyes. She was certain that stories of the shabbily dressed ninny would have the entire court laughing by this time tomorrow.

"Please come back."

The request was so ridiculous, Meg laughed.

"Play for the queen."

Meg produced a handkerchief. She dried her nose and eyes. "There's been some kind of mistake," she said.

"You don't play the virginals?"

"Yes, I do," Meg stammered, "but I was summoned here by the bishop. He has news of my husband."

Now it was the lady-in-waiting who wrinkled her brow in confusion. "But you arrived with the guards I dispatched," she said.

"You sent those guards?"

"Yes."

"The bishop didn't send them?"

The young lady shook her head. "They're the queen's guards."

"Then my husband . . ."

It was clear from the perplexed expression on the young woman's face that she had no knowledge of Pernell. All Meg's fears had been baseless. But that didn't explain how this woman knew about her.

"How did you know I play the virginals?" she asked.

The young woman's face brightened as though she had found a clue to the mystery. "One of the bishop's men recommended you."

While it was a piece of the puzzle, it was far from a solution. How had it become common knowledge among the bishop's men that she played the virginals?

"Will you come back with me?" The young woman was hopeful.

Meg shook her head. "The queen made her feelings about me clear."

"Her Majesty the Queen is distraught. She doesn't know what she wants. Sometimes we're called upon to serve her despite her expressed wishes."

Meg pushed up from the bench. She stared at the young woman incredulously. The poor thing was serious.

"I . . . I just couldn't do it," Meg said.

"But you will be doing Her Majesty a great service."

There was an earnestness to the young woman's plea that was touching, until an image of the angry queen came to mind.

"I'm sorry. You'll have to find someone else."

"But that would be impossible at this late hour! You are our only hope." The young woman touched Meg's arm. Her eyes begged.

"If I return dressed like this, she'll only throw me out again."

"She won't even see you!" the young woman cried. "Her Majesty the Queen is being dressed for bed even as we speak. All you need do is wait a few minutes, then slip into her bedchamber, and begin playing. Once she hears the music, she'll not care how you're dressed."

Meg felt her heart sinking within her. She was wavering when she wanted to be strong and go home.

"The entire court will be grateful to you," the young woman pleaded.

Meg grimaced at her own words. "The queen won't see me?"

"I am sure of it."

Meg couldn't believe the words that next came out of her mouth. "Take me to the queen's bedchamber," she said with a sigh.

Flashing a grateful smile, the young woman grabbed Meg's hand and pulled her back down the hallway and into the presence room, the site of Meg's humiliation. The room was empty. The pale woman instructed Meg to wait near the throne, then disappeared through a door at the far end of the room.

Minutes later a half dozen ladies-in-waiting emerged from behind the door. They stared at Meg with amused grins. The pale lady-in-waiting was the last to emerge. She motioned for Meg, then took her by the wrist, and pulled her through the doorway. "You are an *accomplished* virginalist, aren't you?" she said.

Meg entered the dimly lit room. As her escort withdrew and began to close the door behind her, Meg whispered, "You're not staying?"

The response was a wide-eyed "Good Lord, no!"

"But you expect me to—"

"The virginals is against the wall next to the mirror."

"I could be beheaded for this!" Meg said, hoping to prompt a word of assurance.

"Yes, you could. But you'll do fine." Stepping back, the pale woman shut the door.

The queen's vaulted bedchamber was illuminated with candles. There was just enough light for Meg to make out a huge English oak bedstead with a canopy that had to be eight feet high. Four pillars carved with intricate designs were polished to a shine; the closest one reflected Meg's trembling image. In the center of the bed was a small mound of covers under which, she assumed, was the queen.

Against the wall, just as she had been told, the rectangular virginals sat on a table. Even in the dim light Meg could see that it was a well-crafted oak box decorated with floral inlays and carvings. The keyboard shimmered with candlelight.

Just beyond the virginals, hanging from the ceiling in a corner, was a birdcage of some kind. It was covered.

Meg walked softly to the virginals and slipped as noiselessly as she could into the seat.

"Who's there?"

Meg said nothing.

Covers flew back and the queen bolted upright. "You!" she cried.

Before the queen could say anything else, Meg placed her hands on the keyboard and began to play. Harpsichord-like chords filled the room. She played a soft, lovely tune that her mother used to play for her on dark nights. It was Pernell's favorite piece.

Meg closed her eyes as she played, afraid of what would happen next.

Beneath the covered cage a linnet began chirping to the music.

The bed made a creaking sound, followed by a rustle of covers. Peaking out the corner of her eye, Meg could see the queen, in her bedclothes, approach the birdcage. She lifted the cover and lovingly studied the bird.

"She likes your music," the queen said.

Meg continued playing without comment.

By the time Meg began playing a third song, the queen had returned to bed. By the fourth song, Meg could hear the rhythmic breathing of a sleeping queen.

Two weeks to the night after she began playing the virginals for the queen, Meg had another one of her episodes. She didn't know what set it off. She seldom did. All she knew was that the demons of the past had once again taken shape and invaded her mind, and Pernell wasn't there to exorcise them.

The irrational fear of his death that had tormented her the night she met the queen had been dispelled, but that didn't mean she didn't worry about his safety. She'd received no word from him and he was more than a week late in returning home.

Meg awoke to the sound of her name, not knowing if it was real or imagined. She only knew it had been spoken by that same sick, sugary voice that terrorized her on the day of the red tulip. The voice brought her upright in a sweat, her heart hammering, her breathing labored.

One thought dominated all others. Hide. Robert was coming for her and if he found her, she'd most surely die. Throwing aside the covers, Meg ran to the top of the stairs. They descended into a black abyss. Had this been where the voice originated? Was he waiting for her at the foot of the stairway?

Retreating into the bedroom, she ran to the wardrobe. Throwing open the doors, she dropped to her knees and began madly grabbing everything, tossing it out—boots, belts, stacks of sewing and fabric she'd been accumulating for a quilt. She stepped inside the wardrobe and began to close the doors when another memory flashed, that of a wedge-shaped space beneath stairs. She could feel the cobwebs brush her cheek. Cramped. Dark. Unable to move. The memory drove her from the wardrobe. She'd have to find another place to hide.

Under the bed? No. Too much like the wardrobe.

Her chest heaving, her eyes wide and wild, she fought to make her mind work. *Think. There has to be a place.*

Maybe . . .

Frantically she gathered up all the clothing, boots, and belts from the floor, stuffing her arms full until every item she picked up caused her to lose another. She threw them onto the bed in a huge pile. Returning to the closet, she grabbed an armful of clothes and dumped them on the bed as well.

Then, certain she heard someone coming up the stairs, she crawled beneath the bedcovers, beneath the pile of clothing. She curled into a ball and lay as still as she could, hoping that the bed piled high with clothes gave the impression that she had grabbed items from the wardrobe and fled the house in haste.

Her labored breathing and hammering heart threatened to give her away. She clutched a feather pillow to her chest to quiet her heart; she swallowed her breaths and listened. For steps. For Robert's voice, in that high-pitched, singsong way he had used to hunt her down. Blinded by the clothes and bedding, she was totally dependent upon her ears to warn her of his presence. But all she could hear was the pounding of her heart in her ears.

Slowly, like a small, burrowing forest animal, her hand inched through layers of clothing and bedding toward the edge of the bed until it had established a little opening—a tiny mouse tunnel just large enough for her to peek out. Retracting her hand, she peered through the hole with a view of the top of the stairs. And waited.

She was certain she could smell chicken burning.

Meg didn't know how many hours she lay beneath the pile of clothes before she drifted to sleep. All she knew was that she awoke to a hand reaching beneath the pile. It had her by the arm.

Screaming, Meg twisted and flailed. The clothing had become a trap, working against her, entangling her arms and legs. She managed to break free from the grip, but only for an instant. He grabbed her by the shoulders and pinned her against the bed.

"Meg—"

"Let me go!" she screamed.

"Meg, it's me—"

"Let . . . me . . . go!"

"It's all right. . . . It's me . . . it's me. . . . Meg."

Only one person spoke her name this way. Tenderly. Softly. Bordering on veneration.

Pernell.

Clawing clothes from her face, she saw the strong, boxlike features of his face in the faint light of early dawn. Only then did she relax and when she did, she dissolved, shaking with tears of relief.

"Pernell! Oh, Pernell," she said, sobbing.

Pernell sat on the edge of the bed and pulled her to him. She sank against his chest and breathed in her husband's familiar scent. His arms closed around her, encompassing her in a circle of security.

"You were having an episode," he whispered.

Meg responded with an exhausted moan. She shook uncontrollably.

Holding her tight with one arm, Pernell scooped armfuls of clothes to the floor with the other and climbed into bed next to her, fully clothed. He propped himself against the headboard and positioned her so her head was on his chest. Meg felt his big hand stroke her cheek and hair. It always amazed her that a man so large and brawny could be so tender.

He said nothing. He simply held her. Meg loved him for that. The steady rise and fall of his chest soothed her. She took a deep breath and lost herself in his embrace. Soon slumber covered her like a warm blanket and she drifted to sleep.

Chapter 5

Go back to bed."

"The bishop is expecting me."

"Did you sleep at all last night?"

She knew he hadn't. When she had awakened, he was in the same position as when she fell asleep, and when he climbed out of bed, he was stiff.

His broad shoulders hunched over the kitchen table, Pernell spread soft cheese on a piece of black bread and munched absentmindedly. Meg set a mug of posset in front of him. He sipped it, testing its heat. An eyebrow raised.

"You used milk."

She turned her attention to the dying fire.

"What's the occasion?" he asked.

"No occasion."

Pernell looked at his wife's back and grinned a half grin. Using milk instead of whey was her way of thanking him for last night. A cold tone of voice was her way of telling him she was still angry with him.

While Meg poked the fire back to life, Pernell ate the last of the black bread. It wasn't like before, when their arguments flared quickly and just as quickly dissipated. Now that he and his wife were middle-aged, their arguments simmered over days. Pernell didn't know how they'd arrived at this juncture. If he had known, it would have made no difference. That's just the way things were. And yet he needed for things to be right between them.

Fifteen years of marriage and still he couldn't look at her without his desire stirring. Even now several auburn curls that had escaped from beneath her cap and lay on the porcelain skin of her neck seduced him. The gentle slope of her shoulders, the mature swell of her hips, were an enchanter's spell. He ached to hold her. But he was certain that if he went to her now, she'd bolt upstairs to do some chore or another that couldn't wait.

Meg turned and removed the pot of cheese and the knife from the table. Pernell lifted his mug as she wiped away the crumbs beneath it with a damp cloth.

"You haven't mentioned your voyage," she said.

An opening gambit. But Pernell wasn't inclined to argue. If he had been, he would have pointed out that his presence at the table was evidence enough that her fears had been unfounded. She didn't have to know he had nearly drowned.

"Unsuccessful" was all he said.

Meg paused in her work. "The heretic Tyndale . . ."

"Escaped." He drained his mug. The chair scraped the floor as he stood.

"When will you be home?"

"Before dark."

Alone in the kitchen, Meg slumped into a chair and squeezed her eyes shut. Her head ached horribly, a lingering effect from the episode. For several minutes she sat motionless, hoping the pain would go away. It didn't.

She went upstairs. The unmade bed beckoned to her—*Give in to the pain, climb in, pull the covers over your head, and sleep until you feel better.* Instead she straightened the covers and fluffed the pillows, plopping them into place. She gathered Pernell's pants, shirt, and coat for washing. As always, he had folded and draped them over the back of a chair. The man was as pigheaded as they come but he was neat.

The throbbing in Meg's head was compounded by every movement she made. She couldn't remember the last time it was this bad.

With a moan Meg surrendered to the pain and slumped onto the bed. She rubbed her temples. The episodes were getting worse and so were the aftereffects. There was a time when a night in Pernell's arms was all she needed. Now, while it helped, it wasn't enough. Her prayer was that now that he was home, things could return to normal.

Home for Meg and Pernell Foxe was a narrow two-story structure on Ironmonger Lane. Formerly a mercer's shop, it belonged to the church, acquired through the will of the mercer upon his death. Pernell Foxe had been granted the use of the house plus a humble amount of cash each month as a stipend for hunting heretics and ridding England of pernicious literature, most notably Tyndale's unauthorized translation of the New Testament.

In a day when a man's social class was measured by the lavishness of his standard of living and the number of his servants, Pernell Foxe was a poor man. He had no servants and his means of living were monklike in their austerity. Such things were inconsequential to him. He had a roof over his head, food in his belly, a wife whom he adored, and direct access to the bishop of London. The work he did was for the spiritual well-being of a nation. At times he'd advised the king himself on matters of heresy, first Henry VII and now his son. Pernell had a solid reputation in both court and church.

It was a reputation of which he was proud, correcting the blight on the Foxe name placed there by his father. Rupert Foxe was a sailor of questionable character who owned a squalid little shack in Plymouth. He spent most of his life at sea, and his days on land at harbor alehouses playing checkers or throwing loaded dice or wrestling or fighting in drunken brawls. His son's academic and spiritual pursuits were inspired by his revulsion for his father's wasted life.

For her part, Meg had known nothing of depravity in her early years. She was raised as the only daughter of a father who hired the likes of Rupert Foxe to build a fleet of merchant ships that traded, among other things, exotic fish from the Caribbean. Like others of his escalating social rank, besides his country estate he owned a townhome on The Strand, the most affluent street in London, and would travel there on occasion, accompanied by his skeleton household, a fashionably large retinue of servants.

Meg had enjoyed a happy, carefree childhood with a promising future until the fateful day of the red tulip, when both of her parents were killed. Like ravenous vultures, her father's creditors picked his estate clean, leaving Meg nothing.

She didn't miss the luxury. Nor did she retain the aspirations of nobility and court presence that had so motivated her parents. Meg was content to be the wife of an academic living in a small mercer's shop at the end of Ironmonger Lane.

Even after fifteen years of marriage the simplicity of their existence gave them the appearance of newlyweds. Downstairs consisted of a single room, which at one time had featured a rainbow of colored cloth—purple, scarlet, green, gray, reddish brown, light blue, red, brown, and slate, in silk, fustian, velvet, serge, wool, and linen. Now it was kitchen, counter, and larder for Meg, with ample room for a dining table and cupboard. At the far end was a large fireplace next to which a brazier hung on a hook, for use on colder days.

The furniture was plain. Chairs and stools. Basins, ewers, patens, and great spoons hung from the rafters and glistened in the firelight. The room smelled of dried herbs and roasted meats.

Upstairs was a cramped bedroom with a curtained bed and a spacious wardrobe made of dark, carved wood, which was the only piece of furniture Meg retained that had belonged to her mother. The walls were decorated with stained cloths, giving the room some color.

Ironmonger Lane, a narrow passageway that rarely witnessed direct sunlight, was a stone quilt of buildings, gilded and painted, some timbered, decorated with carved signs and wrought iron poles bearing lamps. Piles of dung and chips, the combination of which was used for firewood, waited to be taken indoors. On the corner stood a house that was the birthplace of Thomas Becket, the most famous of all London saints and martyrs.

It was in this urban setting that Meg and Pernell Foxe passed their days, poor in possessions, rich in prestige and marital love.

Confessing to his wife that he'd failed to capture Tyndale was one thing. Admitting it to a roomful of his peers was quite another. Unaccustomed to failure, Pernell was not looking forward to this.

It was a short walk to Ludgate Hill and Saint Paul's Cathedral. As he approached the imposing edifice, he drew strength from it. Burned to the ground in 1087, it had risen from its ashes larger and more glorious than before. Struck by lightning in 1447, its 489-foot-high spire, like a scarred finger, still pointed Londoners to God.

Pernell prayed he could be as steadfast and faithful.

Bishop Stokesley presided over the meeting that would hear Pernell's report. The bishop wore the trappings of his office—robe, mitre, ring—comfortably as he oversaw the business of his London diocese from an elevated platform. Mostly, though, he was the same old John Stokesley Pernell had known when Pernell was a fellow and tutor at Oxford University.

An ocean of water had passed under the campus bridge since those early days. Stokesley had gone on to become vice president of the college at Magdalen Hall, then principal of Magdalen Hall, and finally, under Cardinal Wolsey's protective wing, bishop of London. All this despite accusations that he had carried on an adulterous affair with the wife of the organist while at Oxford and that he had baptized a cat, supposedly to discover a treasure by magic.

On top of all that, he had a rogue of a brother-in-law who loved women who were not his wife, and frequently ran into trouble attempting to smuggle spices into England to avoid the tax man. These frequent family scandals were not only a continual embarrassment: they almost cost Stokesley his appointment to the bishopric.

But somehow he managed to survive these many accusations and scandals, despite the vitriol of the Oxford rumormongers.

Seated around the perimeter of the vaulted meeting room were the local suffragans, assistants, auxiliaries, coadjutor bishops, and archdeacons. When Pernell had entered the room, he spied a friendly familiar face among the archdeacons. The two men exchanged nods. Now, as Pernell narrated the account of his picking up the heretic's trail, following him aboard ship, and seeing him survive the shipwreck, to the man the entire assembly listened spellbound.

"While the heretic escaped," Pernell concluded, "I managed to snatch this from the sea."

He offered a single sheet of paper to the bishop. Torn, stained, and ragged, it gave every appearance of having been through a shipwreck. A young assistant leaped from the bishop's side, took the paper from Pernell, and delivered it to his overseer. Stokesley held the pieces of the paper together with both hands and studied it in silence. He raised a critical eyebrow.

"A page from the book of Deuteronomy," the bishop said.

"Translated into English," Pernell announced for the benefit of those seated around the room.

A din of murmurs arose from the assembly.

"Proof," Pernell expounded, "proof that this desecrator of all that is holy is expanding his seditious publication to include the Old Testament."

The murmuring escalated, even to shouts for the heretic's head. The bishop's upraised hand brought order back to the room. Laying the page in his lap, he leaned forward and fixed his attention on Pernell.

"Dr. Foxe, you are indeed to be commended for bringing this new information to our attention," he said. "And before we continue, allow me to express, on behalf of all the saints in this assembly, our dismay at learning about your trial by sea."

A chorus of amens affirmed the bishop's sentiment.

"Furthermore, allow me also to express our gratefulness to God for sparing such a devoted crusader of the holy church."

Another chorus of amens sounded.

The bishop sat back and chuckled at what he was about to say next. "It appears that through this ordeal, you now share a common experience with the apostle Paul. A dubious honor indeed."

It was the bishop's attempt at humor. He never was good at it. However, from the response, one would have thought an accomplished jester had just delivered his best joke.

Pernell acknowledged the bishop's comment with a polite nod, then said, "In reference to the translation, Your Excellency . . ."

While he didn't want to appear unappreciative, Pernell was anxious to press forward. Prior to arriving, he had given this juncture of the meeting careful thought. The shipwreck was an unavoidable affirmation of his failure, and he wanted to move past it quickly. The key to accomplishing this was the page from Deuteronomy. It wasn't by caprice that he had presented the document when he did. He'd used it as a fulcrum to swing the conversation from the shipwreck to the task at hand.

He said, "The evidence before you makes clear our next course of action. The heretic Tyndale was undoubtedly seeking a printer in Hamburg. Since we have no reason to believe his plans have changed, logic dictates that we will find him—or clues to his whereabouts—in Hamburg. With Your Excellency's permission, I will sail to Germany and ere many days have passed will deliver this renegade to you in chains."

There was a moment of silence as the bishop thoughtfully digested this information. He leaned forward, his eyebrows huddled in concern. "You look tired, Pernell," he said. "I wonder if you've fully recovered from your harrowing ordeal at sea."

The bishop's comment had a false ring to it.

"I assure you, Your Excellency," Pernell said, "a good night's sleep and I'll be ready to sail."

The bishop appeared to weigh Pernell's words before replying. "I believe your weariness goes much deeper than that. You show all the marks of a man whose soul is tired."

"Your Excellency, I assure you—"

"Tell us," the bishop interrupted him, "what was it like for you, bobbing in that sea, watching your ship go down? You must have experienced a certain amount of fear, not knowing whether you would live or die. Add to that the utter agony you must have felt in your soul as you watched helplessly while the criminal you were sent to apprehend eluded your grasp."

Pernell stared at the man he'd known for years. A trusted colleague. Why was he doing this?

The bishop feigned weariness at what he was about to say next. "That man floundering in the sea is not the Pernell Foxe I know. The Pernell I know would have arrested the heretic at Antwerp. He never would have allowed him to board that ship. An error of such magnitude can only be the result of one of two things: hidden sympathies for the fugitive or cloudy judgment caused by the weariness of advancing age."

Two of the bishop's words sparked Pernell's powder keg of emotions. "Hidden sympathies?" he thundered.

His outburst caused the bishop's assistant to jump back a foot's distance.

The bishop, however, was ready for him. He countered Pernell's anger with his own. "In the name of the almighty God, forget not your place, man! Neither forget to whom you are speaking!"

Pernell instantly regretted the outburst. "Forgive me, Your Excellency."

The bishop maintained the appearance of wrath long enough to assert his holy position. Then, as if changing masks, he replaced his expression of anger with a gentle smile. "No one," he said, "not even the bishop of London, would insinuate that Pernell Foxe held sympathy for godless heretics."

Pernell felt the fool. He'd been outmaneuvered. Baited into denouncing one of two possibilities, he had unwittingly affirmed the other. He should have spotted the timeworn tactic instantly. But he hadn't. Maybe he *was* growing weary.

But not weary enough to give up without a fight.

"Your Excellency," Pernell countered, "allow me to prove myself to you, to this holy assembly, to England herself. Send me to Germany. As God is my witness—"

The bishop's smiled widened. In a fatherly tone he said, "Pernell, you have nothing to prove. We know you to be a godly man who has only the church's best interests at heart."

Like a chess master, Stokesley was blocking his every move. Why?

Pernell tried a different approach. "Your Excellency, there is no one who knows this heretic better than I. It would take six months to a year for someone else to acquaint themselves with the man's ways and movements. I implore you, send me to Germany. Allow me to—"

"The heretic Tyndale is not in Germany."

The news cut Pernell short. "Your Excellency?"

"The heretic is not in Germany. He's in Antwerp, residing at the home of one Thomas Poyntz."

Bishop Stokesley smiled. Check and mate.

"May I inquire as to the source of your information?" Pernell asked.

The bishop's obvious victory put him in a gracious mood. "Indeed," he said.

With a motion of his hand, a door opened and in strode a young man with a confident bearing. He approached the bishop and greeted him with the proper decorum.

"May I present Henry Philips," the bishop said.

While Pernell had never met the man, he was familiar with his reputation, that of a weasel.

The son of a wealthy landowner and member of Parliament, Henry Philips had exchanged his noble birthright for disgrace and poverty. The way Pernell had heard it, the boy's father entrusted him to deliver a large sum of money to an associate in London. The boy stole the money and gambled it away. Not daring to go home, he spent the next several years begging from patrons and writing letters to relatives, asking for money—including his mother and father.

Philips was well known as a fawning, self-pitying braggart who frequented alehouses, making traitorous remarks against the king, calling him a tyrant and spoiler of the commonwealth. He openly proclaimed he would rejoice on the day Emperor Charles V scourged His Highness along with his council and friends. In short, Pernell had never heard a good word and the name Henry Philips used in the same sentence.

Pernell locked eyes with Stokesley. "Is it my understanding that you intend to replace me with this man?"

"Replace you?" said the bishop. "Good Lord, no. No one could ever replace Pernell Foxe. Again, my dear Dr. Foxe, are you not like the apostle Paul when he said, 'I planted, Apollos watered, but God giveth the increase. Every man will receive his own reward according to his labor'?"

The bishop's attempt at diplomacy was no more accomplished than his attempt at humor. And it wasn't fooling anybody. Not the gallery of clerics and certainly not Pernell.

"In all humility, Your Excellency, I would prefer to conclude this matter myself. And I believe I have earned the right to do so. There is no one who knows the heretic's ways as well as—"

The lines on the bishop's face hardened—not to the point of anger but in warning, just enough for Pernell to know that he was approaching a line that should not be crossed. "You have made your position clear," the bishop stated. "And I have made my decision."

Henry Philips stood nearby, watching the interchange with unconcealed amusement. His hands were clasped innocently in front of him, while his lips formed a thin, mischievous smile.

Pernell didn't know where Philips had gotten his information regarding Tyndale's location, but it was clear that he was selling it to the bishop for money or position or both. Maybe the boy was able to bring pressure on the bishop in other ways as well. Pernell could only speculate. But he knew one thing for certain: the situation as it stood was intolerable.

"Your Excellency—"

"The matter is closed," the bishop said.

Pernell had reached the line drawn by the bishop. He knew it, the bishop knew it. Another word, another plea, another gesture, and Pernell would cross it.

Pernell opened his mouth to speak.

Bishop Stokesley rose. Two steps forward and the men were on equal ground.

"My friend," the bishop said, "your personal interest in this matter has not been overlooked." His tone was that of the old Stokesley speaking colleague to colleague. "I well recall our Oxford days. I can still hear the pride in your voice as you spoke of your students, how you felt privileged to be training three men in particular who, you were certain, would ensure the course of Christianity in England for ages to come. Who would have known then that one of those men would become unbalanced and that another would turn his back on orthodoxy and go the way of a heretic? Pernell, those destructive seeds were planted in them at birth. You did all you could. Jesus had his Judas Iscariot; you have your William Tyndale."

"Your Excellency . . . ," Pernell said.

The bishop's gaze hardened to stone.

"... at least grant me permission to accompany Philips."

The request took the bishop by surprise.

"For what purpose?" he asked.

"That I might be there when Tyndale is arrested. I give you my word that I will not be a hindrance. All I ask is that he see me. I want William Tyndale to know that I had a small part in bringing him to justice for his heresy."

Stokesley shook his head slowly. "There is this matter of the English New Testaments hitting our shores in great numbers. We have a lead on one of the ringleaders. A man named North. I think it best if you—"

In a whisper so low that only the bishop could hear him, Pernell said, "John ... don't make me beg. I'm asking you, colleague to colleague, grant me this one request."

There was a long silence as the bishop gazed intently into his eyes. "Granted," he said. "Go with God."

"Pernell?"

"Hm?"

He was seated on the edge of their bed. Meg had just finished brushing her hair, as she had every night for fifteen years. She walked over and sat next to him. He recognized the expression. Something was on her mind and she didn't know how to tell him.

Holding the brush in her lap, she stared at it as she spoke. "While you were gone, palace guards came for me."

"Guards?"

"They took me to see the queen."

"Really? While I was away, I was invited to have tea with King Neptune, myself."

She hit him on the shoulder with her brush. "I'm serious!" she cried.

He was too but she would never know that.

"I played the virginals for her. Somehow she heard—"

"The bishop."

"What?"

"Bishop Stokesley. I told him how much your playing soothes me. He mentioned that the queen couldn't sleep without someone playing the virginals."

"So it was you."

Pernell rested his hand on top of hers. It never failed to amaze him how large his bear paw was compared with her delicate hand.

"I should have told you. But I really didn't think anything would come of it."

"You offered my services without asking me?"

"It's the queen. Besides, like I said, I didn't think anything would come of it."

"I see," Meg said, staring at his hand on top of hers.

"That must have been an adventure for you."

From her expression, it was clear Meg didn't appreciate the humor of the situation. "They came for me at night," she said.

Pernell understood. "Oh, Meg, I'm so sorry. You must have been—"

"Beyond terrified . . ." she said. Tears glazed her eyes.

Pernell put his arms around her. She lay her head against his chest. He rocked her gently. Placing his cheek against the top of her head, he smelled her hair and felt the warmth of her body next to his. He held her to comfort her, but he wondered if she realized how much she in turn brought comfort and satisfaction to him.

Which made what he had to say all the more difficult.

"Meg?"

"Hm?" She sounded relaxed. Sleepy.

There was no easy way to say this, and he hated doing it right now, but there just wasn't time to put it off.

"I sail again in the morning."

She stiffened.

It amazed him how quickly things could change. Instead of holding his beloved wife, he now held a stone replica.

"It can't be helped," he said. "The wind . . . the tide . . ."

She said nothing. Neither did she move. He couldn't even tell if she was breathing, or listening.

"I don't know for certain how long I'll be gone. Possibly a couple of weeks. Maybe a month."

The stone stirred. She broke from his grip and climbed into bed, her face to the wall. Once settled, she didn't move.

Pernell knew that tossing words at her now would be a wasted effort; his words were ceramic and she was a rock. With a sigh he busied himself packing his seabag. That done, he dressed for bed and doused the light.

He found it difficult to sleep. Even though Meg buried her face in her pillow, he could still hear her sobs.

Pernell rose before dawn. Meg was in the same position as when he had climbed into bed. She lay still. He couldn't tell if she was awake or asleep, so he quietly dressed and gathered up his seabag.

At the bedroom door he stopped to take one more look at his wife. He purposely shuffled his feet and cleared his throat, in the hopes that she'd turn over and bid him good-bye. But she didn't, so he descended the stairs and made his way to the wharf.

Chapter 6

The residents of Antwerp have a saying: "The Scheldt River owes its existence to God, and Antwerp owes its existence to the Scheldt River." Therefore it seemed only fitting to use God's river to ship his New Testaments to England.

Two shadowy figures, mere silhouettes against the light of a single candle, skulked through the cavernous warehouse. Saturated air wafted through numerous cracks in the boarded walls, making everything moist to the touch.

After several minutes of holding the candle up to the side of one wooden crate after another, their search was rewarded.

"This one."

The candle bearer stepped aside as the larger of the two men picked up the crate with huge, meaty paws. Had the two been seen strolling through the Grote Markt, the difference in their sizes would have appeared comical. The smaller candle bearer led his partner through the stacks of merchandise, this time looking for wooden barrels. His lips moved silently as he read the words stamped on their sides. His bear-sized partner followed him silently.

"Found it," the candle bearer said, rapping the wooden barrel with his knuckle.

No further instruction was needed. His partner set the wooden crate atop an adjoining barrel, pulled an iron bar from his pocket, and pried open the lid of the crate. A canvas bag was inside, looking as though it had been tossed in hastily. Reaching inside the bag, the large man pulled out two or three small books at a time—they looked like wafers in his huge hands—until there were two stacks of ten.

He felt the bottom of the bag for more. "Is that all? Not very many."

"There was a raid at the print shop."

A meaty paw fingered the damaged corner of one of the books. "That would explain this," he said.

The lid to an empty wooden barrel was removed. With great care the two men wrapped each of the New Testaments in hide and deposited a half dozen of them at the bottom of the barrel. That done, they removed the lid of another barrel, this one heavy with grain.

Hoisting the barrel, the larger smuggler poured the grain on top of the New Testaments while his partner stared into the billows of dust to monitor their progress.

"That's enough," he said when the level of grain reached the one-third mark.

They placed more New Testaments inside the barrel and repeated the procedure, covering them with wheat. A third placement and pouring topped off the barrel, which was then sealed.

The smaller man produced a piece of chalk and, beneath the markings identifying London as the barrel's destination, printed, *JOAN.*

"His dead sister's name," the larger man said.

"Yeah. His idea."

"A fitting memorial," said the large man.

"The *Prince* sails in the morning," said the smaller man, clapping the dust from his hands. "You're sure you can get the barrel aboard?"

The larger man nodded absentmindedly. He was still staring at the woman's name in chalk.

"Niels?" he said.

"Yeah?"

"I think we should pray."

Niels turned back and looked up at the big man. "You sense something?"

"Just seems the right thing to do."

The two men stood over the barrel, their heads bowed. There was a long silence.

"Well?" Niels said.

"I'm not good with words."

A pause.

"All right."

The two men bowed their heads again. Niels prayed.

"Almighty God, Father of our Savior and Lord Jesus Christ, guard these Bibles as they sail for England. May they be a light of truth to all who read them. Amen."

There was a shuffling of feet.

"It was a bit flowery," the big man said.

"Flowery?"

"Yeah. Flowery."

"There wasn't anything flowery about it."

"Yeah, there was."

"Next time you pray, then."

"I didn't mean anything by it. You don't have to get mad. All I said was that it was flowery."

"And all I'm saying is that if you don't like the way I pray, don't ask me to pray."

"You're mad."

"I'm not mad." Niels turned and walked away.

"Don't be like that," the big man said, following him.

"I'm not being like anything," Niels called over his shoulder. "I'm going home."

"You're going home mad."

"I'm not mad!" Niels shouted.

"If you're not mad, why are you shouting?"

There's something about the way men walk when they're propelled by a sense of purpose. Their steps fall into rhythm. Their boots click with synchronous authority. Such was the scene on the Antwerp waterfront.

Grim faces all, they marched toward the house where the heretic was lodging. Pernell matched strides with the procurer general. They followed two officers who pursued the man who would deliver Tyndale to them.

Philips was tall, comely, and confident. In the short time Pernell had come to know him personally, he'd come to despise him. To call the man a weasel would be discourteous to egg-sucking carnivores everywhere. Pernell found him to be a braggart, a liar, and a gambler. He wore malice, self-pity, and deceit as medallions around his neck. Worst of all, he was an incessant whiner. Pernell couldn't stand to be around him.

Philips was motivated solely by greed, even in the matter of the heretic Tyndale. Rumor had it that Philips had been backed in this venture by an anonymous benefactor. Pernell suspected it to be Stokesley himself.

As distasteful as this pairing was to him, Pernell was willing to suffer it for the greater good. God willing, he would be rid of both knave and heretic by the end of the day.

The five men weaved their way through the afternoon waterfront traffic—broad shoulders bearing sacks of produce bound for cargo holds, cart wheels creaking under the strain of heavy loads, barrels rolling up bouncing planks, and booms hoisting pallets high overhead. Horse-drawn passenger carriages inched their way through the human maze while merchants sat astride horses and supervised the loading and unloading of their wares.

Commerce was king in Antwerp. Fortunes rested on these docks. Here the product of Belgium's famous guilds awaited distribution to the world. The seas had become the lifeblood of the nations.

And while Pernell could appreciate the importance of a healthy economy, he was more concerned about the souls of nations and the spirit of error that was presently infecting them; most notably, by the writings and actions of the apostate German monk Martin Luther and then further perpetuated by Pernell's own profligate student, William Tyndale.

Pernell's fist was clenched. God help him—this time he would not fail. The spiritual well-being of the nations depended upon their success. What good was a bustling commerce if the people lived on a slippery slope leading down to hell?

A half dozen strides ahead of him Philips doubled back. He approached Pernell.

"Care for a wager?" he asked.

The weasel grinned, an insidious glint in his eyes.

"Not interested. Proceed with the task at hand," Pernell replied.

"You don't believe I can deliver Tyndale, do you?"

"It doesn't matter what I believe. The events of the day will prove or disprove your boasts."

Philips laughed a squeaky laugh. He put his hand on Pernell's shoulder. Pernell swept it away. The weasel was undaunted.

"I'm willing to wager that not only can I deliver Tyndale to you, but I can get him to pay me to do it."

It was all Pernell could do to keep from thrashing the grinning face in front of him.

"Let's get on with it," he said.

"Yes, let's get on with it," agreed the procurer general.

"No takers?" Philips asked.

He turned to the accompanying officers, who met his offer with faces of stone.

Philips shrugged. "Just trying to make the day a little more interesting."

With a flick of his hand the procurer general gestured for Philips to move along, which he did, but not without a parting shot.

"As the Good Book says, 'Man shall not live by betrayal alone . . .'"

Pernell made a move toward Philips. The procurer general restrained him.

"If he fails, then we thrash him," said the procurer general. "For now we need him. As distasteful as it seems, I have learned that ridding the world of filth often incurs wallowing among the refuse."

Once again they fell into step behind the man who would hand over the heretic to them.

According to Philips, Tyndale was lodging with a man by the name of Thomas Poyntz, who was an English merchant living in Belgium. Philips had learned that it was Tyndale's custom to dine among the merchants. It was this practice that had afforded Philips an opportunity to make the heretic's acquaintance.

Over a period of days Philips had managed to burrow his way into the heretic's confidence and gain an invitation to visit Tyndale at his place of lodging. There he dined with Tyndale and was shown the heretic's work and the secrets of his study.

Philips had learned that Tyndale's Hebrew was now as good as his Greek, if not better, that he was making minor revisions to his 1534 New Testament, was almost finished with the Old Testament's historical books, and was looking forward to translating Ezra, Nehemiah, and Esther.

Poyntz, however, had grown suspicious and had proved to be a problem. A shrewd man and an able discerner of character, he took a disliking to Philips and said as much to his houseguest. Tyndale rose to Philips's defense, calling him an honest man and handsomely learned. Being the good host he was, Poyntz said no more against Philips.

While Philips insisted he was gaining Poyntz's confidence by intimating that he was a man of means, it was thought best to wait and arrest Tyndale on a day when Poyntz was away from the house. After a couple of weeks a business trip developed and the merchant left Antwerp for Barrois, eighteen miles distant. This provided the occasion Philips needed to betray Tyndale.

The five-man squad reached the merchant's house. The entryway was long and narrow, so narrow that two men could not walk down it abreast. The officers were positioned on opposite sides of the opening. Pernell and the procurer general took up position in an alley across the street that provided them a view of the house.

When all was ready, Philips prepared to lure Tyndale out of the house. "Last chance for a wager, gentlemen," he said. "The heretic and forty shillings. Any takers?"

"Mind your business," snapped the procurer general.

With a grin and a shrug, Philips crossed the street on jaunty legs. He disappeared down the long entryway.

Pernell and the procurer general settled in and waited.

"How did you ever come to be associated with him?" asked the procurer general.

"Philips or Tyndale?" Pernell asked.

The procurer general's eyebrow raised. "I was inquiring of Philips but now I'm curious as to both men."

Pernell took a deep breath. Without taking his eyes off the entryway, he said, "Philips is my punishment for failing to capture the heretic when I had the chance; Tyndale is my punishment for failing as a teacher. He was my student at Oxford."

"Double penance," mused the procurer general. "You don't strike me as a man much acquainted with sin."

"Of all men, surely you're aware that sins of omission are just as damning as sins of commission," Pernell replied. "God willing, today my penance ends and my conscience is cleared."

Pernell could feel the procurer general's gaze steadily upon him. It mattered little to him whether or not this man understood the demons that haunted him. What mattered were the events that were about to transpire in the entryway across the street.

He had waited and prayed for this day, imagining what it would be like once again to look William Tyndale in the eyes, finally to confront the man with his heresy, to see the shame in his eyes, his guilt, and to know that once and for all this man's pernicious pen would be stilled. Just as importantly, though, he wanted William Tyndale to know that it was he, Pernell Foxe, who had had a hand in his capture.

For years he had envisioned this moment of confrontation. He'd imagined the triumph he would feel when justice and truth finally prevailed, and the satisfaction of seeing evil defeated. In a sense it was a precursor of what judgment day would be like.

"On earth as it is in heaven," Pernell whispered.

The sound of footsteps echoed down the narrow entryway. Both Pernell and the procurer general straightened in anticipation.

A short, unassuming man appeared.

"It's him," Pernell said.

He could see his former student striding down the walkway, completely unaware of what was about to happen to him. Behind him walked a grinning Philips. Like a little boy showing off, he pointed a finger at Tyndale's head to indicate that he had fulfilled his boast to deliver the heretic.

No sooner had Tyndale cleared the entryway than he was seized by the officers. A moment of shock, then fear, crossed Tyndale's face as he was apprehended. As Pernell stepped out of the shadows and crossed the street, their eyes met and Tyndale's expression became one of understanding.

Pernell closed the distance between them with long, confident strides. He wanted to savor this moment.

Tyndale greeted him. "Dr. Foxe," he said. "I trust that you're well."

No further words were exchanged between them. None were necessary. They both knew the import of what was taking place. All that was required now was for Pernell to witness the man's shame, to see it in his eyes. Then righteousness would be served.

But the eyes that gazed back at him were not the eyes of a man ridden with guilt. Or of a coward. There was no shame in them at all. Neither were these the hardened eyes of a criminal. On the contrary, Tyndale's eyes were clear and untroubled, the eyes of a man at peace with himself. In fact, if there was any emotion present in them, it was sadness.

Pernell searched deeper. Like a man frantically rummaging through a cluttered attic, he looked for arrogance but found none, for a haughty spirit but it was not there, for culpability but he came up empty.

He saw only peace and resignation.

Pernell's spirit simmered with rage. Could this heretic be so dimwitted as not to understand the significance of his criminal acts? Did he not realize that he would most surely be put to death for his treason? Pernell knew better. As a student, Tyndale had a quick mind and a good grasp on theology and its political ramifications, which made his lack of fear or remorse all the more infuriating.

The officers bound the heretic's hands and led him away, followed by the procurer general.

"Eh? What did I tell you?" a grinning Philips said to Pernell. He waved a money pouch in front of Pernell's face. "Forty shillings. Didn't I tell you? The fool just handed it to me. I made up this story about how my purse got lost or stolen between here and Mechlin. Easiest money I've ever made. For such a slippery fellow, he certainly isn't very smart, is he?"

It was all Pernell could do to keep from striking the man. Instead he moved to step around him. Philips blocked his way.

He wasn't done boasting. "Guess where we were headed? He was taking me out to dinner. Can you believe that?" Philips laughed his weasel laugh. "I come to turn him over to the authorities, and he gives me a pouchful of money and offers to take me to dinner! Joke's on him, wouldn't you say? But then, right about now I doubt he can see the humor in it, eh?"

Pernell made another attempt to step around him. Philips put a hand to his chest to stop him, the hand that held the money pouch.

"Hold!" he said. Screwing up his face in a comic expression, he said, "You know, I just realized I played this thing all wrong! I should have handed him over to you fellows *after* dinner!" He laughed. "I cheated myself out of a free meal!"

Pernell made one more attempt to step around him.

"Somebody owes me a dinner! Wouldn't you say? The procurer general or possibly the king of England himself, since I did him such a great favor today. Don't you think? Somebody owes me a dinner and I'm going to collect!"

With an upward swipe of his arm, Pernell knocked Philip's hand aside, sending the money pouch flying. It opened when it hit the brick street. Coins scattered everywhere.

"Hey! Now that was uncalled for!" Philips whined. He dropped to his knees to recover the coins. "What's got into you? I delivered him right into your hands. Easy as pie, I did. Where's the gratitude?"

Pernell wasn't listening. He strode away.

For the rest of the day and into the evening Pernell spoke to no one. The only company he entertained was his own thoughts. The bustling Grote Markt might just as well have been empty of people, as far as it mattered to him.

He couldn't get the look in Tyndale's eyes out of his mind. It drove him mad.

This was the man Thomas More had called a beast, one of the hellhounds that the devil had in his kennel. The work Tyndale did was a discharge of filthy foam out of his brutish, beastly mouth. Pernell agreed with More. The heretic was a deceiver, a hypocrite, a man puffed up with the poison of pride, malice, and envy.

So why didn't Tyndale look and act the part?

Pernell had invested years of his life in the pursuit of this heretic. All those years he'd dreamed of this day. And now it was here. The renegade was in chains. No longer could he abuse God's Word and produce his filth. So why did Pernell feel so unsatisfied?

Pernell walked the streets of Antwerp all night long. He made his way to the harbor, which was situated at the entrance of the city, alongside the riverbank. There he stared at the Steen castle. Constructed completely of stone at a time when most houses were built of wood, it continued to stand tall, while all the structures around it had long since decayed. Pernell drew strength from it, as he did from Saint Paul's Cathedral, with its scarred-finger spire that forever pointed heavenward.

The righteousness he stood for was made of rock and pointed men to God, and no matter how many Tyndales rose up to assault it, it would stand. Of this he was certain. To this he had committed his life.

Early the next morning Pernell Foxe boarded the *Prince* and set sail for London.

Chapter 7

"Mm. That's lovely."

Meg lifted her hands from the keyboard as the last chord faded. "Thank you, Your Majesty," she said.

Queen Anne Boleyn occupied the center of the gilded dressing room, her eyes closed. An appreciative smile graced her lips.

A buzz of activity surrounded her as a dozen or so attendants dressed, primped, and preened their queen. The queen stood with outstretched arms, as stoic as a marble statue and nearly as pale, coming alive only to correct or rebuke unsatisfactory performance.

Her entire demeanor softened whenever Meg played.

"Play another selection," the queen commanded.

"Yes, Your Majesty."

In recent days the queen had summoned Meg frequently, which in a strange way proved helpful. Meg no longer felt overwhelmed by the court and its surroundings. That wasn't to say she felt comfortable in the queen's presence. No one ever did. But once Meg began playing, her hands moved with increasing confidence.

The appropriateness of her clothing aided her confidence. Under the guidance of Lady Jane Seymour, Meg had acquired the approved garments. This tutoring seemed only right, considering it was Lady Jane who had summoned her to the queen for that initial nightmarish appearance.

According to Lady Jane, the queen's tantrums were increasing in both intensity and frequency and were exasperating the attendants and the court. This was where Meg made her contribution to king and country. Her music soothed the temper of the queen.

A noticeable change could be seen in the queen's demeanor within three or four songs. By the sixth selection the queen's internal fire was quenched and harmony was restored. Unless of course some blockhead stoked the queen's anger with a bit of disagreeable news, or an attendant daydreamed and provided inferior service, in which case Meg's efforts were for naught.

Whenever Meg arrived, it wasn't uncommon for her to see a wave of relief and gratitude wash over a roomful of haggard faces. The appreciation she felt was food for her own soul. She knew, though, that whatever part she played at court was a small one.

The mood of the court reflected the mood of the king, and at present everything was going Henry VIII's way. The Star Court was holding the pretentious and demanding nobility in check. The king had emerged victorious from a hard-fought battle with the pope to have his marriage to Catherine of Aragon annulled, though he had to break with the church to do it. Nevertheless, the recent Act of Succession, which ordered his subjects to accept his marriage to Anne as "undoubted, true, sincere, and perfect," was in place, and there was legislation pending in Parliament that would soon make him and all future kings of England the supreme head of the Church of England. The crown's treasury—which he had depleted with elaborate pageants and distant battles—found a fresh source of income from the sale of monastery lands that the king had confiscated from the Roman Catholic Church. And there was hope that a male heir to the throne would soon be forthcoming. Something Henry's first wife had failed to do. While Anne had failed in her first attempt at birth—producing a female—the birth had proved she was fertile. A male heir seemed just a matter of time.

While the king and court were in an optimistic mood, the queen was feeling the strain of their expectations. Anne was now aging visibly. Her once vivacious eyes now regarded the world with suspicion, her smiling lips were pinched and tight, and her cheeks were beginning to sag.

She stood motionless as two of the attendants silently adjusted her dress, while another pair brushed the queen's dark brown hair, which was long enough for her to sit on. At the moment her face was serene as she anticipated Meg's next melody.

The door burst open with a bang. Everyone in the room jumped, including the queen. Two of the younger attendants added voice to their surprise. Meg's fingers, hovering over the keyboard, froze in place.

A dozen men poured through the doorway and spread throughout the room. They wore costumes and masks. They brought with them laughter—partly, no doubt, from the surprised expressions on the ladies' faces—and singing and musical instruments.

As for the ladies, startled expressions were exchanged for smiles of delight. Several of them clapped their hands joyfully. The queen was not one of them.

A masked man boldly stepped forward.

With a booming voice he said, "A loyal gentleman who loves a lady whom he fears and respects would be guilty of great wrong were he to allow himself to die in silence of his passion. It is his duty to explain his feelings to the lady of his choice before allowing himself to come to such an extremity. I advise men everywhere, therefore, to make known their affections and to request their ladies to retain them as their cavaliers. If the lady be prudent and courteous, she will not take it amiss. Far from considering your request dishonoring, she will esteem you the more for it. Indeed, such is your worth that there is not a lady in the world, even were she a queen or an empress, that ought not to consider herself happy in having such as one for her knight."

Approaching the queen, the actor lowered himself to one knee and bowed to the applause of the ladies.

The room fell silent as the unsmiling queen looked down at the actor. She hovered there, her face a placid mask. She said nothing.

The actor glanced up. His movements expressed surprise. "Why, you are the queen!" he cried. "May the saints have mercy on me! You are the queen of England!"

He threw himself at her feet.

"My queen!" he exclaimed. "Make me your knight! I pledge all that I have, all that I am, to you!" With that he kissed her feet.

With seeming reluctance the queen said flatly, "Consider it so. You are my knight."

The actor stood in triumph—but not without difficulty in one knee—doffed his mask, and invited applause from everyone in the room. It was granted him generously.

This was the closest Meg had ever been to the king of England. She'd seen him from a distance and was always struck by his size, but never more so than now. At six foot three, Henry VIII was taller than Pernell. His whole frame was big, muscular, and admirably proportioned, which came as no surprise to Meg, considering the king's legendary athletic prowess.

The man accepting applause appeared heavier than he was the last time Meg saw him. He had a round, clean-shaven face. (The last time she'd seen him, he wore a beard. If the gossip she heard was accurate, he'd shaved it off while courting Anne, who preferred him without it.) His countenance was rather angelic, Meg thought. He was fair of skin, with piercing blue eyes, a high-bridged nose, and a small, sensual mouth. His head, which sported straight auburn hair, was balding at the crown.

For an actor, Meg thought, the king's voice was high-pitched. As for his difficulty rising from a kneeling position, it was well known that the king had recurring trouble with one leg, following a nasty fall from his horse. Despite his aging and his ailments, there was a presence about him, a charisma that not only commanded respect but left a person feeling good for having basked in the emanation.

"I love good friends!" the king cried, his arms raised, his smile infectious. "I love good friends, good cheer, and handsome presents. I hate parsimony, a friend who fails me in the day of need, the man who speaks evil of dice, and the sorry fellow who refuses to play."

Another performance. Another hearty applause.

The king was in a frisky mood. One that wasn't shared by his queen. Anne held her place, unmoving, arms crossed, looking at her husband the king as a mother would a little boy who was acting up.

The king didn't seem to notice.

"We bring you a story!" he boomed.

With a grand gesture, he signaled for the designated storyteller to come forward. A handsome man, young, fair, and festively dressed, appeared. He was the owner of a smug expression, which he wore proudly.

"Hush now. Hush, little children," he said.

The younger attendants giggled at his patronizing approach, which only served to validate the storyteller's smugness.

"Hush now and I will tell you a story."

The king motioned for a chair to be brought for his queen. Two chairs appeared and king and queen sat side by side. The king reached over and took the queen's hand. While she let him have her hand, she did so without so much as a glance or smile in his direction. Her eyes were fixed forward, her demeanor cool and regal.

The attendants found various places to roost, some on chairs, the younger ones spreading their dresses and sitting on the floor. The noise from their giddiness and playfulness was enough to earn them a sharp glance of displeasure from the queen.

Meg swiveled in her chair, sitting with her back to the keyboard. When all was ready and the storyteller deemed the room to be hushed sufficiently, he began his tale.

"In Neustria there was once a high mountain on which there was a relic to two children, whose legend is unknown. Yet despite its unknown origin, the relic attracted much attention. To accommodate the great crowd of pilgrims who came to see it, the king of Neustria built a fair nearby.

"Now this king had a daughter who was kind and fair of feature. She was loved greatly by the townspeople and her father the king, since he had lost his queen several years previous. And as this fair maiden gained in years, word of her beauty grew and became known throughout the land. But the king was not anxious to see her wed, not wanting to lose her. This angered the townspeople, who wanted their beautiful princess to know romance and happiness. So the king made it known that the princess would not be wed to anyone unless the suitor could, without rest, bear her in his arms up to the top of the great legendary mountain.

"When the people of the land heard of the king's proclamation, worthy men from throughout the known world arrived to test their strength and possibly win the hand of the beautiful princess. Yet without exception, strive as they might, the mountain and the weight of the princess proved too much for them. After a time, because so many worthy men failed the test, no one came forward to vie for the hand of the beautiful princess.

"Now it so happens that in this country there lived a squire, the son of a count. Being a frequent guest of the court, he had known the princess since the days of their childhood. This squire loved the princess with all his heart."

Swooning sounds erupted from a couple of the younger attendants. Their sighs brought a smile to the face of the king. The queen was not amused.

"As for the princess," the storyteller continued, "she returned the squire's love, finding him handsome and kind. But fearing the king, the two of them kept their mutual affections a secret.

"It pained them that the world should be so cruel toward their love. So the squire, convinced he could never win his love's hand by carrying her up that impossible mountain, asked the princess to elope with him.

"While the princess loved the squire with all her heart, she feared her father's anger and the resulting punishment the squire would face should they elope. 'There is another way,' she said. She told the squire about her aunt, who for thirty years had studied medicine and knew everything about herbs and what they could do. The princess suggested they go see her aunt and ask her if there was a potion that would make the squire strong enough to climb the hill. The squire smiled at the cleverness of his love's plot. And so they went to inquire of the princess's aunt.

"After hearing their story, the aunt proclaimed the king's task unfair without question, and she agreed to help them. She mixed a potion, poured it into a small flask, and gave it to the squire, saying, 'No matter how worn or tired you may be, by drinking from this flask, you will feel all your bones and your heart and your blood revive greatly. All you must do is drink it when the time arrives.' Happily the lovers returned to the castle with the potion, confident that they would soon be wed.

"The day arrived for the contest. When it was announced who the suitor would be, the king and townspeople scoffed because of the squire's slight build, his slender arms, and his inability till now at proving himself a champion even at sports. But the reaction of the king and townspeople did not deter the squire.

"With the flask and its potent drink tied by a string around his neck, he lifted the princess in his arms and proceeded at a good pace up the mountain. His confidence swayed the crowd and a great cheer went up for him.

"Soon he was halfway up the mountain. The cheers of the crowd had long since faded. The squire began to feel his muscles tighten, yet he continued at a pace that pleased him. His strength came from the pleasure he felt in enduring hardship for the one he loved. He saw no need for the potion now.

"The princess, while admiring her love for carrying her farther than either thought he was capable on his own, grew concerned. She felt him tire and his arms grow slack. She suggested that now was the time to drink from the flask.

"The squire refused. He told her that he'd come this far fueled by courage and love and that it would be foolish to trade that strength for an unknown medicine now.

"They reached the two-thirds milestone on their way up the mountainside. By now the squire's strength was extremely fragile. The princess was worried. She pleaded with him to drink the potion. The squire grew angry that she would break his concentration. The princess kissed him on the cheek and pleaded with him again, but the squire continued on, convinced that he could succeed without the aid of a drug.

"The summit of the mountain was just ahead. The squire's strength was spent. Again the princess pleaded for him to drink from the flask. But the squire was afraid of what the unknown drug might do to him now that he was so close. Fixing his eyes on the summit, he continued on under his own strength.

"Stumbling now with each step, squeezing the last ounce of strength from his legs, with one mighty push after another, he succeeded in reaching the final plateau and stepped onto the peak of the mountain. But as he did, his body collapsed and his heart burst.

"The beautiful princess fell to the ground beside him. She saw he was no longer moving. Checking his pulse, she found him dead. Her cries of pain became so unbearable, many in the crowd had to turn away.

"Finding the flask around his neck, the princess threw it against a nearby rock and shattered it. Her lamentable wails filled the air. She took her dead lover in her arms and held him, kissing his eyes and mouth dearly. Her sorrow was too great for her young heart, and her grief brought her to the brink of exhaustion and beyond—she died.

"When the townspeople heard the news of the two lovers, it saddened them greatly. Finding both the princess and the squire lifeless yet wrapped in each other's arms, they dared not remove the bodies. So they brought a beautiful marble coffin to the plateau and laid the couple to rest on the mountaintop. There the two lovers remained forever alone, surrounded only by the flowering herbs that grew nearby from the contents of the flask.

"The mountain that had previously been known for its mysterious relic to two unknown children now became known throughout the land as the Mountain of the Two Lovers.

"And thus our story ends."

A chorus of sobs from the younger attendants followed. "How sad!" one of them pined.

"Tell it again," cried another, "but this time make it a happy ending."

"Yes! A happy ending!" they all agreed.

"Agreed!" cried the king, bounding out of his chair. To the storyteller he said, "Your squire was a dolt! While he had a big heart, he had no head! And what is courage without the wisdom to use it? Is it not a wildfire, when what we want is a glowing hearth?"

The attendants applauded their king, who in turn fed off their applause.

Suddenly he swept Lady Jane Seymour off her feet, surprising everyone, including the lady-in-waiting herself, who let out a squeal.

"If I were that squire, I'd use any and every means to reach the top of that mountain and claim my heart's true desire! For love will always find a way."

While the other attendants applauded him, the king twirled his fictional princess around a couple of times until his weak knee buckled. With masterful agility he managed to set her on her feet without collapsing. He called for a song.

Not everyone noticed the buckling of the knee. Meg did. She was impressed with the smooth manner in which the king covered it up. And the queen noticed. She was scowling, though Meg couldn't tell whether the expression was in reaction to the king's attempt to prove his virility or to his choice of partners for the little drama.

"A song! A song!" the king cried, looking to his band of revelers.

One of them stepped forward. "Your Majesty," he said, "'tis you who have prepared a song."

For an instant the king was taken aback. Another act? Meg wondered.

"I believe you are right!" the king cried with a huge smile. "Now all I need is a musical instrument to accompany me."

On cue the male revelers parted and out stepped a grinning youth carrying a lyre.

"No, no, no, no, no!" said the king. "Entirely unsuitable. Get back. Back, back, back!" He shooed the musician back into the ranks.

The young man was clearly surprised and displeased with the king's change of mind.

"I think the virginals!" the king cried.

He turned on his heel and strode directly toward Meg.

Shocked to the point of immobility, Meg sat, doe-eyed. Then, her senses returning, she slid off her chair and onto her knees. "Your Majesty," she said.

"What's this?" the king said.

The next thing Meg knew, her chin was being raised by the king's cupped hand. "How can you play if your face is pressed to the floor?" he asked, laughing.

He raised her to her feet. Holding her face in his hands, he studied her appreciatively for a moment. "My, we are lovely, aren't we?" he said.

Meg felt her face flushing.

"And do we play the virginals?" he asked her. "Or do we merely warm the seat?"

Meg tried to speak. Tension in her throat cut off her words. Her second attempt fared better. "I play, Your Majesty," she said.

"Outstanding!" boomed the king. "Do you know 'If You Would Know the Reason Why?'"

"Yes, Your Majesty."

"Grand!"

He released her.

Meg positioned herself before the keyboard, all the while avoiding eye contact with the queen. The memory of the queen's fury when her husband swept Lady Jane Seymour off her feet was a fresh one.

She played a few introductory chords. "Does this range please Your Majesty?" she asked.

The king smiled at her, a smile that was more than consent. Facing the assembled revelers, he placed one hand casually atop the virginals. He sang,

"If you would know the reason why
    But half a song I bring,
I have—alas, I must reply—
    But half a theme to sing!
'Tis I alone that feel the spell;
    'Tis I alone that burn:
The lady that I love so well
    My love will not return.

"I'll take the 'No' she deigns to give,
    Since she withholds the 'Yes';
Better with her in hope to live
    Than elsewhere to possess!
Since with my fate I cannot cope,
    Shall this my solace prove—
To dream that she, as whispers hope,
    May one day learn to love."

The applause was for the king more so than the singer. Regardless, the king reveled in it. With hands folded and head bowed, Meg sat as still as a church mouse, praying that he would not direct any of the attention toward her. Mercifully, he did not.

"And now, dear friends, sadly we must away!" the king cried.

The revelry continued as the men left the queen's chamber, until the last of their merry sound faded as the door was shut. Without any instruction, the ladies returned to the tasks that had occupied them before the arrival of the revelers.

Queen Anne stood.

"Everyone out!" she shouted.

A few of the ladies stood motionlessly, perplexed by the queen's order, since they had not finished dressing her.

"Out! Everyone out!"

Meg rose to leave.

"Not you!" said the queen.

Hearing the voice alone, Meg hoped against hope that the queen was directing her command to someone else. She glanced at the queen and met the monarch's steely gaze head-on.

"You stay," she ordered.

The room emptied quickly. Filled with music and laughter a short time ago, it was now unnervingly silent.

"Would you like me to play for you, Your Majesty?"

"No."

The queen paced back and forth. Meg stood silently by, fearing the woman's wrath. The king's philandering ways were no secret. Indeed, for years before their marriage, Anne Boleyn herself had masterfully played romantic games with the king to her advantage. Having caught the king's eye while a member of Queen Catherine of Aragon's court, Anne played a perilous flirting and rebuffing gambit. She encouraged the king's advances up to the edge of intimacy but no further, knowing that once she gave in to him physically, she would lose her advantage. Denying a king who was accustomed to having whatever he wanted proved to be the ultimate seduction. Henry did everything within his power—including challenging a pope who refused to annul his marriage to Catherine—to have his way with the flirtatious Anne.

As Anne had expected, in time after they were wed Henry's infatuation with her waned. His eyes began to roam and the rest of him was sure to follow. While it hurt Anne that the king would seek the favors of other women, she took comfort in knowing she was now queen of England, a position she would solidify once she gave birth to a son.

When her first child proved to be a daughter, the king sought comfort in other women's arms. And when, not more than a month ago, Anne learned she was pregnant again, she heard rumors of the king's further indiscretions. The pregnancy was troubled from the start. Anne's baby was stillborn. And for the first time she feared for her position.

"The king has taken a liking to you," the queen said to Meg.

"Your Majesty, the king may have taken a liking to my playing, nothing more," Meg said, trembling.

"No, there was more," the queen said matter-of-factly.

While Meg agreed with her, she was frightened to admit it. The king had gazed at her in a way unbecoming a married man. His touch was sensuous. And while she could feel the warmth of his charisma, there was more.

"Has the king ever spoken to you before?"

"No, Your Majesty."

"You've never been in his presence before?"

"No, Your Majesty."

"Not even publicly?"

"At a great distance, Your Majesty."

"How long have you been in my court?"

Meg counted the time silently. "Six weeks, Your Majesty. Maybe seven."

"And in all that time, the king has never approached you?"

"Oh, no, Your Majesty! I am a married woman."

Meg's comment seemed to amuse the queen. "The greater the attraction," she said under her breath. To Meg she said, "The king has a way about him. I'm sure you noticed."

Meg hesitated. "No, Your Majesty, I didn't . . ."

"Now I know you're lying!"

Flustered, Meg searched for the right words. "Granted, Your Majesty, the king is a powerful man. What I mean to say is that I could never see him as anything but my king."

"A woman of your position would be unable to resist his charms." It was a casual statement, nothing more.

"Please, Your Majesty," Meg said, "do not doubt me in this. I would die rather than be unfaithful to my husband."

This gave the queen pause. She studied Meg as though she were examining some strange new form of animal life.

"Who is this man to whom you are so devoted?"

"My husband? His name is Pernell Foxe."

"Pernell Foxe?" the queen said, surprised.

"You've heard of him?"

"The heretic hunter?"

"Yes, Your Majesty."

The queen's gaze darted toward a small table upon which rested an open book. She took a step toward it, then seemed to change her mind.

"Pernell Foxe," she repeated.

"Do you know him, Your Majesty?"

"The entire kingdom knows of your husband, madam," said the queen. "Especially the followers of Luther and Tyndale."

It was an odd comment. Meg didn't know what to make of it. But learning she was married to Pernell seemed to ease the queen's mind regarding her suspected indiscretions. To Meg's relief, the queen changed the subject.

"What was your impression of the disguising?"

"Disguising?"

"The king's little spontaneous pageant."

"Oh! If I may say so, the king seemed to enjoy performing in it."

The queen laughed loudly. "That he does."

"Does he do them often?"

"Not as often as he used to."

Meg regretted the question when she saw the pain it brought the queen.

"And what is your impression of our young ladies?" asked the queen.

Meg thought for a moment, unsure as to where this was leading. "They are full of life," she replied.

The queen laughed. "You choose your words with the care of a diplomat."

"Your Majesty, it's not my intention—"

"Their giggling and squealing and unruly manners are a disgrace to this court," the queen pronounced. "If they'd spend as much time practicing court etiquette as they do in gossip and the affairs of courtly love, they'd know this. When I was their age, I was trained in the French court. The French know how to train a lady."

Meg stood quietly as the queen spoke, grateful that the topic of conversation had passed from her to the attendants.

The queen cocked her head in thought. Squaring her shoulders, she looked Meg up and down. To Meg's relief, the queen's expression was one of approval.

"I remember the first time you came into my court," she said. "Someone has taken the time to educate you in appropriate court dress."

Lady Jane Seymour's name made its way to Meg's lips. It got no further. Meg thought it best not to say anything more at present.

The queen reached for Meg's dress, just as she had done the first night Meg appeared in court. As before, Meg didn't step back. At least this time the entire court wasn't present.

Just as the queen's fingers were about to touch Meg's dress, they stopped. The queen pulled back. Meg interpreted this as an act of respect. She felt flattered.

"I like you," said the queen.

Meg was astounded at the compliment. The queen did not hand them out freely.

She continued. "You're a mature woman with high morals and ideals. A man such as Pernell Foxe would not have married a woman with any lesser qualities."

"Thank you, Your Majesty," Meg replied.

"The younger attendants," the queen said. "Do you think you can teach them to be like you?"

"Your Majesty?"

"I want you to tutor them. Three in particular. Do you think you can do it?"

Meg didn't know what to think. "I'm honored, Your Majesty."

"Can you do it?"

How does one say no to a queen? "I'm unsure of my qualifications," Meg stammered.

"You begin next week."

Business done, the queen called for her attendants.

As the attendants reentered the room, they looked from the queen to Meg and back, curious as to the conversation that had passed between them.

Chapter 8

Broken Wharf was shrouded in fog. A London smuggler's night.

"What are we looking for again?"

"Joan."

There were three of them on the docks, bent over, examining the markings on barrel after barrel, their silhouetted heads bobbing up and down among the rows. Suddenly from the river came voices. Simultaneously the heads ducked out of sight.

On the river there was a slapping of oars. A misty ring of light encompassing a hanging lantern illuminated two male occupants in a wherry.

A voice boomed mid-river. "Good Lord, man, had I known it would take you this long to row me, I'd have swum the blasted river. My Aunt Orabelle has more arm strength than you and she's nigh unto sixty years old."

"Yeah? Well, I've seen your Aunt Orabelles" came a gruff reply, "and she's twice my size."

"Put your back into it."

"Listen, mate, next time I'll lounge and you row."

Moments later there was a hollow wooden sound as the boat and dock met. The wherry's passenger disembarked and tossed a few coins into the bottom of the boat.

"Next time I expect you to earn it."

"There won't be a next time, mate! Not with me, leastways. You can walk across the Thames for all I care!"

Heavy footfalls hit the dock and echoed in the fog as the wherry passenger hurried toward the road; from the river came the sounds of muttering and oars once again slapping the river. Soon they were gone. After a time three heads dared raise above the columns of barrels. Without comment the search resumed.

"What are we looking for again?"

Two voices replied in unison, "Joan!"

"Well, you don't have to get so huffed about it!"

Several minutes later: "Over here."

The three smugglers stood before a single barrel which only that afternoon had been unloaded from the cargo hold of the *Prince.* One of them, obviously the leader, bent low to confirm the markings. The word *JOAN* was printed in bold chalk letters beneath the destination markings.

"Let's load her up," he said.

Within ten minutes the three men had delivered the barrel to its destination, the back room of a small bakery shop on Elbow Lane. One of them pried off the top. Hands dug into the grain. There were a few moments of searching.

"Here's one."

A hide-wrapped package was pulled from the grain. The packaging was peeled away to reveal a New Testament of convenient size. The leader and shop's owner, an average-sized man with large forearms, examined the illegal book. One corner of the cover was damaged. He flipped a few pages to see if there was any other damage. There was none. Except for the damaged cover, it was a handsome volume.

Such an unassuming little book, he thought, *to create such a worldwide furor.*

He looked at the two men standing with him and was struck by the thought that common, ordinary men like them would willingly risk their lives to smuggle the forbidden books into England. Raedmund, a simple fishmonger, honest, loyal to a fault, husband, friend, a true Englishman. His son, Bink, a good boy on the verge of manhood. Strong. Young. Idealistic. The boy was at the age when his chin needed shaving, but only once every fortnight.

The baker wanted to tell them that they were foolish for taking such a risk. Unlike him, they had too much to lose. They should be home, warm and comfortable with their family. Didn't they realize that there were men who would gladly strap them to a stake and burn them alive for possessing this barrel of New Testaments? He wanted to tell Bink that he was too young to be caught up in this kind of activity, that he should go home, find a girl, fall in love, and raise a bunch of little Binks.

Instead he held up the damaged book and said, "Let's get the rest of 'em unloaded."

One by one they pulled the hide-wrapped packages from the grain and stacked them on a counter. They removed loose bricks from the back of an old oven, revealing a cavity in which several other copies of the New Testament had already been hidden.

"Supply's gettin' low," Bink commented.

"God will provide," Raedmund replied.

After the books were safely tucked away, they replaced all the bricks save one.

"You makin' a delivery tonight?" Raedmund asked.

"At the king's kitchen."

Bink liked that. He grinned.

The light was doused and the three men made their way through the back door of the bakery shop into an uncertain London night.

"No . . . no! I've no time for this!"

Meg steadied herself with a hand against the front door. She was dressed to go out, when the episode danced on the edge of consciousness, threatening to take center stage. She tried to stop it by sheer willpower.

It had been this way for several weeks now. Her nightmares had returned with a vengeance while Pernell was in Antwerp. Worse still, so had the day frights. All it took to set her off was the sight of a kitchen knife or a chicken or the opening of a closet door. There were times when her heart would beat so fast, she thought she would faint. At night she was afraid to put out the candle or close her eyes.

She thought they'd go away when he returned. They didn't. A week had passed and they were just as frequent, just as strong. At night

Pernell would hold her. But it was as though the magic had left his arms.

At first she thought it was he. He'd returned from Antwerp angry, despite the successful capture of the heretic. This disturbed her. She thought that once he caught Tyndale, this dark obsession that drove him would dissipate. If anything, he was worse. Now he said that once England was rid of the heretic's insidious Bible translation, he'd rest easy. Meg hoped so. She found it increasingly difficult to live with the black mood that shadowed him like a demon.

Upon reflection, though, she realized that her fears had begun to revive before his return. Something else had to be stoking them. And as soon as she made the connection, it was obvious. The source of her agitated condition had three names: Lyssa Winter, Enid Paget, and Birdie Dormer, the attendants she'd been ordered to tutor.

The underlying horror of it all was that she was tutoring mirror images of herself at that age. She had been just like them. Foolish. Selfish. Immature. Obsessed with the intrigues and melodrama of courtly love, which elevated flirtation and romance to a religion, complete with a code of conduct for the affairs of the heart. Like these young women, she had been groomed and schooled to be a court attendant, by a father who dreamed that his daughter would one day attend the queen. In the end it got him and his wife killed. For it was Meg's parents who selected Robert Culpepper to be her husband.

Robert was an obvious choice. He cut a dashing figure. He was sleek, well groomed, the product of a prominent family, intelligent, and debonair. Mostly he was heir to a fortune and available. Which meant he would require the hand of a beautiful wife to drape over his arm to complete this portrait of English elegance. Meg was raised to be such an adornment.

The introductions were tastefully arranged and no one was surprised when the heir to the Culpepper estate responded by turning his attentions to Meg. The storybook was opened and the tale of romance began.

They were a stunning couple. Robert was British aristocracy reborn. Meg was England's flower. He courted her with flourish. Handwritten sonnets hidden in bouquets of flowers appeared mysteriously on her balcony. The better ones were sung at intimate gatherings or read to the accompaniment of a lute, the conclusion of each bringing a flurry of feminine fluttering—teary eyes, gloved hands raised to lovesick hearts, sighs combined in chorus.

Meg lived a dream. And while she liked Robert, she loved the romance. Almost as much as did her mother. Together they savored each romantic overture, giggling in Meg's bedroom like simple country maidens. For each public appearance they planned Meg's wardrobe, her hairstyle, her entrance, her every word, with an attention to detail that would have put a military strategist to shame. Meg laughed, sighed, pouted, looked bored, fluttered her eyelashes, stood, sat, crossed the room, and cleared her throat all on cue.

She pouted when Robert attended to his studies at Oxford, and accused him of caring more for his dusty books than he did for her. It was a woman's ploy, pure and simple. And Robert, being a hapless male, responded appropriately to his training by bringing her gifts and roses and pleading his love.

Meg's wedding was a coronation. For the event the laws of the universe were altered, making the bride its center, with her mother in closest orbit. Robert was at best a distant planet. At the end of the day all that was left was for the storyteller to write a happy ending.

Only the story proved to be a tragedy, for the characters were so enthralled with the trappings of courtly love that they failed to recognize the wolf inside the groom.

Standing now at the door, Meg fought back the unpleasant memories of the past by concentrating on her preparations to go outside. She adjusted her bodice and skirt and checked her hood, making sure it was firmly pinned.

While the wolf had been slain, its tormented spirit was still very much alive. It padded boldly back into her life on the heels of the queen's attendants, with their incessant silliness and obsession with courtly love. Meg pushed open the door and strode down Ironmonger Lane, determined to do battle with her past.

Pernell paced impatiently in the courtyard of Lambeth Palace. Either Stokesley had nothing better to do than to flaunt the power of his position or there was indeed a pressing matter of business that demanded his immediate attention, as Pernell had been told. Pernell didn't know which it was. He only knew that he'd been waiting to conclude his business with the bishop for several hours.

They had been five minutes into their meeting when a pock-faced page scurried into the Great Hall and whispered something in the bishop's ear. Pernell was immediately ushered to the hallway. There he waited.

He waited while a flock of grim-faced clerics flew in and out of the Great Hall. He waited while page after page hit the doorway and then dashed down the hallway in a half-run, half-walk. When a gaggle of red-cloaked bishops arrived, Pernell concluded he was tired of waiting. At least in the hallway. He took his vigil outside to the courtyard, where the shadows of Lambeth's legendary towers grew long while Pernell's not-so-legendary patience grew short.

He strolled past the eastern tower with its winding staircase and ambled over to the red-brick gateway. The fresh air from the river did him good, as did the buildings themselves. He hadn't really looked at them when he arrived, rushing into the Great Hall with business on his mind. Now that he'd been forced into this unhurried state, the Lambeth facade presented itself to him in all its historical beauty. So much of England's past was tied to the building.

A piece of that history came to mind. He smiled at the thought. *It occurred one hundred and fifty years ago, in this very place,* he mused.

He attempted to re-create the scene. A gathering of bishops and scholars had assembled to question a rogue scholar and preacher, one John Wycliffe. Like Tyndale, in the foolishness of his own reasoning, Wycliffe had translated the Bible into vulgar English. It was here that he mounted an unsuccessful defense of himself and his heresy. Though condemned, he continued with his pernicious translation and thus was born the Lollard heresy. Country preachers expounding from the illegal English text, secret fellowships sprouting up in houses where the outlawed Bible was read aloud. Like a troublesome weed, the heresy seemed to spread with the wind and proved just as difficult to eradicate.

A century and a half later, though hundreds had been arrested and had recanted, pockets of Lollards and their sympathizers could still be found in the country.

Pernell stared at the twin towers and pledged that Tyndale's rogue translation would suffer a much quicker demise. He pledged that fifty years hence William Tyndale and his devilish translation would be so obscure, they wouldn't warrant a footnote in English histories.

A page came running from the building.

"Dr. Foxe?"

Pernell acknowledged the boy and prepared to reenter the Great Hall.

"Bishop Stokesley sends his sincerest apologies. He said to inform you that his business will be concluded shortly, and has requested that you wait."

Pernell was peeved. He tried not to show it.

"Tell His Excellency that I await his good pleasure."

By now the shadow of the building had engulfed the courtyard. It would be dark before Pernell made it home. He grew concerned for Meg. Her episodes had been coming with increasing frequency and he was at his wits' end as to how to deal with them.

In the past the episodes would come more frequently when he was away, but they'd always go away after he returned. Not now. And before, all he had to do was hold her for a couple of hours and her fears would reside. Now he seemed to have little or no calming effect.

Pernell looked up at the fading sky. He'd hoped to be home before nightfall. He was tempted to find that page and tell him to relay a message to Stokesley, telling him he'd come back tomorrow. And if it were just Stokesley, he'd have done it without a second thought—but one doesn't treat the bishop of London that way.

He looked again at the sky. All he could do was hope they could conclude their business quickly and he could get home.

He wished he could take Meg's pain from her. He'd willingly take it upon himself. And—he grinned at the thought—he was sure she'd willingly give it to him.

From the moment he first saw her, Meg had become the center of his universe. He remembered that day. The day he fell in love with her. It was her wedding day.

At thirty years of age, Pernell had been an entrenched scholar. His was a measured world of academic degrees. Beauty was a well-structured argument and one's offspring were published essays. He knew nothing of springtime abandonment or amorous bliss. A perfect day for him consisted of uninterrupted hours in his study with stacks of books gathered at his feet like grandchildren.

He was totally unprepared to meet glamour incarnate. His suffering began with an introduction.

"Professor, I'd like you to meet my wife."

Robert Culpepper stood proudly beside his seventeen-year-old-bride. Thick auburn hair cascaded from beneath a simple floral headpiece and curled naturally at her shoulders. Her complexion was pale and flawless. Round brown eyes lifted briefly in greeting, then lowered shyly.

The sensual impact of her nearness blindsided Pernell. So consuming was his attraction to her that he feared the entire wedding party could sense it. Then he glanced at the grinning bridegroom and a wave of shame doused all other feeling.

Hadn't he just witnessed the granting of the dowry, the exchange of promises, and the blessing of the ring? Hadn't he watched as the bride's ring was placed on three successive fingers in the name of the Father, Son, and Holy Spirit—this to protect her from demons? Didn't that same ring now reside on her left hand? Having just witnessed all this, what kind of wretch would now covet the bride?

Pernell's words tripped over themselves as he made an effort to extend his best wishes. "Pleased I am . . . um . . . it is indeed my pleasure . . . great pleasure, that is . . . to congrat–congratulate you, Mrs. . . . um . . . Mrs. Culpepper, on your wedded . . . wedding day."

Hearing her married name brought a blush to the bride's cheeks. With a quick glance at her husband, she thanked Pernell. Then she flashed him a smile that would frequent the scholar's thoughts for months to come—a smile so alluring, it would torture him with no small amount of guilt and anguish.

"Professor," Robert said happily, oblivious to the suffering his bride was causing, "you haven't taken a bride's lace yet."

Pernell was so lost in the bride's smile, he didn't hear the bridegroom.

"The bride's lace," Robert repeated.

Meg turned sideways, aiming her shoulder at Pernell. Tied to her arm were short lengths of blue ribbon binding sprigs of rosemary. Tokens for the male guests.

"Oh . . . yes," Pernell said. "The bride's lace."

Wearing newlywed smiles, the couple watched as Pernell took one of the sprigs.

His hand did not linger. Of this he was sure. He played it out in his mind a hundred times afterward, and he could state unequivocally in a court of law if necessary that his hand did not linger. Yet at the moment he took the sprig, he felt the warmth of Meg's flesh beneath her dress, and inside him stirred feelings he didn't want to own. So ashamed was he that he could not look the bridegroom in the eye.

"You're supposed to put it in your hat," Meg said.

"My hat," Pernell repeated. His hand went to his head and found only uncovered hair. He offered the bride a sheepish grin. "Seems I've misplaced it. But I promise, as soon as I find it . . . the hat . . . I'll be sure to put this in it. I promise."

Meg laughed gaily at his absentmindedness.

The days and weeks following the Culpepper wedding were non-stop bouts of guilt and self-flagellation. But try as he might, Pernell could not erase Meg's image from his mind. If he closed his eyes, he saw her smile. If he left his thoughts unguarded for but a moment, remembrances of the ease and grace with which she moved took center stage. Nights were the worst. In that uncontrollable moment between consciousness and sleep, she would visit him. In his dreams he heard her laughter, lost himself in her eyes, and reveled in the warmth of her touch.

It was a sin.

He knew it. He confessed it. He scourged himself for it. But he couldn't stop it. Nor could he stop himself from doing things he knew were wrong.

He carried the sprig of rosemary in his pocket, and in guarded moments he would lift it to his nose and she would be as real to him at that moment as she was the day he met her.

He even wrote a poem about her. In it she was a delicate maiden, bright and airy, a mixture of mirth and sunlight, while he was a hideous stone gargoyle with large, clumsy paws. Having wandered into the magical forest in which he guarded a castle, she became lost and frightened, especially when she first laid eyes on him. How desperately he wanted to tell her she had nothing to fear from him, but because he was stone he could not speak. Then a miracle happened. Her tears brought his stone heart and limbs to life and he was able to comfort her with his words. He became her guardian, traveling beside her, protecting her from dangers inherent in a mystical forest. She was grateful to him. And that was enough, for her gratitude warmed him in a way he'd never experienced as a gargoyle.

Pernell rewrote the poem five times. Five times he destroyed it. Each successive rewrite was longer and more detailed than the previous.

When Robert Culpepper returned to his Oxford studies, he frequently spoke of his wife and married life to Tyndale and Thorndyke, his fellow students. Pernell would eavesdrop on the conversations. And for the first few weeks following the wedding, the anecdotes came frequently. Then as the weeks turned into months, there was less talk of Meg as their conversation reverted to theology and Latin. There were times when an entire week would go by without a single mention of Meg. So Pernell, assuming the role of a concerned father of sorts, would talk to Culpepper privately and inquire into his home life, seemingly concerned as to how the boy was adjusting to the responsibility of having both a wife and university studies. Afterward Pernell would feast on every tidbit of information concerning his student's wife.

His interest in the couple prompted invitations to dinner, which he never failed to accept. The couple lived with her parents. Robert used his professor's presence as an endorsement of his studies, which seemed to be a point of contention in the household. Pernell got the impression that Meg's entrepreneurial father disdained Robert's theological bent and dependence upon his father's wealth. So during dinner and after dinner, as they moved from the table to Meg's father's favorite room, in which the walls were covered with animal heads large and small, Pernell would dutifully sing his student's praises and describe future employment opportunities that studies in theology would afford. Clandestinely he would luxuriate in Meg's presence.

Then, as faithful as the seasons, on the ride home he would flog himself, calling himself every imaginable name, and—with tears and great anguish—he would swear he would never accept another invitation. But a week or so would pass and another invitation would come and he would give in to his weakness and accept.

"Dr. Foxe?"

The same page who had appeared before stood in front of him again. It was dark now and he was hard to see. The boy should have brought a light.

"Bishop Stokesley has asked me to extend to you his sincere regrets," the boy said. "But due to unforeseen circumstances, he will be unable to grant you an audience ..."

Without waiting for the remainder of the message, Pernell turned toward home, leaving a stuttering page standing in the dark.

"Do ... do you have ... what should I tell ... when he asks?"

Chapter 9

While Pernell was pacing the courtyard at Lambeth Palace, Meg stopped at the imposing entrance to the girls' quarters. The only thing keeping her from turning around and going back home was that she feared the queen more than she feared the girls on the other side of the twelve-foot door.

The gnawing in her stomach nearly doubled her over. This was to be her third session with the girls. The first two had been disasters. At best her three charges were indifferent; at worst they were rude and obscene. It didn't matter that she had been appointed by the queen; the girls resented the implication that they were less than refined.

Placing a hand on the door, she listened before entering. At first she heard nothing. Were they gone? Had the queen required their services?

Then she heard voices. Hushed voices.

Meg sighed.

They didn't hear her enter. Sitting on the edge of Mistress Winter's gilded canopy bed, with their backs to the door, the girls were hunched over something. As usual, Lyssa Winter was in the middle of things, with Enid and Birdie on either side.

Lyssa was the most beautiful of the three and all of them knew it. Her flawless black hair was impeccably coifed. She had alabaster white skin, arched cheekbones, and lips that were thin and mischievous.

Enid Paget was unattractive. No amount of facial powder could hide poor skin and a bulbous nose. A moody girl from a wealthy family, Enid was accepted among the other attendants because of her relationship to Lyssa.

Birdie Dormer was the plain one. Skinny as a sapling, with twiglike arms, she was a silly, brainless flirt.

There was a fourth girl in the room, standing a discreet distance apart from the others but just as much infatuated with whatever it was that was holding the girls' attention. Meg didn't recognize her. By her patched and worn dress, Meg could clearly tell she was not a member of the queen's court. Her hair was plain brown, short and straight. She kept looking from whatever it was Lyssa was holding to the girls and back again.

Lyssa was speaking so low, Meg couldn't hear what she was saying.

Birdie bolted upright. "I don't understand! What does *begat* mean anyway?"

Lyssa said condescendingly, "You are a backwoods simpleton, aren't you? I'd wager even Alfreda knows!"

All heads turned to the servant girl.

"Of course I do," she said.

The girl's speech was coarse. Being put on the spot made her nervous. She took an awkward step backward. It was then that Meg noticed her deformity. The girl had a clubfoot.

"She's just saying that!" Birdie cried.

"I know!" the servant girl insisted.

"Then tell us," Birdie said.

There was a moment of silence.

"It's a nasty word. Mum would strike me if I said it aloud," Alfreda said.

Birdie scoffed. "I told you she didn't know!"

Lyssa and Enid fell against one another laughing.

"No . . . she's right!" Lyssa said. "It is a nasty word. Deliciously nasty!"

"Tell me!" Birdie insisted.

Lyssa stalled. Meg had seen her in this position before. The center of attention. If she knew Mistress Winter, the girl would milk it for all it was worth.

"I don't know if I should tell you," Lyssa said.

"Tell! Please tell!" Birdie pleaded.

Lyssa was getting the exact response she wanted. She shook her head.

"You've got to tell me!" Birdie cried, bouncing up and down on the edge of the bed.

"Go on, tell her!" Enid said.

"All right," Lyssa conceded. "If you must know."

She leaned toward Birdie. Cupping her hand over the girl's ear, she whispered.

Birdie covered her mouth with her hands and laughed wickedly.

"Tell me too!" Alfreda squealed.

The three girls ignored her. They laughed. Squealed. Whispered. And laughed some more.

"Every one of them?" Birdie cried, pointing to whatever was in Lyssa's lap.

"That's what it means!" Enid said.

"How many are there?"

The girls huddled again. While Lyssa pointed, the girls counted in unison.

"... thirty-one, thirty-two, thirty-three ..."

Meg had seen enough.

"... thirty-four ... thirty-five ..."

She made her presence known.

Four shocked faces whirled around.

"Mrs. Foxe!" Enid cried. "We didn't hear you come in!"

While the two girls shielded her, Lyssa slipped whatever she had in her hands beneath the bedcovers.

Meg made her way to the girls. She employed a tactic her mother used to use on her. She said nothing. She looked each of them in the eye and simply held out her hand. The message was clear enough.

"What?" Lyssa said.

Bold defiance. Meg expected it. She stood her ground and kept her hand extended.

"What is it you think we have?" Lyssa asked.

Defiance wasn't going to work; neither was diversion.

Meg motioned with her fingers.

Lyssa knew she held a losing hand but she refused to admit offense. Reaching beneath the covers, she pulled out a small book and handed it to Meg. "It's not ours," she said.

Meg looked at the book. It was small as books go, barely six inches tall, one and a half inches thick. The top corner of the cover was damaged.

She opened the book to a random page.

> The Gospell off Sancte Jhon
>
> The fyrst Chapter
>
> In the begynnynge was that word / ad that worde was with god; and god was thatt worde. The same was in the begynnynge wyth god.

When she realized what it was she was holding, she dropped it on the bed. The book fairly flew from her fingers, as though it were a hot coal.

"It's illegal to have this book," she said.

"It's not ours," Enid said. "It's hers. She brought it in here." Her finger pointed at Alfreda.

The clubfooted girl's expression was one of horror and betrayal. She stammered, backed away, looked at Meg, the girls, the book, then fled the room, hobbling across the polished floor.

The three girls laughed at her exit.

"You find a deformed peasant girl amusing?" Meg asked.

Lyssa replied smartly, "She provides us entertainment."

Still furious with the girls, Meg entered her house and dumped the contraband New Testament on the kitchen table. Not knowing what else to do with it, she'd carried it home with her in a shopping basket. Concealed, of course. And she'd had Lyssa place it in the basket so she didn't have to touch it.

The walk home had proved to be the longest walk of her life. She could just imagine herself—Pernell Foxe's wife—getting caught with a heretical book. Every eye on Cheapside looked at her suspiciously. At any moment she expected to be stopped and questioned. Of course they'd find the book and cart her off to the Tower.

What would Pernell do? Her knees felt weak at the thought. Pernell would die a thousand deaths. His reputation would be ruined. She wouldn't blame him if he abandoned her and never spoke to her again.

But what else was she to do? She couldn't leave the book with the girls or just lose it somewhere in the palace. Nor could she give it to anyone. How would she explain it? Merely having it in her possession was a sin. The only thing she could think of was to bring it home and let Pernell dispose of it.

Meg crossed herself and breathed a prayer of confession. In her heart she knew she meant well. God knew that too, didn't he?

She stared at the offending volume. A new thought came to her, something she hadn't thought of before now. Didn't the book's very presence in her house invite demons?

Saints above, protect me! she prayed quickly.

All of a sudden she felt dirty, vulnerable for having been in contact with the volume this long. What had she been thinking? Would she bring a rodent into her kitchen? How much worse was bringing in this spiritual infestation? Meg couldn't believe what she'd done. She had to dispose of the book quickly.

Without turning her back on the book, she grabbed a poker and stirred the ashes of the kitchen fire. They were cold. Falling to her knees, she tossed kindling into the fireplace, and in short order a fire of sufficient size crackled lively.

All this because of those three girls. At the thought, Meg's anger blazed as hot as the fire.

Now the problem was how to get the book into the fire?

Another thought struck her. Was it safe to burn the book in her kitchen? What if it released its unholy spirits into her house while it was being consumed by the flames? Was that why they always burned books outside, away from buildings?

Pernell . . . where are you? I need you!

She stared at the book on her table, more afraid of it than ever. It was too much of a threat just to leave it sitting there. But she didn't want to risk touching it. She could sweep it outside, but what if one of her neighbors found it?

Best to burn it and be done with it. She'd watch from the doorway. If any demons were released, she'd flee the house and wait for Pernell. They could get the priest to come and exorcise them.

Meg inhaled deeply to prepare herself for the task. Using fireplace tongs, she reached for the book. The tongs were too blunt to slip under it, and with each effort she managed only to slide the book farther away. She tried scooping the book up. The tongs proved unsuitable; they only shoved the book across the table.

Meg stepped back to rethink her strategy.

Maybe if she just grabbed it with her fingers, with one quick move she could toss it into the fire. Or maybe she could wrap a towel around it first, the way she would a hot pot. But there was something about reaching for the book with her hands that unnerved her.

She decided to give the tongs another try. The book slid to the edge of the table. Meg smiled. The edge of the table! She slid the book so half of it extended over the edge. Now she could grip it with the tongs!

Sensing triumph, Meg clamped the tongs on the book and lifted it. Now all she had to do was get it to the fire. Slowly she carried the offensive book toward the flames.

Just then the tongs slipped in her hands. From nervousness? From squeezing too hard? Or was it her sweaty hands? She didn't know. All she knew was that the book escaped the grip of the tongs and sprawled onto the kitchen floor just short of the fire.

Its pages lay faceup. The cover was slightly arched. Enough that she could grab the book again with the tongs and toss it into the fireplace.

She bent over, tongs at the ready.

Blessed art thou among women . . .

Meg backed away.

The words had leaped up at her.

The tongs clanged to the floor. Her hands covered her mouth. Her eyes were wide with fright, but for some reason she couldn't pull them away from the page.

Blessed art thou among women . . .

The words gripped her and wouldn't let go.

Blessed art thou among women . . .

"Pernell . . ." she whimpered.

Blessed art thou among women . . .

Sorcery. She clamped shut her eyes and tried to force the words out of her mind. She knew she should never have brought this heresy into her home. Now she was possessed by its evil.

But the words didn't feel like evil. She expected them to spread through her like venom. But they didn't. In fact, she felt a measure of comfort from them.

"Blessed art thou among women . . ."

"Blessed . . ."

"Blessed . . ."

"Blessed . . ."

"Blessed . . ."

Demons didn't bless people. They tortured and haunted people. What was happening to her?

Blessed art thou among women . . .

Meg moaned and rocked. Such things were too difficult for ordinary people to understand. That's why they had priests and scholars.

Pernell, where are you?

A sense of urgency came over her. She had to get the book into the fire before she lost her mind. With one hand Meg grabbed the fire poker to protect herself from an unholy spirit that might try to escape from the book; with the other she grabbed the tongs.

She turned her head aside to keep from looking at the text while she reached for the book blindly. Her first attempt merely nudged the book. She tried again, attempting to slip the tongs under the spine and grip it and toss it into the flames. But with each effort she was just missing.

She risked a quick glance, just enough to get her bearings and grab the book.

Fear not, Mary . . .

Again the words seemed to leap up at her, command her attention.

Fear not, Mary . . .

Meg froze. Her eyes locked onto the text.

Fear not, Mary; for thou hast found grace with God.

Her weapons clanked to the floor.

Fear not . . .

Meg fell to her knees.

. . . for thou hast found grace . . .

A strange warming sensation filled her bosom.

Fear not, . . . for thou hast found grace with God.

The room was growing dark. Behind her the fire cast a dancing shadow across the room. It flickered across the book. Meg didn't know how long she'd sat on the floor, staring at the open New Testament. All she knew was that she was alternately horrified by it and attracted to it.

She curled up, hugging her knees, and stared at it. While she didn't want to surrender to any demons that might reside in the book, she was tired of fighting.

A thought came to her.

Why would a demon possess someone with blessedness? That didn't make sense. Besides, wasn't this the Bible—translated into English, to be sure, but still the Bible? It wasn't as though this were a book of black magic.

Meg stared at the offending volume. She leaned closer toward it to read some more.

She backed away, scared.

This is ridiculous. You're acting like a stooge. Either scoop the thing in the fire or read it, but don't sit here and do nothing.

Inching a little closer, Meg hovered over the open New Testament.

Blessed art thou among women . . .

There they were again. The same words she had seen before. She looked farther down the page.

My soul magnifieth the Lord.
And my spirit rejoiceth in God my saviour.

She gasped. The words took her breath away. What a beautiful thought!

She looked again.

And Mary said:
My soul magnifieth the Lord.
And my spirit rejoiceth in God my saviour.

Mary? The Virgin? These were the words of the Virgin? How wonderful!

Meg looked for something that would identify the person uttering these wondrous words.

Mary arose in those days . . .
Elizabeth was filled with the Holy Ghost . . .
Then Mary said unto the angel . . .

Here it was!

And in the sixth month the angel Gabriel was sent from God unto a city of Galilee, named Nazareth, to a virgin spoused to a man whose name was Joseph, of the house of David, and the virgin's name was Mary.

She kept reading.

Lo: thou shalt conceive in thy womb, and shalt bear a son, and shalt call his name Immanuel.

Meg sat back in wonder.

The Virgin Mary's own words!

Her heart was strangely warmed. Except for the light in the fireplace, the room was engulfed in darkness.

And she wasn't afraid.

The door latch rattled.

Meg started.

Pernell!

He saw her sitting on the floor. His face, already concerned, grew alarmed. Leaving the door open, he rushed to her.

Having no time to consider her actions, Meg closed the book and slid it beneath the folds of her petticoat while the table partially hid her from her husband.

He said nothing about her sitting on the floor. He didn't have to. There was only one reason why she would be sitting on the floor in the dark.

"I'm so sorry," Pernell apologized. "I was delayed. I didn't want you to be alone when it got dark. Are you all right?"

Meg's heart pounded wildly. Her skin was instantly chilled, but not for the reason Pernell assumed.

He sat beside her, taking her in his arms, rubbing the chill from her arms. "Was it a very bad episode? How are you doing now? How long have you been on the floor?"

"I'm better now," she said.

And that was the straight-out truth. She felt good. Comforted. Inspired by the words she'd been reading. Only now she felt guilty.

Should she tell Pernell she'd been reading an English New Testament?

Just the thought gave her chills. Pernell sensed them and held her closer. "I'm here now," he said.

Indeed he was. And that was Meg's dilemma.

Wrapped in Pernell's arms, a heretical New Testament hidden in the folds of her petticoat, Meg frantically tried to figure out how she was going to stand and gather up the book without Pernell seeing it. For now, though, she didn't require the aid Pernell was giving her. She sat there, held tight in his embrace.

Chapter 10

Meg slept little that night. Not because of fear but due to an exalted sense of wonder. The words from the heretical book warmed her like no elixir ever could.

"My spirit rejoiceth in God my saviour."

Not only did the words themselves soothe her, but there was a rhythm to them that kept her saying them over and over again in her mind.

The words that captivated her most were "My soul magnifieth the Lord."

Such a noble thought. She wondered what it felt like for a woman to magnify the Lord with her soul. How odd it was that all her life she had seen the Virgin Mary depicted in stained-glass windows—colorful and serene—but not until now had she known what Mary felt when she was told she would bear the Christ child.

The hours slipped by peacefully until sleep finally overtook her. When she awoke, she felt refreshed. Refreshed and guilty.

That morning it seemed as if Pernell would never leave the house. He dawdled while dressing. He dawdled while eating his oatmeal. He dawdled through his morning prayers. It seemed to take him twice as long to walk to the door and explain that he would probably be late returning home again that night. Even his kiss was slow.

All this time Meg couldn't keep her mind off the heretical New Testament, which she'd managed to hide in the bedroom wardrobe. It had been a stroke of good fortune that the night before, the room was dark save for the fireplace. When Pernell stood to light some candles, it allowed her the chance she needed to sweep the book up with her petticoat and run upstairs. She said she was getting a handkerchief. Instead she burrowed into the bottom of their closet and hid the book in the back corner, beneath her mother's prized tulip bulb, which was wrapped in a dirty burlap bundle.

It lay out of sight all this time but was never far from her mind. Every time Pernell made a move toward the wardrobe, her heart leaped into her throat.

What would she say to him if he found it?

The thought alone left her stammering.

Relief came over her in waves when the door closed behind Pernell and he was finally gone. One thing was certain. She had to get that book out of her house before he returned.

Lambeth Palace was a good hour's walk from Pernell's house. Most days he enjoyed it, especially on days like today, when the sun was warm and the sky clear. Cheapside and the riverfront were bustling as usual with market business. He stopped for a parade of beer casks being rolled down the middle of the street, then crossed the Thames at London Bridge. The colorful buildings lining both sides of the bridge offered him a diversion from his thoughts. So did the activity. Public riders on horses. Mules pulling carts on creaking wooden wheels. Merchants peddling baskets of bread and meat and cheese. A little girl rolling a hoop into a chicken coop, resulting in feathers and squawking and cursing and crying.

It kept his mind from his anger at being kept waiting at Lambeth the day before. As he approached the familiar twin towers, he was determined to put the previous day behind him, to not take offense even if it was intended, and to concentrate on the business at hand—namely, to secure the necessary authority and documents to rid England of every last one of Tyndale's heretical New Testaments.

No sooner had he entered the courtyard than his resolve was tested once again. Bishop Stokesley was indisposed. Would Pernell be so kind as to wait in the hallway? So for the second time in as many days, Pernell began a vigil in the hallway just outside the Great Hall.

For two hours he waited. Standing. Pacing. Sitting. Looking at paintings, rugs, walls, and ceilings. Then a page appeared. The same pock-faced page from the previous day. Pernell was getting sick of that face.

He was told that Bishop Stokesley had been summoned to Whitehall; would he be so kind as to return this afternoon for an audience with the bishop?

Pernell clenched his jaw so tightly, the muscles quivered. He turned and left the building before he said something that would injure his Christian character.

Why was Stokesley being so casual about this matter? Did he not understand that England's very soul was at stake? Would a physician be so nonchalant about treating a poison? And wasn't that what this heresy was, a poison in the bloodstream of a nation?

He crossed the courtyard and exited through the gateway. He wasn't about to waste another day hoping that the good bishop would somehow manage to find time for him. But then, it wasn't as though he had a choice.

Hands on hips, Pernell gazed across the Thames at Whitehall. There was nothing for him here. At least not until this afternoon. But he didn't want to walk all the way home just to depart an hour or so later.

Making his way to a livery, he paid four pence for the rental of a horse and rode off. He'd spend the early afternoon with Meg and still have time to be back for an audience with the bishop.

As he approached London Bridge, a smile crossed his face. Meg would be surprised. He hoped pleasantly so. Women were often odd about having their daily schedule disrupted.

Pernell had said he wouldn't be home until late. Good. That gave her the day to dispose of the book. Meg's first impulse was to get rid of the book immediately. That way it would be done with. Then she decided to take care of her morning chores first. That would give her time to decide what to do with it.

Strapping on her hood, she grabbed the wooden buckets and made her way down narrow Ironmonger Lane to the water conduit. For as long as she could remember, Pernell had been promising her that someday they'd be able to afford a water carrier. He hadn't spoken of it lately. But then, how many wealthy heretic hunters were there?

After hauling the water, Meg returned to Cheapside with her shopping basket to buy the day's food. But as she wandered among the booths, her mind was on the book in the bottom of her wardrobe.

Every time she caught herself thinking about it, she felt guilty. At the same time, it gave her pleasure to think about it. She found herself standing at the fruit vendor's stand, holding an apple in her hand and thinking, *My soul magnifieth the Lord.* Her heart beat happily, as though she were in love.

"Do you want apples or do you just like holding 'em?"

The fruit merchant, an angry man with an unkempt mustache that curled over his lip and into his mouth, stared at her as if she were addled. In a way she was, for it took a moment for his words to make sense.

"Do you want apples or not?" he shouted.

"Yes," Meg said, her senses returning. "Four."

"Four! What good fortune!" he cried.

Meg took her apples and continued her shopping. A pound of balled sweet soap. Needles, thread, and buttons from the haberdasher's booth. Eggs. And finally fish for the evening meal.

The entire morning she walked as though under a spell. All she could think of was how the words in that book made her feel as if she were glowing inside. As she weaved her way through the narrow street that led to home, she came to a decision. She would look at the words one more time, then dispose of the book.

Meg sat on the edge of her bed with the book in her hands. It no longer frightened her. At least not in the sense that she was afraid to touch it. She was still uncomfortable with the forbiddenness of it.

She couldn't begin to describe the aftereffect the words from the book had on her. The only feeling that came close to it was the warm peacefulness she felt in Pernell's arms. Only this was stronger. It went deeper.

She found it impossible to comprehend how such feelings came from a book that generated such hatred. Yet there was no mistaking its power over her. When she read it, she felt as though the angels of heaven were embracing her. What was wrong with her that she could find such comfort in such a horrible book? It was foolish even to consider keeping the book inside the house.

She knew she had to get rid of it . . . as soon as she took one more look. Laying the book in her lap, she lifted the cover. Her fingers explored its damaged corner.

For several minutes she sat there. Immobile. Wanting to read more of the words, then not wanting to.

She fingered the edge of the first page and slowly turned it. Then another. She saw a name.

William Tyndale

The heretic.

Then Meg's eyes stumbled on this paragraph:

> For the nature of God's word is, that whoseover read it or hear it reasoned and disputed before him it will begin immediately to make him every day better and better.

She could almost hear Pernell's voice in her head. *The heretic's defense, no doubt. The reasoning of a criminal as to why he would defy king and country.*

The heretic sounded as if he were a physician and this were his prescribed cure for the ails of humanity. Better and better. Every day.

How could a book of heresy do that?

Yet she knew it was true. She'd already experienced the book's healing power.

She read further.

> Here thou hast (most dear reader) the New Testament or covenant made with us of God in Christ's blood . . . that I might be found

faithful to my Father and Lord in distributing unto my brethren and fellows of one faith, their due and necessary food: so dressing it and seasoning it, that the weak stomachs may receive it also, and be the better for it.

A covenant. In Christ's blood. Due and necessary food. Weak stomachs will be the better for it.

Yes . . . yes . . .

Meg grabbed a thumbful of pages. She began searching for the words that had affected her so positively the night before, not knowing where to begin looking. As before, the words on one of the pages leaped up at her:

Let not your hearts be troubled. Believe in God and believe in me.

Meg slammed shut the book, frightened.

It was as though the book were speaking to her directly! She sat there on the edge of the bed, numb. Tears welled in her eyes. Yet the damage had been done.

As on the night before, the words had been planted in her mind. She could feel them taking root. Spreading. Soothing. Healing. Strengthening her.

A hundred sermons could never begin to produce the same effect on her. A year on her knees in penance could not make her feel more exalted than she felt at this moment.

Dare she repeat them aloud?

"'Believe in God . . .'" she whispered.

Would God strike her dead? She waited.

No fire came from heaven. No avenging angel appeared. The floor didn't open to swallow her.

"'Believe in God,'" she whispered again. "Let not your heart be troubled. Believe in God."

For the longest time she sat there, immersed in the words, embraced by arms she could not see.

"'Let not your hearts—'"

The front door opened and slammed shut.

"Meg?"

Pernell!

Meg jumped up from the bed, the book of heresy in her hands. She slid it under the bedcovers.

No. What if Pernell wanted to rest? Or sit on the bed?

Throwing back the covers, she snatched up the book.

"Meg? Are you here?"

She could hear the sound of his boots on the hardwood floor.

Should she say something? If she did, he'd come straight for the bedroom.

Pernell's boots hit the stairs.

"I'm in the bedroom!" she shouted. What choice did she have?

She had to get the book into the wardrobe.

With the sound of Pernell's steps getting louder, Meg threw open the wardrobe doors, dropped to her knees, dove toward the back.

"Meg? What are you doing?"

There was more concern in his voice than accusation.

Meg withdrew halfway from the wardrobe. She looked up at her husband. He was a tower. He always had been.

A look of concern crossed the tower's face and he began to tumble to his knees.

"No!" Meg cried. "I'm getting up!"

"Are you all right?" Pernell asked, his face marked with worry.

"I'm all right!" Meg cast a quick glance into the wardrobe, making sure that he couldn't see the book. He couldn't. The corner to which she'd thrown it was dark. "I was just, um . . ."

She grabbed the rag bundle encasing the tulip bulb.

"I was just getting my mother's tulip," she stammered. "I thought it was time I planted it."

With one hand she held up the dirt-crusted rag as evidence; with her other hand she swiped back a strand of hair from her cheek, marking her face with a dirt smudge.

Pernell looked at the bulb, then at her. The silence between them seemed longer than necessary. He suspected something, didn't he?

He offered her his hand. She took it and stood. It was difficult for her to match his gaze.

"You're certain you're feeling well?" he asked. His eyes searched hers.

"Oh, yes," Meg said. "Just getting the bulb." Again she held it up as evidence.

He smiled. Long arms encircled her and drew her against him. Meg lay her cheek against his chest.

"For a moment you had me worried," he said.

"Worried?"

He hesitated. "When I came in and saw you half inside the wardrobe . . ."

He paused. Meg could hear his heart racing.

". . . it reminded me of the foot of the stairs at your father's place."

Where she hid from Robert.

"I thought maybe you were reliving it again."

"No, dear, I'm fine. Believe me. I was just getting the bulb."

He placed his cheek atop her head and hugged her more tightly.

"Thank God," he said.

"Are you hungry?" she asked, speaking into his chest. She didn't wait for a response. "I'll fix you some eggs."

She closed the wardrobe door and, carrying the rag-covered tulip, hurried down the stairs into the kitchen, making certain that Pernell was following her.

Over a plate of eggs Pernell related how the bishop had once again set him aside for other matters.

"But you're returning this afternoon?"

Pernell took a forkful of eggs and nodded. Meg hadn't joined him at the table. She kept herself busy around the kitchen.

"I did hear some news from Antwerp, though," he said. "Things that happened after I sailed."

"Oh?"

"The procurer general saw to it that the heretic Tyndale made it to Vilvorde Castle."

"Where's that?"

"Six miles north of Brussels. He'll be safe from meddling hands there until his trial."

"What will happen to him?"

"He'll get what he deserves," Pernell said matter-of-factly. "He'll be formally condemned as a heretic, degraded from the priesthood, and handed over to the secular authorities for punishment. Most likely burning at the stake."

Meg, who had been stirring the fire while he was speaking, stopped and set the iron poker aside.

Pernell began to chuckle. "But there's better news," he said.

"Oh?"

"No sooner had I sailed than Philips shows up at the procurer general's door, as frightened as a trapped animal."

"Frightened? Of what?"

"The English merchants in Antwerp. The news of Tyndale's arrest spread quickly."

"They're defending a heretic?"

"Many of them have Lutheran sympathies; that's why it was important to move Tyndale to Vilvorde. But what riled them most was that Philips had abused their corporate diplomatic privileges to find and befriend Tyndale."

"What did the procurer general do?"

"Bade him Godspeed."

"He didn't help him?"

"Philips made his own bed. A fool shouldn't be protected from his own foolishness."

Meg glanced at the stairway.

Pernell chuckled at his own story. "Particularly when, having been warned, he persists in his foolishness. The way I heard it, just after we closed in on the heretic, Philips sent his secretary to England to demand more money for the capture of Tyndale."

"Didn't you already know the man was greedy?"

"This goes beyond greed. You have to remember, his benefactor in all this has chosen to remain anonymous. Naturally, following the capture Philips is going to want to inform that benefactor of his success. Sending a secretary as he has done is like pointing a finger."

"Do you know who the benefactor is?"

"I have my suspicions."

That's all he said and Meg chose not to press him. If he wanted her to know, he'd have told her outright.

"So where did he go?"

"Philips? Apparently, he's still waiting around for the money, hiding from the merchants, and hoping he can stay alive long enough to run away to Paris."

Pernell chuckled, pleased at the thought of Philips's predicament. He thought Meg was quieter than usual, but then, he did surprise her and interrupt her routine.

Late afternoon he rode back to Lambeth, praying that his meeting with the bishop would not be delayed again.

Meg stood alone in the kitchen, trembling. It unnerved her to think about what would have happened had Pernell caught her reading the heretic's New Testament. Keeping the book in the house was simply too dangerous.

She went upstairs and dug the book out of the bottom of the wardrobe and brought it back to the kitchen. Book in hand, she stood before the fire. All that was left to do now was to toss it into the flames.

She didn't want to but she had to. Who was she to argue against the wisdom of the king and the church and scholars, even that of her own husband? If they said the book was dangerous, it must be dangerous. If it was a sin to have it, she shouldn't have it. The law was clear.

The flames danced happily, unaware of her struggle.

Meg looked at the book in her hands. A finger traced the corner. Damaged. Just like her.

Why should this be so hard for her?

A surge of willpower came over her and she tossed the book into the fire. The flames embraced it.

"No . . . no . . . no!" she screamed.

Dropping to her knees, she reached for the book. There wasn't time for tongs or pokers or anything else; she had to rescue the book from the flames. The fire burned her hand and she pulled back instinctively. Then reached again.

She fought the flames and the pain.

Get the book out of there. She had to get it out.

She managed to grab it and pull it out, dropping it onto the hearth. Coals spilled out with it. She picked at the book until it was free from them. The edges were smoldering but otherwise the book was intact.

For a long time she stared at it lying on the floor, free from the fire. Her right hand was burned. It began to blister and hurt. Of greater concern to her was the book on the hearth.

Why was she doing this?

All she knew was that it seemed the right thing to do. The book didn't belong in the flames.

Nursing her throbbing hand, Meg took the New Testament upstairs and hid it again in the bottom of the wardrobe, where she had stored her mother's red tulip bulb all these years.

Chapter 11

The infamous day of the red tulip occurred at the beginning of a new term at Oxford, when Robert Culpepper's increasingly strange behavior blossomed and bore horrific fruit.

Pernell noticed that the boy increasingly seemed to be having difficulty concentrating in class. Neither his comments nor his papers showed any of the brilliant logic of which he was capable. Tyndale and Thorndyke noticed the change, too. They expressed their concern for him to their professor.

At first Pernell feared he was responsible for Robert's peculiar behavior. He was convinced that his feelings for Meg had finally been exposed, that during some unguarded moment he'd said or done something to give himself away, and that Robert had seen his attentions for what they truly were. At every encounter with Robert, Pernell expected the boy to confront him with his illicit feelings.

Each day became judgment day in Pernell's mind. Every morning he expected a visit from a superior accusing him of acts unbecoming a Christian and an Oxford professor. Each night Pernell would experience a strange brew of relief and dread for the coming day. With tears he would confess his sin. At times he even welcomed exposure. Maybe under the harsh light of academic and public condemnation he would finally be purged of his obsession.

But the accusation never came. Meanwhile Culpepper's condition grew worse. His appearance became increasingly disheveled. His attention span during lectures was nonexistent. His eyes darted madly from side to side as he sat in his chair. Perspiration trickled down his cheeks. If anyone spoke to him, he ignored them. If they touched him, he'd deflect their hand.

He began making chicken sounds.

"Bawk, bawk, bawk."

His unfocused eyes darted here and there. His cheeks glistened with sweat.

"Bawk, bawk, bawk, bawk."

He rocked back and forth in his chair.

Thorndyke was sitting to the left of him. He reached over and touched Culpepper's arm.

Reaction was instantaneous. Culpepper jumped up and threw off Thorndyke's hand. He stood there, shuffling his feet uncertainly; then he sat and continued rocking and clucking. A minute later he got up and left the room, leaving behind a half dozen theology students staring after him and at each other.

Instructing his students to continue discussing the lesson without him, Pernell went after Culpepper. The boy was nowhere to be found.

After class Tyndale and Thorndyke volunteered to ride out to their classmate's residence to check on him. Pernell told them he thought it best if he went—alone.

As Pernell approached the house, it appeared deserted. No one came to greet him.

He announced his presence.

Silence answered him.

A pair of doors stood open on one side of the house. He walked toward them, announcing himself again. He saw or heard no one. He entered the house.

That's when he saw the first indication that something was horribly wrong.

Just inside the door lay a dead chicken. At least that's what it appeared to be. There were feathers and blood, but little else remained to distinguish it. Pernell would later remember thinking how he pitied the dog that had killed the animal and dragged it into the house.

He stepped over it.

"Robert?" he called. "It's Professor Foxe."

He stood in the center of the room, facing the stairs, expecting someone to respond to his hail. When no one did, he called again, this time louder.

Hands on hips, he debated what to do next. His options were the stairway and a door. Not having been in this part of the house, he guessed that the stairs led to private living quarters, and so felt more comfortable choosing the door. As before, he announced himself before opening it.

The kitchen. It too looked deserted.

At the far end of the room three fowl were burning on a stilled spit, one side reduced to charcoal. In the center of the room, a long wooden table was laden with bowls of food in various stages of preparation. The garden greens in the bowl nearest him were starting to wilt.

An eerie feeling chilled Pernell's flesh. This entire incident was decidedly odd. First there was Culpepper's behavior. Then the dead chicken in the doorway. And now this. The kitchen gave every evidence of having been abandoned in haste.

Pernell edged his way along the table toward a door that he supposed led outside.

"Good Lord, no!"

He saw them.

The cook.

Meg's mother.

Meg's father.

All of them dead.

Faceup, lifeless, dead.

His thought immediately turned to Meg's safety, unless he was already too—

The door in front of him burst open as though the hinges had exploded, knocking him backward, bowling him over, landing him on the floor against the other door.

The force behind the explosion entered as unstoppably as a wall of water through a bursting dam.

Robert!

He was screaming. Frenzied. Sweat flew from his hair and spittle from his mouth as he moved. He carried an ax in his hands.

Pernell had never seen a mad dog before, but he couldn't imagine it being much different from the creature coming at him. The boy's eyes were charged with pain and fury, his clothes caked with mud and blood. His scream was more of a howl. He lunged wildly, mindlessly, forward with the ax raised over his head.

He swung the ax at Pernell. The weapon missed its mark, splintering the wooden floor next to Pernell's ear.

Robert was bent over, inches from him. Perspiring heavily. Panting. Pernell grabbed his shirt, and before the boy could reverse his momentum and dislodge the ax, he placed a foot in the boy's chest. With one good shove his attacker flew backward. The ax dislodged and tumbled to the floor.

Pernell scrambled to his feet, intent on grabbing the ax. But there is something about madness that quickens the flesh. Robert beat him to it. With a triumphant grin he waved it in circles between them.

Pernell retreated, inching his way around the table, hoping to keep it between him and his attacker. He stumbled over the cook's lifeless arm. It was a stumble that saved his life, for he collapsed against the table just as the ax blade swished where his head had been and buried itself in the table's edge. Robert pulled to dislodge it.

With the seconds allotted him, Pernell climbed over the three corpses on his hands and knees. He pulled himself up, his back to the wall, the full length of the table between him and his attacker.

The ax head struck again and sent bits of bowls and containers and a variety of utensils tumbling everywhere.

Pernell spied a knife on the floor. From the looks of it, it was the one used to kill the cook and Meg's parents. But he couldn't think about that at the moment. It was a weapon. And he sorely needed a weapon right now. He grabbed it.

He pointed the business end of the knife at Robert, who was raising the ax for another blow. Pernell hoped that the sight of the weapon would deter the boy.

The ax came down on the table with a vengeance, sending clouds of flour and spices into the air.

"Robert! Robert! Can you hear me!"

Pernell had to jump back to avoid the next blow.

"Robert! It's me, Professor Foxe! You don't want to do this!"

The ax struck again.

Pernell was moving from corner to corner at the far end of the table, keeping its length between him and his attacker. Robert was lunging at him, his reach with the ax nearly as long as the table itself. The last two blows cut huge, wedge-shaped notches out of the table's edge. Each time Pernell managed to avoid the blow, each time he felt the whoosh of the ax head as it came down, and each time the wall prevented him from retreating any farther.

"Stop, Robert! Stop! In the name of God, put down the ax!"

Robert paused. The entreaty to deity somehow penetrated the madness and struck a rational chord in his mind. His eyes softened. He blinked, and with each blink a measure of sanity filled his eyes.

It was momentary.

With a howl that chilled Pernell's flesh, Robert lunged at him again.

The blade buried itself in the edge of the table, deeper than the others, closer to its human mark. Pernell invoked God's name over and over without effect. There was no pause, no change; it had no effect on his attacker except to make him angrier.

Pernell knew he had to do something. He couldn't dodge these blows forever. They were getting too close and he was winded, his arms and legs heavy.

Think! Think! What are your options? The wall was to his back. There were two doors. To reach one, he'd have to go through Robert; to reach the other . . .

He eyed the door to his right.

Pernell saw the ax coming out of the corner of his eye. The blow hit the corner closest to the door. He pulled back, inching away from the door, backing into a corner.

With animal quickness Robert lunged again.

Pernell slumped to the floor. He eyed the back door over the three bodies. Even before he could move toward it, Robert was there, standing at the end of the table, blocking his way.

There would be no escape. Robert was too quick.

His attacker looked down on him, sensing the kill.

Pernell lifted the knife. It was a futile effort. The range of Robert's weapon was too long. He'd be split in two before the knife blade ever reached its target.

Robert stepped toward him. His foot stubbed against the cook's ribcage. He glanced down, his eyes meeting those of his dead victim. Robert viewed the man no differently than he would a fallen log in the forest.

Pernell gripped the knife in his hand.

Robert's head snapped up. Their eyes locked. The hunter and the hunted. The ax head raised and as it did, a shrill, high-pitched sound emanated from behind the attacker's bared teeth.

He stepped over the cook's body. Then Meg's mother.

The ax head hovered at its peak.

Robert took one last step. His foot got caught up with Meg's father's arm. It was as though, even in death, her father were making one last effort to stop the rampaging madman.

The killer stumbled, lost his balance, and fell forward. The ax, already started on its downward arc, fell short of its mark, but not short enough; Pernell shouted as it bit into his leg.

Right behind the ax was Robert. Off balance. Falling.

He landed on Pernell, his sweaty face slamming against Pernell's cheek.

Then everything was still.

Pernell's chest was heaving. He saw the ax on the floor beside him and grabbed it before Robert could get it. But there was no longer any competition. Robert made no effort to reach the ax. He made no effort to do anything at all.

With his free hand Pernell pushed his attacker off him. Robert fell lifelessly to the side. The boy's chest was red and sticky wet. The knife he had used to kill the others protruded from his chest.

For Pernell the shaking started. First in his hands, then in his arms and legs and face. He'd never killed one of his students before.

Meg!

Everything he'd seen argued that she too was dead, sprawled somewhere on the floor like her parents. But he didn't want to believe it.

He tried to get up. Pain held him down. The cleaved flesh of his leg burned like fire. Scooting to the table, he pulled himself up, using his arms and one good leg. The blood drained from his head and he felt woozy. He fought to keep control of his senses. He told himself that Meg needed him now. This was no time to pass out.

Wrapping his leg tightly with a kitchen towel, he hobbled through the door that led to the stairway and, he presumed, the living quarters.

He made his way upstairs and hastily checked each room, not knowing whether or not time was a factor. For all he knew Meg was alive but wounded. When he found no bodies initially, he inspected each room again, this time more carefully. The absence of a corpse raised his hopes. Maybe Meg had escaped this gruesome scene altogether. Maybe she was visiting a friend or relative. He had to be sure.

Standing in the center of what he assumed was Meg and Robert's room, he carefully searched every space large enough to hide a human being. Under the bed. In the wardrobe, where he recognized a couple of Meg's dresses. He stood on the balcony overlooking the garden and scanned the foliage below. He found nothing out of the ordinary, save a splash of red from a rare tulip.

The outcome of the search repeated itself in the other rooms upstairs. In one room—the bedroom of another female, who, judging by the clothing and finery, was probably Meg's mother—there was a staircase leading downstairs. He went down it.

At the landing he stared down the length of the hallway. From the way the house was laid out, he assumed it led outdoors. For a time he stood there. Go back upstairs and search again, or go outside and search the grounds?

As he pondered his next step, he spied something curious at the foot of the stairs. Arch-shaped scratches on the floor. The kind a door would make. Only there was no door. A wooden panel enclosed the space beneath the stairs. Odd, though. The top corner of the panel was broken off. He stuck his finger in the hole.

Something smashed it from the other side.

He cried out and pulled back his hand. As he did, the panel crashed open, knocking him backward. A figure tumbled out of the space beneath the stairway and moved quickly toward the stairs.

Meg!

Pernell grabbed her by the hips from behind. She screamed and kicked. He called her name. She couldn't hear him over her screams. In her hand was a scuffed black shoe that she used repeatedly to strike him in the face. Then an elbow to his chest and neck.

Pernell managed to restrain her and pull her against him, encircling her with his arms, holding her tight, shushing her, saying her name over and over, telling her the danger was past, that she had nothing to fear, promising her he would see to it that nothing would harm her ever again.

Chapter 12

Meg knelt over a planter of dirt outside her house on Ironmonger Lane. The sun was making a brief appearance down the middle of the lane, warming her back as she bent over the planter. She hadn't had her hands in the soil since her parents were killed. It felt good to flex her hands in the earth again. There was something optimistic about planting; it was a statement of sorts that said you had hope for the future. Maybe even more than a statement.

She had removed the bulb from the bottom of the wardrobe to draw attention away from the New Testament she was hiding there. Having told Pernell that's what she was after, what choice did she have but to plant it now? It had lain in the bottom of the wardrobe these many years, wrapped in burlap and fear. She had been certain that handling it would prompt one of her episodes. Scooping the dirt aside to form a crater in which to bury the bulb, she realized now her fears were unfounded.

Meg sat back on her heels. She looked down at the planter box of dirt and the hole she'd dug. Philosophy and unfounded fears aside, it felt good to have the sun on her back, to have her hands in the soil, and to anticipate once again seeing her mother's prize tulip in full bloom.

The door opened.

"I'll only be gone an hour," Pernell said, shrugging on a black cassock. "Two at the most."

"Saint Paul's?"

He nodded, squinting into the sun and adjusting the brim of his hat.

Meg stood and brushed the dirt from her skirt around the knees. She put her arms around Pernell's neck and kissed him. He squirmed.

"Meg, please," he said, glancing behind her down the street.

Meg turned to look herself. Ironmonger Lane was empty of traffic all the way to West Chepe. She held her ground. The two of them met nose to nose in the shade of the hat brim.

"Tonight after dinner I thought we could make an early night of it," she said.

For a moment Pernell forgot they were embracing in public. He smiled.

Meg rose to her toes and kissed him.

"Dr. Foxe!"

A middle-aged, squat woman emerged from the cobbler's shop halfway down the lane.

"Mrs. Dauncey," Pernell greeted her. Meg was still draped around his neck, with her back to the woman. She giggled.

"Shameful!" she heard the woman cry. "A man of your stature? Shameful! In full view of God and children! Shameful!"

A door slammed and they were alone again.

Meg buried her face against Pernell's chest and laughed.

"I don't see what you find so funny," Pernell said, breaking her grip. "If she speaks to the priest, we could be charged with public indecency."

"I don't care," Meg said, feeling bold. "My defense will be that I love my husband."

"And you'll be ordered not to make a public display of it; then they'll give you a couple of days in the stockade to think about it."

"Oh, bother," Meg said.

She caught a whiff of rosemary. She found a sprig pinned under his doublet.

"I love that you still carry it," she said.

"I always will."

She rose quickly and pecked him again on the lips.

"Meg!"

They both checked the lane. No one was in sight.

"Hurry home," Meg said.

Pernell adjusted his lapel, his hat, and brushed off his shoulders to remove some dirt from her hands. With a nod he headed down Ironmonger Lane.

She watched him go. As he passed shop after shop, greetings were called out. He returned each one by touching the brim of his hat. A moment later he disappeared around the corner.

Meg returned to her work. She placed the bulb in the earth and covered it, once again anticipating the day when it would bring a splash of red into her life.

Taking the watering can, she sprinkled moisture over the freshly planted bulb. All that was left now was to watch, water, and wait.

She bent down to get the rag that had held the bulb all these years, and was struck with a delicious thought. Pernell was gone. He said he'd be gone for at least an hour. Time enough to . . .

No . . . Meg shook aside the thought and entered the house. She washed her hands, checked the fire, and put on the kettle to heat water for some tea.

He'd be gone an hour.

At least.

Alone for an hour . . .

Meg looked at the stairs leading to the bedroom. With Pernell no longer traveling for extended periods of time, she couldn't count on having many opportunities like this. She took a step toward the stairs, then pulled back. The water was coming to a boil. Was she going upstairs or was she staying downstairs and having tea?

She pulled the kettle off the fire and looked again at the stairs. Her heart beat like that of a maiden in love, and with the feeling came guilt for keeping a secret from Pernell. But it didn't keep her from climbing the stairs.

A moment later she was on her knees, reaching into the back corner of the wardrobe, searching until her hand felt pages. She pulled the New Testament from the recesses.

She had only an hour.

Moving to the edge of the bed, she held the book up to the light of the window and opened it, anxious to see what she would find in it today.

Pernell stood before a massive oak table, his hat doffed and his hands folded in front of him. Papers and books and writing instruments littered the surface of the table. Two attendants with boyish faces stood at the bishop's elbows. Several more lined the stone walls, awaiting his bidding.

"There's been a development since our meeting at Lambeth," the bishop began.

"Development?"

The bishop leaned back in his chair. He made a steeple with his two index fingers. Pernell didn't like the look on his face. It was the look of a man about to deliver unpleasant news. This was just like Stokesley. Pernell thought everything had been decided at their Lambeth meeting. Now Stokesley wanted to change things.

"We're getting on in age, Pernell," the bishop said.

Pernell's jaw set in anticipation of what was coming.

"We're not as young as we once were. Not as agile. Not as spry."

Pernell wished he would just get on with it, but Stokesley had a habit of walking a person through a verbal rose garden just before springing some unpleasantness on him, in the hopes of somehow making the news less offensive. It was having the opposite effect on Pernell. He tensed.

"And while our intentions are good, and our determination as strong as ever ..."

Get on with it! Pernell screamed inwardly.

"... sometimes our age gets in the way."

Pernell decided a more aggressive approach was called for, not only to speed things along but to assure Stokesley that everything was under control.

"Your Excellency," he said, "it's true we're not as young as we once were. However, let me assure you that there is enough strength in these old bones to —"

The bishop cut him off with an uplifted hand.

"No need to feel defensive, my friend."

My friend. Now Pernell knew Stokesley had something up his clerical sleeve.

"The task of ridding England of the heretic's New Testaments is still yours," said the bishop with a placating grin. "And I will grant you the resources you need to complete that task."

"Thank you, Your Excellency."

"Including . . ."

Pernell's relief was short-lived.

". . . including an associate."

The bishop wouldn't do this to me again, would he? Visions of Henry Philips walking through the door unnerved him.

"Your Excellency," Pernell objected, "the resources of the church are all I need for this task. Age aside, I do my best work alone."

Again the bishop raised his hand to cut him off. Pernell fell silent. The bishop motioned to one of his attendants, who exited the room.

Pernell felt hard-pressed to put a stop to this before Philips entered the room.

"Your Excellency," he pleaded, "while I concede to the wisdom of your appointment in the capture of the heretic Tyndale, having an associate in this matter will only serve to slow the progress of the task."

The bishop wasn't listening. His eyes were trained on the doorway.

He didn't have to wait long. His attendant reappeared and, with a nod to the bishop, resumed his place against the wall. The door was left open.

With a sense of doom Pernell watched the doorway.

A young man stepped through.

"Dr. Foxe," the bishop said to Pernell, "allow me to introduce . . ."

"Master Kyrk Thorndyke," Pernell said with a tone of pleasant surprise.

The two men exchanged nods. The young man was tall and slimmer than Pernell remembered him being. His clothing was as colorful and striking as his red, wavy hair. He strode into the room like a thoroughbred.

"Master Thorndyke came to me, requesting to work under your tutelage," said the bishop. "He was quite vigorous in his argument." The bishop was obviously enjoying his part in arranging this reunion.

Pernell smiled. "Oral debate is one of his talents."

"Then I take it you have no objections to his appointment as your assistant?"

"Your Excellency, I would be most pleased to have Master Thorndyke as my assistant," Pernell said.

"How is Dr. More?" Pernell asked.

Kyrk Thorndyke walked beside him. He looked older, more mature. No longer a boy. There was an air of confidence in his stride, his eyes, and his speech. The professor inside Pernell was proud.

The two men strolled among the shadows of clouds driven by an ocean breeze while the Thames lazily lapped its riverbanks. Their meandering conversation, mostly reminiscing about Oxford, had found a steady bearing in the trial and imprisonment of Thomas More, Pernell's friend and fellow scholar and Thorndyke's teacher.

"When did you see him last, Professor?"

"I regret to say it's been several months. I've been away."

"Tyndale," Thorndyke said, nodding. He squared his shoulders and looked distant. "Dr. More's spirits are high," he said, "though, as you can imagine, it's difficult for him being away from his family."

It was also More who, as chancellor of England, had commissioned Pernell to continue the fight against Lutheran heresy by seeking out and arresting William Tyndale. The two men shared a common intellectual and theological passion to save England from Luther, Tyndale, and their kind. And now it seemed that Kyrk Thorndyke had joined their ranks.

"Does Thomas see any hope of release?" Pernell asked.

"Only if he signs the Act of Succession, thereby recognizing the king's right to wed Queen Anne."

"He'll never do that."

"No, he won't."

They walked a distance, each lost in his own thoughts. While he couldn't say it aloud, Pernell was in full agreement with More. The king had gone too far, having allowed his lust for the vixen Anne Boleyn, and his desire for a male heir, to overcome all reason.

Thorndyke spoke. "Rumor has it that the queen's sympathetic to Luther's teachings, that she's given the king Tyndale's treatise *The Obedience of a Christian Man.*"

Pernell clenched his teeth. "Only rumor?"

Thorndyke shrugged. "For the moment."

They walked a little farther.

"It was Dr. More who suggested I work with you."

Pernell smiled. That sounded like More, always the teacher.

"I think he sees the end close at hand," Thorndyke said.

"We must pray for him, then."

They walked with only the sound of street hawkers coming between them.

"Tell me, Master Thorndyke, what are your thoughts regarding your former classmate William Tyndale?"

Thorndyke's eyes hardened. "I agree with Dr. More," he said, "when he calls William the leader of a false sect and an evangelical English heretic. He and his kind are a plague. They're abhorrent in doctrine and troublemakers politically. I believe they're responsible for the Peasants' Revolt in Germany. Their heresy is a poison, an infection, a contagion that attacks the whole of Christendom. They scorn the sacraments of the church and deride the notion of purgatory. They encourage sexual license, deny the Eucharist, and revile the Mass. They believe that the Church of Christ is fundamentally corrupt and should be swept away. The spread of their teachings is tantamount to the collapse of world structure. Master William Tyndale is in league with the Antichrist and will someday answer for his sins on the Day of Judgment."

Pernell gave the satisfied nod of a professor. "And the flow of English New Testaments into England?" he asked.

"Must be stopped at all costs," Thorndyke said without hesitation. "Every one of them . . . burned."

"And those who import them, distribute them, and harbor them in secret?"

"Burned as an example to others who would introduce pestilence into a peaceful society."

Pernell felt like hugging his new assistant.

Six days later Pernell was ready to renounce his English citizenship. Sir Thomas More, a saint if there ever was one, was scheduled for execution. England made preparations to slaughter its best and most courageous scholar to satisfy the king's lust.

According to reports, More was given one final chance to recant. But recant what? Having principles? Being a man of high moral character? Pernell knew his friend too well. The man would embrace death rather than betray his beliefs. And he knew the king too. Here was a man who thought nothing of altering centuries of English history and turning his back on his church and his faith simply to have his way with a maid.

The injustice of it all made Pernell sick.

But the facts remained. Henry was king and the object of his lust was Anne, who was now the queen. To get her, Henry defied the pope, raped church properties, and established himself as the head of the church in England. Moral qualifications for this ecclesiastical position didn't seem to be a factor to him.

Like the spineless worms they were, one by one the king's advisors fell in line. All except the chancellor of England, Pernell's honorable friend Thomas More. To the king it didn't matter that More was a man of wisdom and righteousness. He was an obstacle to the king's desires and had to be removed.

For the last six days of his life More fasted and prayed. Both Thorndyke and Pernell joined him. They visited him as often as the king would allow, which was infrequently. Pernell was with More when a barber came to cut More's beard and hair. The prisoner declined.

"The king has taken out a suit on my head," More said, "and until the matter is resolved, I shall spend no further cost upon it."

Pernell was praying with him when news came that the king had commuted More's sentence from disembowelment to beheading. The sentence read that this was granted him because of More's long service at court. Upon receiving the news, More closed his eyes in relief. At least he was spared the worst pains this world can offer.

The day of his appointed death was kept from him until the last moment. Pernell and Thorndyke were with him for early morning devotions when the news came by way of Sir Thomas Pope, a representative of the king's council. He informed the prisoner that he was to die at nine o'clock of that same day.

More: "Master Pope, for your good tidings, I heartily thank you. I am bound to His Highness that it pleases him so shortly to rid me out of the miseries of this wretched world. And therefore I will not fail earnestly to pray for His Grace, both here and in another world."

Pope: "The king's pleasure is further. That at your execution you shall not use many words."

More: "I am readily obediently to conform to His Grace's commandments."

Pernell could take no more. Nor could he bring himself to witness the execution of so fine a man. In tears, leaving Thorndyke behind, he wished More God's blessings as he entered eternal rest. Then he fled the room.

—

It was nearly noon. Pernell stalked the house like a caged beast. He refused all comfort. Meg stood by with a heavy heart, respectfully silent, slicing boiled potatoes for their afternoon meal. She doubted Pernell would want anything to eat, but she thought it best to have something ready for him all the same.

Pernell went upstairs for the hundredth time.

She heard him rummaging around.

Her heart leaped.

The New Testament!

What if he should find it?

She reached for a towel and headed toward the stairs just as he came back down. There was nothing in his hands. His mouth was the same grim line it had been for the last week. His eyes were fixed, hardened.

Meg stepped out of his way as he passed. His anger weighed on his shoulders like a heavy woolen shawl. Wordlessly she returned to her meal preparation.

"Let not your heart be troubled . . ."

The words came to her unbidden yet so clear she couldn't be certain someone hadn't spoken them.

She glanced around the room.

Pernell had taken up a book and was leafing through it. He gave no indication of having heard anything.

"Let not your heart be troubled . . ."

The words sounded again, but this time softer, in her mind. For many days now they had been a personal comfort to her. Mentally she completed the thought.

"Believe in God and believe also in me."

Her emotions stewed within her, a curious mixture of comfort and anguish. Comfort from the words she'd come to treasure, anguish over not being able to share them with Pernell when he was so obviously in need of them.

Dare she?

No. No! It was unthinkable! How did such a thought even enter her mind? It would ruin everything!

A thudding at the door interrupted their silence.

Pernell answered it.

The door blocked Meg's view of the messenger. She only heard his voice.

"He's in glory now."

Pernell took the news stoically. He closed the door softly. For a long moment he stood there, bracing himself with a hand against the door.

There was a shuffle of feet as he turned around, then the sound of the kitchen chair as it scraped across the wooden floor. Pernell slumped into it. He took a deep breath. Then another.

He lifted his eyes to look at Meg.

"A good man was killed today," he said, "for getting in the way of another man's selfish desires. What kind of country do we live in that would allow such a thing?"

The man of stone crumbled. Sobs shook his frame. His huge hands covered his face, then balled into fists and pounded the table so hard, the bowls and utensils jumped.

Meg moved to his side. He leaned into her and she cradled his head.

"Let not your heart be troubled," my dearest . . .

How she ached to say these words to him.

She pulled him harder against her.

"Let not your heart be troubled . . ."

Pernell shuddered uncontrollably.

Meg held him. She wept with him and for him. But mostly she wept because for fear, she could not bring herself to say aloud the words she yearned to say.

Chapter 13

The chamber into which Meg walked that next Sunday was a room of mystery. It always had been. Wax tapers and tallow candles flickered and smoked against stone walls. Incense and charcoal commingled with the body odors of the throng that pressed against her. Without exception they came for a single purpose—to witness the miracle.

High overhead, plaster images stared down at them, players known and unknown in this ancient drama.

Meg glanced up at Pernell standing beside her. His face was fixed. Solemn. She envied him. He knew the secrets. The language. The symbols. The magic behind the drama. His serenity bespoke an assurance she lacked, and craved. But it wasn't her place to understand. Merely to attend. To watch in wonder. To stand and sit, to speak and be silent, all at the proper times, and to feel blessed for the interlude the drama brought to the toil and tedium of her everyday existence.

Once, when they were newlyweds, Meg had asked Pernell to explain it all to her. His voice firm, as though he were speaking to a child, he patted her on the hand and told her it was enough for her to look at the pictures in the windows. The images of stained glass were there for her and they were sufficient. At the time she concluded he was right, of course. The cravings she felt were unnatural. Unhealthy. She felt ashamed for having them. Who was she to covet the knowledge of the saints?

The New Testament in her wardrobe had resurrected those cravings. Was it sinful of her to want to understand spiritual things? The things she read in the book were enlightening. Inspiring. She felt closer to God after reading it. Was it wrong for her to enjoy the sensation, to want to lift the veil that obscured God?

As it did every week, the drama began with a procession. Priests followed by ministers and servers. They approached the altar and took their customary positions.

For reasons unknown, the clamor of vendors in the nave behind them increased to the point of distraction. Meg glanced over her shoulder. Guild merchants were hawking their cloth wares; farmers from the outskirts of town bartered with women over poultry; aldermen examined weights and measures.

The noise distracted Pernell too. He scowled. At times the market grew so loud, it drowned out the words of the priests. What did it matter? Even when Meg heard the words, she didn't understand the language in which they were spoken. The nave activity reminded her she needed to stop at a fishmonger's cart on the walk home. She'd promised Pernell salmon for dinner.

"Kyrie eleison.

"Christe eleison.

"Kyrie eleison."

The priest turned to the congregation and raised his hands. *"Gloria in excelsis Deo,"* he said, and the Mass officially began.

The secret ritual progressed with a parade of crucifixes, candlesticks, chalices, and patens, with much of the ceremony conducted at the high altar, which was hidden from the people by a rood screen. Some of the proceedings were deemed too holy for the common person. Instead they were given prayers and devotions with particular attention to the hours of the Virgin.

Meanwhile the priest and his assistants moved in and out of view, their every gesture and word cloaked in obscure sacred truth. Careful to perform the ceremony exactly as it had been passed down to them, they worked the magic of the Mass, speaking the phrases that would invoke the miracle.

At the climax of the ceremony the priest stepped from behind the rood. In his hands he held the host, which he lifted high for all to see. It was done. The miracle for which they had gathered. The host had become the body of Jesus, the Christ.

At that instant candles and torches were lit to illumine the scene. The sacring bell rang, as did the church bells, so those in neighboring streets and fields might be made aware of this solemn moment. For Christ was present in their midst once more, and time and eternity were reconciled.

In concert with the other worshipers, Meg knelt and held out her arms in adoration.

—

At the conclusion of the service, having received God's saving grace through the partaking of the wafer host, Meg and Pernell made their way through the assembled throng. A blue light fell upon them, drawing Meg's attention to its source—sunlight, filtering through a stained-glass window.

Her gospel.

She stared at the image immortalized in thin sheets of blue and red and yellow glass. The Madonna, looking serene as always, cradled an equally serene Christ child in her arms. Angels hung suspended overhead, looking down on both mother and child in reverence. At her feet a little lamb stared up at her in adoration.

The holy mother's head was adorned with a halo that resembled a rising sun. Even the colors of the window portrayed a simple serenity, primary and unmixed, juxtaposed magically to evoke the emotion of the scene—a woman, content with child, fulfilled, at peace with herself and her world while heaven and earth looked upon her with wonder.

Meg's expression matched that of the adoring lamb. For now she knew the Madonna's thoughts.

"My soul magnifieth the Lord. And my spirit rejoiceth in God my saviour."

Then something—a passing cloud?—moved behind the window, cutting off the light. The colors turned dark. Disturbing. Threatening.

A chill came over her.

"Meg? What's wrong?"

Pernell looked at her with concern.

A few feet from them, two men had just laid hands on a third man, accusing him of being a cutpurse and hauling him away to the authorities.

"Meg?"

She licked her parched lips. "It's nothing," she said. "Nothing. Just lost in thought, that's all."

"Are you certain?"

"I was just looking at the window."

The sun reappeared and once again the colors of the glass came alive. The Madonna looked down on her with her never changing expression of serenity.

A crowd was gathering around the plume of black smoke as Pernell stepped from the church nave into the sunshine. A safe distance from the fire that fed the smoky column, Bishop Stokesley sat prominently atop a raised scaffold with several other bishops, abbots, and a couple of priors. Their elevated position afforded them a good view of the proceedings, and the crowd a good view of them.

Standing at the edge of the platform was a squat, round-faced rector who was addressing the assemblage. Pernell recognized him as Geoffrey Chapman, an ardent preacher and well-known opponent of the German heretic Martin Luther. As befitting the rector's reputation, his voice rang clearly, well beyond the reaches of the sizable crowd.

"Many children of iniquity, maintainers of Luther's sect, blinded through extreme wickedness, wandering from the way of truth and the Catholic faith, have craftily translated the New Testament into our English tongue, intermeddling therewith many heretical articles and erroneous opinions, seducing the common people; attempting by their wicked and perverse interpretations to profane the majesty of Scripture, which hitherto had remained undefiled, and craftily to abuse the most holy Word of God, and the true sense of the same. Of this translation there are many books printed, some with glosses and some without, containing in the English tongue that pestiferous and pernicious poison, dispersed in our diocese of London."

Pernell nodded. Pestiferous and pernicious poison. He couldn't have said it better himself.

For nearly an hour Chapman railed against Tyndale's New Testament, with a summary exposition of the errors of the translation, two thousand by his count. Choosing wisely not to enumerate the errors at length, he contented himself with labeling the English translation of the New Testament accursed and damned, and called for its destruction.

Carts of the condemned New Testaments appeared. With the assembled clergy's approval, the books were tossed by the armful into the fire. Bishop Stokesley looked particularly pleased, this entire event being his doing. Pernell considered it to be a dubious victory at best. It was a matter of contention between them.

The books that were being consigned to the flames had not been confiscated. Stokesley had purchased them. He sent men into the streets and marketplaces to purchase every Tyndale New Testament they could find for this display. The bishop argued that the end result was worth the cost.

Pernell opposed the tactic. The idea of criminals profiting from smuggling contraband, regardless that it was now off the street, was repugnant to him. Lawbreakers should be punished for wrongdoing, not bribed into handing over the filth in which they traffic. It further enraged Pernell to think that the bishop's money eventually found its way back to Tyndale's followers, who used it to print more New Testaments. But no matter how passionately he argued, all the bishop could see was a public bonfire that gave the impression that he was ridding England of heresy.

"Pernell?"

Meg touched his arm.

"I'll meet you back at the house," she said.

Pernell looked at her. She looked pale. Her lips were a thin, grave line.

"Are you ill?" he asked.

"Tired."

"Give me a few moments and I'll walk you home."

"You stay," she insisted.

"It'll only be a moment."

Meg's lips pursed. "Do you want salmon for lunch or not? If you do, I have to begin preparing it."

"Salmon? Yes . . . salmon would be nice."

Meg turned and walked away. "I'll meet you at home," she called over her shoulder.

Pernell looked after her, not certain as to what to make of their conversation. Meg hadn't been acting herself lately and he was unsure what to do about it. She had always had spans of time when her past haunted her, but they usually came and went like a summer storm. Something deeper was troubling her.

For now Pernell turned his attention back to the pyre of books. A practical man, he set aside the issue of Meg for the time when he could do something about it. There was something else he wanted to do now.

Reaching into his coat pocket, he pulled out a single sheet of paper, torn and crumpled from travel and stained with the salt of the sea. The word *Deuteronomy* appeared boldly at the top of the sheet. Pernell worked his way through the crowd toward the fire. The heat of so many burning books was intense. Still Pernell approached the flames, pleased at the sight of so many pages of English text curling up with black edges. Standing toe to toe with the fire, the heat turning his skin red, Pernell tossed the Deuteronomy page on top of the books.

He thought of Thomas More, the only other man he knew who felt as passionately as he did about the threat the works of Luther and Tyndale presented to the kingdom. Now he stood alone in the task.

Watching the flames consume the page, Pernell breathed a heartfelt oath: "In the presence of God and all that is holy, I vow that I will not rest until every copy of this heretical work, together with every person who aids in its distribution, suffers the same fate as this single page. May God give me strength."

He stood until the page was nothing but ashes.

"Thy will be done," he said.

Chapter 14

Meg stood with her hand on the gold-plated latch, feeling dwarfed by the huge door. She dreaded going in. The door was cracked just enough for her to see Lyssa, Enid, and Birdie huddled on Lyssa's bed, in full court dress. The three were in rare form. As usual, the two drones were circling their queen bee.

"He's so adorable!" Lyssa gushed, fanning her face with the flat of her hand as though she would faint. "Those *incredible* blue eyes of his looked up at me, and he said,"—she imitated a dreamy male voice—"'Excuse me, miss. I do believe you dropped this.'"

Enid and Birdie squealed in delight.

"'I do believe you dropped this,'" Enid mimicked, using the same inflection.

"Did you?" Birdie asked.

"Did I what?"

"Drop it?"

"Of course I dropped it!"

"I mean on purpose. Did you drop your glove on purpose just so he'd notice you?"

Lyssa delayed her response for no other reason than to torture her audience. When she did speak, her tone was worldly-wise. "How else was I going to get his attention? Show my ankle?"

Enid and Birdie covered their mouths in shocked delight. Their squeals elevated to a new pitch.

Meg stepped into the room.

"Time for your lesson, ladies," she said. "Her Majesty the Queen has instructed me to review with you the proper etiquette for this week's royal tennis match."

"Did he touch you?" Birdie asked Lyssa.

"What a dumb question!" Enid spat. "What do you think he did? Kiss her in full view of the court?"

Birdie's back straightened defensively. "It's not a dumb question! He could have touched her ungloved hand!" To Lyssa she repeated, "Did he? Did he touch you?"

"As a matter of fact . . . ," Lyssa said.

"Ladies!" Meg said sharply.

The three turned disapproving glares at her, offended by her interruption.

Behind Meg the door to the chamber opened and closed. Alfreda, who Meg had learned was the daughter of the scullery maid, hurried across the floor as quickly as her clubfoot would let her.

"Not now, Alfreda," Meg said. "The ladies are occupied."

Alfreda walked straight toward Meg. "'Scuse me, mum," she said. "They's not who I needs to talk to."

From her canopied throne Lyssa dismissed the girl with a wave of her hand. "Go back to your kitchen, you wretched monster," she said.

Enid and Birdie thought the dismissal hilarious.

"Mistress Winter!" Meg cried.

"It's awright, mum," Alfreda said. "They treated me worst afore."

"Then they were wrong before," Meg said. "It's unkind of them to speak to you that way and they know it."

The three girls on the bed gave no indication they took Meg's chastising to heart. They turned to primping and preening themselves.

Meg would deal with them later.

"What is it you need, Alfreda?" she asked.

"I needs to talk at you," the girl said. She looked past Meg at the girls. "Bys ourselves."

"Don't worry about them," Meg assured her. "Tell me what you need."

The clubfooted girl inched a little closer to Meg. Covering her mouth with a hand, she said, "I needs the book you tooks from them."

"The book?"

Lyssa spoke up from the bed. "That Bible book," she said, pleased to show that she'd overheard. "The one that listed all those men having marital relations."

The other two girls giggled openly. Lyssa smiled, proud of herself.

Meg felt the color rising in her neck, for Lyssa's rude behavior, but also for reasons unknown to the girls. She turned Alfreda toward the door.

"Let's talk in the hallway."

"It's all right to talk about it," Lyssa said. "The queen has one too. I've seen it in her room."

"The queen has one of *those* books?" Birdie cried.

"Haven't you seen it?" Lyssa said. "It's in her bedchamber on that small table."

"You've been in the queen's bedchamber?" Enid asked.

Lyssa donned her most superior tone of voice. "Of course! Haven't you?"

Meg led Alfreda from the room. The sound of the three chattering magpies ceased when she closed the door.

"I needs the book," Alfreda insisted.

Meg didn't know what to do. She hadn't anticipated anyone asking her for the New Testament.

"You know you're not supposed to have that book, don't you?" she said.

"I knows dat."

"Then why—"

"I's not suppose to haf it 'cause it belongs to me mum. And if she finds out I's the one who taked it, she'll tan my backside beet red!"

"Your mother doesn't know I have it?"

Alfreda shook her head. "When she looks for it, I tols her I never touch it."

"You lied to your mother?"

Alfreda was a slow girl. It hadn't dawned on her until too late that she'd just confessed to lying. With her sin revealed, she became flustered.

"I din lie! I din lie!" she shouted. "Pleas' don' tell me mum I lied. She'd beats me fur sure."

Meg put a hand on the girl's shoulder to calm her down.

"I needs dat book. I needs it now."

"I don't have it," Meg said.

Alfreda's eyes grew wide with alarm. She began to dissolve on the spot.

Meg felt sorry for the girl. "I don't have it here . . . with me. Do you understand? I can't give it to you right now, because I don't have it with me."

"You can git it?" The girl's eyes were hopeful.

"Yes."

"Today?"

"Tomorrow."

Darkness passed over Alfreda's face like a cloud. "Tomorrow?" There was a distant look in her eyes as she envisioned the implications of this. She looked up at Meg. "Promise?"

"I'll do my best."

Alfreda seemed confused. "Is your best as good as a promise?"

Meg nodded.

This satisfied the girl. Wiping her cheeks with the back of her hand, she hobbled down the hallway.

The next morning it seemed as if Pernell would never leave the house. With the kitchen still smelling of breakfast bacon, Meg wiped the table for the third time. Pernell was still in the bedchamber. She could hear him stomping about but had no idea why he was taking so long to get going this morning.

Meg tossed the cleaning rag aside. With hands on hips she stared at the ceiling, as if by willing so she could make Pernell move faster. She was expected at court and was ready to leave, except she didn't have the scullery maid's New Testament and couldn't get it until Pernell departed.

Finally heavy boots on the stairs signaled that Pernell was coming down. His steps were slow, his eyes preoccupied in thought.

"Will you be wanting supper tonight?" Meg asked. Maybe if she got him thinking about coming home, he'd be reminded that first he had to leave.

His steps slowed. He came to a stop one step shy of the landing.

"Kyrk Thorndyke is a remarkable young man," he said.

"The young man you've already told me so much about . . . ," Meg said. "I can see why Thomas was so taken with him."

Not wanting to appear anxious for him to leave, Meg picked up her cleaning cloth and began wiping the table again, all the while mentally urging him to take the final step down the stairs.

"He was one of the most determined of my students," Pernell mused. "Persistent. A rare quality in a man so young. And conservative too. He recognizes the value of deep spiritual roots in society. Another rare quality."

With the rag cleaning a clean table, Meg stared at Pernell's boots. She urged them forward. One more step. Just one more step.

"He has some interesting ideas as to how to stop the flow of pernicious literature into England. How to locate and apprehend those who are smuggling and distributing Tyndale's wretched translation."

Meg stopped wiping.

"Give me ten young men like Kyrk and not only will I rid the isle of that filth, but I will see that every person caught with it will rue the day they strayed from the path of righteousness."

Flustered, Meg suddenly didn't know what to do with her hands. They wrung the cloth, then tossed it onto the table, then brushed a wayward strand of hair from her eyes, then settled on her hips, then reached again for the cleaning rag.

"Well . . . ," Pernell said in conclusion. He descended the final step, covered the distance between him and his wife in three strides, gave Meg a hug, and headed for the door. He called over his shoulder, "Sorry I have to rush off. I'll be late coming home tonight."

The door closed behind him.

Meg stood frozen for a time. Then, her voice weak, she said to the door, "I'll keep your supper warm for you."

She sat on the floor, the doors of the wardrobe opened wide like an angel's wings. On her lap was the New Testament. She didn't want to give it up, but she was taking too great a risk hiding it in the house.

A noise came from downstairs. Her heart jumped. Her muscles tensed. Every other sense lent its energy to her ears as they strained to hear the sound of the door or footsteps on the stairs. Perhaps Pernell had forgotten something?

When she heard nothing after several seconds, she allowed herself to breathe again, but she was still tensed; her hands were shaking.

Just put the book in the basket and be done with it, she told herself.

But it wasn't that easy. Knowing she would never have another chance like this one, a part of her longed to open the book one last time. She caressed the cover. She didn't have time for this. Then again, how long would it take just to read a few more words?

She pulled the pages back with anticipation.

> Rejoice in the words always, and again I say rejoice. Let your softness be known to all men. The Lord is even at hand. Be not careful: but in all things show your petition unto God in prayer and supplication with giving of thanks. And the peace of God which passeth all understanding, keep your hearts and minds in Christ Jesus.

Meg exhaled. The tension drained from her neck and back; her shoulders slumped, relaxed.

"*... the peace of God which passeth all understanding ...*"

It was hard for her to think of this book as anything but magical. Whenever she opened it, it was as though the book knew exactly what she needed to hear at that moment.

Her eyes closed. Her head tilted back as she luxuriated in the passage. Then after a time she craved more.

> Furthermore, brethren, whatsoever things are true, whatsoever things are honest, whatsoever things are just, whatsoever things pure, whatsoever things pertain to love, whatsoever things are of honest report; if there be any virtuous thing, if there be any laudable thing, those same have ye in your mind, which ye have both learned and received, heard and also seen in me: those things do, and the God of peace shall be with you.

Meg walked to the palace with mixed feelings. Her basket, with its contraband concealed under bread and cheese, weighed heavily on her arm. She avoided eye contact with the people she passed, lest her eyes betray the struggle she felt in her soul. She wanted to give the book back to the scullery maid so she'd no longer be tempted to sneak readings behind Pernell's back, yet she didn't want to give up the passages that had come to mean so much to her.

For the length of her journey the sky overhead was a gray slate and the wind had a bite. Meg's cheeks felt its nip.

Entering the palace grounds, Meg deviated from her usual route and made her way toward the kitchens. The tension in the hallways was palpable. Conversations were hushed and clipped, mannerisms strained. Given the state of the kingdom, she supposed it was understandable.

Catherine of Aragon, the king's first wife and a favorite of many in the court, had recently died. This while the court was still reeling over the death of Sir Thomas More. Many of the king's staunch supporters thought he had gone too far in executing More. Added to all this was the queen's failure to give Henry a son. In this matter, though, hopes were high; Anne was big with child again.

The king had been still of speech and action, and the court reflected his mood. Rumor was that he was thinking he'd made a mistake in marrying Anne. The birth of this child would tell. The queen had aged visibly under the strain. But as Meg walked the palace hallways, she sensed there was more. Something had happened that had charged an already volatile environment.

"There you are!"

Madge, one of the queen's ladies-in-waiting, caught up to Meg from behind. She was a small woman. Petite. Not beautiful but usually pleasant. Meg had always found her to be a polite, reserved lady in a sea of sharks. At the moment she was flushed and worried.

"Her Majesty the Queen is in a frightful mood!" Madge cried. "She's been calling for you! Where have you been?"

Guilt pounced on Meg for dallying on the floor of her bedroom, reading her forbidden book.

"What's happened?" she asked.

Madge looked at her in astonishment. "Haven't you heard?"

"Tell me!"

Madge swallowed hard, either to work up her courage or to keep down her emotions.

"His Majesty was thrown from his horse while jousting!" she cried. "He's been unconscious for two hours!"

Meg raised a hand to her throat. "God be with him," she whispered. "This news is certain?"

"The duke of Norfolk informed Her Majesty a short time ago. She's been calling for you ever since."

"Where have you been?" the queen thundered the moment Meg was introduced.

Meg didn't attempt an explanation. She didn't think the queen wanted one. She bowed. "At your service, Your Majesty."

The scene into which she'd walked was a frightful one. The pregnant queen was pacing, her hands bracing her back. She perspired heavily. Her entourage buzzed about her helplessly, their eyes frozen in fright.

The queen herself looked near death. Her mouth was drawn. She flitted about like a caged bird.

Conscious of the basket on her arm, Meg laid it aside and approached the virginals.

"No, no, no, no!" the queen bawled. "Not here. In my bedchamber."

The queen waddled toward the bedchamber, a dozen attendants trailing behind, each offering her advice at the same time. Meg fell in step with them, then remembered her basket. She dared not leave it unattended. Running back, she grabbed it. From within the bedchamber Meg could hear the queen bellowing for her music.

Rushing past the stragglers, Meg dropped the basket beneath a table and took her place at the keyboard.

As Meg played song after song, the attendants readied the queen for bed. It seemed to take an inordinate amount of time, but eventually Her Majesty lay in bed with her head propped up on pillows, her eyes closed.

The entire room held its breath as the chords of the virginals anointed the bedchamber. The queen let out a sigh and with it the room breathed again.

However, their smiles of relief were premature.

The queen popped up.

"Out! Out! All of you, get out!" she ranted. Her arms waved hysterically. "Out! Quickly! I want to be left alone!"

The doorway wouldn't have been more jammed had a fire broken out in the room. Meg rose from the virginals to leave.

"You! Stay!"

Meg closed her eyes, hoping the queen meant someone else. Cautiously she looked over her shoulder. Anne Boleyn was pointing at her.

Dutifully Meg took her seat, her foot kicking the basket under the table. She nudged it until it was out of sight, then resumed her playing as the last of the attendants left the room. From the golden cage in the corner the queen's linnet began to sing.

"She's always liked your playing," the queen said.

Meg began another song.

"That'll be enough," the queen said.

"Yes, Your Majesty," Meg said. She stood to leave.

"I haven't dismissed you," said the queen.

Chapter 15

Robert Culpepper.

William Tyndale.

Kyrk Thorndyke.

Three students who had altered the course of Pernell's life. He thought it ironic. In their hands he had envisioned the spiritual course of England righted and back on course, with God at the helm. Unforgiving reality had other plans.

Culpepper was dead and Tyndale was in Vilvorde prison, charged with heresy. Pernell glanced at Thorndyke. He alone held any hope of a professor's dream coming true. Yet the situation in which Pernell found himself was eerily reminiscent of Antwerp and that rogue Philips.

They awaited heretics and Thorndyke was in charge. At least for tonight. Before they were paired together, Thorndyke had done some infiltration of his own into the smugglers' lair on Broken Wharf. He'd learned that a shipment of New Testaments had been delivered and that they'd be picked up for distribution tonight.

"You're certain of your information?"

Thorndyke was peering through a space between the slats of a shed. He'd been sitting there, motionless and silent, for over an hour. Without looking at Pernell, he replied, "My source is reliable. I can't vouch for the validity of the date, though. These men are smart. They circulate several dates and places. About one in three is an actual time; the others are phony."

"In other words, there's a one-in-three chance we're wasting our time."

"Yes. But I don't think so."

"Why not?"

"A feeling."

There was no apology in his explanation. Sharp, eager eyes concentrated on the dark dock.

Pernell sat back and waited with mixed feelings. He didn't know whether or not he wanted Thorndyke's information to be correct. That he wanted to capture smugglers and confiscate New Testaments wasn't part of his dilemma. He wasn't sure he wanted Thorndyke to succeed this easily, this quickly. More to the point, without him. If he did and Stokesley heard about it, Pernell could find himself in the same position he was in at Antwerp with Philips. A mere spectator.

If something was going to happen at the docks tonight, it would happen with or without Pernell staring with Thorndyke through the crack in the slats. So he let his mind wander back to their Oxford days. Exactly what did he remember of Thorndyke?

Pernell was in his second year of teaching at Oxford when Culpepper, Tyndale, and Thorndyke walked into his Latin class. Like all first-year students, they were idealistic, confused, and disoriented. And like all first-year students, their anxieties about school life drew them together. Wherever one was found on campus, you would find the other two.

As the term progressed, their academic abilities became apparent. Pernell drew them aside for special sessions and was himself soon drawn into their circle, first in the role of professor, later as a confidant.

They were a professor's dream and he found himself looking forward to every moment with them—answering their questions, challenging them to think for themselves and defend their opinions, seeing their eyes open with delight when the light of truth broke through adolescent, muddled thinking. Pernell had never known such a comradeship with other men, let alone students, before or since.

He remembered how similar Culpepper, Tyndale, and Thorndyke were in their passions, yet how different in their abilities. Culpepper was brilliant and articulate. Tyndale had a gift for languages. And while Thorndyke was the least gifted of the three, he made up for it with persistent, almost Herculean effort. Pernell had never seen such bull-headed determination in a man so young.

At his post Thorndyke tensed. He leaned forward, trying to see through the darkness. Pernell didn't have to ask. The smugglers had made an appearance.

The professor in him surfaced. Shedding his own fears for the moment, he was most interested in watching how Thorndyke handled himself in this situation.

The younger man stood. He was calm. Confident. He even took time to brush the warehouse dust off his clothes before saying anything. When he spoke, he was brief.

"It's time," he said.

Pernell followed him the short distance through the warehouse and into the night. Ahead of him Thorndyke took a deep breath of London's moist night air. He was in no hurry.

Too confident? Pernell thought.

With measured strides Thorndyke led the way to the end of the wharf. As he did, he raised his right hand and made a circular motion in the air. The signal to his men.

They were not as quiet as he. No sooner had he signaled than from two positions not far from the wharf, armed men and horses appeared, some of the men carrying torches.

The quiet lapping of the river gave way to their racket, and the torches lit the faces of two men on the wharf, one much younger than the other. At first they both wore identical masks of fright, then as the realization of what was happening took hold, the elder of the two men became resigned to his fate, while the younger man grew angry. Balling his fists, he set himself to charge.

"Bink! Don't be a fool!" the older man said. "They have weapons!"

Clearly the two men were overmatched. Half a dozen swords were pointed at them by the first row of men, with an equally armed row behind them. While the two smugglers had no weapons, the younger one's eyes darted from side to side. He was not ready to concede defeat.

He looked behind them at the river.

Thorndyke saw what he was thinking. "You won't get far swimming for it," he said.

As he was speaking, a boat approached from upriver, laden with armed men and more torches. Thorndyke had covered every escape route.

"You have no place to go," Thorndyke said to them. "We can capture you whole or in pieces; it matters not to me."

The older smuggler caught the eye of his younger partner and said, "We'll not resist."

In quick order the two smugglers were bound.

"Now let's see what we caught." Thorndyke pointed to a large barrel. "Open this one."

He stepped back as two of his men pried open the barrel's lid. They stepped back.

Thorndyke looked at Pernell. "Would you like to do the honors?" he asked.

"This is your night," Pernell said.

Removing his glove and rolling up his sleeve, Thorndyke plunged his hand into the grain. He fished around for a while, his eyes working from side to side as though he were seeing through the ends of his fingertips. Then his eyes locked into place. He grinned.

Grain spilled onto the wharf as he removed his hand. In it was a small, rectangular package wrapped in hide. With great relish he unwrapped it.

A book. Thorndyke called for a torch. Holding the book up to the light, he examined the first few pages. "The work of the heretic Tyndale," he proclaimed.

Pernell nodded approvingly.

The two smugglers looked on, defeated.

Thorndyke started to toss the book back into the barrel, when he had a thought. To Pernell he said, "Care to celebrate our first success?"

"What did you have in mind?"

"Our own little book-burning ceremony."

It was a dramatic flair. Needless, really, but somehow appropriate. More than that, satisfying.

"Proceed," Pernell said.

Drawing his sword, Thorndyke draped the book over the blade. He held out his other hand and a torch was handed him. Holding both at a distance, he touched the flame to the pages. It didn't take long for them to catch fire.

A cheer went up from Thorndyke's men.

"May God forgive you," the older smuggler said.

Pernell approached him.

"What is your name?" he demanded.

The man brazenly looked him in the eye. "Raedmund," he replied.

"And yours?" Pernell asked the younger man.

The older man answered for him. "That's my son. His name is Bink."

"How do you make your living?"

"I sell fish."

"Fish," Pernell repeated. "And tell me, Master Raedmund, what does a fishmonger know of theology? Tell me! I wish to know!"

Raedmund didn't answer him. The man's lack of response angered Pernell.

"Are you aware that England's greatest theologians have declared this book to be heresy?" he thundered. "That the king of England has outlawed it? That by your association with it, you have condemned not only yourself but also your son to death?"

The man's silence was irritating, his lack of remorse infuriating.

"Speak, man! What do you have to say for yourself?"

Raedmund looked him in the eye. "How can it be wrong," he said, "to crave the very words of God? How can it be wrong to desire for your family to know his commandments?"

"So you would do away with the church altogether? You would appoint yourself and your son as priests?"

"I can trust the word of God," Raedmund said. "I don't trust corrupt priests."

It was useless arguing with the man. It was obvious he was possessed by a demon of error. Pernell felt pity for him.

"By your error," he said, "you have condemned yourself and your son to death." To the guards he said, "Take them away."

The fishmonger and his son were led away. Pernell joined Thorndyke at the end of the wharf as the last of the heretical New Testament burned on the end of his sword and fell in blazing pieces into the Thames.

"There's no reasoning with them," Thorndyke said of Raedmund and his kind.

"It's a shame they've been deluded as they have," Pernell replied.

Thorndyke ordered the confiscation of all the barrels on the wharf. He and Pernell watched as one by one they were rolled away and loaded onto wagons.

"You're to be commended for your work tonight," Pernell said.

Thorndyke smiled. "Thank you, Professor. Coming from you, that means a lot to me."

"You'll make the appropriate report to the bishop?"

Thorndyke looked puzzled. "That would hardly be my place," he said.

"Oh?"

"I am merely your assistant. You should be the one to report to the bishop."

Pernell felt his chest fill with pride. This wasn't to be Antwerp and Philips again after all. His reservations about working with a partner dissolved.

When the last of the barrels was loaded, the two men departed the wharf. Pernell felt comfortable enough with Thorndyke to reveal some information of his own.

"Have you heard the name North mentioned on the docks?" he asked.

"No, sir."

"Keep an ear cocked for the name. The bishop believes he may be the leader we're after."

"North," Thorndyke repeated. "What do we know of him?"

"He's intelligent. Always seems to be one step ahead of us. He has connections in the palace."

"The palace?" Thorndyke said, surprised.

"Possibly a nobleman," Pernell said. "Educated. Good connections. Wealthy."

"I'll see what I can find out."

"Good."

They'd come to the end of Ironmonger Lane.

"Good night, Professor," Thorndyke said.

"Good night." Pernell stepped into the lane. He stopped and turned back. "And, Thorndyke?"

"Yes, sir?"

"Good work tonight."

Chapter 16

The queen's bedchamber had no windows, so Meg could only guess that it was dark outside by now. There was one thing of which she was certain, though: in the time she'd spent in the room, she'd used up her supply of anxiety for a week of days.

Shortly after the queen had ordered her to stop playing the virginals, the duke of Norfolk appeared with news of the king. It was good news. The king had regained consciousness and was sitting up and speaking. His head still hurt but he was hungry. The doctor was most encouraged by that.

A flurry of attendants appeared in the wake of his departure, buzzing about, each inquiring as to the queen's wishes and thanking God in her presence for his watched care over king and country. The queen's spirits rallied somewhat, but by her mood it was clear something was still troubling her.

Her short temper and sharp tongue were a pair of daggers that she bandied about with expert skill. When the attendants left the room, most of them did so in tears.

Meg was certain the queen had forgotten her. It was as though she were invisible. Attendants came and went, with as many as a dozen of them hovering over the queen at one time; then it would be the queen and her alone in the room. But not once since the news of the king's improved condition did the queen give any indication she knew Meg was still there.

Yet Meg dared not leave until she was dismissed. So she sat and waited. There was little else she could do.

The queen called successively for her personal physician—ordering him to leave the room when he tried to attend her—her personal secretary, an advisor, and three attendants by name, only to dismiss each of them curtly and abruptly. Between each one's arrival she would moan and rub her hands over her swollen belly. Meg turned away, certain she shouldn't be witness to such things.

She felt like a piece of furniture. Or more correctly, like the linnet in the cage. The only difference between her and the bird was that the bars of Meg's cage were invisible.

"Come here," the queen said.

Meg stood. There was no one else in the room. She approached the bed, keeping a proper distance between her and royalty.

"Is it always like this?" the queen demanded. Her dark eyes were half closed in pain. Tucked between the covers, devoid of jewels and ruffles, she looked like a scared child. However, her voice was still that of the queen.

Meg was uncertain as to what was expected of her, or even as to what the queen was referring to.

When no answer was immediately forthcoming, the queen looked up at her. "Being with child," she snapped. "Is it always this difficult?"

Meg's uncertainty compounded. What did she know of bearing children? While the queen had never delivered successfully, she'd been with child before. That was more than Meg had ever experienced.

"I'm surrounded by imbeciles!" the queen shouted. "How many children have you had?"

"Why . . . none, Your Majesty," Meg stammered.

"None? You've never given birth?"

The queen stared at Meg's wide hips. Meg understood now how the queen had come to assume she'd had children. She did have the figure of a woman who had birthed children.

"No, Your Majesty. I've never given birth."

A look of disgust took hold of the queen's face. "Then what good are you to me?" she snapped. A dark mood flowed over her as visibly as a black veil.

That was the very question Meg had been asking herself for hours. What was she doing here if she wasn't playing the virginals? What did she have to offer the queen save her music?

"Let not your heart be troubled . . ."

The words just came to mind, as they had in the kitchen with Pernell. They came with such intensity and volume that Meg was certain the queen heard them, too.

The queen had turned her face to the pillow, brooding. Meg so wanted to console her with the very words that had been her own consolation. But how could she? This was the queen! And the words were from a book that the king had declared heretical!

Just then she remembered something Lyssa said. *"The queen has one too. I've seen it in her bedchamber."* One of the forbidden books in the queen's bedchamber? No, certainly Lyssa was mistaken, or possibly she had fabricated the whole thing to shock Enid and Birdie.

Still, Meg couldn't help but let her eyes roam the room. In the corner was the linnet, its cage covered; next to it was the table with the virginals, and of course her basket hidden beneath it. On the far side of the room was a wall of mirrors stretching floor to ceiling, in the corner closest to the door an enormous wardrobe, and in the other corner a small mahogany table with French legs.

Meg caught her breath. Could it be? Atop the table was a single candle. At its base was a small book, lying open. How could she have been in the room this long and not noticed it? Still, it was just a book. From here there was no way she could be sure that it was a—

"What are you staring at?"

The queen's eyes were fastened on her.

"Forgive me, Your Majesty; it's not my place to . . ."

The queen looked over at the French table, then back at Meg. An amused grin appeared on her face, the same kind of naughty grin Lyssa and the girls wore when they whispered among themselves about matters of courtly love.

"Have you read it?" the queen asked.

Meg lowered her head. Her fingers played nervously with the folds in her dress. A lie rose quickly to her lips. What choice did she have but to lie? To do otherwise could mean her death. She glanced toward the doorway. How desperately she wanted to flee the room and never return.

"I . . . forgive me, Your Majesty, but I don't know to what you are referring . . ."

The queen's eyes narrowed in thought. She made no immediate reply. Meg stood there, her hands trembling. She dared not look at the queen, lest her eyes betray her. She dared not move, lest her knees fail her. Fear froze everything—her breathing, her thoughts, her heart, time itself.

"You have read it, haven't you?" the queen said.

The words were her death sentence; Meg was certain of it. A cell and a fiery pole awaited her.

"Look at me," the queen said.

The judge was demanding the prisoner to admit her guilt to the court.

"Meg, look at me," the queen said again, only this time her tone was softer, no longer demanding. Not judge to prisoner, or even queen to subject, but woman to woman.

Feeling there was nothing more to lose, Meg took a deep breath, filling her lungs with resolve. She raised her chin and looked at her queen.

With a soft voice Meg said, "'Let not your heart be troubled . . .'"

The queen cocked her head. "What did you say?"

Meg began again, this time louder. "I said, 'Let not your heart be troubled. Believe in God and believe also in me.' These are the words of our Savior."

"You have read the book!"

"Yes, Your Majesty."

The house was dark when Pernell entered it. Not only was it absent of light, but it was equally absent of life and the odors of his supper.

"Meg?"

He tossed his hat onto the table and lit a couple of candles.

"Meg?"

Taking two steps at a time, he bounded up the stairs. The bedroom was as dark as the kitchen.

"Meg? Are you here?"

By now it was clear she wasn't, and he really didn't expect an answer. His words were the futile cry of a hungry man who was accustomed to having his supper waiting for him when he returned home.

Pernell went back down to the kitchen. The fireplace cupped a handful of dying coals in its hearth. He stirred them to life and added some wood.

Coming home, he'd heard of the king's eventful day, which had sent the entire kingdom into shock. While the news was unexpected, Pernell didn't think it surprising. All his life King Henry had been proud of his physical prowess, eager to show it off to other men as well as to the ladies. But there came a day in each man's life when advancing age stared him down. It was inevitable in the life of every man. Today was simply the king's day.

Given the circumstances, he wasn't surprised that Meg was not at home. The queen would need comforting at a time like this, and Meg's playing would be required.

A loaf of bread sat in the middle of the table. He reached for it and, instead of getting up to get a knife, tore a piece off and tossed it into his mouth to fend off his complaining belly.

It was rare for Meg not to be home. He tried to console himself with the thought of her faithfulness in caring for him over the years, but his rumbling stomach made it hard for him to be sympathetic to that argument. Beside, Meg had always been his confidante and he had a niggling need to brag to her about Thorndyke. Theirs was going to be a righteous partnership; he was certain of it. The two men were cut from the same cloth. They were of one mind and purpose.

Today, because of Thorndyke, a fishmonger and his son were brought to justice for their heresy, and soon so would all who boldly defied both king and church.

"North."

Pernell said the man's name aloud, the name of the heretic who dared walk the halls of the king's palace while inviting heresy to England's shores. A nobleman, possibly holding a position in the court. A traitor. A disgrace.

"North."

Pernell spat the name in derision. It was only a matter of time before he too would be brought to justice, and all who followed him. He took another bite of bread and chewed furiously, the beat of his heart in tandem with his resolve, building steadily at the thought of wickedness stalking the king's hallways.

Reaching for more bread, Pernell helped himself to another bite. An inspired thought crossed his mind. Meg had access to the queen's chamber. Would she know to mention to him if she saw any heretical literature there? Maybe she'd heard of this North fellow. When she returned home, he'd ask her.

Meg crossed to the other side of the room. She approached the small book on the stand.

"Hand it to me," the queen ordered.

Meg complied.

"You know this book?"

"I've found words of comfort on its pages," Meg replied. "Words from our Master's lips," she hastened to add. "They have soothed me when I was troubled."

The queen held out the book to her. "Show me," she said.

Meg took the book. Her eyes fell on the upper right corner. Unlike her copy, it was undamaged.

With a calmness that surprised her, she opened the book and began searching for the words as a woman would search a chest for a precious heirloom. She said the words again as she searched: "'Let not your heart be troubled . . .'" Page after unfamiliar page turned. "I know they're in here, Your Majesty, if you'll just be patient."

She regretted the words as soon as she had spoken them. Had she really just told the queen of England to be patient? What was she thinking?

Meg risked a glance at the queen. There was no indication of offense; the monarch's eyes were focused on the turning pages. Relieved, Meg kept looking.

She found the Gospel of Saint John. That was a start. The words she was looking for were buried somewhere in his gospel. At the moment, though, it was proving to be a rather large gospel, and she was well into it and still nothing looked familiar. Had she passed it?

Meg could feel the eyes of the queen on her. How long would she let her continue her search before concluding that Meg was incompetent for the task? Page after page showed nothing familiar. Maybe she should start over at the—

"Oh!" Meg cried.

"Did you find it?"

Meg scanned the page. "No . . . no . . . " Her eyes snatched the words from the page like a hungry person would snatch crumbs of bread. "This isn't what I was looking for," she explained, "but . . . oh, my . . . oh, my!"

"Read them aloud!" the queen said eagerly.

Meg nodded. With her finger she traced back to the beginning of the section.

> These words have I spoken unto you, that in me ye might have peace. For in the world shall ye have tribulation: but be of good cheer, I have overcome the world.

Meg looked up.

"Who spoke those words?" the queen asked.

"Let me see . . ." Again Meg placed her hand on the page and began tracing the sentences backward. She looked up.

"The Master," she said. "These are the words of the Master to his disciples!"

"Read them again. Slowly."

The queen lay her head back against her pillows. She closed her eyes. As Meg read, the queen savored every word. When Meg finished the section, the queen said, "Continue reading."

Meg stood beside the queen's bed and, tilting the open pages of the book toward the candlelight, read Saint John's account of Jesus asking God to glorify himself through his Son and protect his disciples from the Evil One and praying for all who would believe in the Son of God through the message the disciples would deliver to the world.

When Meg was finished, the queen opened her eyes. They had a calm quality that Meg had never before seen in them. She recognized the feeling, only this time she was seeing it from the outside.

"Query," the queen said.

"Yes?"

"You're Pernell Foxe's wife, yes?"

The question was lightning to Meg's calmed heart. Just when she was feeling safe again, fear of discovery struck. She tried to formulate a response. None was forthcoming.

The queen said, "I find it oddly amusing that the wife of the legendary Pernell Foxe would be acquainted with seditious literature."

There was a smirk on the queen's face that unnerved Meg. She made a second attempt to say something. Fear trapped every word before it could escape.

The queen's smirk widened. "He doesn't know, does he?"

Meg managed to shake her head.

"Delicious!" the queen squealed, and for a moment she was an adolescent girl again, like Lyssa and Birdie and Enid.

Meg smiled weakly.

"So tell me," the queen said, "how is it you came to be acquainted with this book?"

Meg set the queen's New Testament down and retrieved hers from the basket under the virginals table. She handed it to the queen.

"My, we are full of surprises, aren't we?" the queen said. Her fingers immediately went to the damaged corner of the book. "And your husband has no idea you have this?"

"It would kill him if he knew," Meg said.

"Kill him? Or would he kill you?" The queen chuckled as she ran her hands over the book. "This . . . is . . . so . . . delicious!"

While the queens word's were spoken in girlish fun, they sent a chill through Meg's very being.

"I gave one to the king."

Meg's head snapped up.

The queen took delight in her shocked response. "Truthfully!" she said. "I also gave him a copy of Master Tyndale's book *The Obedience of a Christian Man.*"

"Has His Majesty read them?"

"I don't know," said the queen. "He hasn't spoken of them to me since."

Meg's hopes began to rise. "Do you think he'll lift the ban on the New Testaments?"

"It doesn't suit his purpose," said the queen.

Meg's hopes deflated.

"But this is good!" the queen said gaily.

"What is, Your Majesty?"

"Your knowing the New Testament as you do. You can read it aloud to me. I can trust you because you have just as much to lose as I have."

At first hearing the thought didn't sit right with Meg, but the more she considered it, the more she liked the idea. What better place to read the New Testament than in the security of the queen's chamber?

"You can begin right now," the queen said. She handed Meg the book and eagerly repositioned herself in bed.

Indicating a chair, Meg asked, "May I, Your Majesty?"

The queen nodded her assent.

Meg pulled the chair to the queen's bedside. She opened the damaged New Testament to the passage with which she was most familiar, anxious to read the Madonna's song aloud to the queen.

The queen listened with her head back and her eyes closed as the birth of the Savior was announced to Mary by the angel Gabriel, then as the young Hebrew girl launched into a song of rapturous praise.

When the passage was concluded, Meg looked up, wanting to know if the queen wished her to continue.

The queen was crying softly.

"What is it, Your Majesty?"

Suddenly the queen was gone and in her place was a frightened girl. Forlorn eyes, wet with tears, stared into the distance. They fastened on something Meg couldn't see.

"I'm so frightened," Anne said.

"Of what?"

"Of the king." She wiped tears from her eyes. They were readily replaced with fresh ones.

Meg wanted to hold the girl, but knew better than to touch the queen of England. She would have to rely on words.

"Surely, the king would never harm you . . ."

"If I don't deliver a son to him this time, I don't know what he'll do to me."

Meg's heart went out to the poor girl. She began to weep with her. She knew what it was like to fear the wrath of a man.

Together the women wept in the face of their unknown futures.

Pernell was waiting for her when she returned home. He was sitting at the table. Crumbs were all that was left of the half loaf of bread. Meg tried to assess whether he was angry. The light was too dim to tell at first glance.

"Sorry I'm late, dear," she said, closing the door behind her. "You must be racked with hunger."

The wicker basket dangled on her arm. Hidden in it was the damaged New Testament. As soon as the queen had dismissed her, Meg hurried home, knowing that Pernell would be waiting for her. There was no time for a side trip to the kitchen. She felt bad about Alfreda and would go to the kitchen tomorrow. But now she wasn't sure she would give back the New Testament.

She hoisted the basket. "I'll take this upstairs and then be right down to fix your supper."

Pernell's chair scraped against the wooden planks as he stood. "I'll do that for you," he said, reaching for the basket.

Meg pulled it out of his reach.

"I'll do it," she insisted. "I'll be just a moment."

"Nonsense. I'll put the basket away; you prepare supper."

His hand was on the handle. If she made too much of a fuss, he'd get suspicious. It was all she could do to let go of the basket. A quick glance revealed that the book was covered. But one bump or stumble and the covering could slip and expose a corner. And any book in her basket would get his attention. Of course he'd investigate. Lift the cloth covering and find—

She didn't want to think about it. She watched as he mounted the stairs. She listened as his boots clomped on the floor overhead.

"Where do you want me to put it?" he yelled from above.

"The wardrobe. In the wardrobe. The bottom. Please."

Her words were charged with anxiety. She chided herself for the tone.

"Pernell?"

"Yes?"

"Can you come down here? Quickly? I have something I need you to do. It's urgent."

The sooner she could get him back down here, the better, at least so she thought.

"Just a minute," he called.

His minute stretched into three eternities. She could hear his boots. A scuffle here and there. And could only wonder what he was doing.

"Pernell?"

"Coming!"

Finally she heard his feet on the stairs. His boots appeared, then his legs, and finally the rest of him.

To appear busy, Meg grabbed a rag and attacked the crumbs on the table.

"What do you need me to do?" he asked.

She looked up, trying to read his face. Surely if he'd seen the book, it would show on his face, wouldn't it?

"Stir the fire, dear," she said as calmly as she could.

"Stirring the fire is urgent?"

She smiled weakly. "It is if you want to eat."

Pernell grabbed the poker and went to work on the fire. It jumped to life at his prodding; the eager flames illuminated his face with an orange light. Meg studied that face while her hands continued working on their own. She was looking for anything that might indicate he'd found the book—a sideways glance, the downturn of his mouth, an angry poke at the logs.

"Was the queen grateful for your service to her?" he asked.

The image that leaped to Meg's mind was that of the queen listening peacefully as she read from the New Testament. Was Pernell alluding to something?

"What do you mean?" Meg asked. She reached for a knife with which to slice a leg of mutton.

"Your playing the virginals, of course," Pernell said. "The queen must have been in a frightful state, given the day's events."

"Oh, that! Yes . . . um, Her Majesty was pleased with my music today. It seemed to comfort her . . . somewhat at least . . . of course, she was still worried, until she received word that the king was all right, but then after that she was relieved . . . comforted . . . by the music . . . my playing . . ."

Pernell put the poker in its stand. His brow rippled with concern. "Are you all right?" he asked. "Did anything happen at the palace that I should know about?"

"No!" Meg said quickly. Perhaps too quickly. "It was just a stressful day, what with the king's accident and all."

She was babbling. If Pernell had seen the book in the basket, surely he would have said something by now.

Just give him his dinner, then excuse yourself and go upstairs and check on the basket. Until then keep your mouth shut and attend to supper.

Pernell pulled out a chair to sit down.

"Put the water on to boil," she said.

Pernell moved slowly, his mind evidently still in thought. He swung the pot of water over the fire. "Have you ever met or heard of a man at the palace by the name of North?" he asked.

"North?" Meg repeated, glad for the change in subject. "Does he have a title or a first name?"

"All I know is that his name is North."

Meg thought for a moment, then shook her head. "Not that I can recall," she said. "Why?"

"We think he's the mastermind behind the smuggling of the Tyndale New Testaments."

Meg was glad to be able to say again that she'd never met the man.

"Possibly a nobleman," Pernell said, thinking out loud now. He sat down at the table. "A crafty man, from what we hear, in an evil way, of course."

Meg said nothing as she gathered items around her cutting board—hard cheese, a fresh loaf of bread, a knife.

"Capture him and we have pretty much broken the back of the smuggling effort," Pernell continued. "Keep an eye and ear open for me while you're at the palace, will you? If you meet a man by that name or hear anyone mention his name, let me know immediately."

"Working in the queen's chamber as I do, I'm pretty much surrounded by women," Meg said.

"Just the same, keep your ears open."

"I will."

Pernell ran the flat of his hand across the table, staring at it as he did so, deep in thought. "What about seditious books?" he asked.

"Books?"

"Banned literature. Like the Tyndale New Testament. Ever see any illegal books being passed around the palace?"

Pernell raised his head and looked at her.

He did find the book in my basket! Meg thought. Her hands stilled, frozen solid, hovering over the cheese in mid slice.

"Why . . . why do you ask?" she managed to say.

"Just wondering. We know that some of them have made their way into the palace. I thought you might have seen something."

Meg forced a chuckle. "I'm pretty much confined to the queen's chamber," she said.

Pernell grinned. "You stay just as you are," he said.

"What does that mean?"

"It means that when it comes to the dark things of this world, you are an innocent babe. Rumor has it that the queen herself has been known to read seditious literature from time to time."

"I find that hard to believe," Meg said, doing her best to make her voice sound incredulous.

Pernell stood. Moving toward her, he encircled her waist with his arms and buried his cheek against the nape of her neck. "Like I said . . . you stay just as you are and I will do my best to protect you from the cruelties of this world."

Chapter 17

The din from the palace kitchen could be heard several hallways away, reflecting the king's improved condition. The palace pulsed with his vigor, especially the center that fed his appetite.

Meg worked her way through the maze of passages toward the great kitchen. As risky as it was, she'd decided to keep the damaged New Testament. She reasoned that she could read ahead and look for passages that would be helpful to the queen, and thus be better prepared when the queen called upon her to read.

She knew this would put Alfreda in something of a predicament, and she hadn't quite figured out how she was going to handle it. She'd just have to assess the situation and attempt to work some kind of compromise.

Knowing that the queen had her own New Testament gave Meg courage. Surely, should any ill circumstance fall upon her in this endeavor, the queen would come to her aid.

A blast of sensations greeted Meg upon entering the kitchen. It was an enormous room with three great fireplaces, a row of boiling pots, two ovens, and table after table of bowls and plates, lined with kitchen workers busily preparing the king's meal, which meant servings for eight hundred people.

The room was heavily humid, as steam and heat and human sweat combined to make the room's atmosphere. Every step Meg took was either gritty from spilled sugar or flour or slippery from grease. Dodging elbows and spoons and rushing bodies, Meg made her way inside. She hadn't imagined there would be so many people in one room. Where to begin looking? All she knew was that she was looking for Alfreda's mother.

She was in luck. She spotted Alfreda at a long table, spooning a mixture of meat into pie shells. At first the girl didn't see her approaching. When she did, her face turned as white as the flour on her apron. Meg gave her a reassuring smile. It had no effect. Alfreda stood immobile, spoon paused mid scoop, as she watched Meg draw closer. Then the girl's head came alive, moving from side to side, attempting to warn Meg away.

Meg was not to be put off.

"Alfreda," she said in greeting.

The girl said nothing. Wide, tearful eyes did her communicating.

Beside her a woman was rolling dough and molding it to the inside of pie pans, then trimming the excess before passing the shells on to Alfreda. Noticing the girl's expression, she looked to the source and saw Meg. An exasperated frown formed.

"What'd the girl do now, mum?" the woman droned.

She was a short woman with muscular forearms and hands. Her complexion was pasty, her expression fixed and inflexible. She was every inch a woman who had lived a hard life.

"Are you Alfreda's mother?" Meg asked.

The woman assessed Meg from head to toe without ever stopping what she was doing. She lifted fresh dough from a bowl, slapped it onto the table, creating clouds of flour, and then attacked the dough with a rolling pin. "If it's just the same to you, mum," said the woman, "tell me what the little wretch did and I'll beat her for it later."

"I've come to talk to you about a personal matter," Meg said.

The woman stopped rolling. An amused expression formed on her lips. "Beggin' your pardon, mum, but what are the chances of the likes of you having personal business with the likes of me?"

Meg persisted. "I need to talk to you about a book. One that I believe belongs to you."

"Book?" the woman said. "Do I looks like the sort of woman what's got time to read?"

Meg was trying to avoid mentioning the New Testament directly. "It's a special book," she said, "if you know what I mean."

Directly behind the woman was another table, this one laden with loaf after loaf of bread set in rows to cool. A man of average stature, obviously a baker, judging by the way his hands and face and apron were dusted with flour, overheard what Meg said. While Alfreda's mum didn't seem to catch her intimation, he did. He cast a curious glance at Meg.

"This is a kitchen," the woman said, her voice and attitude becoming testy despite Meg's elevated social position. "If you want books, mum, I suggests you go finds yourself a nobleman."

Alfreda was about to become undone. She fidgeted back and forth, from her good foot to her clubfoot. Her mother shouted at her to get back to work. She did.

Meg considered leaving. She'd tried to return the book, hadn't she? The woman clearly didn't want it, despite what Alfreda had told her. Nevertheless, Meg decided to make one final effort. She leaned closer to the woman, catching a hint of currant from the meat mixture. She said, "The book I'm talking about is a . . ." She glanced in the direction of the baker. He was looking straight at her. Meg lowered her voice even more. "It's a New Testament."

This Alfreda's mother understood. She recoiled. Her expression matched that of her daughter.

"I don't know what you're talkin' about!" she shouted.

Meg held up a reassuring hand. "It's all right. I'm not here to—"

The woman was no longer listening. She shook her head furiously. Then, with a vicious glance at Alfreda, she hefted a rolling pin as if it were a weapon.

"You need not fear me," Meg assured her. "All I want is to—"

"Who are you?" the woman shouted. She shook the rolling pin at Meg.

The baker watched the events with concern but held his place.

It was Meg's turn to step back. A voice inside told her simply to turn around and leave. If the woman wouldn't admit to owning the New Testament, how could she possibly offer to replace it? Meg had tried to do the right thing—at great personal risk. The wise thing to do now would be to walk away.

But for reasons reason cannot fathom, Meg didn't do the wise thing.

"I mean you no harm," she insisted.

The woman's expression remained hostile. She didn't believe Meg.

"Tell me your name!" the woman barked.

"Meg."

"Meg what?"

Meg spread her arms wide in an inviting gesture. "I know your daughter from upstairs. She often—"

"Meg what?" the woman shouted louder.

"Meg F—" Now she understood. Her shoulders slumped. "Meg Foxe," she said.

The baker's eyebrows raised. He then had the strangest reaction. He grinned.

The woman, on the other hand, was more frightened than ever. "We's heard all about the way you've been sneakin' your way into the queen's chamber so's you can spy. And we knows all about what your husband does to those who are caught with those books. Whatever you think is mine ain't. I can't get any clearer than that."

Meg felt defeated. No amount of assurance was going to convince this woman she meant no harm. She should have known that the woman would be suspicious of a lady of the court coming down to the kitchen.

"You're Pernell Foxe's wife?"

The question came from the baker. He stepped toward her with an odd expression on his face. If Meg was reading it correctly, it was a mixture of disbelief and humor. And something else. She couldn't be sure but she thought she detected a glint of infatuation in his eyes.

"Do I know you?" Meg asked.

The baker bowed slightly. He had a winning smile and warm brown eyes. His hands were folded in front of him. A servant's posture. "Please forgive the lack of formalities," he said. "After all, you did catch us at a busy time."

"I noticed you didn't give me your name," Meg said.

His smile grew larger. "No, I didn't. And I noticed that you didn't confirm your identity, though there is little doubt that you are indeed Meg Foxe."

He said her name with a warmth that was alarming.

"And you are?" Meg prompted.

"My name is Nicholas."

"That's it? Just Nicholas?"

"Nicholas the baker, if you prefer," he said, jesting.

His gaze never faltered. Unaccustomed to looking men in the eyes, Meg lowered her gaze. There was nothing left for her to do now but leave.

"If you'll excuse me," she said.

"I was the one who gave this woman that Tyndale New Testament," he said.

Meg halted in mid turn. His comment was so matter-of-fact, she wasn't certain how to respond. Why would a man admit such a thing, knowing who she was?

"If I remember correctly," he said, "it has a damaged cover. The upper right corner."

Meg blinked, completely off balance now.

"You have the book?" he asked.

"Yes."

"Pernell Foxe's wife is in possession of a seditious book?"

Meg's face grew warm. This was the second time someone had found amusement in her predicament. "I did not come here to be made sport of," she said. Once again she turned to leave.

"Keep it with my compliments," the baker called after her. "I'll see that Edyth gets another one."

Speaking over her shoulder, Meg replied, "As you wish. It is no longer any concern of mine."

Stepping smartly, she weaved her way through the chaos of the kitchen.

"You're welcome," the baker called out to her.

Nicholas stepped from the kitchens into the waning sunlight. His work done, he arched his back and stretched his arms wide. They reached nearly as wide as his grin.

It had been years since he'd seen her.

He chuckled to himself.

"Do I know you?" she'd asked.

He had wanted to say, "No, but I know you and have admired you from afar for lo these many years, all the time knowing I could never converse with you or get to know you, yet all this time you have fueled my dreams."

"I noticed you didn't give me your name," she'd said.

He'd wanted to say, "No, but you've captured my heart—a heart that has wept silently over the tragedy of your life countless times over the years, a heart that has never stopped praying for your happiness."

But all he'd said was, "My name is Nicholas. Nicholas the baker."

Did it matter? Today he had stood just a few feet from her. He gazed into her eyes and she into his. They spoke. It was more than he had ever dared hope for.

With a little skip to propel him on his way, Nicholas shouted at the sun, "Oh, blessed, blessed day!"

Chapter 18

They lay side by side, encased in a black tomb. Neither was asleep but neither were they restless. The ropes that held the mattress and groaned every time one of them turned had been silent for more than an hour.

"Are you awake?" Pernell asked.

It was an obvious question. He knew she was awake. His query was merely an invitation to conversation.

"Just thinking," she said.

The ropes groaned. While she couldn't see his face, his voice was now directed at her.

"You've been distant lately," he said.

She had. For two days now. She'd been preoccupied ever since her encounter with the baker. It wasn't that she felt threatened by him, at least not in the sense of being discovered. But it disturbed her that he seemed to know all about her yet she was certain she'd never seen him before in her life. Absolutely certain. She'd gone over it in her mind countless times. She was as certain as it was possible for her to be.

And then there was the coolness with which he handled the matter of the New Testament. While Alfreda's mother saw her as a spark to a powder keg, he stepped forward ever so casually, without so much as a nod to the situation's explosive nature, and went so far as to admit that he dealt in seditious books. This after learning that she was the wife of heretic hunter Pernell Foxe.

"The mood in the palace is uncertain," she replied to Pernell's question. "The queen is afraid of what will happen if she fails to deliver a male heir to the king."

"She has every right to worry."

"Are you certain?" Meg asked. "Look at the great lengths to which the king went just to have her as his wife."

Pernell chuckled. "My point exactly."

"I don't understand."

"You're granting the king characteristics he does not possess."

"Such as?"

"Nobility of character."

Meg pondered this. Weren't kings born of noble character?

"The way to get the king's attention is to tell him he can't have something. He wanted Anne and she would not give in to him until he got rid of Queen Catherine and married her. Now that he's had her, the polish is off the apple. His thoughts have returned to what he doesn't have."

"A male heir."

"Exactly."

"Then she has every reason to fear."

"That she does. The king has already demonstrated that he's not going to let marriage vows stand in the way of what he wants."

Meg thought of the queen—not the bombastic Anne but the frightened little girl huddled in her bed.

"In this world you will have trouble . . ."

"Did you say something?"

Meg started at the sound of his voice. She hadn't said those words out loud, had she?

"I didn't say anything," she said.

A few moments of silence settled between them. Then, "You haven't had one of your episodes lately," he said.

"No . . . no, I haven't," she said.

He was right. The fact surprised her until she realized one doesn't miss an unwelcome guest

"I've not been away as often," Pernell said by way of explanation.

"For that I'm grateful," she said.

But there was also the New Testament in the wardrobe to consider. She'd continued having episodes even after Pernell returned, but not since she found consolation within the passages of the Bible.

"Remember I told you about that fellow North?" Pernell asked, changing topics.

Meg didn't reply. She was still thinking about how the Bible had calmed the turmoil of her inner life.

"The one smuggling the seditious books?" Pernell prompted.

"Yes, yes, I remember," she said, pulled back into the conversation.

"And I told you there was possibly a palace connection . . ."

"Oh? . . . Yes, I remember now."

The baker came to mind. Could he be the man they were looking for? For some reason the thought of his capture disturbed her.

"We've set a trap for him."

"A trap?"

"Tomorrow night."

"So then, you'll be late coming home." Meg decided that was the kind of question an uninvolved wife would ask.

"Actually, the way it turns out, the lead was confirmed by one of the queen's attendants. Kyrk has been courting her." Pernell laughed. "I don't know what kind of powers she has over him, but she's all he talks about. Sometimes to the point of distraction. If I didn't remember exactly how it felt, those early days when I was infatuated with you, I'd probably speak to him about it. But I know it would do little good."

"What's her name? This temptress?"

Pernell had to think for a moment. "Lyda? . . . No, that's not it. Lyssa. Yes, Lyssa Winter. Do you know her?"

Meg cringed. "Poor Master Thorndyke," she said.

"This woman is that bad?"

"A seductress."

"Should I warn him?"

"Do you think it would do any good?"

"No."

"I wouldn't think so, either."

Pernell thought for a moment. "Is he in any danger?"

Meg laughed.

"If your Master Thorndyke is the young man Lyssa is mooning over, he's already hooked, gutted, and on the grill."

"That bad?"

"The girl knows how to get what she wants."

"Is she reliable?"

"In what sense?"

"North. The heretic. Do you think her information is reliable?"

Meg stifled a cry with her hand. The implications of what they were discussing suddenly hit her. Lyssa was talking to Pernell's assistant! Lyssa, who knew all about Alfreda's confiscated New Testament. Lyssa, who knew about the New Testament in the queen's bedchamber. Had she said anything to Master Thorndyke about these books?

"Is something wrong?" Pernell asked her.

"I don't know," she answered.

Chapter 19

The noise and bustle of market day in Cheapside used to get on her nerves. Today, as Meg strolled down the middle of the wide street, she was amazed at how calm she felt. Positively relaxed. The sun was bright and warm against her skin, sails drifted lazily on the Thames, and in spite of the incessant cries of the hundreds of vendors who lined both sides of the street, it was peaceful.

Maybe familiar was more what she felt but she was enjoying it. With no responsibilities at the palace, she took advantage of the day to do some much needed shopping. She found it relaxing to be surrounded by ordinary people again. Women who had nothing more on their mind than to buy a few cod and a leg of mutton and then hurry home to clean the house or care for their children and husband. Such a simple life compared with life at the palace.

It felt good to walk once again with people who had no palace pretense, no social position to promote or protect, no reason for maneuvering this way or that to support one's status in the court or undermine another's. There were no ruffles here. No one was looking down her nose in disdain. Haughtiness and pride had no place among squawking chickens, fresh fish, barrels of ale, and hanging sides of beef. Life on Cheapside was reduced to existence. Politics here was diversionary talk, not a way of life. Even the air smelled more honest. No perfumes and powders, only the open, moist air from a timeless river.

It was like coming home. Meg remembered when market day was the most stressful day of her week. Now it was a relief, an escape from the tensions that came with being associated with royalty. She made a promise to herself. Today she would not think of anything related to the palace. No thoughts of the palace or the queen or Lyssa and her brood or anything related to royalty. Today she was housewife Meg again. Nothing more.

Oh, except for later. With Pernell coming home late, she wanted to read from the New Testament, in hopes of finding a few sentences she could share with the queen. But that was all. She'd do that and nothing more. Today she was housewife Meg, just like old times.

With Saint Paul's Cathedral at her back, she scanned the vendors lining the street. Skinned rabbits hung by their feet at one booth. It had been a while since she'd bought rabbit for Pernell, and she was tempted to do so now. There were booths with pheasant, partridge, lark, and quail; fruit stands with apples, pears, peaches, and medlars; an herb stand; a butter and cheese stand; and of course a long row of butchers' stands.

The queue at the water conduit was particularly long. The gossip today must be good.

She'd come back for water later. Right now she needed to pick up some vegetables, herring to pickle, and some eggs. Oh, and a loaf of bread.

The frugal side of her winced at the thought of buying bread. She'd never bought bread in her life and never imagined she would. For a housewife, making bread was like breathing. It was simply something she did without thinking.

But then, Meg had never imagined she'd spend untold hours with the queen, either. So today would be a first.

Stepping spryly, housewife Meg headed toward a vendor selling garden vegetables. Soon her basket was heavy with goods as she made her way toward Elbow Lane and the bakery shop.

Crossing the threshold from cobblestone to wooden floor, Meg paused while her eyes adjusted from the sunlight to the dim interior of the bakery shop. The smell of baking bread had greeted her well before she reached the shop, and now inside she saw the wares that created the aroma she associated with home and warmth and security.

Bread was stacked neatly, like logs, on tables. There were buns and a variety of pastries on shelves. Meg chose a loaf of bread, once again cringing at the thought of having to pay for it, and a strawberry tart that she and Pernell could share for dessert.

"Could I interest you in some whole wheat buns?"

Meg looked up.

Familiar brown eyes met hers. They registered surprise, just as hers did.

"You!" she said.

"Me," he replied.

"What are you doing here?"

"I could ask the same question."

In response she hefted her shopping basket.

"This is my bakery shop."

Meg tried not to look flustered but she was. She'd never expected to see those eyes again.

"Your shop?"

The lines that framed the baker's eyes matched the lines at the corners of his smile.

"Is that so hard to believe?"

"But aren't you one of the king's bakers?"

"The king's cook hires me when he needs extra help."

Meg kept squeezing the loaf of bread in her basket. The ease which had accompanied her all morning had vanished the moment she saw him. She was staring into the same expression of familiarity that had haunted her all night long.

"You're mauling your bread," he said.

"Excuse me?"

He pointed to her basket.

She looked at the loaf in her hand. It was mangled.

"Here," he said. He took the loaf from her and gave her a fresh one.

"Thank you," she stammered.

She pulled a couple of coins from her purse and offered them to him for the bread and tart. She set her eyes on the door, wanting desperately to satisfy her compelling urge to flee.

He stepped to one side. He just happened to step in the same direction she did. Her basket crunched as she ran into him.

"Pardon me," he said.

"My fault," Meg replied.

They stood there, each waiting for the other to move. Neither did.

"I'll . . ." He motioned with a hand to one side.

"Thank you," she said.

He stepped out of her way.

The path to the doorway clear, she shot through it like an arrow. With winged feet she rounded the bend in the lane and flew toward the open expanse of Cheapside.

The thing that most flustered her was that she had no idea why she was flustered. She dismissed the idea that it was because he knew she owned a New Testament. In that matter he was as vulnerable as she. It was the way he looked at her. As though he'd known her all her life. Yet try as she might, she could not remember ever seeing him.

It was maddening.

And he seemed like a nice man, not at all the kind of man she pictured when Pernell described the heretics he . . .

Pernell!

The trap.

The thought brought Meg up short. Cheapside and the market and all its market-day hustle and bustle stretched in front of her.

What if the baker was one of the men walking into Pernell's trap tonight? For the first time the heretic had a face, and it was a friendly one. Maddening but friendly. He didn't seem the evil sort. He was a baker who trafficked in New Testaments. She also knew a queen who harbored seditious literature. And she herself . . .

A shudder shook her to her frame. It reached so deep, she had to steady herself against the stone corner of the candle shop that bordered Cheapside.

How many times had she worried about Pernell catching her with the New Testament? Hundreds? Thousands? But in her mind it was a husband catching his wife doing something of which he disapproved. Painful, certainly, but not until now had she thought of herself as a . . .

She couldn't even think the word in relation to herself.

The queen and the baker were just like her. Were they evil people simply because they had found comfort in the words of an English translation of the Bible?

The law said they were.

Pernell said they were, and he'd dedicated his life to rooting out such people and punishing them.

If you're going to be one, you ought to have the courage to own up to it, she told herself.

The realization was too painful. Meg turned her back to the stone wall and slumped against it.

Say it!

She turned her head toward Cheapside. Blue sky overhead. A splatter of color in motion as people moved every which way. Going about their business, buying food, exchanging services, worrying about sick children or elderly parents, complaining about taxes, feeling the aches and pains of age . . . little knowing that slouched against the candlestick shop there stood a . . .

Say it!

She looked in the other direction. A winding lane of shops and guilds. Businesses on the ground floor, residences above. Built who knows how many ages ago on the River Thames, London's liquid highway. What would the men who built these shops think if they knew that at the corner of their lane stood a . . .

Say it!

She couldn't.

Say it!

If she formed the words, she would become it.

Say it!

But how long could she go on denying the obvious?

Say it!

Tears came to her eyes.

Say it!

"Heretic! I'm a heretic! A heretic," Meg cried softly.

"You again!"

Meg stood in the doorway of the bakery shop, her basket in her hands. "Me again," she said.

The grin on his face revealed that he was not displeased to see her so soon.

"Did you have second thoughts about my buns?"

Meg blushed.

"My whole wheat buns," Nicholas said quickly.

Meg looked around the shop. They were alone for the moment. She could hear voices and the clattering of pans in the back. She stepped closer to him. What she had to say required a quiet voice. Lives depended on it.

"May I speak with you privately?" she said.

Nicholas looked around. "This is as private as it gets."

Meg took another look around. It would have to do.

"Do you wish another copy of Master Tyndale's—"

"Shh!" Meg hushed him. Danger signals clamored in her head. One just didn't speak so openly about such things. How did he know she could be trusted? He didn't know. Did he?

"Or possibly his book *The Obedience of a*—"

"Shhh!"

This time she was more forceful.

"Are you always cavalier about treasonous matters?" she cried.

His face sobered. It was the first time she'd ever seen it that way. His features were strong with character.

"Believe me when I say, madam, that I am daily aware of the dangers of what I do."

"But how do you know you can trust me? You speak so readily about things that—"

He held up a hand. It was thick, attached to an equally thick wrist and forearm. "Any moment, a customer could come walking through that door and our conversation will be cut off. Let me ease your fears. Though you may not be able to understand it now, know this: I would trust you with my life."

There it was again. A familiarity that went beyond her understanding. She vowed that one day she would know the source of it, but he was right—now was not the time.

"Very well," she said, nervously glancing at the doorway. "I'm taking a great risk telling you this." She glanced a second time. "And I'm hoping that you'll be able to—"

"Madam. Just tell me."

Meg swallowed hard. She could still back out. She hadn't told him anything yet.

"All right." She swallowed again. "If you are in any way associated with Lord North, your life is in danger."

"Lord North?"

"Yes. Pernell, my husband . . ." Saying his name brought her emotion rushing to the surface, compounding her offense.

"I know who your husband is," Nicholas assured her. "And believe me, I'm familiar with Dr. Foxe's work."

"A trap," Meg managed to say. "Tonight. For Lord North. Can you warn him?"

Nicholas lowered his eyes in thought.

This wasn't the response Meg had envisioned. She was expecting open gratitude for the risk she was taking.

"Can you warn him?" she cried.

"I'm not certain," he said.

Meg was beginning to think she'd made a mistake.

Nicholas glanced up and read it in her eyes.

"This is helpful information," he assured her.

She felt a little better.

"Truthfully," he insisted. "I know how difficult it was for you to tell me this."

Did he?

"Then you'll pass the information along?" she asked, still needing affirmation that she had done the right thing.

Voices from the doorway interrupted them. Two middle-aged, very plump women, chattering away, passed the shop, then, realizing they'd walked past it, giggled and retraced their steps.

Nicholas grabbed two whole wheat buns and handed them to Meg.

"Please come again," he said to her. "And express my regrets to your husband. Tell him my uncle Lord North will be unable to meet with him tonight. Possibly some other time."

Nicholas abruptly turned his attention to the ladies.

"Ah, Mrs. Cassidy. I have your pies in the back. Please excuse me while I fetch them."

"I'll need a boy to carry them for me," she called out to him in a matronly voice.

"Certainly, Mrs. Cassidy."

While Nicholas disappeared into the back of the shop, Meg placed the buns in her basket and hurried out the door. The eyes of Mrs. Cassidy and the other woman followed her all the way.

Meg was shaking uncontrollably by the time she reached Fortier's Candle Shoppe. She steadied herself on what was now a familiar corner. She found it difficult to breathe. Her mind was a swirl of conflicting thoughts.

She felt dirty. Unfaithful. Ashamed. At the same time, she felt as though she might have saved a life.

The life of a heretic.

But then, that's what she was. A heretic.

How could she face Pernell? Would she ever be able to look him in the eye? For if she did, he'd know, wouldn't he? He'd know.

Meg pulled herself upright. What was done could not be undone. She would have to find a way to live with herself. And Pernell.

It was odd. Even though she was a heretic, she didn't feel like one. Except for the guilt, of course. But she didn't feel as if she were doing something that could cause the destruction of English civilization, as Pernell so often said it could.

She took a deep breath. Why couldn't life be simple?

Once again she stood in the shadows and looked out across the expanse of Cheapside. It hadn't changed since she looked upon it last. But her world had changed and it could never be the same again. All she'd wanted to do today was to be a good wife. Instead she became a heretic in league with other heretics.

Meg the heretic stepped from the shadows into the bright sunlight. In her basket she carried a tart for her husband, and two whole wheat buns, a gift from another heretic.

Chapter 20

Kyrk Thorndyke paced back and forth, nervous with anticipation. It was a rare sensation for him.

He despised it.

The crescent moon overhead in the clear sky, the carefree babbling of the pond, the array of flowers cast in the bluish light of night—all failed to calm him.

His first experience with nervous anxiety had marked him for life, and he'd vowed never to experience it again. He was six years old. It was his first week of grammar school. Having already learned his alphabet at home, he attended the school with his two older brothers and fifteen other boys whose fathers paid a monk from the abbey at Malmesbury to serve as schoolmaster. The money came through the lease of several corn mills.

The school day began at six o'clock in the morning and ran for twelve hours. By four o'clock, especially on warm days, he would tend to nod off. He would jab his pen into the back of his hand to stay awake, but despite his every effort, sometimes he was awakened by a leather strap across his back. That wasn't the worst of it, though.

The worst beating he ever received at school was for being unprepared. It was the last day of the first week. The boys had been instructed to be prepared to recite the final stanza of *Beowolf.* Memorization did not come easy for Kyrk, and he was hoping that since he was the youngest boy, all the others would be called up before him.

That way he could hear it seventeen more times and hopefully it would stick.

The schoolmaster called his name first.

Even now as he paced back and forth, Kyrk could remember the anxiety of that moment. He remembered thinking he was going to fail. He remembered thinking he'd get a beating. And there was nothing he could do about it.

Admitting to the schoolmaster he was unprepared did him no good. The wiry monk stood him in front of all the other boys and for half an hour attempted to withdraw forcefully from his mind words that had never been deposited there in the first place. Then Kyrk was punished with blows his father never would have allowed on their farm animals.

But fleshly wounds on the young heal all too quickly. The deeper scars from that day had never healed. He had failed because he had not prepared. The feeling he had as he shuffled to the front of that class was like having a colony of carnivorous ants gnaw away at his insides.

They chewed at his insides even now as he stood alone in the pond garden. He hated the feeling. To calm himself, he quoted lines from *Beowulf,* which after his initial failure he had memorized. Not the last stanza only but the entire story. It was his way of gaining mastery over his anxiety.

> Around the barrow the battle-brave rode,
> Twelve in the troop, all true-born aethelings,
> To make their lament and mourn for the king;
> To chant a lay their lord to honor.
> They praised his daring; his deeds of prowess
> They mentioned in song. For meet it is
> That men should publishe their master's praise,
> Honor their chieftain, and cherish him dearly
> When he leaves this life, released from the body,
> Thus joined . . .

A rustle interrupted him, not of wind and leaves but of layered petticoats. He turned toward the sound. A fairy-sprite glided toward him on a silver ribbon of stone. She was bathed in night's radiance, a vision of courtly beauty if ever there was one.

The ants in Kyrk's belly summoned reinforcements.

He smoothed his doublet and adjusted first his left, then his right turned-back cuff. Being tortured by a grizzled monk in front of a classroom of grammar school classmates was easy compared with this.

He bowed at the waist. "Mistress Winter."

The lady paused, bowed slightly, then drew closer to him. "I've only a moment," she said breathlessly. "The queen is in a frightful mood, even for her."

Kyrk heard only every other word. In between words he was struck senseless by Lyssa Winter's smooth skin and elegant dress and captivating perfume. Lavender, if he wasn't mistaken. He concluded it was unfair that women had so many weapons at their disposal in the battle called courting.

The folds of her satin blue skirt shimmered in the moon's light. A crescent of pearls in her hair created the illusion that she was the mythical Diana. Matching ropes of pearls lay in perfect harmony against her pale bosom.

"A moment in your presence," he said, "could sustain a man through a hard winter."

He seemed to have caught her by surprise. She flashed him a coy smile. This pleased Kyrk. It had taken him two days to compose that line.

They exchanged silent glances, a peacock and a peahen sizing each other up. Lyssa took small steps leading nowhere in particular. Kyrk shifted from foot to foot.

"What did you wish to say to me?" Lyssa said softly. Her head at a demure angle, she gazed at him invitingly.

"Must there be a reason? Isn't being with you reason enough?"

Another rewarding smile.

Kyrk had based the line he'd composed on an element of truth. He fed off her beauty. Her seductive eyes, thin ruby lips, and flawless skin were his feast.

"Surely you didn't invite me here simply to ogle me."

He hadn't, though he could have.

"Of what shall we speak?" she asked.

It was Kyrk's turn to smile. He had come prepared. "We could speak of the moon and stars," he said.

That earned him a frown.

"The heavens bore me," Lyssa replied.

"We could speak of the beauty that surrounds us." He waved his hand at the pond. "We could speak of how the water that glistens with the light of yonder moon traveled three miles simply to sparkle for you. And how these cornflowers"—he cupped one in his hand—"that bloom twice each year cannot compare ..."

Lyssa yawned.

"I bore you?"

"The pond? The flowers? You speak of ponds and flowers?"

"Only if it pleases you."

"It does not."

Kyrk stared, crestfallen, at the cornflower still cupped in his hand.

Lyssa's thin eyebrows raised in understanding. "The pond ... the flowers ... You made a study of this garden to impress me, didn't you?"

She was quick-witted; he had to give her that. A sheepish grin was his confession.

"Pond water that travels three miles. Cornflowers that bloom twice a year."

Kyrk gazed at her defenselessly.

Suddenly all coyness and flirtation were gone. "All right," she said. "Let's see how good a job you did. The cornflower. How high does it grow?"

"One to three feet."

"How much moisture does it need?"

"Average to dry."

"What other name is associated with it?"

"Bachelor's button."

"How did it get its name *cornflower*, then?"

"Because it grows wild in grainfields."

Lyssa appeared impressed. So was he. Her questions reflected her own education.

But she wasn't finished. She pointed to a yellow and red flower near her feet. "And what is the name of this flower?"

"Primrose."

"And this one?"

"Marigold."

"And this?"

"Gillyflower." Before she could point to the next row, he said, "Those are Sweet Williams. They're a relative of the carnation."

Lyssa grinned. But she wasn't ready to concede. "The pond. It was originally encompassed . . ."

". . . by striped poles, each supporting the head of a heraldic beast."

A nod indicated her concession. "One more question," she said.

"At your leisure."

"Why?"

"Simple. Direct. But do you really want to know?"

Folding her arms, she waited for his answer.

"Because you make me nervous."

The surprise on her face indicated this wasn't the answer she was expecting.

Kyrk locked his hands behind his back and toed the edge of a stone on the path as he explained. "I don't like surprises. I like to be prepared for things. So I prepare. The more I know going into a situation, the more control I have over it."

"Control over the situation," Lyssa repeated.

Kyrk smiled. "And the people," he confessed.

"So all this is an attempt to control me?"

"I would not be so foolish as to think anyone could control you," he said. "My study of the garden was merely an attempt to control myself. For I've learned that whenever you're around, all sanity eludes me and I'm but a helpless victim."

Lyssa liked that.

"I must go," she said. "I really shouldn't have come."

She took a few steps back the way she'd come. He followed.

"Would you leave so soon?"

"I'm afraid I cannot see you again," she said.

Kyrk positioned himself between her and the palace. "Why would you say such a thing? Is there another?"

"No other."

"Then why?"

A troubled look visited Lyssa's face.

"I could never give myself to a man who is interested in an ecclesiastical career."

Kyrk reached for her. She backed away. A mistake. In his eagerness to please her, he was being too familiar, too fast.

"You are mistaken about me," he said.

"Do you not associate with Bishop Stokesley and Dr. Foxe?"

"A means to an end," he said.

"What end?"

"Wealth. Status. Courtly position."

Lyssa's eyes brightened.

"I admit, at first I was swayed by theological ideals and visions of utopian societies. But the more I studied, the more I realized that such things are the dreams of fools."

"But you have continued in the church."

"Because in it resides great power," Kyrk explained.

"Not as great as in the court," Lyssa said.

He took her comment as a reference to King Henry's victory over the pope.

"The tide of power ebbs and flows, my lady," he said. "Wise is the man who has cultivated power within both realms."

Lyssa smiled, impressed.

"As for my studies at Oxford," he said. "Dr. More? Dr. Foxe? Bishop Stokesley? Fools. What did Dr. More's ideals get him? Beheaded. Bishop Stokesley at least enjoys the power and money and prestige of his office. But I have no desire to become a bishop."

"And Dr. Foxe?"

"The greatest fool of all. The man has no money, no power, only a dream of a righteous England. And we both know that will never come to pass."

"Then why are you his associate?"

Kyrk smiled at her. "He's a stepping-stone to greater power and authority. Through him I will earn Bishop Stokesley's favor by convincing the bishop that Foxe is a useless relic of the past. Once I earn the bishop's favor, I will seek an appointment to the court as a liaison between the king and the bishop. With the confiscation of the pope's properties, there's a need for men who understand both court and church. There is power and wealth and property to be had in both realms."

Lyssa no longer seemed in a hurry to leave.

"So you see, Mistress Winter," Kyrk said, his eyes sparkling, "I'm not what you would call your typical theological pundit. I have no grand theological misconceptions. Wealth and power are my deity."

Lyssa Winter strolled casually up the pathway. There were three tiers in the garden, each one step deep; the pond gurgled at ground level. The edge of her dress swished against the stone pathway as she walked. She ascended to the next level not so much by stepping as by floating. She paused and looked back at him over her shoulder. The signal from her eyes was clear.

Kyrk rushed to her side.

"You speak of wealth and power," she purred. "How soon?"

Kyrk grew warm with passion.

"Key events are at hand," he said. "Thanks in large part to you."

"Me?" she said, fluttering a hand. "Why, how could I have possibly been of any help?"

"Lord North. He'll be arrested tonight."

"Because of what I told you?"

He grinned.

"And his arrest will bring you wealth?"

"It will provide me the key to the treasure-house."

"The key?"

"After tonight, based on Dr. Foxe's own testimony, my leadership will be well established. For the second time in his career, Dr. Pernell Foxe will be replaced by a younger man."

"And the fortune?"

Kyrk laughed.

"All in time, my lady. Once I have achieved Dr. Foxe's position—a position of authority normally reserved for doctors of theology—it will earn me the bishop's ear."

"And the king's ear?"

"Is just a whisper away."

A flash of pleasure crossed Lyssa's face. It was gone as quickly as it appeared, hidden by a layer of practiced composure.

She moved along the pathway and floated up the next step. This time Kyrk didn't wait to be summoned; he was right behind her when she turned around.

Lyssa stared in the direction of the palace. There was a faraway look in her eyes. She sighed. "A lady could be an old maid before such a plan bore fruit."

Kyrk winced. He had spent years formulating this plan and it was based on one thing—patient persistence. Impatience had never been a factor. Now it was. And it wore a silk dress and pearls.

"Believe me, my lady, the treasure is worth the dig."

Wrong answer. Displeasure flared in Lyssa's eyes. She moved toward the final step leading back to the palace.

"My lady," Kyrk persisted.

She stopped but didn't face him.

He moved to her side.

"The distance between me and my fortune is a mirage. It only appears distant. In truth, it will be mine soon."

Even as he said it, he regretted it. The promise had no foundation in truth. While he was confident his plan would bear fruit, it would take time. Yet he had to say something, didn't he? He couldn't just let her walk away.

Lyssa said nothing.

"It would be a cruel world indeed that did not reward a lady for the passion she incited in the heart of an ambitious man."

He was grasping now. Devoid of facts, he resorted to flattery.

It worked.

Lyssa turned to him. Approval sparkled in her eyes.

Chapter 21

Birdie and Enid were waiting for her.

"Tell, tell, tell!" Birdie squealed.

"Leave nothing out!" Enid cried.

Lyssa entered the room like a queen. She lacked the entourage, but by the way she carried herself, it was easy to imagine her surrounded by underlings.

Her two worshipers did all but kneel before her in their attempt to learn what had transpired in the garden.

"You're killing us with suspense!" Enid said.

"Don't be cruel, Lyssa. Please tell us!" Birdie said.

Lyssa took her time crossing the room. She removed the pearls from her hair and tossed them onto the bed, a self-satisfied expression on her face. She raised a hand to silence her following. Then after a dramatic pause that further tortured Birdie and Enid, she spoke.

"Masterful," she said.

"Him or you?" Birdie asked.

Lyssa shot her a look that made her feel the dunce.

"*I* was masterful," Lyssa droned.

"I would have been a puddle of emotions," Enid said. "One gaze into those luscious eyes and it would have been all over for me."

"Children, children, children . . . ," Lyssa said, "come sit at my feet and I'll tell you everything."

Lyssa lit on the edge of her bed. Her two adoring subjects did exactly as she'd instructed. They sat at her feet.

“I knew I had him the moment he looked at me,” she began.

Birdie and Enid squealed.

“Did he kiss you?” Birdie asked.

“He would have if I’d let him.”

“Why wouldn’t you let him?” Enid cried.

“He hasn’t earned it, my dear. He hasn’t earned it.” She sighed heavily. “I don’t know . . . I just don’t know.”

“Don’t know what?” Birdie asked.

“If he’s worthy of me.”

“But he’s so luscious!” Enid cried.

Lyssa shrugged. “He has yet to prove himself.” She stared into the distance in thought for a moment, then said, “But tonight was delicious. He was a little puppy dog, begging for my attention.”

A solitary candle lit the page. The wardrobe stood open, ready to embrace its secret once again at a moment’s notice.

Meg’s thoughts and emotions made for a curious stew. How had she ever come to this place? Here she sat on the edge of her bed, with a book of sedition open on her lap. A book she loved all the more every time she read it. Yet as usual when she read the book, she sat with one ear cocked for the sound of the downstairs door latch because her husband had dedicated his life to seeing every copy of the book destroyed.

Pernell. The New Testament. She loved both of them. To ask her to choose between them was like asking her to choose between air and food. Both sustained her in ways the other could not.

And then there was the baker. How strangely he had entered her life. What did she know of him other than his profession and that he trafficked in New Testaments, which made him an enemy to Pernell? She knew he was kind; she could see it in his eyes. She knew he was brave, because of the risks he took so the people of England could read the Bible in their own language, and by the way he handled himself in this task. When she told him of the trap set for Lord North, he never lost his composure.

But then, there was the disturbingly familiar way he looked at her. She felt powerfully attracted to him. Not in a romantic way, but it was an attraction nonetheless. One that intrigued and thrilled her. How was it that he seemed to know all about her?

Meg shook these thoughts from her head. She couldn't think about such things now. It was too much. Wasn't it enough that she had to contend with both Pernell and Nicholas?

It seemed odd to use his name, especially in the same thought as her husband.

They were both out in the night somewhere, on London's dark streets. In her mind she could see Pernell lying in wait. Would Nicho— the baker and Lord North elude him? And if they did, would it be because of her warning? And if it was, how would she feel, knowing she was responsible for Pernell's failure to capture them?

Meg groaned. How did she ever get to this place?

She sighed, knowing all too well the answer to her question. It lay open on her lap. And as if her mental stew didn't have enough ingredients in it already, it had added one more.

She didn't know why she'd turned toward the back of the book. Possibly because it was largely unexplored. But it didn't take long for the words to leap from the page at her as before.

> Beloved, let us love one another: for love cometh from God.

And as so often before, the words warmed her like an elixir. More than that, they seemed to hover over all that was happening between her and Pernell and the baker and cover it with hope, if not perspective. Were these not God's words? And if so, did they not express his desire for this contentious world?

She read the words again.

> Beloved, let us love one another: for love cometh from God. And every one that loveth, is born of God, and knoweth God. He that loveth not, knoweth not God; for God is love.

Meg's eyes closed. Her head turned heavenward. How much she wished all England could hear these words. How much it needed to hear these words. A country where the queen feared the king. Where the king exchanged one wife for another as easily as he would a suit of clothing. Where the king would behead a godly man like Dr. More for speaking his mind and calling for righteousness.

"Beloved, let us love one another."

These were the words that had caught her eye in the flickering candlelight. But it was the words farther down the page that pierced her soul.

> There is no fear in love, but perfect love casteth out all fear, for fear hath painfulness. He that feareth, is not perfect in love. We love him, fore he loved us first. If a man say, I love God, and yet hate his brother he is a liar. For how can he that loveth not his brother whom he hath seen, love God whom he hath not seen? And this commandment have we of him: that he which loveth God, should love his brother also.

She spoke the words aloud: "'If a man say, I love God, and yet hate his brother he is a liar.'"

Pernell.

She had never known a man so devoted to God. She had never known a man more passionate. For his wife. For his God.

The baker.

There was no hatred in the man. She'd only met him twice yet she was certain of it. Hatred. Vengeance. These things were foreign to him.

She could not say the same for Pernell. His hatred drove him. At times possessed him.

"If a man say, I love God, and yet hate his brother he is a liar."

The thought was a ladle that stirred a stew of emotions. Two men walked the streets of London. Their destinies were two strands of a single rope. One, her husband. The other, a baker she hardly knew. Pitted against each other in a battle over the fate of the book that sat on her lap.

Meg found herself praying for the success of the baker.

Nicholas hugged the shadows of Hog Lane. He paused to catch his breath. Everything was quiet up and down the dark road. The air was heavy with moisture from the river, settling on cobblestones, buildings, and late-night travelers alike.

Under his arm he carried his package, which consisted of three loaves of bread.

How quickly things had changed. He remembered Hog Lane being a country road with a few tenements between the fields. He used to fetch milk from the farm run by the nuns of the Minories. Now the city had caught up with it. Both sides of the road were lined with elm trees. The lane was one continuous stretch of garden houses and cottages.

Checking once again for signs of movement, especially behind him, he stepped out of the shadows and half ran, half walked up the lane.

"You're late," Pernell said.

"I stopped to check on the position of the guards on the north side," Thorndyke explained, sidling up next to him. "Anything yet?" he asked.

"Not yet," Pernell said. His nose twitched. "You say you were checking the guards?"

Thorndyke nodded. "Never take anything for granted."

Pernell sniffed. "And which of the guards is wearing lavender perfume?"

Color rose in Thorndyke's cheeks. He sniffed his sleeve and grinned. "I didn't say I only checked on the guards. They were my most recent stop."

"But not the lengthiest."

Thorndyke chortled. "If it were, what would you think of me?"

Pernell grinned.

"Does the scent bother you?" Thorndyke asked.

"Lavender irritates my senses."

"My apologies."

The two men were concealed from the adjacent lane by a stack of barrels beside a cloth merchant's warehouse. Thorndyke had reached the position without threat of detection by entering the warehouse on the opposite side.

"There!" he whispered.

A silhouetted figure stepped from the shadows and scurried up the lane.

"We've got him!" Thorndyke said.

"We have him in sight," Pernell cautioned. "Seeing him and capturing him may prove to be two different things. Let's see where he leads us."

Nicholas slipped into the garden that fronted the modest cottage. Rows of basil, parsley, leek, fennel, coriander, mustard, sage, and safflower made the night air pungent. It was a simple herb garden for a simple family.

He approached the door and lifted his hand to knock. Before his knuckles met wood, a feminine voice came from within.

"Who's there?"

"Nicholas," he whispered.

There was a pause.

"Go away!"

"Please, let me in . . ."

"Go away!" Louder. More insistent.

Nicholas wanted to tell the woman on the other side of the door how much his heart grieved over the capture of Raedmund and Bink. He wanted to offer assurances, to tell Raedmund's wife that no harm would come to her husband and son. But he knew she wouldn't believe him. Nor should she. He wanted to tell her that should God require them to sacrifice themselves in this life, they would surely be rewarded for their courage in the next life. But all he said was "I've got bread."

"Leave it and go!" the faceless voice shouted.

In the background Nicholas could hear a baby crying and two children squabbling. Unwrapping the bread, he took his coin purse, placed it inside the package, then wrapped it up again. He placed the bread at the threshold.

"May God grant you a measure of peace," he said.

Nicholas was a half dozen steps from the door when it flew open. He turned back and was met by three books that flew through the opening. The moment they were launched, the door slammed shut, the bread still on the threshold.

Nicholas caught one of the books. The other hit him on the shoulder. The third landed among the mustard plants. Undelivered New Testaments. He picked up the two on the ground.

With nothing to conceal the books, he tucked them under his arm and stepped back into the lane. He felt vulnerable, like a foist with his hand stuck in a gentleman's pocket, or a nip with a knife in one hand and a purse with severed ties in the other.

He considered hiding the books somewhere and returning for them later but decided against it. With a final glance at the Raedmund cottage, he entrusted the family to God's care, then set off down the lane, in the opposite direction from which he'd come.

"Was that a woman he was talking to?" Thorndyke asked.

"I didn't get a good look," Pernell replied. "Make a note of the house."

Their quarry was on the move again.

"Let's nab him now," Thorndyke said.

"No. I want to see where he'll take us." Pernell studied his young charge. "Why so impatient all of a sudden?"

Thorndyke looked away. "No reason," he said. "I'm just anxious to bag him." He moved to follow their target.

Pernell restrained him with a hand to his arm. "Give him some distance."

"I don't want to lose him!"

"We won't."

Thorndyke wasn't listening. Stepping from behind their cover, he followed the man from shadow to shadow down the lane.

As Nicholas neared the bakery shop, his thoughts turned to Meg. How precious she was to warn him. It took a lot of courage for her to do what she did.

He chuckled at the way she'd abused the loaf of bread in her basket. And the way she'd looked when she first recognized him and shouted, "You!"

He'd wanted to say, "Whom did you expect? Did you think you'd rid yourself of me that easily? One who has admired you from a distance all these years? One who is cursed from birth because he was not born of a station sufficient to allow him to court you?"

But all he'd said was "Me."

His reminiscing was cut short by a sound behind him. A cough or the scuffle of a shoe; he couldn't tell which. Without stopping he glanced behind him. The lane was deserted. He wasn't convinced. He knew he'd heard someone.

Suddenly he felt as if the books under his arm were stone and he were swimming in deep waters. He stepped to one side of the lane and waited.

No one appeared.

"Show yourself," he said.

No one did.

He began to doubt himself. Could he have been mistaken? He scanned the street for a place to hide his illegal cargo. Household refuse lined one side of the alley, shattered crates and discarded boards and broken bricks the other.

His only recourse was to make it back to the bakery.

"Why is he going in there?" Thorndyke asked.

Pernell squinted into the darkness. "There's only one way to find out," he said. "Master Thorndyke, I think it's time you summoned your guards."

"We've got him!" Thorndyke cried.

Chapter 22

Meg had dozed off and didn't awaken until Pernell was halfway up the steps. She awoke to the realization that the New Testament was still on her lap. Fighting the fog in her mind, she willed herself into action. The marching sound of Pernell's boots foretold imminent disaster should she be caught.

She flung the book into the wardrobe and closed the doors, leaning against them and stretching in a sleepy way just as Pernell walked into the room.

"You're still awake," he said.

Meg finished her stretch, faked a yawn—her heart beating wildly—and said, "I slept for a while, then awoke when I heard you coming."

Pernell groaned the groan of a tired man as he sat on the edge of the bed and removed his boots. He stood and approached the wardrobe. Meg was still standing guard in front of it. She blocked his way.

Boots in hand, he looked at her oddly. She smiled back at him.

"I'd like to put my boots in the wardrobe," he said.

"Oh! Of course . . ." Instead of moving aside, though, she reached for the boots. "Let me do it for you while you get into your bedclothes."

For a moment they both held the boots. Pernell looked at her, puzzled. The look didn't last long, just long enough to indicate that he thought she was acting strangely. Meg winced inwardly, then concluded it was better to have him think she was acting strangely than to let him open the wardrobe and find the New Testament.

He released the boots and began untying his doublet. Meg delayed long enough for him to turn his back to her; once he did, the wardrobe doors were opened, the boots were tossed inside, and a clean skirt was tossed onto the floor of the wardrobe, covering the New Testament. Closing the wardrobe, she resumed her guard position, her back pressed against the doors. Had Pernell known what she was doing, he surely would have thought she was afraid the book might leap out of the wardrobe on its own.

But Pernell didn't know what she was doing, and was preoccupied with getting himself ready for bed. When he was ready, he stood at the head of the bed and looked at her expectantly.

"Well?" he said.

"Well, what?"

"Are you going to climb in or are you going to climb over me?"

Ever since they were married, she'd slept on the side of the bed that was pushed against the wall. Of course she had to climb in first; what was she thinking?

She made a feeble attempt to explain by saying "I was going to douse the candle."

"I'll douse the candle. You get into bed."

For fifteen years it had been that way. She felt a fool suggesting otherwise.

"Thank you, dear," she said and climbed across the sagging center of the bed to the far side.

Pernell extinguished the candle. The bed rocked like a boat on the river as he climbed under the bedcovers.

Meg allowed him time to get settled. She was anxious to learn what had transpired tonight, but didn't want to appear too eager. While Pernell undressed, she had tried to read his face. It revealed little other than that he was tired.

"Did it go well tonight?" she said to the dark.

"We had something of a setback," he said.

Pernell didn't always talk to her about the day's events. He would after a long voyage, but rarely at the end of an ordinary day. Normally that was just fine with her. Tonight was different. But she wanted to be careful not to press him to the point where he'd become suspicious.

"A setback?" she said.

Pernell groaned as he turned and pulled on the covers in an attempt to get comfortable. When he spoke, his voice was thick with fatigue. He'd be asleep in a moment.

"Thorndyke was given bad information."

Meg's hopes rose.

"Bad information? Then you didn't capture a heretic tonight?"

Though half asleep, Pernell chuckled. "We nearly arrested Bishop Stokesley's brother-in-law."

Meg waited for an explanation. The pump of information was drying up; she'd have to prime it again.

"Bishop Stokesley's brother-in-law is a heretic?"

Another chuckle. "Not a heretic. A philanderer but not a heretic. We followed him to several women's houses. Caught him . . ." He paused to search for the right words. "Let's just say we caught him in a compromising position and leave it at that."

"Oh, my!" Meg cried.

"Exactly. Needless to say, Lord Northrup will have a word with the bishop. Kyrk will undoubtedly have some explaining to do."

"Lord Northrup?" Meg said. "I thought you were looking for a—"

"Lord North," Pernell said. "Hence the error. It's my fault. I'm aware of Lord Northrup's philandering. Just didn't put the two together."

Meg grinned at the error, trusting the darkness to conceal her smile from her husband—that is, if his eyes were open, which, judging by the increasing slur in his speech, she doubted.

An error. That meant Nicho—the baker was safe. Her smile widened. It was so big, she doubted even the darkness could hide it. Unable to suppress it, she turned her face to the wall.

"Very uncharacteristic of Kyrk to make such an error," Pernell said. "Something must have distracted him."

With his next breath he was asleep.

Pernell was still at the house when Meg left early for the palace. She made up an excuse about needing to look in on the girls before going to the queen's chamber. In truth, her walk to the palace would take an indirect route through the bakery shop on Elbow Lane.

She felt bad about lying but Pernell seemed in no hurry to leave the house, and she felt a need to make sure that the baker had indeed emerged unscathed from the previous night's activities. She reasoned that she'd already asked Pernell too many questions. Any more would make him suspicious. As for the increase in her heartbeat as she made her way down Elbow Lane, she reasoned that the wind was cold as it rushed between the buildings. She pulled her cloak tighter.

As before, the warm, homey odors of freshly baked bread and pastries greeted her long before she reached the door to the shop. When she entered, she looked around for the baker. Everything was exactly as it had been the last time she was in the shop, except for his absence.

Meg walked the length of a bread table as if shopping for bread. When she reached the end, she examined the pastries and buns on the back shelves. Still no one came from the back to wait on her. She could hear muffled conversation and the general clatter of a working kitchen, but nobody seemed to be aware that there was a customer in the shop.

"Hello?" Meg called into the back room. "Hello?"

A stocky man appeared, wiping his hands on a towel. "What can I help you with today?" he asked in a businesslike way.

His appearance flustered Meg.

Furrowing her brow, she walked to the table laden with loaves of bread. "Um . . ." She pretended to examine the bread. "I . . . um, I have a question for the baker," she said. "Would you please send him out?"

"I'm the baker," the man said. "What's your question?"

"You're the baker? Oh, you're the baker . . ." She stared again at the bread, hoping a bakery question would pop into her head. "Um . . . is this bread . . . um, fresh?"

The man scowled at her. He took her question as a veiled implication. "Of course it's fresh!" he barked. "It's still warm!" He held his hand over the bread. "See? Feel for yourself!"

Meg stretched out her hand. "Yes . . . I can see that it is. Warm. That is, fresh. It must be fresh because it's warm."

"How many loaves?" he said, picking up one and reaching for another.

"Well, actually . . ."

She had a choice: admit she was there to see Nicholas by asking for him by name, something she didn't want to do, or purchase a couple loaves of bread.

"I guess I'll take—"

"My, my . . . and once again we meet."

The familiar voice came from the doorway. Nicholas sauntered in, all smiles. Meg returned his smile, genuinely glad to see him, for a couple of different reasons.

Nicholas held out his hand to the other man, a few coins in his palm. "You take care of this," he said, "and I'll attend to our customer."

The stocky baker glanced at Nicholas, then at Meg. He tossed the loaf of bread back onto the pile, took the coins, then disappeared into the back of the shop with a grunt.

"And to what do I owe this honor?" Nicholas asked. "It's unlikely you need another loaf of bread so soon."

Now that she was here and he was standing in front of her, Meg felt foolish, completely unprepared for this conversation. She felt like a little girl daring to talk to the object of a childish infatuation.

"I simply . . . I wanted to make sure . . . well, to see that . . ."

Nicholas folded his arms, which emphasized the size of his muscular forearms.

". . . well, to make sure you avoided . . ."

"The trap," he said.

"And now that I see you have, I'll be on my way."

She brushed by him on her way to the door and was at the threshold when he spoke.

"So there really was a trap."

She stopped, perplexed. She whirled around.

"What do you mean by that?" she asked. "Of course there was a trap."

"I would have thought your husband would have told you his nets came up empty last night," he said.

The familiarity that had been so deliciously annoying was gone, replaced by a smugness that went beyond annoying. It was infuriating.

"My conversations with my husband are none of your business," she said.

His grin turned sarcastic. "Being the subject of those conversations just might give me the right to inquire."

Why was he acting like this? A part of her wanted simply to walk out the door and have done with it; another part of her wanted to knead the grin off his face and toss him into his own ovens.

Again she turned to leave. Again he stopped her.

"It's comforting to know the great Pernell Foxe is fallible," he said. "I'm certain it gives his prey a measure of hope."

Meg whirled around again. "It just so happens," she fumed, "that the information he'd been given was in error. His source was unreliable, not him."

"The way I heard it, he tried to arrest the wrong man."

"A reasonable mistake," she shot back. "Lord North. Lord Northrup. You have to admit, the names are similar."

Nicholas howled.

"You find humor in that?"

"Lord Northrup? Are you telling me that the great and mighty Pernell Foxe captured Bishop Stokesley's wayward brother-in-law? Why, yes, I can say with certainty I find that humorous."

The tide of Meg's defensiveness rose, and with it her anger.

"Well . . . you tell . . . you. . . . This isn't over," she sputtered. "You inform Lord North that he'd better watch his back because Pernell will be looking for him. Now, good day."

"He knows," Nicholas said.

Meg was halfway out the door again. "He knows? How could he know?" she asked.

"You just told him."

Meg cocked her head.

"I'm North."

Meg didn't believe him. "You're Lord North?"

The baker laughed. "That's what was so perplexing," he said. "There is no Lord North. There's Lord Northrup—your husband made his acquaintance last night. And then there's just plain North."

She stared at him questioningly.

"Nicholas North. My name. I'm the man your husband is hunting."

"And you're telling me this for what reason?"

"Just thought you might like to know who you've been associating with."

Meg stammered, wanting to say something clever, only her mind and mouth could not seem to come up with anything at the moment.

North said, "Thank you for your warning, though. I don't take it lightly. Nor do I take your husband lightly. Pernell Foxe is a dangerous man."

Meg's defenses, already in place, were quick to respond. "My husband is no such thing. He's a man of principle and integrity."

"Who enjoys killing innocent Christians."

"He does no such thing!" Meg cried.

North unfolded his arms. He walked toward her. All humor had drained from his face. "Do you want to know where I was last night while your husband thought he was tracking me down? I was visiting a good Christian woman. Taking her bread. Was she grateful? No. She threw books at me. Do you want to know why?"

Meg didn't reply. Her glare was glacial.

"It's because both her husband and her son are in prison awaiting execution. Guess who put them there?" North took another step toward her. Now he was uncomfortably close. "I know these men. They're good men. They're my friends. So don't stand there and tell me your husband is a man of principle and integrity, when he wants to roast my friends in the public square."

"They wouldn't be in prison if they hadn't broken the law," Meg said. "Pernell is merely enforcing—"

"Bah!" North shouted. "Do you expect me to believe that Pernell Foxe is merely enforcing the law? That he has no personal feelings in this at all? Let me ask you this: Would a man who is merely enforcing a law track another man all across Europe, as he did William Tyndale? Would your husband do the same to catch a cutpurse? Or a thief? Or even a murderer? Pernell Foxe hunted down William Tyndale as he would a boar in the forest, and for one reason and one reason only: because he doesn't believe a common man should be allowed to read the Bible for himself. It's not a matter of enforcing the law; it's a matter of control. He wants to keep godly Englishmen from reading God's truth for themselves, because if they do, they might discover that the clerics have been lying to them for years."

"I'll not stand here while you defame my husband," Meg said. "Good day."

North grabbed her arm.

"Unhand me!" Meg cried.

"I'm not finished," North said.

"I think you are, sir."

Meg tried to wrench her arm free. He was too strong for her.

"What do you think your dear husband will do when he discovers that you've been secretly reading the New Testament?"

Meg stopped struggling. She avoided North's eyes.

"I don't know," she said softly.

"I think you do."

In truth, she didn't. While she feared being found out and knew it would hurt and anger Pernell, she hadn't thought about what he would do. She didn't want to think about what he would do.

"He'll turn aside," North said. "He'll look the other way."

Meg met North's gaze.

"When it's his wife, it'll be different."

"No . . . ," Meg said without conviction.

"You know I'm right," North said. "Unlike everyone else, you have the luxury of dabbling in a little New Testament reading, because you know that if your husband finds out, all he'll do is take your book away from you and slap you on the back of the hand."

"No . . ." She didn't want to believe it.

"Do you know what it's like for the rest of us?"

Meg turned her head. She tried to break free. His grip was unyielding.

"I'll tell you. Our future is that of a young Oxford student named James who fell under the suspicion of Drs. More and Pernell, then professors at the university. More ordered the student's house searched. In it they found letters and treatises that implicated James, his wife, Joan, and four others. James's house was burned to the ground. He and the others were summarily imprisoned in the fish cellar at Cardinal

College. They were shut away for months. They were finally released, but not before three of them died."

Tears welled in Meg's eyes.

"Joan was one who died," North said, choking back tears of his own. "She was my sister."

Meg felt all the fight drain from her.

"That's what awaits the rest of us should Pernell Foxe ever catch up with us."

North released her arm and left her standing there. He disappeared into the back of the bakery.

Nicholas North stormed into the working end of the bakery, past the baker's dozen of workers who were mixing dough in huge wooden bowls, kneading it on large tables splashed with flour, using long-handled peels to pull finished loaves from the three large brick ovens, and decorating a variety of pastries with raisins and nuts.

"Nicholas," the stocky baker said, "we're running low on . . ."

"Master North," said another worker, "do you want all of these pastries to be . . ."

He didn't hear them.

He rushed through a doorway to a smaller room with a single oven that hadn't seen a fire in years. It was the oven with which he'd started his bakery business. Now it held the fire of God—Tyndale New Testaments hidden behind loose bricks.

He slapped the bricks in frustration. Within seconds the flat of his hand and the bricks were identical in color.

His mind was stuck on his encounter with Meg. At the moment, he could think of nothing else, as though his entire existence consisted of their heated exchange. He relived the moment when he saw her standing in his shop as he walked through the door.

He'd wanted to say, "Do you realize how my heart leaps every time I see you? How for years you have captivated me in my dreams? Do you know that since my youth you have been the model of the perfect woman for me?"

He'd wanted to say, "I can't stop thinking about how you took the chance to warn me about the trap your husband was setting, and although I knew he was operating on a false assumption, nevertheless it was stirring that you would be so concerned about my well-being that you would risk warning me."

He'd wanted to say, "Do you realize what joy it gives me simply knowing that you have one of the New Testaments I helped bring over from the continent? Do you know how often I wonder what portions of it you read, and fantasize that someday we might read portions of it together? Do you know how much I ache to share some of my favorite passages with you?"

Instead he'd said, "Pernell Foxe is a dangerous man."

Despite the redness of his hand, North slapped the bricks again.

Pernell emerged from Ironmonger Lane, his thoughts on Thorndyke and his morning meeting with the bishop. He couldn't suppress a smile. The boy had acted on bad information. It was as simple as that. Very uncharacteristic of him, though. But he was young. Driven sometimes by things other than wisdom. In this case distracted by the pretty face of a seductress.

That's what prompted Pernell's smile. Everyone had a weakness. From all indications, feminine beauty was Thorndyke's weakness. It was Pernell's weakness too.

He'd have a talk with the boy. Tell him how he learned not to let his physical passions control him by finding the right woman and focusing all his passion on her and her alone. To learn to be content with one good woman was the only way to keep from being undone.

How many men had he seen ruined by unbridled lust? As of last night, one more. Lord Northrup, with the help of his influential brother-in-law the bishop, might be able to contain the damage from last night, but from what Pernell had seen, he was a man who had surrendered himself to his passions too many times. He no longer controlled them; they controlled him. How many times can someone cover up a stink before the odor sticks to him for good?

He'd speak to the bishop too. Intercede for the boy. Assume the blame for the night's fiasco. Do what he could to help the boy out so his image wouldn't be tarnished in the bishop's eyes.

These were Pernell's thoughts as a crisp morning breeze whipped around the corner of Ironmonger Lane, cutting through his cloak and chilling his flesh. He adjusted his coat to protect himself.

That's when he saw her.

Meg.

Emerging from a bakery situated at the bend in Elbow Lane. Her head was down. She walked with angry strides, noticeably upset by something. A man learned to recognize his wife's moods over fifteen years of marriage. Especially anger. And Meg was angry.

He started toward her, then stopped. What was she doing here anyway? She'd left the house some time ago, saying she was going to the palace. While she was headed in that direction now, Elbow Lane was in the opposite direction.

Shopping for bread? That would be the obvious explanation. Only she'd picked up a loaf and some buns yesterday. And wouldn't it make more sense to pick up bread on the way home from the palace? Besides, she was not carrying her shopping basket and there was no bread in her arms.

He followed her at a distance for a while. She made straight for the palace, acknowledging no one.

As she rounded Saint Paul's, Pernell let her go. He stood in the shadow of the marvelous stone edifice, in thought. Then, turning, he retraced his steps. Meg's steps.

To Elbow Lane.

To the bakery shop situated on the bend in the lane.

He stood at the doorway and looked in. He saw plenty of bakery products but no people. He crossed the threshold.

A stocky man emerged from the back, wiping his hands on a towel. "Can I interest you in some of our fine pastries?" he said.

Pernell looked at him suspiciously. What could have possibly happened in here that would have upset Meg?

"Are you the baker?" Pernell asked.

Exasperation stretched one side of the man's mouth, as though the question were a sore point with him.

"Do I not look like a baker?" he said.

His point was a valid one. Dough was crusted on his arms and hands. His shoes were splattered with flour.

"Your name?" Pernell asked.

The man's eyes squinted in suspicion. "William Royden," he said. "Are you here for baked goods or not?"

Pernell looked around the shop. Everything was in order. There were shelves of baked goods everywhere. The unmistakable sounds and smells of a bakery kitchen wafted through the doorway leading to the back room.

He considered asking the man directly about Meg, inquiring of her business there, but then thought better of it. If this man had harmed her in any way, he'd undoubtedly deny it. That would give him the rest of the day to do whatever he thought he could do to cover up any indiscretion. No, he'd ask Meg tonight when she came home; then if necessary he'd return here and settle matters.

"I've changed my mind," Pernell said in answer to the man's question. He turned to leave.

With a grunt the baker turned on his heel to go back to work.

"Just one more thing," Pernell said, catching him just before he disappeared into the back room. "Are you the proprietor?"

"No."

"And who might the proprietor be?"

"Nicholas North."

Chapter 23

Meg was not prepared for what was awaiting her at the palace. The gloom was so heavy when she stepped through the northern gate, it was like entering a horticulturist's hothouse. Her spirit had already been bruised by North's verbal assault; she didn't know if she could take another blow. Still, she pressed on.

She deduced the news before she heard it. The somber faces. The huddled conversations, all with an identical theme. Listen for just a short time and two words inevitably would be heard.

The queen.

There was only one conclusion to draw.

Meg went straight to the queen's chamber. There would be no tutoring today. She found the ladies of the court gathered in one of the outward chambers. Madge approached her as she entered.

The small, soft-featured woman reached for her. Meg offered her hands.

"You've heard?" Madge asked.

"A miscarriage?"

Madge nodded. Her cheeks showed evidence of recent tear tracks. Her eyes were filled with fresh tears ready to spill over at any moment.

"Does anyone know what caused it?" Meg whispered.

No one in the room spoke above a whisper.

"It was horrible," Madge said. "Yesterday afternoon the queen caught a young maiden on the king's knee. She flew into a frenzy. I've never seen her in such a state—and you know how the queen can get sometimes."

Meg nodded. She had indeed witnessed some of the queen's frightful moods.

Madge drew closer to her. With her lips nearly touching Meg's ear, she said, "It was Lady Jane Seymour. She was on the king's knee."

"God help us," Meg said.

It made sense now. While the king had a reputation of being friendly with the ladies, there were some who posed a greater level of threat to the queen. On the top of that list was Lady Jane Seymour.

While the queen's court was divided over their feelings toward Lady Jane, Meg was one of the few who had not chosen sides. It was Lady Jane who had summoned her to the palace to play the virginals for the queen. And it was Lady Jane who had personally instructed her in the matters of court dress and etiquette. Personally, Meg liked the girl but thought she was overly flirtatious, which, given the present court atmosphere, was like a flame to gunpowder.

And now the unavoidable explosion was history.

Meg scanned the room.

"She hasn't shown her face," Madge said, reading her eyes. "Then last night the queen miscarried."

"God have mercy on her," Meg said.

Again Madge leaned close to her ear. "It was male," she said.

Meg fought back tears.

"And the queen?" she managed to ask.

"Has been sobbing fearfully all night long."

"God have mercy," Meg said. "Has she called for anyone?"

Madge shook her head sadly. "Except for her doctors, she's been all alone."

Until the queen assigned her tutoring responsibilities, Meg's entire reason for being in the court was to soothe a troubled queen. Now the queen needed soothing more than ever, and Meg found it difficult to stand in the outward chambers and do nothing. Especially since she could do so much more than play the virginals.

"'Let not your heart be troubled,' Your Majesty," Meg muttered in a barely audible voice.

"Did you say something?"

"A prayer for the queen."

Madge crossed herself.

Suddenly the door to the outward chamber slammed open. King Henry, his eyes fixed on the door leading to the queen's bedchamber, stormed through the room. The sea of ladies parted before him.

His face was cold, unforgiving.

Throwing open the bedchamber doors, he strode in, stood there for a moment, then slammed the doors behind him. For the brief time the doors were open, Meg could hear the queen weeping.

The undercurrent of whispers that had filled the room only moments before gave way to complete silence. The bedchamber doors did little to mute the voices of the king and queen.

The king complained repeatedly about "the loss of his boy." He flung harsh words at his queen, blaming her for the child's death.

The queen yelled that fault lay with him, for his cruelties to her.

The king refused to accept responsibility and shouted that she would have no more boys by him.

The queen, tossing aside all caution, cried desperately that he had no one to blame but himself for his disappointment, which he had caused by her distress of mind about that wench Jane Seymour. She sobbed audibly, then shouted, "Because the love I bear you is so much greater than Catherine's, my heart broke when I saw you loved others."

There was a moment of silence, after which the king spoke.

"I will speak to you when you are well."

Everyone in the room jumped collectively as the doors to the queen's bedchamber flew open. The king made no effort to close them. His eyes as hard and cold as ice, he crossed the room and was gone.

The bedchamber doors were closed. The sobbing continued. As the hours passed, the ladies began filing out of the room. Madge excused herself, saying there were duties that required her attention.

Meg found herself alone in the outward chamber. She found a bench and took up a silent vigil, alternately praying and waiting for the queen to summon her.

As the day turned out, Thorndyke proved to be the least of Pernell's problems. The rumors he heard while crossing the bridge on his way to his meeting with the bishop were confirmed shortly upon his arrival at Lambeth. The queen had miscarried. The king was beside himself. The kingdom was in turmoil, for its hopes of a male heir to the throne were once again dashed.

The mood at Lambeth was somber. The queen's miscarriage was all anyone could talk about. Including the bishop. Pernell wouldn't have been surprised had the bishop chosen to meet with them another day. He didn't. However, the meeting was brief.

Thorndyke was wisely quiet. Lord Northrup had indeed approached the bishop privately and pleaded his case. From the few references Stokesley made, Pernell surmised that the lord's defense was basically that he was visiting the estranged wife of a friend in an attempt to convince her to reconcile with her husband. In short, a case of misinterpreting an innocent act of kindness.

The bishop was not fooled. But neither did he choose to embrace a family scandal at this time. On behalf of his charge, Pernell replied that the incident was entirely his fault and should not have occurred in the first place had he insisted that Kirk Thorndyke double-check his sources before initiating a course of action.

The bishop was placated. Thorndyke was mildly admonished, while Pernell received the brunt of the bishop's displeasure, after which they were in essence charged to carry on with their work and warned not to let such a grievous error against an upstanding citizen of the realm occur again.

All in all, Pernell was not troubled by the outcome of the day's events. At least not nearly as troubled as he was regarding the mysterious actions of his wife.

She wasn't home when he got there. While he could count on one hand the number of times that had occurred in fifteen years of marriage, it was now becoming a regular occurrence. Suspicious.

He lit some candles.

Until now he'd accepted her word that when she wasn't at home, she was at the palace. Why not? He had no reason to believe she was deceiving him.

Until today.

Now he wasn't sure what to believe. Considering the events of the day, it would make sense that she would be late in coming home. The queen could conceivably require Meg's services on the virginals.

Then again, this morning she said she was going to the palace, and only by accident did he learn that she first went to the bakery on Elbow Lane, on unknown business.

And the proprietor's name was North.

Coincidence?

He could only hope so.

He heard steps outside the door. The next moment Meg entered. Her face was drawn, her shoulders slouched.

"I suppose you heard?" she said.

She took off her cloak and draped it over her arm, smoothing it unconsciously.

"I heard," Pernell said.

Their eyes met. Was it Pernell's imagination or were they the eyes of a stranger?

"I'll put my cloak away and make you some supper." She moved toward the stairs.

"You're tired," he said.

"Weary to the bone."

"You've been at the palace all this time?"

He had to ask. There was no way he could keep himself from asking. He watched her response. She gave no indication that she was suspicious of the question.

"I waited all day in the outward chamber should the queen call for me."

"Did she?"

Meg's eyes glazed over with tears. "No."

She took the first two stairs as if she were carrying the weight of the kingdom on her shoulders.

"Go to bed," Pernell said.

"I'm fine," Meg said, smiling weakly. "I'll get your supper."

"Go to bed. I can hunt up something for myself."

"Are you sure?"

"You're tired," he replied.

She didn't argue. She trudged up the stairs. Pernell could hear her scuffling overhead.

Her eyes disturbed him. It could be fatigue. She wasn't used to the burden of kingdom politics. But then again, it might not be fatigue at all but a wall. A wall behind which she was hiding something from him.

Rummaging around the kitchen, he found a hunk of boiled beef. He sliced it. He cut up some cheese, bread, and cabbage. Into a mug he poured some swish-wash, a water and honey mixture to which he added a pinch of pepper.

Overhead the scuffling stopped. Ropes groaned and then all was silent.

Pernell sat down at the table. The beef was tough. He chewed and chewed and chewed some more. Even then he swallowed prematurely. A large lump of beef worked its way down his gullet. He helped it along with a swig of swish-wash.

The cup in his hand suspended above the table, he agonized over what to do about Meg. Should he let the incident go unexplained? She'd never given him cause to mistrust her. Never. There was probably a simple explanation. He should just ask her outright.

He took another swig.

Still, there were two things that bothered him. First, whatever had occurred in the bakery, it had disturbed her; surely if such was the case, she'd mention it, wouldn't she? Any other day and it might have been the first thing out of her mouth when she came home. But today was not any other day.

Second, North. He couldn't get the name out of his mind. For all he knew, Meg had never met the proprietor.

He lifted the slice of beef for another bite.

Tomorrow he'd find out all he could about Nicholas North. That would give Meg another opportunity in the morning to voluntarily tell him about the incident in the bakery—

A shriek from upstairs stopped his heart cold.

His chair crashed backward when he stood; the mug tumbled onto the table, spilling swish-wash across the surface and onto the floor; the table itself rose and fell as Pernell struggled to clear his legs from beneath it and scramble up the stairway.

His long legs took the stairs two at a time.

It was a shriek; there was no doubt about that. Not a shout. Not a yell. Not even a scream. A shriek. And it was Meg, and she didn't stop with a single shriek; she was still shrieking.

The darkness upstairs did not slow him. He flew through it toward his wife. As he neared the bed, he could see the barest outline. She was sitting upright, hugging the bedcovers to her chest, her eyes wide with terror, her mouth stretched open in a ghastly shape, her chest heaving, and with each heave came another shriek.

Pernell threw his arms around her. Buried her face in his chest, muting the shrieks but not stopping them. He looked around the room for signs of anything that might be frightening her—a predator, human or animal, a bat, a rat, anything that would explain her terror.

There was nothing.

No movement.

No scurrying.

No animal eyes.

Nothing.

Meg continued to rise and fall in his arms with each heaving breath. He pulled her even tighter.

"Hush, I'm here now," he said in a soothing voice. "Hush . . . hush . . . "

She turned her head to one side so her face was no longer pressed into his chest. The volume had gone out of her shrieks but her breathing was still labored. She was regaining a measure of control.

"Hush now. Hush. Hush."

She shuddered one great convulsive shudder. After that she began to calm down, though she continued to sob and whimper.

"What was it? What frightened you?" Pernell asked, though he was fairly confident he knew the answer.

Meg sobbed; her knuckles at her mouth were wet with tears and saliva. She hadn't calmed down enough to speak.

"Was it Robert?"

She was afraid to respond. He'd seen her this way before. She was afraid that by saying his name, it would somehow summon his presence.

"It was Robert, wasn't it?" Pernell said.

After a few shivering sobs, she nodded her head, but only once.

"It's all right," Pernell said, lowering his cheek onto her hair. "You had another episode. It was a dream. You're all right now. Hush. You're all right now."

He shifted his legs to get comfortable. Meg let out a cry and clung to him.

"I'm not going anywhere," he said. "I've still got you. You're safe. Everything will be all right."

Pernell positioned himself for a long night, never once letting go of Meg. Fully clothed, with his boots still on, he settled onto the bed.

Meg settled against him. Her sobs had turned to sniffles.

In the darkness Pernell held her, as he had so many nights in their marriage. Only it had been such a long time since her last episode, he couldn't help but wonder what it was that had set off this one.

CHAPTER 24

"Do they have to be here?"

Thorndyke motioned with his head toward Enid and Birdie, who were perched at the edge of the pond garden. While their distance may have been discreet, their stares weren't.

"They look like a couple of drunken magpies," he quipped.

Lyssa laughed appreciatively. It was true. They stood shoulder to shoulder, their heads tilted together, their mouths moving at the same time. Her glance in their direction prompted a new round of giggles and a finger-wiggling wave from Birdie.

"They're harmless," Lyssa cooed. "Besides, are you suggesting we meet in full view of God and king without some sort of chaperone?"

Her eyes were playful. They worked their intended magic on him.

"We did the other night," he whispered.

Lyssa giggled deliciously.

In contrast to the heavy pall that suffocated the court because of the queen's miscarriage, Lyssa's mood was positively giddy. She touched Thorndyke's forearm. It was a bold gesture on her part, in public, in full daylight. He knew she did it to give the two girls something more to squeal over, which they did, but he didn't mind. The warmth of her touch through his sleeve was electric and exciting.

"You are whimsical today," he said.

She flashed a smile, which, together with her sparkling eyes, formed a one-two punch that staggered him.

"And why not?" she said lightly.

"Recent events with the queen come to mind," he said, though he didn't know why. The last thing he wanted to do was to douse the fairy-sprite that was flitting in front of him. To his relief he hadn't.

"The queen's troubles are the very source of my giddiness!" Lyssa said, twirling her dress about playfully.

"Oh?"

"She deserves everything she's getting," Lyssa said, sobering for but a moment. "Anne Boleyn is a calculating witch. And God willing, the king is finally seeing her for what she is and will burn her at the stake."

Thorndyke took a quick glance around. It was foolish to say such things aloud in a public place. Though it was common knowledge that many in the kingdom had always felt this way about the queen, she was still the queen.

Thorndyke shushed her. "Someone might hear you," he said.

"I don't care," Lyssa said airily. "Let them hear me!"

"What makes you think you're immune to the queen's wrath?"

Lyssa grinned slyly. This time she did lower her voice. "Because I'm a favorite of the next queen of England."

"The next queen?"

"Lady Jane Seymour."

The rumors were circulating freely. It was well known that Lady Jane Seymour was frequently in the king's company and occasionally on his knee. However, while Thorndyke did not pretend to know the will of the king, he knew men. And for a man to have a lover and to take her as his wife were two entirely different things.

"You can't be certain he'll dispose of Queen Anne," he said.

"Can't I?" Lyssa said with a grin that suggested she knew something. "Besides, the king has already divorced himself from a virtuous wife; what's to keep him from disposing of a harlot and a witch?"

Again, rumors. Thorndyke wondered how much of it was true. He said, "And Lady Jane . . ."

". . . will be the next queen of England."

"You're certain?"

Lyssa answered him with a wicked smile.

Thorndyke began to share her giddiness. He could only hope that half of what she was telling him was true. If he was to be the consort of a woman who had the queen of England's ear, there was no telling how great a position he might be able to reach in the court.

This bejeweled, pale-skinned fairy who excited him every time he was near her was also a golden key to riches and position. His heart swelled with the possibilities.

"And your news for me? Is it good?" his fairy princess asked.

As quickly as his heart had inflated, it deflated.

"Good news," he said, doing his best to put on a positive face. "Not nearly as good as yours but not bad either."

Displeasure cast a shadow over Lyssa's features, muting her glow. Seeing it, Thorndyke fought a rising sense of panic. He hurried to explain.

"Not bad news," he insisted. "Just not as good as I was hoping for."

The displeasure was settling in; he had to talk fast.

"We didn't catch the smuggler we were after." He chuckled. "It's really sort of humorous. We were trailing the wrong man. His name turned out to be Lord Northrup, not Lord North, and he happened to be the brother-in-law of the bishop, and we caught him in . . ." He chuckled again. "Well, with his britches down."

Fleetingly he considered mentioning that his lack of success was due in large part to faulty information—information she had given him—but he wasn't sure how she'd react. Defensively was his guess, possibly even hostilely. He chose not to mention it.

"So as you might expect," he hurried on, "I did not receive the accolades I was expecting from the bishop. But be assured, it's only temporary. An insignificant delay. Certainly nothing that should concern—"

"Lord Northrup." Her brow wrinkled as she said the name.

"Not a smuggler. The bishop's brother-in-law," he reiterated. "But it doesn't matter. Listen to this. That old codger Pernell Foxe? He stood up for me before the bishop. Took the blame. Can you believe it?" Thorndyke forced a laugh.

"I could have heard wrong," Lyssa said, not listening to him. "She stammers when she speaks . . ."

"So as I said, you needn't worry—"

Lyssa's eyes snapped back to the present moment.

"His wife has one of those books," she said.

"What?"

"So does the queen. One of those illegal books with all the familiar relations listed. Meg Foxe reads it to the queen in her bedchamber."

"Familiar relations?"

"Begones . . . beguiles . . . be . . ."

"Begats."

"That's it!"

"A New Testament. The queen has one? You know this for certain?"

"Lady Madge listens at her door. She's heard Meg Foxe reading it to her. I told you the queen was a witch."

"And you say Meg Foxe has a New Testament of her own?"

"She took one from Birdie and Enid and me."

"You had one?"

Lyssa shrugged. "We were curious."

"Does she still have it?"

"I don't know."

"Where did you get it in the first place?"

"The book? Alfreda."

Thorndyke cocked his head and waited for an explanation.

"A dumb, clubfooted girl who loiters around our room. We make sport of her."

"She's a palace servant?"

"Kitchen servant. Her mother's a scullery maid."

"And where did this clubfooted servant get an illegal New Testament?"

Lyssa was getting bored and, as it always did, her face displayed the emotion. But this time Thorndyke didn't leap to appease her.

"Two things," Thorndyke said, drawing her back to the conversation. "Think. Meg Foxe—is there anything that would lead you to believe she still has the New Testament?"

Lyssa shrugged. She yawned in his face. "I already told you. I think it's time I . . ."

"The clubfooted girl," Thorndyke pressed. "I want to talk to her."

"... returned to the palace. This conversation is getting frightfully—"

Thorndyke grabbed her by the shoulders.

His actions sent the two magpies into a tizzy. Had they truly been birds, feathers would have flown everywhere. Even the unflappable Lyssa became alarmed.

"She might know who delivers the New Testaments to the palace," Thorndyke explained.

Lyssa's fear gave way to a knowing grin.

"Can you show me where to find the girl?" he asked.

"No," Lyssa replied. A glint of wickedness flashed in her eyes. "I can do better. I can bring her here. Wait for me."

Lyssa stepped purposefully up the stone walkway. A concerned Birdie and Enid fluttered down to her, meeting her halfway. The three girls huddled. All Thorndyke was able to hear of their conversation was Lyssa shushing them, then, "I don't care how you do it! Bring her here. Now!"

Skirts raised, the two magpies flapped their way toward the palace while Lyssa returned to him. Her usual feminine glide was more of a swagger. She wore a superior smirk. Thorndyke loved her all the more. A man of authority needed a strong woman by his side, a woman who knew what she wanted and knew how to get it.

He smiled approvingly at her. The two of them were going to go far together.

Birdie and Enid returned with surprising speed. They dragged a disheveled, reluctant girl between them. Standing between two courtly ladies who'd spent untold hours getting their hair coifed, having their faces painted, picking out the best dress for the day, and being primped and preened, the scullery maid looked like a clod of dirt. Compared with the way the two ladies of the court carried themselves, even while dragging her between them, she hobbled and lurched like the cripple she was.

They brought her to the edge of the pond garden.

Thorndyke took a step toward her.

"No," Lyssa said. "Allow me."

Thorndyke started to object.

Lyssa grinned. "I know her weaknesses."

He found a wooden bench and sat down and watched the interrogation.

Lyssa leaned into the girl's face and said something he couldn't hear. The girl shook her head.

So much for the direct approach, Thorndyke thought.

The three court ladies began circling the kitchen maid. They reminded Thorndyke of the birds circling the battlements above the stone gateway of London Bridge, picking at the severed heads of traitors displayed on poles. In the same way, the girls were circling the kitchen maid and pick, pick, picking away at her.

The girl began to weep and they didn't stop. She grew angry and lashed back and they didn't stop. She sank to her knees and covered her face and they didn't stop. Mercilessly they circled and picked and circled and picked and circled and picked.

This went on so long, Thorndyke concluded that the girl didn't know anything, but he did nothing to stop it. He folded his arms and inhaled the garden's fragrance, watched the rippling pool of water, and lifted his face to the warmth of the sun while Lyssa and her girls continued their circling.

Then Lyssa cocked her ear to the girl. She spoke and listened, then spoke again and listened again. Turning to Thorndyke, she glided toward him with a freshness that suggested she was seeing him for the first time that day. He rose to accept her.

"Meg Foxe never returned the New Testament," she said.

"Then she still has it?"

"It would seem so. She had a chance to return it and didn't."

Thorndyke thought on this a moment. She could have turned it over to Pernell, who would have destroyed it. But if that was the case, he also would have gone after the source, wouldn't he? Why didn't he? Maybe his wife hadn't told him about the book. After all, she was reading it secretly to the queen.

"As for the man who delivers the books to the palace—the girl knows who it is?"

His heart stuttered. The right answer in the next moment and he could turn everything around to his favor once again.

"She does," Lyssa said with a grin. Now she was playing with him. And though it was agony for him, it was an exciting form of torture.

"Tell me!" Thorndyke cried.

"No," Lyssa said.

Thorndyke grinned. "Oh, you are a wicked one."

"Never forget that," she cooed.

Thorndyke stepped back and folded his arms. "I can wait," he said.

"Oh? You're not going to torture me?" she asked.

He could feel the glint in his eyes. "The thought has merit," he said.

"Yes, it does," she said seductively. Then, as quickly as a coin can be flipped, another side of her appeared. A light, breezy, carefree side. "But not today," she said and glided past him.

"Wait!" Thorndyke called after her.

But she didn't stop.

He ran past her and blocked her way.

"Tell me!" he cried.

"No."

"Tell me!"

"No!"

"You know you want to!"

Her mouth began to form the word *no* once more, but it never sounded. Instead she said, "How badly do you want the information?"

"I'll do whatever you say."

This brought a squeal from her. "Oh, my dear, you have no idea who you're speaking to; otherwise you'd not say that so lightly."

Though her warning was spoken in a playful tone, after what he'd just witnessed, he realized that there was an element of truth to her statement. And it frightened him.

However, the fear lasted but a moment; it was swept aside by the sparkle of her eyes, the sensuousness of her lips, and the playfulness of her voice.

"Get on your knees and plead," she said.

Thorndyke looked over his shoulder at the two magpies. They were totally absorbed in the drama that was playing out before them.

In the spirit in which it was asked, Thorndyke dropped to one knee.

"Now plead."

He again looked over his shoulder. The magpies were giggling uncontrollably.

"My lady," he said, "I implore you . . ."

"Louder."

Thorndyke made a silent plea to her with his eyes. She ignored it. He began again.

"My lady, I implore you . . ."

"Louder!"

"Lyssa!" he cried.

"I want Enid and Birdie to hear you," she said.

He cleared his throat. Fairly shouting, he said, "My lady, I implore you. Show favor on me. Grant that I would know the information I seek."

"Now kiss my hand."

She dangled a delicate white appendage in front of him.

The kiss he performed quite willingly, savoring the softness and scent of the back of her hand.

"Nicholas North," she said.

He was so caught up in the pleading and the kissing, he nearly missed the name.

She said it again. "The man you're looking for is Nicholas North. He's a baker."

"In the king's kitchen?"

"How am I to know? Must I do everything myself?"

Nicholas North, he thought, gazing at the ground. *A baker, not a lord.*

He looked up and got a faceful of sun, for Lyssa had moved. He turned to see her hurrying up the stone walkway toward the palace. Her entourage of magpies greeted her excitedly, both talking at once as they fell in step.

"When will I see you again?" Thorndyke cried after her.

If she heard him, she ignored him, leaving him in the middle of the pond garden on his knee.

The biggest grin of his life stretched wide his face. "What a day!" he shouted. "What a day!"

A baker named North. A smuggler of Tyndale New Testaments. This man would be his stepping-stone into the confidence of the bishop of England. One of two stepping-stones. One of two. For he would also use Meg Foxe.

A shiver ran through him. This was too good to be true. Pernell Foxe's own wife somehow caught up in the very smuggling effort Pernell sought to destroy. She would be his key to remove Pernell from the scene.

He rose to his feet with such excitement, he leaped. A whoop sounded across the garden. If Lyssa was correct, she would soon be the favorite of the next queen. And if only half of this new information was true, he would be the favorite of the bishop. This was more than he could ever have hoped for!

But this time he would be cautious. He'd learned his lesson from the Northrup fiasco. He'd do his research. He'd find out all about this baker and Pernell's wife. Then when the time was right, he'd spring the trap of all traps.

With one final whoop Thorndyke took a deep draft of fragrant air from the pond garden. His mind already working a plan of attack, he stepped spryly through the garden, completely oblivious to the sobbing kitchen servant who lay like a lump of soiled laundry on the stone steps.

Chapter 25

Meg had no way of knowing if she would ever again play the virginals for the queen or read aloud to her in the royal bedchamber. The queen's miscarriage was seen by her enemies as an opportunity to move against her. Plans were made and carried out quickly, with the full knowledge of the king.

That the king could turn against the queen surprised no one; that he did so with such speed and blatant fabrication shocked even the staunchest enemies of Anne Boleyn.

The palace was bedlam as winds of rumor, suspicion, accusation, and intrigue blew through the palace hallways. Normal activities were swept aside, including Meg's tutoring duties and virginals playing, as thoughts of daily service gave way to thoughts of how to weather the approaching storm.

Her services at the moment no longer required, Meg found herself falling back into her previous household routine. As for news about the queen's fate, she had to content herself with market gossip by day—which was unreliable and often in bad taste—and updates from Pernell by night.

What she heard was disheartening.

The problem at hand seemed to be, how to invent a crime that would accomplish three things—inspire revulsion for the queen, create sympathy for the king, and provide a legal basis for her death? Adultery was a convenient charge, given the queen's record of flirtation and her fascination with courtly love. However, it fulfilled only two of the three objectives. It painted the queen with scandalous colors while portraying the king as a spurned yet faithful husband. Its failing was that it wasn't high treason. Adultery didn't carry the death penalty for a queen.

Still, it was an easy foundation upon which to build, and charges were soon made against three men—Mark Smeaton, one of the queen's musicians; Sir Henry Norris, a prominent courtier; and one other. These men were quietly arrested and secretly spirited off to the Tower of London. There they were charged with being the queen's lovers.

Norris was promised a full pardon if he admitted to having criminal intercourse with the queen. Unfortunately, he proved to be uncooperative, vowing that he would die a thousand deaths rather than plead guilty to a crime he did not commit.

Smeaton, on the other hand, proved more cooperative. After two days of torture on the rack, he confessed to being the queen's lover.

A few days after the arrests, while the queen was watching a tennis match—and silently chastising herself for not placing a bet on her champion, who was winning—a messenger arrived, summoning her to present herself to the Privy Council. Upon her arrival in the council chamber, a panel of grim-faced men charged her with having committed adultery with Norris, Smeaton, and another man, who remained unnamed. She was told that Norris and Smeaton had confessed their guilt, though this was not true in the case of Norris.

The queen took the news calmly and allowed herself to be escorted to her chamber, where she was placed under guard. Her concern was more for the men than for herself. She reasoned that other queens in the past had been accused of adultery and had even been found guilty. They suffered little more than confinement. She feared nothing worse than divorce, imprisonment, or exile. The men, however, would face death.

Later that afternoon, while the queen was dining, the door opened to admit several lords of the Privy Council. They bowed. A scroll of parchment was unrolled and the queen was read an official warrant for her arrest. She was told that she was to be taken to the Tower, where she would abide at the pleasure of His Highness. Committing herself to their custody, she was conducted to her barge. It would be the last time she set foot in Whitehall Palace.

The conveyance of state prisoners to the Tower of London normally took place under cover of darkness. The queen was transported in broad daylight. It was a harrowing journey by barge down the Thames, and by the time she reached the Tower, she was distraught.

In a state of near collapse, she had to be assisted from the barge and up the steps into the Tower. She sank to her knees on the cobblestones, praying for God to help her.

It was while she was in the Tower that she first learned that the third man who was accused of having sexual intercourse with her was George Boleyn, her own brother.

These were the facts of the queen's predicament as Meg knew them when once again she was summoned to play the virginals.

It was with tentative steps that Meg crossed the drawbridge spanning the Middle Tower and the Byward Tower. She had never been to the Tower of London before. Nor had she been to Tower Hill to witness an execution. There had been no reason to go. And no desire. Until now.

The anxiety she was feeling was similar to that she felt the night she was first summoned to the palace. As long as she lived, she would never forget that awful night. Awakened in the dark. The repeated pounding at the door. Realizing she was alone, defenseless. Then the march behind two guards through the night streets of London to the palace. Believing Pernell was dead. The trip to the Tower, while made without guards and in daylight, was no less ominous.

As she crossed the drawbridge, she was filled with an apprehension of a darker kind. Those who resided behind the walls that stretched before her were leading suspended lives at best. Most of them dwelt in the shadow of impending death.

All her life Meg had heard stories of the Tower. Who in England hadn't? Built by William the Conqueror for defense nearly three centuries ago, it had been used as a citadel, a treasury, an armory, a menagerie, and a prison.

Then there were the persons associated with the Tower. William Wallace, the notorious Scottish rebel, had been imprisoned here. King Richard II hid within its walls while ten thousand peasants revolted in the London streets over his introduction of a crown tax. Edward IV held lavish courts in the Tower's town-sized rooms. And here Richard III presided over splendid celebrations for his coronation.

It was in Wakefield Tower that King Henry VI was murdered while praying between the hours of eleven and twelve o'clock on the night of May 21. And in this place the two boy princes, Edward IV's sons, heirs to the throne, were brutally murdered by assassins, smothered in their beds, their bodies hidden, never to be found.

On a more personal note, it was here, only months ago, that Pernell's colleague Sir Thomas More had been imprisoned. Housed in the Bell Tower. Executed on Tower Hill. His crime? He refused to recognize the king's marriage to Anne Boleyn. And now the queen herself was an unwilling resident behind these same walls.

Meg walked under the archway of the Byward Tower. Its sides were slotted for the portcullis, which was pulled up to allow passage. In the event of an attack or attempted escape, the huge iron grating was lowered to secure the gate. Meg had to go under four portcullises and cross two moats, and that was just to pass through the outer defenses of the Tower's land entrance.

She was stopped by warders at the Byward Tower and had to endure the winks and crude grins they exchanged while her papers were examined. For passage within the Tower walls, the guard in charge of the gate, a middle-aged man whose right eye was squinted shut, said he would escort her. He turned. She followed.

The man led her between the walls of the Outer Ward. Past the Bell Tower. Toward the Wakefield Tower. He turned left, and she followed him across tiled floors through the Garden Tower and into the Inmost Ward.

Emerging into the sunlight, Meg gasped involuntarily as the conqueror's infamous White Tower loomed before her. It was there, in its basement, that Mark Smeaton had been tortured into giving false witness against the queen.

"This way," the warder barked. His good eye looked her over suspiciously, trying to discern why she had slowed. Having assured himself that she was not signaling or plotting or in any way a threat, he proceeded. He led her to a timber-framed structure called the Lieutenant's Lodgings. This was Anne Boleyn's prison.

The warder knocked, identified himself and Meg, then stepped aside to allow her passage into the houselike structure. He didn't leave until it was clear that his responsibility for her was officially concluded.

The warder had entrusted her to an unsmiling, gaunt matron who looked as though she had no flesh on her at all; she was only a skeleton wrapped in wrinkled skin. If the woman was one of the queen's attendants at the palace, Meg had never seen her before.

"Follow me," the woman said with a voice as dry as paper.

Meg was momentarily reminded again of her first meeting with the queen at Whitehall, of how the guards led her down long corridors gilded and lined with paintings. This time it was nothing like that. Meg was led to the next room, where she saw Anne Boleyn sitting in a chair before a fire.

"Meg Foxe," the matron announced.

Only one other time had Meg seen the queen in such a pitiable condition, in her bedchamber when the pains of bearing a child had worn her down. Now her pains were of a different sort. But they had succeeded in chipping away all pretense and trappings of royalty, leaving behind a vulnerable, frightened girl.

"Meg!" the queen said. "How kind of you to come."

"Your Majesty," Meg said, bowing.

"That will be all, Altilda," the queen said to Meg's escort.

The shroud of a woman gave no sign of having heard the dismissal—no movement of the thin, lipless line that was her mouth, no nod of her skull-like head, not even a flicker of acknowledgment in her eyes. She simply turned and vanished into unknown parts of the lodging.

"Come closer," the queen said to Meg, extending both hands. "Let me look at you."

Maybe it was the trouble she was in, or maybe the setting, but there was a warm quality to the queen that Meg had never seen before.

It was attractive on her. Though her power and presence was intimidating at the palace, in the back of Meg's mind there was always an image of a little girl dressing up in grown-up clothes and playing queen.

The queen gazed hungrily at Meg. "You don't know how good it is to see a friendly face," she said. "As you can see, I've had a virginals placed in the room."

Meg followed the queen's gaze to the corner of the room, where the virginals sat on a table, just as the queen said.

"Would you like me to play for you now, Your Majesty?" Meg asked.

"That would be nice."

Meg moved obediently to the instrument. She seated herself, but before she could play the first chord, the queen interrupted her.

"While I was able to persuade my keepers to allow an instrument in my room, I fear to ask them about the other item that has become dear to both of us."

Meg knew immediately to what she was referring.

"I was hoping you would bring yours with you," the queen said.

The thought had crossed Meg's mind. Hide it in the basket as she would when taking it to the palace. But surely, she thought, the warders would want to know what she was carrying. What would they do to her if they found a New Testament in her basket?

"My apologies, Your Majesty," Meg said. "I didn't bring it with me."

The queen smiled with understanding.

"They allow me a prayer book," she said. "Which is of great comfort," she added quickly. "It's just that you were so kind to read to me in my bedchamber, and the words and your voice had such a calming effect. Given my current circumstances . . . the anxiety of it all . . . not knowing what my fate will be . . . I long for a measure of peace . . . a kind word . . ."

The woman in the chair was no longer the queen; she was a desperate soul in pain. Seeing her like this made Meg's chest heavy with sympathy.

"*'Let not your heart be troubled. Believe in God . . .'*"

Then, before she knew what she was saying, Meg said, "I know where to get another New Testament for you."

The queen's face brightened, like embers in a fireplace sparking to life. Her eyes brimmed with hope and joy.

"Do you think you could? And would you read to me? Oh, Meg, I can't tell you how desperately I need to hear words of comfort in these trying days."

"It would be my pleasure to serve you in this way, Your Majesty."

With a nod of thanksgiving, the queen repositioned herself in her chair. Closing her eyes, a smile on her face, she waited for the musical chords to wash over her and ease her pain.

Meg played all the songs that over the months had seemed to be the queen's favorites. But while her fingers moved skillfully, her mind was distracted.

What ever made her make such a promise to the queen? Getting the New Testament would be bad enough, but sneaking it into the Tower of London? What was she thinking? The more she thought about it, the more she regretted making the offer.

While she played song after song, she thought of a hundred ways to retract her offer, each one sounding like a pitiful excuse to cover her cowardice. She considered leaving and never returning again to the Tower. She could send the queen a message saying she was ill and unable to come. She could say she attempted to procure a New Testament but Pernell had succeeded in confiscating all the recent shipments.

She had just about convinced herself to withdraw her offer before she left the room, when she was haunted by a conversation.

"You can dabble in a little New Testament reading because you know that if your husband finds out, all he'll do is take your book away and slap you on the back of the hand."

Meg closed her eyes in an attempt to force the unwanted words from her mind. And the face of Nicholas North that was attached to them.

"Do you know what it's like for the rest of us?"

She didn't want to hear this again.

"All he'll do is take your book away and slap you on the back of the hand."

This is different, Meg thought.

"Joan was one who died . . . my sister. That's what awaits the rest of us should Pernell Foxe ever catch up with us."

Meg thought of the New Testament hidden in the bottom of her wardrobe. Of sitting on the edge of her bed and rejoicing in its words. She remembered wishing all England could hear those words. But those were thoughts made in the security of her bedroom.

"Do you know what it's like for the rest of us? . . . Joan. My sister. . . . That's what awaits the rest of us."

Playing the song's refrain without conscious thought, Meg gazed at the queen. She could think of no one in all England who needed to hear the words from the New Testament more.

Pernell was careful to maintain a safe distance as he followed his wife down to the wharf. He'd read the letter summoning Meg to the queen's presence at the Tower, and he had no doubt that's where she was going. But he couldn't get it out of his head that the road to the Tower just happened to pass by way of the wharf and the bakery shop on Elbow Lane.

He had offered to escort her to the Tower, but when she learned he had business at Lambeth, she declined. It was daylight, she said. Besides, what could possibly happen to her with all those warders standing about?

He conceded to her wishes, then wondered why she was so insistent upon going alone.

Minutes after she left, he followed her.

Her course was steady, her step determined. He watched as she exited Ironmonger Lane and stepped into the shopping traffic of West Cheap. While the expanse was wide, he figured there were sufficient bodies to allow him to follow her undetected. Unless of course her activities were suspicious, in which case guilt would cause her to glance over her shoulder occasionally.

He hung back. Skills honed by years of hunting heretics came into play with barely a thought. Even if she suspected him of following her, she'd never see him.

Never once did she look over her shoulder. Neither did her steps betray a secret destination. When she reached the turn to Elbow Lane, she passed it by without any visible hesitation. Not even so much as a glance.

Pernell breathed easier. He kept her in sight until she reached the drawbridge leading to Lion's Gate. Then with a contented sigh he turned back.

His thoughts turned to Lambeth and his scheduled meeting with Thorndyke. Ever since the Lord Northrup fiasco, the boy had seemed distant, reluctant to share his thoughts. He'd lost his confidence and with it the aggressiveness a hunter needed to succeed. No doubt the boy was embarrassed for humiliating Pernell in front of the bishop. Pernell would talk to the boy. Encourage him to learn from the incident, then put it in the past and press forward.

A stumble interrupted his thoughts. It was as though a stone in the street had come loose. Pernell caught his balance. He looked down. The cause of his stumble wasn't a stone but the heel of his shoe. The nails had worked loose and the heel dangled from the shoe, attached by a single remaining nail.

Pernell hobbled to the side of the road. Steadying himself against a cart, he examined his shoe. He could press the heel back in place but it wasn't going to stay. Plucking it off completely, he limped his way back across West Cheap, down Ironmonger Lane, into the house, and up the steps. He had an old pair of shoes he could wear while these were being repaired.

Sitting on the edge of the bed, he removed his shoes and tossed them to one side. Opening the wardrobe, he began rummaging around the bottom, looking for his old shoes.

His hand hit a sharp corner. He winced. A box of some sort? It was buried beneath some folded blankets and towels. Lifting them, he saw not a box but a book.

What was one of his books doing in the bottom of the wardrobe? He didn't recall placing one there, though he could have long ago and forgotten about it.

A sweet curiosity filled him. Finding a forgotten book was like finding an old friend. He reached for it, eager to be reacquainted. He lifted the cover and read the title page.

Chapter 26

With the Tower to her back, Meg headed straight for Elbow Lane. If she was going to get a New Testament for the queen, she had to do it now. If not now, she'd surely talk herself out of it.

The sun was still high as she stepped into the shadow of the lane. With the walls of the shops so high and the lane so narrow, the sun's visit was less than an hour at best each day. She felt the chill of the stone, the same chill she'd felt in the interior portions of the Tower.

With the threshold of the bakery only steps away, she still hadn't worked out in her mind how she would broach the subject of a New Testament. Especially considering that her last visit to the shop had ended on an unpleasant note. But then, where else could she get a New Testament? While she would prefer not having to talk to Nicholas again, at least she felt she could trust him.

As she entered the shop, one of her concerns vanished instantly. Nicholas was in front with the baked goods. She wouldn't have to ask for him again.

When he saw her, his face registered surprise. The pleasant kind.

"I wasn't sure if I'd ever see you again," he said.

A girl, about ten years old in Meg's estimation, was paying for a loaf of bread. Hearing the baker's words, she turned to see to whom he was speaking. A silly, girlish grin formed on her face as she hurried out the door.

Meg stood silent, still unsure how to begin.

Nicholas relieved her of her dilemma by saying, "I want to apologize for my behavior. I said some things I regret . . ."

She walked toward him. When she crossed the invisible decency barrier—society's acceptable distance separating a man and a woman in public—he stopped talking. She leaned close to him and whispered, "I'm not here for bread."

She was close enough to him that he had to lean back to meet her eyes.

"You're not?" he replied.

"No."

Meg was hoping her remark would be sufficient for him to understand what she was asking. His eyes were playful, not discerning. He didn't understand. Before making another attempt, she glanced around the shop, making sure someone hadn't slipped into the room unnoticed.

"I'm here for something else," she said.

"Oh."

Again she waited. Again he just stared at her dumbly.

"Well?" she asked.

"Well what?"

Meg sighed in frustration. Once more she leaned close to him, close enough to see the stubble of a half day's growth of whiskers on his cheeks.

"I'm here for a book," she whispered.

"A book . . ."

Either he wasn't trying, or . . .

"Ah! A book! You want a New—"

"Shh!"

Without thinking, she placed her hand on his lips to keep him from blurting out the words. Then when she felt his breath on her fingers and realized where her hand was, she pulled it back quickly and just as quickly stepped back, reestablishing an acceptable distance between them.

The grin on his face indicated he was enjoying her discomfort entirely too much.

"I understand now," he said, assuring her.

She smiled weakly at him.

He didn't move.

"Well?" she said.

"I don't have any."

"You don't have any?"

"No. I don't have any."

She studied his face. "Is this because of who—"

He laughed. "If you're asking if I think you're trying to trap me, the answer is no."

"You don't have any?"

"I really don't have any."

Meg was deflated. All this anxiety for nothing.

"Six days," he said. "I should have some in six days."

She furrowed her brow in thought. Six days. Could she wait that long? But then, what else could she . . .

Apparently, he read her expression as one of doubt or displeasure, because he said, "That's the truth. Six days. I wish it were sooner, but . . ."

"It's not that," she said. "I just don't know if I have six days."

This intrigued him. "Not have six days? You're not expecting to leave suddenly, are you?"

"It's not for me," she said, still pondering her choices.

"May I ask who?"

Meg's response was not immediate. Should she tell him? She couldn't think how the information could hurt the queen, since it was known that she had one at the palace. And if she told him who it was for, maybe he would think of a way to get one sooner.

She stepped across the invisible barrier again, leaned close to his ear, and said, "It's for the queen."

"The queen?" he fairly shouted.

Meg jumped back. "Why not step out onto West Cheap and shout it?" she cried.

"The queen?" he said again, this time softly. "Of England?" Amusement covered his face; then as quickly as it appeared, it disappeared, replaced with an expression of shocked terror when he realized what Meg was up to.

"You can't do it. I won't let you," he said. "You'll never get it past the warders."

"She needs it," Meg said simply.

"It's too risky," he said. "Do you know what they'll do to you if they catch you?"

"Look the other way," she said, using his own words against him. "Slap me on the hand."

He shook his head. "I won't let you do it. I have no book for you," he said. "Not now. Not in six days."

"I'll tell my husband about the shipment," she said.

The words came out before she could stop them. But even had she given thought to making a threat, she probably would have done it anyway.

"Go ahead. Tell him. Tell the bishop. Tell the whole palace guard. Tell the king. I'll not be part of a plan that puts you in that kind of risk."

"Fine, then," she said. "I'll take a dozen muffins."

He looked at her incredulously. "A dozen muffins," he repeated.

"You do have them, don't you? Or do I have to return in six days for them as well?"

"I have a batch in the oven," he said.

"Good. I'll be back for them within the hour."

She turned and left the shop.

Before she left the bakery shop, Meg had decided what she would do; by the time she reached her house, she was certain it was the best plan.

"Pernell?"

She closed the door behind her.

"Pernell? Are you here?"

Not taking any chances, she searched the house. When she was certain she was alone, she opened the doors of the wardrobe and sank to her knees. Moving things aside, she reached for the New Testament.

The moment she had it in her hands, something inside her confirmed that she was doing the right thing. Then just before getting up, she paused. Something didn't seem right. She scanned the bottom of the wardrobe. Everything was as it should be. Unable to identify the cause of her feeling, she stood, closed the wardrobe doors, and prepared herself to return to the Tower. If she hurried, she could still return home before Pernell.

Nicholas was waiting for her when she entered the bakery shop.

"Are my muffins ready?"

"What do you plan to do with them?"

Taking her basket from her arm, she handed it to him. "Place them in here, please," she said.

"You didn't answer my question."

"Do you always inquire of your customers what they're going to do with the wares they buy?"

"When I think they're going to do something foolish, I do," Nicholas said. He made no move to take the basket from her.

"Are you going to sell me the muffins or not?"

His answer was to fold his arms.

"Fine. You're not the only baker in London. I'll get my muffins elsewhere."

She turned to leave.

"Wait!"

She turned back. There was a look of deep concern on the baker's face. He held out his hand for the basket. After removing a cloth from the bottom, she handed it to him. No sooner did he have the basket than he inspected it.

"If you don't mind," she said, "I'm in a hurry."

"Meg, don't do this," he pleaded.

"A dozen muffins, please."

"The warders will inspect the basket," he said. "And I doubt you can bribe them with muffins."

Meg said nothing. She simply waited for him to fill her order.

Throwing up a hand in resignation, Nicholas said, "Fine. I'll get your muffins." He disappeared into the back room, returning a few moments later with the basket laden with muffins.

She took the basket from him and covered it. She reached for her purse.

"No charge for the muffins," he said.

She looked him in the eyes and saw undisguised pain. "Be careful," he said.

"Thank you."

Exiting the bakery shop, Meg set on a course toward the Tower of London.

Nicholas watched Meg leave. His heart was stone heavy. He wanted to follow her. To protect her. If necessary, to sacrifice his own freedom to ensure that she would remain safe and unharmed.

When she walked in the door, he'd wanted to say, "I'm concerned for you and I want to help you. How can I convince you that you're dealing with things that excite great passion in men, driving them beyond reason, beyond compassion. You don't know who you're dealing with. If they catch you, they'll imprison you, as if doing so proves they're right; then they'll kill you, all the while claiming that they're acting on God's behalf."

He'd wanted to plead with her, to take her in his arms and hold her so she couldn't go, to convince her to let him go on her behalf if it was that important to her.

Instead he'd said, "What do you plan to do with them?"

North slammed his hand down on the bread table, ruining three loaves.

Meg stepped from the shadows of Elbow Lane with determined resolve. She felt that the risk she was taking was justified. It wasn't as if she were carrying something degrading or disgusting. These were God's words. Powerful words. Healing words. It didn't matter whether she was delivering them to the queen of England or a street beggar; someone desperately needed this book and she was going to see that it was delivered. Or forfeit her life in the attempt.

That's what it comes down to, isn't it? she thought. *Is the book I'm carrying worth a life? My life?*

As the answer came to her, she was filled with a greater sense of purpose. Not simply to live but to live for a cause that was greater than herself. If necessary, even to die for it.

Meg felt giddy and she laughed self-consciously. She'd never thought of her life in this way before. She was on a mission. A mission of mercy to the queen of England. God willing, she would be the instrument God would use to comfort another woman's sorrow.

As she approached the Lion's Gate for the second time that day, her steps were empowered. She didn't know if it was the danger or her newfound sense of purpose, but everything seemed sharper, clearer. The odor of freshly baked muffins was stronger. She could feel the heat on her arm as it rose from beneath their covering.

Yet with all her heightened senses, she failed to see the dark figure of a man standing in the shadows of Elbow Lane, watching her as she made her way to the Tower.

Chapter 27

The squinty-eyed warder did not look happy to see Meg. He was equally displeased by the effect her presence had on his men. An attractive woman carrying fresh muffins created an unnecessary stir at the Byward Gate. Just as Meg hoped it would.

"I'm here to see the queen," she said. "Would you like to see my papers again?"

"Won't be necessary," he said gruffly. He turned on the warders gathered around them and began shouting oaths and orders. He didn't stop until he and one other warder were the only ones remaining at the gate.

Meg endured his ranting, glad that it was directed at them and not her, even though she was the cause of the man's tirade. She knew, however, that once they were gone, she would become the sole focus of his attention. Sure enough, her time came.

The warder turned his gaze on her. Whether he practiced it or it just came naturally, she didn't know, but the man's one good eye emanated enough vitriol for two.

"Will you escort me or should I go alone?" she asked. "I know the way."

"Whatcha got in the basket?" A dirty finger poked at the covering.

She raised a corner for him to see. "Muffins. The queen has asked me to bring her some."

"Has she, now?" said the warder. "What else is in the basket?"

Meg took a breath before answering. "Nothing. Only muffins." She recovered the muffins. "May I go now? I don't like to keep the queen waiting."

The warder nodded.

That was all Meg needed. She started for the Outer Ward.

"Get back here!" the warder bellowed.

Meg froze in her steps.

"You really didn't think I was goin' to let you pass, did you?" he bellowed.

She turned to him. Doing her best to appear calm—a task that grew increasingly difficult with each passing minute—she said, "You indicated that I could pass."

"Gimme the basket," he demanded. He extended his hand.

The other warder, a young man with a mustache, winced in sympathy as he watched the interaction. Meg wished it were he who was in charge and not Warder Squinty-Eye.

She handed over the basket.

Setting it on a table, the senior warder threw back the covering to reveal a fragrant mound of muffins.

"I smell cinnamon," the younger warder said with a grin.

"Who asked you?" the older man shouted. "If I want a list of ingredients, I'll ask for it. Until then keep your blowhole shut."

He started to upend the basket on the table.

Meg stared in horror. "Wait!" she cried.

The basket stopped, suspended in midair. The warder's good eye trained on her suspiciously.

Meg approached the table. Taking the covering, she stretched it out on the table. "If you must empty the basket, at least do it onto the cloth. I can't very well serve the queen muffins that have been rolled all over your filthy table, can I?"

Without answering her, the warder dumped the contents of the basket onto the table. Muffins tumbled out. One of them took a healthy bounce and fell onto the floor. The young warder reached for it, and in doing so nearly got his fingers stomped.

The boot of the senior warder thumped loudly, muffled slightly by the muffin. The warder lifted his boot to reveal a decimated muffin. The sole of his shoe bore its imprint in crumbs.

"That one's yours," he said to his younger charge. He laughed hoarsely at his own joke.

Turning his attention to the basket, he searched it with his hands as well as his eye, looking in the bottom, turning it over, then searching the bottom again. Finding nothing to arouse his suspicions, he slapped it down on the table.

"See?" Meg said. "No knives. No secret papers. Just muffins. May I go now?"

The warder ignored her. He now turned his attention to the muffins spilled on the table. He picked one up and examined it. Then he sniffed it.

"Oh!" Meg wrinkled her nose in disgust. "I can't give that to the queen now!" she complained.

The warder looked at her, then took a bite of the muffin. He chewed with crumbs dangling on his lower lip. "Mmm. Tasty," he said. He turned to the other warder. "Not poisonous." He laughed again, spraying bits of muffin across the floor.

"Those are the queen's muffins!" Meg protested.

He took another bite and reached for a second muffin.

"You're not going to handle them all, are you?"

The second muffin he placed on the bare table.

Meg cried, "That table's filth—"

His fist hammered the muffin, startling both her and the young warder. Then one by one he took the muffins, placed them apart from the pile, and pounded them.

He took a bite of the last muffin before destroying it. Now there was nothing but crumbs on the tabletop. Still chewing, he said, "You didn't really believe I was goin' to let you walk into my tower with these muffins, did you?"

The younger warder, staring at the field of muffin crumbs, said, "But there wasn't anything hidden in them."

"We know that now, don't we?" his superior said sarcastically. "They are tasty, though." As though to prove his point, he pinched some crumbs from the table and dropped them into his mouth.

Meg straightened herself in defiance. "I demand you come with me and explain to the queen what you did to her muffins!"

"Come," the warder said. He headed toward the Outer Ward.

"What about my basket?" Meg asked.

"You can pick it up when you leave," he said.

As before, Meg followed her escort down the alley of the Outer Ward, past the Bell Tower, through the Garden Tower, and to the Lieutenant's Lodgings. And as before, he knocked on the door and handed Meg over to the gaunt attendant, but not before saying, "Thanks for the muffins."

"Explain yourself to the queen," Meg demanded.

"Don't know what you're talkin' 'bout."

"The muffins," Meg said.

"Oh! Thanks. They was good." The warder laughed as he turned and strode away.

The elderly matron ushered Meg to the queen. She was standing in the sunlight beside the window when Meg was introduced. She was surprised, though pleasantly, to see Meg again.

The two of them waited until they were alone before speaking.

"Your Majesty," Meg said, curtsying.

As before, she was struck by the queen's quiet demeanor, so unlike the queen of the palace.

"Forgive me for intruding, Your Majesty," Meg said, "but I wanted you to have this."

Meg untied the back of her dress down to her waist while the queen looked on, amused.

It was awkward to reach behind her as she was doing and she struggled, but eventually was able to pull the hand-sized book from the small of her back.

She handed the New Testament to the queen.

At first the queen couldn't take her eyes off it. They glassed over with tears as she stroked the cover with the flat of her hand. Her fingers moved to the damaged upper corner.

"This is yours," she said.

"Yes, Your Majesty. I present it to you as a gift."

The queen glanced up. The look in her eyes had the emotion of a thousand thank-yous.

"If you had been caught . . . ," she said.

"The best way to get a man's attention, or to distract him, is with food," Meg said.

The queen held out a hand to Meg and led her beside the window, where there were two chairs.

"Read to me before you go," she said.

"It'll be my pleasure, Your Majesty."

That night, despite her second trip to the Tower, Meg returned home and had enough time to prepare supper before Pernell came home from Lambeth. To say he was in a surly mood would have been an understatement. He shuffled into the house as though his shoes were made of lead. His face was drawn. He looked ten years older than when she had seen him last. He looked at her with tired eyes. He said little, and when he did, he spoke as if each word had to be drawn from a deep well.

Meg thought it best not to press him regarding the events that had depleted his life's resources so. He'd tell her when he was ready. Besides, considering the secrets of her day, it was to her benefit that he didn't feel like talking. The less they talked, the less lying she'd have to do.

Supper was an exercise in silence, punctuated occasionally by the thud of a knife against a cutting board, or the hollow clink of a spoon against a wooden bowl. He'd taken fewer than a dozen bites when he pushed away from the table and trudged up the steps.

With a heaviness in her chest, Meg watched him until he was gone, then busied herself with the after-supper cleanup. Pernell's condition was a strain on her emotions as well. At times like this she understood why marriage was often referred to as a yoking. Over the years they had pulled through life like two workhorses. When one grew weary, it was a burden to the other. She had seen the weight of the burden often enough on Pernell when she had one of her episodes. At such times he took up the extra burden without complaint. Tonight it was Pernell who was weary, and her turn to bear the extra burden. It was something she did dutifully.

Having finished storing the food and cleaning the bowls and utensils, Meg wiped her hands and ascended the stairs herself. When she entered the bedroom, her heart catapulted into her throat.

Pernell was on the floor, his upper half swallowed by an open wardrobe. Weeks of secrecy had set such an image firmly in her mind, and when she actually saw it, it was like touching powder to flame. An instant later rational thought caught up with her fear, and she realized how fortunate she was.

The New Testament wasn't there. It was in the queen's possession. Surely the angels had been guiding her this afternoon by insisting that she take the book to the queen immediately. Had she waited until tomorrow . . .

It took a second for the effects of her anxiety to dissipate. When they did, she spoke.

"What are you looking for?"

Pernell pulled himself out of the wardrobe. He had a blanket clutched in his hand. It was one of the blankets under which Meg had hidden the New Testament.

He wasn't quick to explain himself. His tired eyes looked at her for a long moment before he said, "I have an old pair of shoes in here somewhere."

She moved toward him. "Is something wrong with your good shoes?"

His reply was to reach into his pocket. He produced the shoe's heel.

"You hobbled around Lambeth all day on that shoe? You poor dear."

If the look on his face was any indication, her words were of no comfort. But then, that was Pernell. Some men look to their wives as substitute mothers, craving their pity and consolation. Pernell was not that kind of husband.

"You're looking on the wrong side." She reached past him and extracted a worn pair of shoes. "Here they are."

She handed him the shoes and as she did, her heart sank from sorrow at the look on his face. Pernell rarely displayed emotion. Yet he was close to tears. So close that a single word or look would push him over the precipice.

The night was nearly gone and Pernell still was not asleep. He had not slept all night, having spent it listening to the gentle breathing of the woman lying next to him. He could not remember a moment when, after meeting her, he didn't love her. He loved her still.

Only she wasn't the woman he thought she was. She was a stranger to him. That was the only explanation he could come up with. Something or someone had changed her. This wasn't his Meg.

His Meg wouldn't sneak around behind his back.

His Meg wouldn't hide things from him.

His Meg wouldn't possess a book that embodied everything he hated, everything he despised, everything he fought against; his Meg wouldn't allow such a book in their house, hide it in their bedroom; his Meg wouldn't soil herself with pernicious, foul heresy and then live as though nothing were different.

What kind of woman could make the beds and sweep the floors and prepare his food and pretend everything was as it had always been, while at the same time dabbling in trash and filth? What kind of woman would accept the love of her husband and then undermine everything he stood for, everything he'd worked for, everything he believed in?

Pernell felt as though he were being ripped in two. There was no one he loved more than Meg. Yet there was nothing he hated more than the heresy of Master Tyndale's New Testament.

To think of her even holding that book in her hands . . . Pernell let out a moan. He turned fitfully in bed.

A day on the rack would have been paradise compared with the day he spent agonizing over finding that book in the bottom of his wardrobe. To discover such a book hidden in his house . . . it knocked his world off center. It sent him reeling for the rest of the day. He could think of nothing else.

And tonight, after struggling all day over what to do, he'd decided to get the book from the wardrobe and confront her with it.

Only it wasn't there.

Did she know he'd found it? Maybe she had a certain way of placing it to indicate that it hadn't been discovered. Front cover up. Or down. Spine to the back of the wardrobe. Had she become that devious? Had someone instructed her? The thought infuriated him. For fifteen years this hadn't been her nature. Why now? Someone had to corrupt her, teach her these things. His Meg would never do something like this on her own.

"Are you awake?"

Her sleepy voice sounded gentle in the twilight of morning.

He grunted, not trusting himself to speak, for if a single word breached the dam, a black torrent would surely follow.

She rolled over, laying an arm on his chest. With a sleepy-warm hand she stroked his face.

For the first time in their married life, Pernell recoiled at her touch. Was that so surprising? That he would find no pleasure in having physical contact with a heretic? She didn't sense his displeasure and continued stroking his cheek with the back of her fingers. Each stroke grated his nerves more than the last.

Pernell had never felt hatred toward his wife and never thought the day would come when he would. But in that moment he hated Meg.

Chapter 28

"We know surely if our earthy mansion wherein we now dwell were destroyed, that we have a building ordained of God, an habitation not made with hands, but eternal in heaven. And therefore sigh we, desiring to be clothed with our mansion which is from heaven: so yet if that we be found clothed, and not naked. For as long as we are in this tabernacle, we sigh and are grieved for we would not be unclothed but would be clothed upon, that mortality might be swallowed up of life. He that hath ordained us for this thing, is God which very same hath given unto us the earnest of the spirit.'"

Meg lay the book in her lap and looked up. The queen stood beside the window, looking out over the East Smithfield Green. She moved sullenly to the four-poster bed dominating the room, and sat on it.

"Do you believe that?" she asked quietly.

"Believe what, Your Majesty?"

"That our mortality will be swallowed up by life."

Meg thought a moment. "It would be a cruel God indeed to promise such a thing if he were unable to bring it to pass. And I don't think God is cruel."

The queen smiled weakly.

"I thought I'd know by now," she said. "I thought I'd be dead now and past my pain." She lifted her gaze to the window, in the direction of the scaffold upon which she would die. Hastily built in front of the

Royal Chapel of Saint Peter ad Vincula, it had been finished earlier that morning.

Twenty separate offenses were listed in the queen's indictment, which was read to the Grand Jury of Middlesex. The indictment charged that Queen Anne, "despising her marriage and entertaining malice against the king, and following daily her frail and carnal lust," had procured by various base means many of the king's servants to be her adulterers. Then came a new and fatal charge. The indictment also alleged that from October 1534 the queen and her lovers had plotted the king's death. And that Anne had promised to marry one of them afterward.

Witnesses were called, among them certain ladies of the court who testified to such promiscuity on the part of the queen that it was said in court that there was "never such a whore in the realm."

When the jury of twenty-six peers was asked to render a verdict, every one pronounced the men and the queen guilty. The executioner then turned his ax toward the queen, signifying that she was condemned to die.

Meg couldn't begin to imagine the anguish the queen was feeling or how she'd endured to this point. As if the trial weren't horrible enough, the events of the last few days had been unbearably cruel for the queen.

Yesterday she was taken to the Bell Tower, whose windows overlooked the East Smithfield Green, where she was forced to watch the execution of the men found guilty of being her lovers. Each was given an opportunity to speak—she was too far distant to hear what they said—after which their sentences were carried out with dispatch. In a surprising display of compassion, the king chose not to display their heads on poles above London Bridge, as was usually the case with those executed for treason.

The queen was much shaken by their deaths, most visibly by the death of her brother.

Then this morning at two o'clock she was informed that her own execution would take place later that day. The good news, if you could call it that, was that the method of execution would not be burning at the stake but the quicker death by decapitation. Further, to ensure a swift and painless end, the king had sent to St. Omer in France for a headsman who was renowned for his experience in cutting off heads with a sword.

The queen had prepared herself by praying with her chaplain for most of the early morning hours. Soon after dawn she offered her last confession and received Holy Communion. Then the wait began.

Meg had heard from others of the poor woman's range of emotions as the time neared, from near hysteria to stoic acceptance to moments of mirth and humor. At the moment, as Meg read to her, the queen was quiet, contemplative.

It was nine o'clock. A knock was heard at the queen's door. It sent a shiver down Meg's spine. Was it time?

"Enter," the queen said.

A man Meg had never seen before appeared in the doorway. She learned later that he was the constable of the Tower. He bowed. His face was stolid. Emotionless.

"Your Majesty," he said. "I have news."

Meg's heart leaped. News at this hour could be only good news, could it not? The king had a change of heart. In mercy the queen's death sentence was to be commuted and she would be banished instead.

These were Meg's thoughts in the briefest of moments between the time the man said he had news and when he made the announcement.

"Forgive me, Your Majesty," he said, "but the headsman has been delayed on the Dover road and will not arrive until noon."

He bowed again and was gone.

The queen placed her hand to her chest. Her eyes closed. "I am sorry to hear this," she said. "I thought I would face death this morning."

Meg wanted to speak words of comfort to her, but at that moment words seemed as straw.

"I'm told there will be no pain, it is so subtle," the queen said. "I have heard the executioner is very good, and I have such a little neck." She put her hands around her neck and laughed heartily.

Meg forced a smile.

The queen gazed out the window at the scaffold. "Read to me," she said. "The words you just read. Read them again."

Opening the New Testament to the place where she'd left off, Meg read through eyes blurred with tears.

"'We know surely if our earthy mansion wherein we now dwell were destroyed, that we have a building ordained of God, an habitation not made with hands, but eternal in heaven. . . .'"

At noon there was another knock on the door and the same man appeared. This time Meg's thoughts were not fanciful enough to imagine it was good news. She steeled herself for the worst. Only the news that was delivered was worse than she imagined it would be.

"Your Majesty," the man said, "it is my duty to inform you that the headsman has still not arrived and that the event has been rescheduled for tomorrow morning at nine o'clock."

As before, the news was delivered without emotion of any kind and he was gone.

Upon hearing this news, the queen swooned. Meg was instantly at her side, catching her before she fell, assisting her to a chair.

The queen's hand gripped Meg's wrist. It was cold, devoid of fleshly warmth.

"Stay with me, please," the queen cried.

"Of course, Your Majesty."

"Through the night."

"Yes, Your Majesty."

"I fear the delay will weaken my resolve," the queen said. "It's not that I desire death . . . and I thought I was prepared to die . . . but now . . ."

Meg knelt beside the queen, holding her hand. A messenger was sent to inform Pernell and she stayed the night, alternately playing the virginals, reading, and praying with the queen of England.

At nine o'clock on Friday, May 19, 1536, there was a third knock on the door, and once again the man who had borne the earlier news appeared.

"Madam, the hour approaches," he said. "You must make ready."

Receiving the news with a nod, the queen said, "Acquit yourself of your charge, for I have been long prepared."

He then approached the queen and handed her a coin purse. "To pay the headsman," he said.

Meg was surprised at how steady was the queen's hand upon receiving the purse.

After he had gone, the queen turned to Meg. As she had seen her before at infrequent times, Meg saw not the royal queen of England but Anne the young woman. Frail. Frightened. Vulnerable.

The queen rose and retrieved the New Testament. She handed it to Meg.

"Oh, no, Your Majesty," Meg said. "It was meant as a gift to you."

"Take it," Anne said. "It will do you more good than it will me. And when you read it, pray for me."

"Thank you, Your Majesty," Meg said.

"May I make another request?" Anne asked.

"I am yours to command."

"No, this is something I wish not to command of you but to request."

"Yes, Your Majesty."

"Attend me to the scaffold."

Meg felt the blood drain from her face and limbs, making her weak. She would have readily agreed to anything but this. She didn't know if she could do this.

"You have been a great Christian comfort to me," said the queen. "And I would very much like you to be with me as I cross heaven's threshold."

"Yes, Your Majesty," Meg said.

The words were there, not the will to carry them out. While the queen of England prepared herself for execution, Meg somehow manufactured the will to accompany her.

She was one of several of the queen's ladies who followed Queen Anne Boleyn into the May sunshine. A small contingent of yeomen of the king's guard were awaiting to escort them to the scaffold. Among them was the squinty-eyed warder. Upon seeing Meg, he winked at her with his good eye.

Meg estimated the crowd around the scaffold to be in the thousands. The structure itself was draped with black cloth. Straw was strewn atop the platform.

The murmur of the crowd increased when the queen and her ladies advanced on the short walk to the East Smithfield Green. The queen walked steadily in a dark gray robe trimmed with fur. From her shoulders flowed a long white cape. There was a dazed look in her eyes, the accumulation of two sleepless nights and weeks' worth of cruel apprehension. She carried in her hands her prayer book.

Awaiting them at the scaffold was the headsman, dressed in black and hooded. He was accompanied by an assistant and a priest. At his feet was a low wooden block.

Meg stood with the ladies beside the scaffold as the queen mounted the steps. Somehow the queen managed a smile as she gazed upon the people who had come to watch her die. She asked that the signal not be given for her death until she had spoken.

Meg clutched the New Testament in her hands. She made no attempt to hide it. No one was paying any attention to her and cared even less about what she held. All eyes were on the queen atop the scaffold.

The queen addressed the crowd.

"Good Christian people, I am come hither to die, for according to the law and by the law I am judged to die, and therefore I will speak nothing against it. I am come hither to accuse no man, nor to speak anything of that whereof I am accused and condemned to die, but I pray God save the king and send him long to reign over you, for a gentler nor a more merciful prince was there never: and to me he was ever a good, a gentle, and sovereign lord. And if any person will meddle of my cause, I require them to judge the best. And thus I take my leave of the world and of you all, and I heartily desire you all to pray for me. O Lord have mercy on me; to God I commend my soul."

She then turned to her ladies. "Do not be sorry to see me die. For any harshness I have done you, I beg your forgiveness. I pray you will take comfort in my loss." She locked eyes with Meg when she said, "I admonish you to be always faithful to her whom with happier fortune ye may have as your queen and mistress."

The queen indicated she had concluded her farewells by handing her prayer book to Lady Lee, who had accompanied her onto the scaffold. She then knelt with the priest for some final prayers.

Rising, she removed her French hood to reveal a coif over her long dark hair, bound high so as not to impede the headsman, who now knelt before her and asked her forgiveness for what he must do. She granted him his request and handed him his fee. Unclasping her necklace, she knelt before the block. A blindfold was tied over her eyes.

A wave of weeping swept through the ladies assembled around Meg.

Unable to watch, Meg turned away. She buried her face against the book in her hands.

From the scaffold she could hear Anne's voice, repeating over and over, "To Jesus Christ I commend my soul: Lord Jesu, receive my soul."

There was a collective gasp from the crowd.

The guns of the Tower boomed. A signal. The queen's death. It amazed Meg how quickly a person passed from life to death. Even royalty. The woman who had both frightened and befriended her was now beyond her reach, though her influence was still very much alive.

The crowd on the East Smithfield Green dispersed quickly. Meg was among them. Finding an out-of-the-way recess in the buildings, she managed to tuck the New Testament once again into the small of her back before filing out of the Tower grounds, one of many.

She walked on legs that no longer had any feeling, guided through the street by instinct alone. A profound sense of loss weighed upon her like a shroud. Her mind was clouded with grief. She couldn't even remember how she got home, only that the door to her house was suddenly in front of her.

That night she had one of the worst episodes she could remember. All the elements were there in graphic detail.

The red tulip, which had bloomed that morning.

The bloody chicken.

The cramped quarters.

And of course the fear. The fear of Robert. Of pain. Of dying.

Hearing him calling her name, getting closer.

The cobwebs in her hair.

Her knees against her chest.

Stilling her sobs, her breath, lest he hear her and find her.

Pernell was there for her. He put his arms around her. He spoke the usual words of comfort.

They were wooden words. Was it just she or were they as hollow as they sounded? It was as if she were in the arms of a stranger.

Since the day of their marriage, never had Meg felt so frightened and alone. It seemed as though the night, the darkness, the fear, would never end.

In the royal palaces, carpenters, masons, and seamstresses set to work removing every evidence that Anne had been queen of England. Wherever her initials were displayed, they were removed. Portraits of Anne were taken down and hidden away.

Meanwhile the king called for his barge. He had himself rowed to the Strand, where Jane Seymour awaited him. There they dined. On the same day Anne Boleyn was executed, the king's betrothal to Jane Seymour was announced to the Privy Council.

Chapter 29

Kyrk Thorndyke could barely contain himself. His reluctance to act until he was certain of his information, which had earned him Lyssa's considerable ire, was about to pay much anticipated dividends. Not wanting another fiasco, he had checked and double-checked his sources, performed personal surveillance, and was now ready to make his move.

The two men stood on the grassy courtyard in front of Lambeth, between the lengthening shadows of the twin towers. The sun was low. The wind was cold, considering the time of year. It had been three days since the queen was executed.

Thorndyke had waited until now to inform Pernell so that when the report was made, it would be clear to everyone—and the bishop especially—that this was his doing and his alone.

He said, "The smuggler's name is Nicholas—"

"North." Pernell completed the sentence for him.

The word was a jagged beam that tore into Thorndyke's sails, leaving the wind rushing out of him. He had purposely withheld this information from Pernell. Was all the sneaking and skulking about for naught?

"You know?" he cried.

"He's a baker," Pernell said. "Has a shop on Elbow Lane."

Thorndyke deflated visibly.

"How did you . . . Oh! Your wife."

Now it was Pernell's turn to feel impaled. He could see Thorndyke piecing things together by the way his eyes shifted from side to side.

"She told you about the New Testament, the one she confiscated from that clubfooted scullery maid. I should have figured as much."

His conclusions were wrong, of course, but Pernell made no effort to correct him.

"I suppose you know about the shipment as well?"

"Shipment?"

Thorndyke brightened. He still might be able to salvage the recognition he craved, after all. The shipment was the key that would lock the smugglers away. And he, not Pernell, had obtained the information about it.

"Tomorrow night," he said. "Broken Wharf. From there the books will be taken to the bakery. Do you know where North hides them?"

"No."

A self-satisfied grin creased Thorndyke's face. Another key piece of information that was his alone.

"An old oven. Behind some loose bricks."

"How do you know this?"

"One of his workers."

"Volunteered the information?" Pernell asked.

"He was persuaded," Thorndyke replied.

Pernell didn't want to know any more, so he didn't ask.

Suddenly he felt very old, very tired.

"Form the guard," Pernell said. "We'll close in once the goods are delivered to the bakery."

"Why not the wharf?"

"Too open. Anything could happen. We got lucky with that fishmonger and his son. The goods could get dumped in the river. North could say he got the wrong shipment by mistake. At the bakery they're confined. We block off front and back. Plus we get all the goods. Those being delivered and any he has stored in his oven."

Thorndyke liked the plan.

"Tomorrow, then," he said.

Pernell concluded the meeting by walking away. Before, whenever he was closing in on a heretic, there was the excitement of the chase; now there was only sadness.

They sat at the table. Light streamed through the windows, framing brilliant elongated squares on the wooden floor. The houses and businesses on Ironmonger Lane being squeezed as tightly together as they were, the home was blessed with direct sunlight for only short periods during the day. Meg and Pernell were enjoying today's brief daily blessing.

Meg had cleared away the lunch dishes and was mending a pair of Pernell's pants. Pernell was hunched over an open textbook. The soft rustle of the occasional turned page was the only sound until Pernell spoke.

"I'll be going out tonight," he said without taking his attention away from the book.

"Before or after supper?"

"After."

Meg continued her stitching.

"Kyrk Thorndyke thinks he has identified another smuggling operation."

"How certain is he? You remember last time."

Pernell chuckled absentmindedly. "I think the boy learned his lesson," he said. He turned a page, sniffed, and guided his vision to the top of the next page with a finger. For a moment all was silent again as he read and Meg worked her needle.

"A local shop," Pernell said.

"Oh?"

"You might know it."

"Possibly. Which one?"

Pernell stopped reading. He looked across the table at her. "Bakery shop on Elbow Lane."

Pricked, Meg's senses jumped to attention, fully alert now. She paused to control her voice before speaking, lest it reveal her anxiety.

"On Elbow Lane?"

"Proprietor is a man named North."

She could feel his eyes on her, so heightened were her senses at the moment. *Keep stitching,* she told herself. *No matter what, keep your eyes on your work and keep stitching.* He couldn't know the effect this information was having on her—that is, unless she betrayed herself.

"You can understand why the confusion with Thorndyke's last effort."

"Certainly. North. Northrup. A misunderstanding. Or simply a word misspoken. Or misheard. Easy enough to see . . . to understand."

She was babbling, and the only way she could stop the flow of words was to press her lips tightly together.

"Do you know the place?" Pernell asked.

"The bakery?"

"Of course the bakery. On Elbow Lane. Have you been there?"

Meg hesitated for what seemed to her to be an eternity, while her mind raced at full gallop. Should she admit to having been in the shop? If she did, he might ask more questions. Which meant more decisions. Possibly more lies. A string of them. If she denied shopping there, it would be over. With a single lie. But it was a lie and she didn't want to lie. And she was taking far too long in coming up with an answer to a very simple question, and if she didn't answer him soon, and very soon, he might sense that something was wrong or that she was hiding something from him, when she had no reason to hide anything from him, at least as far as he knew; still, she didn't want to . . .

"No," she said.

Pernell returned to his book. "I thought you might have bought some bread there once or twice."

"Ouch!"

Meg stabbed herself deliberately with the needle to keep from having to lie a second time. Pernell looked up with concern, both of them focusing on the cherry droplet that formed on the tip of her finger. Meg sucked on her finger. Pernell resumed reading.

"Can't remember the last time you did that," he said.

Meg said nothing, her finger in her mouth giving her the excuse she needed.

Each returned to their projects and several pages turned lazily, enough so that Meg concluded that their conversation was finished. She set her fingers to work on stitching the pants and her mind to work on how she could get word to Nicholas. She must warn him.

"I may be late returning home," Pernell said.

"Hmm?"

"Tonight. The raid. Word is that the shipment will be picked up at nine o'clock. So the hour may be late by the time I get home."

"Oh."

"You'll be all right?" he asked.

She looked up from her mending. His eyes were set on her, brimming with concern.

"Your episodes," he said.

"Oh . . . that."

For a moment Meg lost herself in his eyes. So kind. They always had been. And so full of love. She couldn't imagine a man ever loving a woman more than Pernell loved her. How many times had he proved his devotion to her? Countless. And yet all this business with the New Testament and the queen and now Nicholas . . . it had put a wedge between them, separating them, putting him at a distance. Meg could feel it and from the look in his eyes, she knew Pernell felt it too, though she was certain he didn't know why.

"I'll wait up for you," she said.

"I'll try not to be too late," Pernell replied.

It was dark when Pernell left the house.

Meg paced the kitchen floor for ten eternal minutes before grabbing her cloak. Then, as an afterthought, she dashed upstairs and retrieved the New Testament from the wardrobe.

As she left the house, a splash of red caught her eye. Her mother's prized tulip. It was blooming.

Half walking, half running, Meg hurried down Ironmonger Lane. The night was warm. A prelude to summer.

Chapter 30

North had to force his eyes to focus on the printing on the barrels at Broken Wharf. His mind was elsewhere. On Raedmund and his son, Bink. Earlier today the church announced their sentences. They were to be burned at the stake in front of Saint Paul's.

"What are we lookin' for agin?"

A bearded face had raised up from among the sea of barrels and wooden boxes to ask the question. An older face. Hairier. With no intelligence residing in its eyes. The man was faithful. Strong. A trusted helper. But not Raedmund. And though he was sounding like Bink, not Bink.

"Joan," North said with a grin.

"Joan. Gotcha." The man snapped his fingers and dove back under, in search of barrels named Joan.

There were three of them. North and two regulars. One of them also worked at the bakery. The other, the hairy one, was a common laborer. Members of a faithful congregation of worshipers who met in secret to read Tyndale's English translation of the New Testament and to distribute it to all England, God willing. Brave men and women. Every one of them. Compassionate. Godly.

North vowed not to allow himself to get close to them, though. It hurt too much when they were captured. Like Raedmund and Bink.

"Found one!" the man with the hairy face said, a little too loudly. The sound skipped across the river and came back as an echo. He winced. "Sorry."

"Two over here," the bakery worker said in a whisper.

"Load 'em up," North said. "There should be one more." He kept searching while the two men loaded three barrels into the back of the wagon. There was room for one more.

North found the fourth barrel at the same time his hairy partner found a fifth barrel. North checked his barrel again. *JOAN* was clearly printed on the side. Each of the other four barrels was checked; each bore the name in bold block letters.

"Five," North said. "I was told four." He pondered this, then said, "Let's get them to the bakery."

"Only room for one more on the wagon."

He was right.

"Load that one up," North said, standing over the fifth barrel. "Deliver them to the bakery; then one of you come back for me."

Minutes later North watched the wagon wobble away under its heavy load, creaking as it went. He slumped down onto a crate to wait.

JOAN stared at him from the side of the barrel.

North thought of his sister and of Raedmund and Bink. A sullen mood came over him. Why was it that everyone he cared for seemed fated to die a horrible death?

Out of breath, Meg hurried down Elbow Lane. On both sides shops were dark. The street was dimly lit from the open windows of living quarters over the shops. Signs jutted out overhead, dangling on iron poles. Meg breezed beneath them until she reached the bend in Elbow Lane and the bakery shop.

Shutters on both sides of the window were drawn. Her breathing labored, she pressed an eye to the crack between them, hoping to see a glimmer of light within. There was only darkness.

She went to the door and raised a closed fist. Before knocking, she glanced up and down the lane. Family sounds, muted with distance, came from second-story living quarters. Other than that all was quiet.

Her knuckles rapped on the heavy wooden door. She waited. When no one came, she knocked again.

Two pairs of eyes watched her from the shop across the way.

"Do you know her?" Thorndyke whispered.

"Yes," Pernell replied curtly.

"Well?"

"My wife."

Thorndyke glared at him in disbelief. "You involved your wife?"

Pernell said nothing. His eyes were fixed on Meg. His jaw muscles tensed.

"You should have told me," Thorndyke objected. "I can't believe you didn't tell me."

The old man is trying to outflank me, Thorndyke fumed. He cursed himself. He should have known better. Every man for himself. That's the way it was; that's the way it would always be. Still, he couldn't help but wonder what the world was coming to when you couldn't trust a man like Pernell Foxe.

"Well? Are you going to tell me what she's doing?" he pressed. "You should know I take offense that you're involving your wife without informing me first."

"Shut up."

The sound of Meg's knocking echoed up and down the street. She thought for sure she'd wake the entire neighborhood. She considered going around to the back, though that would mean working her way through an alley with which she was unfamiliar. In the dark. Alone. At night.

She knocked again. Her best, persistent, come-to-the-door-now knock.

Time was a masher breathing heavily down her neck. If someone didn't come to the door soon, she'd have to—

The latch on the other side of the door sounded. Meg's breath caught in her throat as the door creaked open just far enough for a man's nose to poke out. She recognized the nose and the eyes behind it. It was the stocky baker.

"Are you mad?" he hissed. "We're closed."

"I must speak to Nicholas," she said.

"He's not here. Come back tomorrow." He pulled back to shut the door. Meg stopped the door with her foot.

"It's vital that I see him!" she cried.

Through the dark slit the baker's eyes examined her. He was a long time in speaking. "You're no good for him," he said.

Meg's emotions flared at the man's effrontery. She did her best to douse them with reason. There wasn't time to take offense. She had to warn Nicholas.

"I know what you're doing here tonight," she said.

The man's eyes turned serious. "Go away," he snapped. Once again he tried to shut the door; once again she stopped him.

"I must speak to him," she insisted.

"I told you he's not here. Go away!"

His tone was hard. Defensive. Bordering on fear. It was clear that words alone were not going to convince.

Reaching under her cloak, she uncovered a small book with a dented corner. She showed it to the man blocking her way.

He recognized it.

The door opened far enough for her to slip inside, then slammed shut and bolted.

Chapter 31

At Broken Wharf, North guessed it was about eight o'clock. The boys were probably unloading the barrels from the wagon about now. He expected that one of them would be returning for him in about fifteen minutes.

He stood and stretched and walked to the end of the wharf. There was little traffic along the Thames. A few lanterns bobbed in the distance.

Thoughts of the fate of Raedmund and Bink reminded him how risky this business was. He felt fortunate to have no family. No wife at home wondering if he'd return every time he stepped out of the house at night. Naturally, he was lonely at times and longed for companionship. But how could he do this and have a wife? How could he love someone, then ask her to live in the valley of the shadow of death? He couldn't do that to someone he loved.

No, it was best this way. Consider Raedmund's wife. She was hysterical over her loss, and who could blame her?

His toe hit a protruding board. The end of a plank had come loose and had warped in the sun. He pushed it down. It sprang back up. He did this perhaps a dozen times—down, up, down, up, down, up—as he waited and thought.

His heart ached over Raedmund and Bink and their family. Something had to be done. But what?

He thought he heard something. A cough.

North looked up. The road in both directions as far as he could see was empty. It must have come from the river. Sound could travel amazingly far on the water at night, especially on a night as quiet as this one.

The stocky baker led Meg through the storefront to the back room housing the ovens. Stacks of bread loaves and biscuits and muffins along the way made for lumpy, aromatic mountains on either side of them.

The back room was illuminated by two lanterns, their light insufficient for baking bread, sufficient for smuggling New Testaments. The door to the alley was open. A large wooden barrel was placed just inside the door. Two men, one hairier than the other, were wrestling a second barrel into the room.

Had it not been for the circumstances, their efforts would have provided the night's entertainment. The barrel being too heavy for them to lift, they attempted to roll it in on its rim. But the barrel rolled at an angle, while the passage through the doorway was straight. Nor was it wide enough for the barrel and a man to pass; it had to be one or the other. The two men, one on each side of the barrel and each gripping their side of the rim, rolled with the barrel, and in doing so took turns wedging each other between the barrel and the jamb.

Their efforts ceased when Meg entered the room.

"What's this?" cried the one. It was his turn to attempt to squeeze into the room between the barrel and the doorjamb.

"Who's she?" cried the hairy smuggler at the same time.

Apparently, he could do only one thing at a time. For, when asking the question, he released his grip on the barrel, and that which was tipped now became level, pinning the other man against the door.

"She was making an ungodly racket at the front door," the stocky baker explained.

"So you just let her in?" the hairy man cried. His partner was busy trying unsuccessfully to free himself.

"She knows North," the stocky baker said in his defense.

"A lot of people know North!"

"But she has this!" The baker grabbed Meg's wrist and held it up. In her hand was the New Testament.

It seemed to be explanation enough. The protest was dropped.

"Help me!" the stuck man hissed with as much breath as he could manage.

He and the hairy man attempted to tip the barrel again, but it had settled and wedged itself and him securely in place. His partner lowered his shoulder and with a couple of loud grunts attempted to shove the barrel through the door. Each attempt succeeded in moving it about an inch, until finally it was in and the stuck man was free.

"I've come to warn you," Meg said. What else could she do? She would have preferred delivering her message to Nicholas, but he wasn't there. So she directed her words to all of them, hoping that at least one would listen.

"Warn us?" the hairy man said.

"You must hurry," she cried. "They know about this shipment and they're coming for it."

"Who?" the baker asked.

Meg shook her head. "Does it matter? They'll be here at nine o'clock. You must hurry."

The three smugglers exchanged glances.

"Please believe me!" Meg cried.

"Where will we hide them if not here?" the hairy smuggler asked. His partner was busy rubbing his lower ribs where the rim of the barrel had caught him.

The stocky baker was shaking his head. "This is a decision for North. She says she wants to help, but how do we know she's not leading us into a trap? No, we wait for North."

"Agreed," said the other. "We unload the last two barrels, go get North, let him make the decision."

Meg had witnessed their unloading effort. It could take them all night to get the other two barrels through the door.

"You have to put the barrels back on the wagon," she said, "and get them away from here. There's no time."

"Nope, nope, nope," the hairy smuggler said, sure of himself now. "We don't even know who you are, lady." He assumed the posture of a philosopher which would have been comical had it not been for the circumstances. "The more you insists on doing things your way, the more suspicious we become. That's the way of things between a man and a woman. Works that way every time. This I know."

Meg looked at them helplessly. How could she convince them? And where was North? He would believe her.

Behind her, from the front room of the bakery shop, there came a thunderous sound of splitting wood and smashing timber. It sounded as though the entire front of the shop had crashed to the ground.

A small cry of fright escaped Meg's lips as she and the others whipped around in that direction.

"Hold! Everyone hold!"

The command, nearly as loud as the crash, came from the direction of the back door, from behind the hairy smuggler. Just as their heads had whipped in one direction, now they whipped back at the voice.

They didn't have time to think about fleeing, let alone make any effort to flee. Guards with lances poured in through both doors, cutting off all access to outside and freedom.

Once the guards had secured the room, two men entered.

Meg's heart failed her.

Pernell!

Beside him was a younger man. Thorndyke, she guessed. Both of them were looking at her, but it was Pernell's eyes she saw.

They held no glint of surprise, nor of questioning, as she might expect. Neither was there sympathy. She wouldn't have been surprised if she had seen disappointment in them—that would have been understandable—but there was no emotion in them at all. They were dark and fathomless. Never had she seen him look at her this way.

She felt numb. Even though she stood in the center of the illegal activity, it was as though she were seeing everything from a distance, peering at events through the wrong end of a telescope. There was only one other time when she'd experienced a situation similar to this. The day her parents had been murdered, when she found them dead on the floor and in her horror distanced herself from what she saw. She remembered thinking that the distance between her and the bodies of her parents was so great, she might never get close to another living soul again. On that horrible day it was Pernell who rescued her.

His eyes today did not look like those of a rescuer.

North eyed the road for the hundredth time.

What was keeping them?

Shoving his hands into his pockets, he walked to the land side of the wharf, to the edge of the road, and peered down it again.

Still no sign of any traffic.

They should have been back by now. He had given them plenty of time to get back to the bakery, unload the wagon, and return. More than enough time. Even for them.

He looked thoughtfully at the barrel, staring at it for a long time, as if he'd asked for its opinion and was now listening to its reply.

Turning toward the heart of the city, he set off on foot for the bakery. As quiet as this night was, the barrel should be safe at the wharf for now. When he ran into the returning wagon, he could simply hop onto it and ride back here. Chances of him and the others missing each other were slim. There was only one direct road between here and the bakery. The circumstances would have to be very unusual for them to take any other route.

His pace was brisk, his senses alert. Maybe it was his imagination but it just felt as if something were wrong. Hopefully, he'd soon see the wagon coming toward him, and the delay would be explained away with some funny story, and the knot that was growing in his stomach would disappear and be forgotten.

The sooner the better, he thought. Because with each step the knot tightened.

"All he'll do is take your book away and slap you on the back of the hand."

Wasn't that what North predicted? Meg thought, looking around. The two smugglers who had wrestled the barrel stood shoulder to shoulder, guarded by the serious ends of the guards' lances. The stocky baker stood apart. He too was closely guarded. Meg alone was without an attending guard.

Thorndyke stepped forward, taking charge. "Let's see what we've got here," he said. Motioning to two idle guards, he pointed at one of the barrels and said, "Open it."

They smashed the lid, then removed the broken pieces. The barrel was filled with wheat flour. The guards stood back, looking stupidly at Thorndyke for further instructions.

"Well, search it!" he shouted, annoyed at their dullness. "Dig into it with your hands!"

So eager were the guards to obey the order, they bumped heads as their hands dove beneath the surface of the flour. They wriggled their hands deeper and deeper into the flour until it was up to their elbows.

One of them grinned. He'd found something. Extracting his arm from the barrel, he held up a small package wrapped in hide and bound with string. It was white and dusty, as was his forearm.

"Bring it to me," Thorndyke commanded.

Trailing flour with each step, the guard handed the package to Thorndyke, who snapped the string.

Meg glanced at Pernell. He wasn't watching Thorndyke, the guard, the barrel, or the package. His eyes were fixed on Meg. His face was stone.

How desperately Meg wanted to fly to him, to throw herself into his arms, to explain herself. How she happened upon the New Testament. How she meant to deliver it to him that same day. How she happened to read a passage. How it came to mean so much to her. How it comforted her soul.

She wanted to ask him what was so wrong about reading a book that contained such wonderful and powerful thoughts, that contained the words of God. She wanted to read some of her favorite passages to him in an attempt to explain, somehow to make him see, to help him understand that the books were not of the Devil.

She wanted to listen to him explain again why he felt the books were so evil—she really did, not just because she'd been caught but because now that she'd had a chance to read the book for herself, to see what its pages contained, she sincerely wanted to learn more about it, to discuss what she read with him, and even to learn the error of her ways if that indeed was the case. But truth be told, she couldn't conceive of being wrong about the book.

Thorndyke peeled back the hide cover to reveal a book identical to the one Meg held in her hands, save for one difference: its corner was undamaged.

Pernell's young charge held up the book victoriously.

The guards cheered. Some of them pounded the wooden floor with the butts of their lances.

"Well done, men! Well done!" he said, clearly pleased with his victory and, in Meg's estimation, even more so with himself.

She had never met the man before tonight but she knew she didn't like him. He had to have some redeeming qualities for Pernell to speak so highly of him; she, however, was repulsed by the arrogant smirk plastered on his face. Lyssa probably had something to do with her attitude toward him, as well. Anyone to whom Lyssa was attracted couldn't be all good.

Thorndyke took the book and held it under the stocky baker's nose. "We have evidence enough to hang you," he sneered. "But I want North. Tell me where North is."

"What would you want with the proprietor of the shop?" the baker said. "He is not one of us. We use his shop without his knowledge."

Thorndyke struck the baker on the nose with the flat side of the book. The man recoiled. His nose began to bleed. "We have a jester in our midst!" Thorndyke mocked.

He walked over to the other two smugglers.

"Where is North?" he demanded.

The hairy one shrugged his shoulders and said, "Dunno."

The other one covered his nose with his hand.

Thorndyke brandished the book, threatening to hit the man on the nose anyway. Then he stepped back and smiled. "The rack will improve your memories," he said.

Pernell seemed oblivious to anything else going on in the room. His eyes were fixed on Meg. He had made no move nor had he said anything since he walked through the door.

Thorndyke turned to him. His very approach suggested a subservient role; however, it was clear that he was the kind of underling of whom one needed to be cautious. He was a puppy dog, but with every evidence of having distemper.

"The important thing is we got the books," he said to Pernell, displaying the New Testament as proof. "And the shop," he added.

An afterthought occurred to him. He swung around and looked at the old oven. He strode over to it and began pulling at the bricks. First at those on the corners of the oven, then working his way toward the back.

A brick moved. Then another.

With the excitement of a child opening a gift, he tossed bricks aside, revealing a two-foot-square recess.

He cursed. "It's empty," he reported to Pernell. "But we got the shipment, the smugglers, and the hiding place. I'll get North. I swear it. I'll get him."

To the guards he said, "Take them away."

He looked at Meg and amended his order.

"All except her," he said.

The guards moved to bind the smugglers for transportation.

That's when Pernell spoke. For the first time since the raid began.

"No," he said.

Though spoken softly, the single word carried enough weight and authority and cold strength to freeze everyone in their tracks.

They all looked to him. The guards. The smugglers. Thorndyke. Meg. They couldn't help but look at him. Suddenly he was larger than any of them, completely in control over everything in the room. No one dared breathe, let alone move, until he told them they could.

Pernell took two steps and he was in front of Meg.

He held out his hand.

"All he'll do is take your book away and slap you on the back of the hand."

Meg handed him the New Testament.

She looked into his eyes, hoping to see something of her husband, something of the man she loved, the man who had loved her all these years and rescued her from the edge of insanity so long ago.

But she saw nothing of Pernell in those black eyes. In fact, she saw nothing human at all.

"Take her too," he said.

Chapter 32

North's premonition didn't do the situation justice. It was worse than he feared. Coming within view of the back entrance to the bakery shop, he saw the prisoners being loaded into a cart. Guards were everywhere. There was nothing he could do.

Helplessly he watched as his three friends stepped up into the cart. Add them to the list of friends captured, North thought, along with Raedmund and Bink. Five now, in such a short time. He felt their loss keenly. He knew their fate and that pained him even more.

Then he saw Pernell. Tall. Even from a distance and in the dark he was imposing. A man to be feared. And thwarted. Somehow, God help him, Pernell Foxe had to be thwarted.

Then the greatest shock. Meg appeared.

North recognized her instantly. His first thought was disbelief. Then confusion. He wondered why she would have accompanied Pernell on such an endeavor; at no time, not even in his deepest consciousness, did he think she had betrayed him.

And then he saw her hands bound behind her back, and the guards assisting her into the back of the cart, and his worst fears were realized.

"Oh, God . . . oh, dear God, no!" he cried.

He sank to his knees. In one night he'd lost three more friends and his bakery shop, but the sight that tortured him most was that of Meg being carted away to prison.

The door closed behind Pernell, and with it his will to live. For the longest time he stood there in the house, unmoving, in the dark, the wretched book still in his hands.

All he wanted was for the pain to stop. Somehow to turn off his mind. If he could just stop thinking, shove all rational thought from his head, maybe he'd stop feeling, stop hurting.

Habit urged him to keep moving inside, light the fire, pull out a chair, rest his feet. But habit also urged him to call out to Meg and tell her he was home. To expect her to have his supper waiting for him on the table. To expect to hear her voice and feel her arms around him in greeting.

But there was no one to call. There would be no supper, no voice, no arms, no companion, because he had just locked her away in a filthy stone prison, with thieves and prostitutes and swindlers, the refuse of society.

He had feared this day would come the night he found the New Testament in the bottom of the wardrobe. He'd imagined the worst and tonight it happened. He baited her. She took the bait and felt the sting of the trap.

Why did she do it?

"No!"

He shouted the word; with all his might he shouted it. He didn't want to know how or why she had come to this. It would be like hearing the details of how one's wife was raped. And she had been raped, at least at first. Someone pressed his advantage on her weaker mind. Forced untruths on her against her will. But it was also clear to him that at some point she became a willing partner. She gave in. Believed the lies. Embraced them. Harbored them.

Enjoyed them.

He knew because she went to the bakery.

Of her own free will.

To protect the one who had violated her.

And for that he could never forgive her.

Never.

She took everything he stood for morally, ethically, and spiritually and made a mockery of it and of him. And did so publicly. Humiliating him.

But the worst . . . she broke the law. And the law without enforcement and punishment was no law at all. Anarchy. How could he turn his head? How could he enforce the law for others and not expect his very own to obey it?

"The law is not mocked!" he shouted.

With all his might he threw the book across the room, and though he couldn't see it in the darkness, he heard it hit the wall, then the floor.

He was not far behind it.

He too hit the floor. First on his knees, then on his face.

With his cheek pressed against the hard wood, he wept bitterly, for his world had come to an end. And the person he loved more than the world had betrayed him and England. To satisfy the law, she must die.

"Weeeheeeee!"

Thorndyke danced a little jig. He felt as light as a feather. With his hands on his hips, he danced full circle around the pool in the garden at Whitehall Palace.

Lyssa approached him warily, her dress shimmering in the light of the moon.

"You got my message!" Thorndyke cried. He ran to her. "And you're alone. No magpies!"

He felt her eyes assessing his sanity. It amused him.

"The message said it was urgent," Lyssa said.

"It is," he replied. "I couldn't wait until morning." His face was stretched so wide by his smile, he had difficulty reining it in to form words.

The vision of her beauty helped him. It had struck him dumb so many times before and did so again tonight. Her complexion was flawless, her lips were red, her eyes sparkled, and her raven curls formed the most exquisite frame to complete the portrait.

"By all that is heavenly, you're beautiful," he said.

Lyssa held the compliment at bay until she could determine the nature of their meeting. She probed with a question.

"I take it things went well tonight?"

"Well?" he shouted joyfully. "*Well* doesn't begin to describe it. They went great! Couldn't have gone any greater. *Stupendous* is an understatement."

This brought a pleased smile to her lips. She folded her hands demurely in front of her.

"So tell me," she said.

"We got the shipment . . . ," he said, then paused. He didn't want to blurt out the news; this news was meant to be savored, one delicious course at a time.

". . . and three smugglers . . ."

"Yes?" she said, beginning to enjoy the game.

". . . and the shop with the hiding place . . ."

"Yes?"

"And a bonus!"

"A bonus?"

He nodded his head enthusiastically. "Not just a bonus but a *bonus!*" He drew out the pronunciation of the word to emphasize it. "The bonus of all bonuses!"

His excitement was contagious and Lyssa was catching it.

"Tell me!" she squealed.

He started to say it, then held back to heighten her anticipation. It had the desired effect.

"Tell me!" she squealed even louder.

"We . . ."

"Yes?"

". . . captured . . ."

"Yes?"

". . . the old man's . . ."

"Yes?"

He held it for several counts, then, ". . . wife! We captured the old man's wife!"

"Meg Foxe?" Lyssa cried in disbelief and lack of understanding. "What do you mean you captured Meg Foxe?"

Now Thorndyke was eager to explain. "She came while we were waiting for the shipment. She came to warn them off!"

"Meg Foxe attempted to warn the smugglers?"

"Yes! And here's the best part!"

"There's more?"

"The old man set a trap for her! He suspected his own wife and he set a trap for her! He told her where the raid was and at what time, only he gave her the wrong hour so she'd think she had time to warn them!"

"I don't believe it!" Lyssa cried. But her face clearly revealed that she wanted to believe it.

"The old man made no effort to stop her from going in. And when we found her inside, there she was with one of the books in her hand!"

"This is just too delicious!" Lyssa said, clapping her hands.

"And when I ordered the guards to arrest the smugglers, I instructed them to leave her alone. And Pernell Foxe said,"—Thorndyke stood tall to mimic Pernell's height and spoke in a deep voice to mimic his speech—"'Take her away. She's one of them too!'"

"Ooh, I can't wait to tell Enid and Birdie!"

"Do you understand what that means?" Thorndyke cried. "It totally discredits Pernell Foxe! Suddenly I'm the hero saving England from spiritual heresy! Me! I'm no longer someone's student; I'm in charge! And the bishop has told me that he is willing to reward me in a compensatory manner!"

"You spoke with the bishop?"

"We went to his residence to report immediately afterward. The bishop dismissed Pernell and then used those very words, 'a compensatory manner'!"

"Sounds like wealth and power to me!" Lyssa cried.

"And he wants me to track down the leader, North. Once I get him—"

"You can ask for just about anything!"

"Precisely!"

Lyssa was clapping her hands again. "With Lady Jane becoming queen and now this . . . ooh, it's perfect, just perfect! And no two people deserve it more than us!"

Chapter 33

Meg's trial was little more than a sentencing. The bishop informed the court that the proceedings had been expedited out of respect for Pernell's meritorious service to church and crown. Her guilt was unquestioned from the start. Her sentence was to die by burning at the stake.

Pernell was conspicuously absent. Meg counted this a blessing. It was difficult enough standing with your hands bound before a roomful of clerics and spectators, with everyone staring at you, sneering, leering, thinking the worst of you. Seeing Pernell there would have been one more burden, because she knew that her shame was his humiliation.

She hadn't seen him since the night in the bakery shop.

Prominent by their presence were Lyssa, Enid, and Birdie. Cheerful. Excited. Carefree. Talkative. They dressed as though the trial were the social event of the spring. Lyssa in particular caught Meg's eye whenever possible and smirked.

Sentencing was almost a relief in that it was an end to the public ordeal. As filthy as her prison cell was, Meg longed to retreat to its privacy. At least on the day of execution the flames would make short work of her, and for that she would be grateful.

She desperately wanted to see Pernell at least once more before she died, but not at her execution. She prayed he wouldn't come to her execution.

Knowing that she would die held little meaning for Meg. The instant Pernell had walked into the bakery, her existence was split in two. It was as though she were both awake and dreaming at the same time.

The night of her arrest, the trial, her impending execution—these things were part of her dream existence. None of them seemed rooted in reality. She walked through these events with a sense of emotional detachment.

Then there was the reality of her existence. Her prison cell. The stone's coldness penetrated her clothing and flesh with a chill that went as deep as her bone and marrow. The stone's hardness pained her joints, making sleep impossible. The straw that was meant to provide a measure of comfort was soiled, stinking, and home for a variety of vermin. The women with whom she shared the space were as hard and crude as the cell. They acted like animals, fighting over food and living space. One night Meg awoke to find a black-toothed crone standing over her, tugging at her cloak, trying to steal it while it was still wrapped around her shoulders.

There were moments, lucid moments, when she remembered how she used to wonder how Queen Anne felt as the hour of her death approached. She wondered no more.

Meg would sit apart from the others, her back against the stone wall, trying her best to remember the substance of the passages she had read to the queen. However, her memory was faulty and she retained only bits and pieces.

How she wished she were allowed to have a New Testament in these her last days on earth. What would it hurt? It had already been determined that she would pay the price for it.

With each passing day she felt a greater need for it. Her soul was becoming as infested with doubt and hopelessness as were her garments with vermin. So when she was informed by a guard that Pernell had come to visit her, she felt flush with excitement.

The visiting area was no more than a stone box roughly ten feet by ten feet. A square block of sky capped the room. On clear days the sky's blue color pulsed with vibrancy and infused the box with a patch of freedom and a desperately needed reminder of happier days, but on cloudy days, such as today, the sky was just another foreboding gray wall, filling the stone container with swirling, bone-chilling wind.

The area had a single entrance, guarded on both sides of the heavy door. Pernell was inside the stone box, waiting for her, when Meg was escorted in.

Breaking free from the guard who held her by the arm, she ran to him, throwing herself against his chest, wrapping her arms around him.

She might just as well have been hugging a stone pillar. Pernell was solid and stiff and unyielding. The only indication that he was human was the warmth of his body as a cold wind off the river encircled them.

Meg clung to him. She began to weep. But neither her passion nor her tears could dissolve his monolithic demeanor. She looked up at him. His eyes—those same black, fathomless eyes she had seen in the bakery shop—stared straight forward, fixed on the guard at the door.

He moved his hands to her shoulders. Large, hard, uncaring hands. Not the same hands that had held her at night in the warmth of their bed, calming her when she was frightened, stroking her cheek with assurance that everything was going to be all right. These hands pulled her off him and set her at a distance.

The wet, frigid wind that had encircled them now came between them, reminding Meg that she stood alone.

Pernell's hands dropped to his side.

"Are you well?" he asked.

His voice held no more compassion than the guards who watched over her day and night.

She thought of the ache in her hips, her chilled flesh, the stench and vermin. "Yes," she lied.

"Good," he said.

"And you?" she asked.

"I'm well, thank you."

"Good," she said.

The wind chose that moment to interrupt by introducing a couple of tree leaves to the stone box. They chased each other around the perimeter a few times before dying atop one another in a corner.

"Can I get you anything?" he asked.

Meg glanced at the guard. "I don't think I'm allowed to have anything else."

"I suppose not."

He fixed his eyes on the guard again.

She felt something move in her hair and reached up to scratch it.

"Well . . . ," Pernell said. He stepped around her toward the exit. "I wanted to check on you, to make sure you were all right."

She pivoted, watching him depart. Was that it? He was just going to leave? With so many things unsaid? She wanted to throw herself against him and beat his chest with her fists until the real Pernell emerged.

Instead she said, "Thank you for coming."

"Yes . . . well . . ." He turned toward the guard, thought of something, and turned back.

"You know that next Saturday is . . ." He didn't finish the sentence.

" . . . is the day," she said.

He nodded. And for a moment, for just a moment, his eyes softened. They became Pernell's eyes. The eyes that had gazed upon her longingly on the day they met. The eyes that grew sad when she was sick or in pain. The eyes that had spoken love to her in ways that were too deep for words. Then, just as quickly as they had softened, they hardened again.

"I'm ready to leave," he said to the guard.

"Pernell?"

He turned back.

"I never meant to hurt you," she said.

"Yes . . . well . . ."

He signaled to the guard and was let out.

When she was returned to her cell, all Meg wanted to do was crawl into a corner and die. But the corners were privileged property, savagely protected by their occupants. And all she could do was collapse in the middle of the cell; her own arms wrapped around herself were her only comfort.

Meg's chest heaved with wave after wave of sobs.

The day of her execution couldn't come soon enough.

Saint Paul's came into view as Pernell walked home. That stony edifice that weathered atmospheric storms without and ecclesiastical storms within and yet remained as ever—steadfast, tall, faithful—as it pointed an eternal finger heavenward.

In front of the cathedral, workers were completing the scaffold for the execution. There were three poles prominent. Two others would share Meg's fate. A father and a son. Pernell had captured them in an earlier raid, though he couldn't remember their faces at the moment.

A mountain of kindling wood rose next to the scaffold.

A few curious shoppers gathered to watch the construction, but for the most part it was business as usual along the market street.

Pernell nodded to those who greeted him, though he didn't see them. He didn't see anything or anyone. To others he looked alive and healthy. But they couldn't see inside him. No one could. He forbade them entrance. For if they could, they would see a man racked with pain, reduced to the merest existence by internal suffering. Like a disease, it had eaten away all life, all hope, all purpose. The shell they saw walking around was animated by reflex only. The life that was once Pernell Foxe no longer existed.

He turned down Ironmonger Lane, hoping to keep up the charade for a few steps more. By willpower alone he made his way toward his destination. If he could just get that far, get through the door . . .

But the strength that came from habit and reflex could only take him so far, and then it ran out.

Pernell collapsed against the front door of his house. He groped for the latch and came up empty. His legs unable to support him, he slid into a sitting position.

Tears came and he couldn't stop them.

His hands shook uncontrollably.

Long legs that had served him well drew up against his chest; his arms held them there.

Up and down Ironmonger Lane neighbors, business owners, and children came out, drawn by the eerie sound of deep-throated wails. A small crowd of gawkers gathered around him.

They gazed down upon what once was a pillar of moral and ethical righteousness, now reduced to a mangle of suffering flesh whimpering his wife's name.

Beside him in a flower box was Meg's mother's prized tulip. Red and brilliant in full bloom.

He didn't know how long he lay there. After a time a measure of strength returned, and he managed to open the door and stumble up the stairs and onto the bed.

He slept.

When he awoke, it was dark. He was fully dressed, lying atop the bed. He didn't know the hour. Groping for the stand next to the bed, he lit a candle. Dim yellow light splashed the walls and furniture.

The doors of the wardrobe stood open.

How long had that wretched book been secreted away in the bottom? How many nights had he slept with it in his room? Had she made love to him knowing that it was but a few feet away?

Pushing himself up, Pernell approached the wardrobe. He shut the doors. Something on the floor of the wardrobe was spilling over the edge, preventing one door from closing. He forced the door shut. It opened slightly, almost at will. He banged the door shut. Still it didn't close. He slammed it again and again and again, pounding it with his fist and kicking it with his boot. Each time it swung back open.

Exhausted, Pernell gave up the fight.

A splash of color from within caught his eye. He opened the door. There, hanging neatly, were Meg's clothes. With a trembling hand, he ran his fingers down one sleeve, then another. Grabbing a fistful, he pulled the clothes out of the wardrobe and buried his face in them.

They smelled of Meg.

The clothes muffled the sound of his sobs.

From that night until the day of execution, Pernell Foxe resided in the guest cell of the Charterhouse, located between Smithfield and Pardon Churchyard, where plague victims and executed felons were buried.

The Charterhouse offered religious living without the taking of vows. It provided a regimen of seclusion, labor, and perpetual prayer. Behind the great oak doors, Pernell sought spiritual peace among the bay trees, ponds of carp, and rosebushes. Adorned in a robe of undyed wool, he arose at five o'clock in the morning to attend Mass, followed by a time of prayer and meditation. In the afternoon he hoed the vegetable gardens. In the evenings he attended Vespers, which was followed by three hours of prayer.

But he found no lasting peace in his retreat. Despite his prayers, he could not stop the advance of time, and the day he'd been dreading arrived all too soon.

Chapter 34

The day of Meg's execution was breathtakingly clear, as though the earth wanted to give her a good send-off. Afternoon sunlight was just beginning to stretch the shadow of Saint Paul's steeple beyond its foundation. The air was as crisp as Meg had ever tasted. But then, perhaps it just seemed that way to her because she'd been living on the fetid air of a prison.

Her hands tied behind her, she stood in a cart as she was paraded through the streets to the execution site. One of the prison guards, a burly man more than twice her weight who smelled of onions, stood beside her, gripping her arm.

The cart jostled from side to side in slow procession. On either side of the street, people lined the parade route three and four deep, shouting at her, throwing rotted food, jeering, cursing. One man held a small boy—seven or eight years old, she guessed—in his arms. He pointed at her while speaking into the boy's ear. She could imagine what he was saying.

"Take a good look, Son. That's what happens to bad women. If you stray from the path of righteousness, break the law, dabble in sorcery or heresy, you'll find yourself paraded through the city in a cart, just like her. People like her deserve what they get."

Wasn't that what they were all thinking of her? She deserves to be burned. There goes a woman who is not worthy to live in the king's England. Do not pity her. Women like her are born to shame. There is no place for them among good, honest Englishmen and women.

The familiar sound of girlish squeals caught Meg's attention.

Lyssa. Enid. Birdie.

The three shared a balcony. They giggled and waved to her. Lyssa looked especially pleased. Watching her burn would be their entertainment for the day.

The cart rounded Saint Paul's and the scaffold came into view.

"Don't look at it," the guard said. "You're better off that way."

Taking his advice, Meg looked away. But she couldn't remove from her mind what she had seen at first glance.

A long scaffold with a set of steps on each end. Three wooden pillars. Two other prisoners. Both male. They were flanked by guards who were tying them to the posts. A lone post remained. Nearest the review stand. Reserved for her.

Meg looked skyward, praying that the sea of endless blue would wash the image from her mind. She caught sight of Saint Paul's spire out of the corner of her eye. It pointed her toward God.

Yes, she thought. *Think of God. Think of heaven. Think of the things you've read in the New Testament.*

But it was humanly impossible for her to think of heavenly things while being pelted by cabbage and tomatoes and apples, and while all around her people were shouting curses, and while—even though she'd been warned not to think of it—the site of her death drew ever closer.

Meg closed her eyes, forcing herself to concentrate. But she couldn't close her ears. And with her eyes closed, the image of the scaffold burned more brightly.

"Dear God, help me," she muttered. "Help me."

Suddenly the noise around her receded. The image in her mind faded to blue. And these words sounded in her mind as though the Savior were speaking to her in a heavenly whisper:

"'Let not your heart be troubled. Believe in God and believe also in me. In my Father's house are many mansions. If it were not so, I would have told you.

"'Let not your heart be troubled . . .'"

The sounds of the crowd told him Meg's cart was coming. The shouts grew louder as it approached.

Pernell didn't look immediately. He couldn't. It would take him a few moments to muster sufficient resolve. He had to be strong.

He was standing on a raised platform reserved for officiating clerics. Beside him was the bishop, seated in a chair. Thorndyke stood nearby, obviously nervous with excitement. Pernell sensed that the boy was curious as to his reaction to seeing his wife executed—as, he assumed, was everyone else.

He determined to show them strength. Dignity. Resolve. Righteousness. Had they come to see a broken man, a man tainted by his wife's shame, they would be disappointed.

In his hands he held the offending New Testament Meg had hidden from him in their wardrobe. The bishop had granted his request that it be burned in the fire with his wife.

After sufficiently steeling himself for what he was about to witness, Pernell turned to view his wife's approach, knowing that just as many people were watching him as were watching her.

As he turned, he caught a whiff of rosemary from the sprig he kept pinned inside his doublet.

"Pernell . . ."

When Meg opened her eyes, the first thing she saw was her husband standing with the clerics. His name escaped her lips involuntarily.

He was looking at her with the same rigidity that had characterized him ever since the night of the raid. This was not her Pernell but a manufactured public image. Her Pernell was strong but tender, and passionate, though few people knew that about him. It was this Pernell whom she would remember for all eternity.

The cart came to an abrupt halt, jerking her back to the moment. The scaffold loomed in front of her. She could now more clearly see the two men who would share her date of death. One was young, the other older, possibly Pernell's age. There was a family resemblance.

Crumpled on the ground in front of them was a woman crying hysterically, holding out her arms to them, pleading for their lives. Two women, one on each side of her, attempted to console her. Their efforts were in vain.

Meg remembered North telling her about his equally futile attempt to console the wife of a fellow smuggler. Didn't he say both the husband and a son had been arrested? Could this be them?

Her arrival caught the attention of the other prisoners. They seemed just as curious as everyone else about the woman who would share their flames.

The guard guided her by the arm to the back of the cart. He jumped down first, then helped her down. She was led to the steps of the platform.

Meg remembered another set of steps. They too led to a platform, one covered with straw in which the blade of a French headsman was hidden. Meg thought of her queen on that fateful execution day.

Now it was she who was climbing the steps. It all seemed so unreal. The crowd. The scaffold, the platform upon which she would die. They were more dreamlike than real.

No, not even that substantial. For she'd had dreams on countless nights that were more vivid and real than were the steps she was now ascending. She could only hope that the flames would be equally dreamlike. For she'd been burned before. When pulling the New Testament from the flames. That burn—a slight one—had hurt for days afterward.

The thought made her chuckle. She wouldn't be feeling anything after today. She knew the thought was morbid. Still, when walking to one's death, one grabbed at anything that would break the tension.

At the top of the steps, she was now on the same level as Pernell, separated by a span of spectators at ground level. Their eyes met. A wave of remorse swept over her.

The guard pulled her away and when she swung around, she came face-to-face with the executioner. He was dressed in black, wearing a black hood that revealed dark eyes set within a circle of flesh. Meg was handed over to him. He seized her free arm before the guard released the other.

The executioner backed her against the wooden post and supervised two other men as they circled her with ropes, pulling them tight. When the executioner grunted that he was satisfied with their work, they hustled to the mound of kindling and stacked it around her.

Meg squirmed. The ropes held. It wasn't that she thought she could break free; the ropes cut into her arms and across her chest, making it difficult for her to breathe. Struggling did not help.

She glanced at the other two prisoners. The older man was still looking at her as the executioner's assistants packed the wood against her, using their feet. The younger man's eyes were closed. His head was back against the post. His lips were moving. He was probably praying.

The executioner signaled to the bishop that everything was ready. With a nod the bishop set in motion the events that would purge the church and the world of three heretics.

Everything from this point began happening quickly.

Charges were read. A simple paragraph accusing the prisoners of heresy, and serving as a warning to all who would be tempted to follow their evil example.

The bishop then commended their souls to God.

With the preamble over, the main event began.

Torches appeared from half a dozen sources. Two men for each post circled the prisoners, poking the dry kindling with fiery brands. Each place they poked came alive with flame. After starting the fires, the torchbearers left the platform.

So this was it.

Meg looked down. Four baby flames flicked their tongues at her, feeding off the wood, growing stronger, eager to taste her. She could feel their heat as the smoke stroked her cheeks. She turned her head from side to side. Smoke caught in her throat, choking her.

She looked in Pernell's direction. He was gone! A movement on the steps of the cleric's platform caught her eye. It was him. He was leaving.

If it's possible to feel relief during your execution, Meg felt it now. She didn't want Pernell's final memory of her to be a gruesome one.

Tears came to her eyes. She wished she'd been able to say good-bye to him. She lost him in the crowd, then spotted him again.

He was coming toward the platform!

Suddenly the approach of Pernell became of greater concern than the growing flames. She watched him ascend the steps. He nodded to the executioner, who nodded back.

Then he was standing in front of her. Just a few feet away. The crowd was in a frenzy. The man who had been wronged was to get his revenge. They were chanting.

"Burn! Burn! Burn! Burn! Burn!"

Meg looked into Pernell's eyes.

It was her Pernell standing in front of her.

Not the righteous heretic hunter. Not the stone-like, unfeeling visitor at the prison. Her husband stood before her, separated from her by a growing wall of flame.

As Pernell lifted his hands, she noticed he was carrying something. Her New Testament.

In a grand gesture, he turned and faced the crowd, holding the New Testament high over his head. The frenzied mob roared.

"Burn it! Burn it! Burn it! Burn it! Burn it! Burn it!"

Without expression he lowered his arms and turned once again until he was face-to-face with his wife. He held the New Testament between them.

Was he doing this to shame her? Did he want an apology?

He caught her eye.

"I have always loved you," he said above the clamor of the crowd.

"I know," Meg replied. "And I have always loved you."

A sadness crossed his face. He said, "May God watch over you." He tossed the New Testament into the flames.

The crowd went wild.

Meg began to cough from the smoke.

Reaching beneath his doublet, Pernell pulled out a knife.

Chapter 35

When Pernell descended the steps from the cleric's platform and made his way to the execution platform, he tried not to appear to be in a rush. The sight of the flames at Meg's feet strained his composure.

The crush of people proved to be more of a problem than he'd anticipated. Like ghouls, they fed on this kind of coarse entertainment, each one pressing forward to get a closer look. Pernell took every inch given to him and without any pretense of courtesy wedged his way through the crowd. By the time he reached the foot of the steps of the execution platform, he was frantic and had to compose himself before continuing.

He mounted the platform. The executioner was familiar to him. Pernell acknowledged him with a nod. By the time he stood in front of Meg, he could see that time was short. The flames were ever so close to her. The smoke was choking her. She turned her head from side to side to escape the increasing heat.

There were so many things Pernell wanted to say to her. The words had stuck in his throat when he visited her in prison, and now there was no time.

He made a show of holding up the New Testament and got the predicted response. Then he turned one last time to speak to his wife.

"I have always loved you," he said.

At that moment all sense of control abandoned him. He was a madman driven solely by his passions. Drawing a knife from beneath his doublet, shielding it from the executioner's view, he stepped into the fire.

The crowd gasped.

Without giving the flames time enough to get hold of him, he kicked a bundle of fagots into the face of the executioner.

The executioner recoiled, shielding his face with his hands. His assistants likewise ducked under the sudden barrage of flaming missiles.

The crowd fell silent, momentarily stunned at the turn of events.

The bishop was on his feet. His face registered shock and disbelief.

Pernell sent another flaming barrage in the direction of the executioner. He had to keep the man off balance. The burning faggots hit their mark but they weren't enough. Bending down, Pernell scooped up another bundle, then another, each one burning his hands, as he advanced on the executioner and his men, forcing them back. When they reached the edge of the platform, he charged.

The executioner and one assistant tumbled backward off the platform, hitting the ground with a dust-raising thud. A blow to the chest of the remaining assistant, a mere boy, sent him tumbling after them.

Pernell swung back toward Meg. His blade flashed in the sunlight as he attacked the ropes that held her. She was thrashing. Weeping. Choking.

"Pernell?" he heard her say between coughs.

The crowd was coming alive. They shouted collectively for someone to stop him, thrilled that this was turning out to be more than an ordinary execution.

With the executioner and his assistants on their backs, the only enforcers remaining were two guards, one stationed at either corner of the scaffold, at the bottom of the steps. Under normal circumstances two guards were all that was needed. The bishop hadn't figured on the staid Pernell Foxe erupting in an act of passion.

His knife slashing furiously, Pernell dispatched with the ropes quickly and Meg was free. She collapsed at his feet.

Pernell checked the guards. Initially as stunned as everyone else, they had been entangled by the sudden surge of the crowd and were now struggling to break free and reach the steps. Pernell scooped up his wife in his arms. He looked to the back of the platform.

A shout distracted him. Accompanied by the thunder of horse hooves and the screams of the crowd, a man's voice was calling his name.

"Here! Over here!"

An approaching horse-drawn cart parted the crowd as efficiently as Moses parted the Red Sea.

"Nicholas!" Meg said.

At that moment four men from the crowd leaped to the platform. A pair rushed each of the two remaining posts, the ones to which Raedmund and his son Bink were tied. It was then that Pernell realized that not one but two rescue attempts were under way.

Nicholas North reined the cart to the front of the platform. The guard closest to Meg's post was pounding up the steps, his lance in hand.

"Hurry!" North shouted.

Pernell hesitated.

North reached toward them to assist Meg into the cart. "Hurry!" he shouted again.

"I have a horse behind the scaffold," Pernell shouted.

"And I have a cart right here!" North shouted back.

"Pernell—," Meg said.

It was at that point he saw that she was clutching the New Testament in one hand. Her voice was weak and frightened.

Pernell carried her to the edge of the platform. North helped her into the back of the cart. Meg moved to one side to allow room for Pernell to jump into the cart.

He didn't.

With a sweeping motion of his arm, he shouted to North. "Go! Get her out of here!"

North had the reins in his hands.

"Pernell!" Meg shouted.

But he had already turned toward the approaching guard.

The guard was a charging boar. Thick. Hairy. The platform trembled as he rushed at Pernell, his lance lowered. Pernell was ready for him.

He stepped to one side, parried the clumsy thrust, and with a shove sent the guard sprawling.

He checked the cart's progress and was dismayed to find that it was still there. "Go, man! Go!" he shouted at North.

Meg was attempting to climb out of the cart and back onto the platform.

The guard rallied. Gaining his feet, he stumbled toward Pernell for a second attempt. The people in the crowd were beside themselves; never had they seen such entertainment at an execution.

Two rescue attempts.

An enraged bishop screaming orders from the cleric platform.

A recognized heretic hunter defending his heretic wife.

At the far end of the platform Raedmund and Bink were free. With their rescuers, they had fought back the remaining guard easily, Bink getting in some eager blows.

Pernell glanced at Meg, then checked the progress of the charging guard. It was another clumsy attempt, reflecting more stubborn duty than skill. Pernell positioned his feet to meet the charge.

This time, however, he didn't parry the lance. He stepped into it.

He doubled over as the lance pierced his stomach.

The crowd roared their delight.

As he collapsed to his knees, Pernell thought he could hear Meg screaming his name, but it was hard to single out one voice amid the cacophony of human bedlam, harder still because of the pain that exploded in his gut, and the resulting wave of unconsciousness that threatened.

He fought back the black wave long enough to take one last glance in Meg's direction. North had spurred the horses. Raedmund and Bink and their rescuers were piling into the back of the cart. From inside the cart Meg was reaching toward him. Calling his name.

Pernell couldn't hear her.

He fell to one side, his shoulder and head banging against the wooden platform. It was at that moment, believing that Meg was safe now, that he let go. His struggle was over. The transaction was complete.

"A life required. A life given," he said.

The last thing Pernell Foxe remembered was being lifted above the crowd, as though he were being carried upward in the strong arms of angels.

Chapter 36

When Meg saw Nicholas coming for her in the cart, she thought he and Pernell had conspired together to rescue her. That such a partnership existed only in the realm of fantasy didn't occur to her. But then, a woman's ability to reason is not at its best when she is tied to a stake with flames licking her legs.

With the ropes no longer holding her up, she collapsed, her legs momentarily unable to support her. She saw the New Testament on the platform, its edges charred, lying next to a tangle of burning fagots. She reached for the book and clutched it to her bosom just as Pernell lifted her in his arms.

When Pernell didn't climb into the cart with her, she was confused. Pernell shouted at Nicholas to go. She urged Nicholas to stay. Ahead, the other men had somehow escaped and were yelling for him to come get them.

"I can't wait any longer!" Nicholas shouted.

"You must!" Meg screamed.

"I can't!"

"Well, I can't leave my husband behind!"

The guard lunged at Pernell. He wasn't very good at it. It looked as if he were going to miss again.

Then Pernell did the inexplicable. He stepped into the point of the lance. Deliberately. At least that's what it looked like to Meg.

She felt rather than heard a scream erupt from within. The tip of the lance protruded from her husband's back. Her mind refused to accept that it was Pernell who was collapsing to his knees on that platform. Without thinking, for no thinking was required in such a situation, she moved toward her husband.

The cart shook beneath her feet as Nicholas urged the horses forward, knocking her off balance. She watched helplessly as the cart pulled away despite her screams, separating her from Pernell when he needed her most.

Images of that moment seared themselves on Meg's memory.

Pernell, a lance protruding from his stomach, blood on his hands and doublet, slumped to one side, motionless, the clumsy guard staring down at him, surprised at what he'd done.

And Nicholas North, shouting to his friends, handing the reins to one of them, storming back to Pernell with the others, knocking the stunned guard from the platform, picking up her husband and loading him into the cart, all the while shoving back a crowd that was now surging onto the platform like waves on the seashore.

And lastly, the receding image of an enraged bishop standing on the cleric's platform, pointing at them, shouting to no one in particular, his face as red as the Devil's.

When Pernell Foxe opened his eyes and saw scarred wooden beams instead of heaven's vaulted glory, he nearly lost his faith.

"Why am I not dead?" he croaked, despite a raw, raspy throat.

No one answered him.

He heard feet scuffling. Then a door opened and closed. Muted voices came from beyond. He couldn't make out what they were saying.

His revived senses took it upon themselves to prove to him he still lived in a world of pain and suffering. His throat was on fire. His head was bursting. His burned hands throbbed. There were no words to describe the white-hot poker in his belly. Despite the pain he shouted.

"Why am I not dead?"

He heard footsteps. Then the door. Meg came into view. She smiled down at him.

"Why am I not dead?" he asked her.

She bent low and kissed him on the cheek. Her hair fell against his cheeks. It was torture.

"Nicholas and Raedmund saved you."

"I should be dead."

She smiled. "Yes, you should be. So should I. But God has been good to us."

He turned his head. He paid dearly for it. Originating in his neck, a lightning bolt struck his brain and gut simultaneously.

"Let me die," he wheezed. "If you have any regard for me at all, you'll let me die."

Meg emerged from the makeshift shack that served as their living quarters. It was a small structure with no ceiling, within a large warehouse. It had once served as a clerk's office.

Nicholas and Raedmund stood as she approached them. They had been sitting on stools next to a bundle of blankets on the floor where Nicholas, Raedmund, and Bink slept.

"How is he?" Nicholas asked.

His concern was genuine. As was Raedmund's. It was Nicholas who had secured a surgeon to treat Pernell's wound. And Raedmund had risked recapture when he sought out an apothecary for a prescription of treacle, a highly prized drug with a mixture of rare ingredients. The drug had to be imported.

For three days Pernell suffered from alternating fever and chills while Meg, following the surgeon's orders, applied a styptic composed of egg white, gum, frankincense, and aloes, bound together with hair, to stop the seeping flow of blood from the wound. During that time Nicholas and Raedmund were her companions and support. She found them to be good men. Compassionate. Spiritual. She didn't have brothers and had never before had male friends. She discovered she liked it. At the moment, however, and through no fault of theirs, she found it difficult to speak to them.

"He wants to die," she said.

"In God's name, why?" Nicholas asked.

"If you knew Pernell, you'd know he means it," she said. "It's the way he thinks."

"He's suicidal?" Raedmund asked.

"You have to understand Pernell," she replied. "He's a man of great conviction. A man whose entire life has been based on righteousness. He says the law has been broken and demands justice."

"That's what he was doing on the platform," Nicholas said.

Raedmund was shaking his head. "I don't understand."

"He deliberately stepped into that lance," Nicholas said. "That's what he was doing on the platform. He set Meg free. In exchange he offered his own life."

"'A life required. A life given.' His words," Meg said, "spoken several times in his delirium."

"Only he didn't die," North said. "And justice goes unsatisfied."

They sat in contemplative silence for a time.

Meg feared what Pernell would do to himself. His mind had always been strong. And he was stubborn. At times his strength and his stubbornness combined and he was a formidable force. At other times they combined and he was worse than a barnyard mule.

"What do you think he'll do?" Raedmund asked.

Meg shook her head sadly. She didn't know. Her head ached. After three days she was still feeling the effects of swallowing smoke. Her throat was raw. It hurt to think, let alone try to figure out Pernell.

"He'll attempt to escape and turn himself in," Nicholas said.

"And us with him?" Raedmund asked.

"If I know my heretic hunters—and I think I do—that's exactly what he'll try to do," Nicholas said.

Raedmund stood. "I'll get Bink," he said. "We'll take turns guarding the door."

North entered the sickroom. He pulled up a chair and sat next to Pernell's bed, which consisted of wooden planks stretched between wooden crates.

"The infamous smuggler, if I'm not mistaken," Pernell said.

"The infamous heretic hunter," North replied.

Lying on his back, Pernell felt at a disadvantage. The man who looked down on him appeared genial enough, but he had already proved himself to be a lawbreaker and a scoundrel. Besides which, Pernell had every reason to believe this was the man who had poisoned Meg's mind by giving her a pernicious book.

"You should know that as soon as I'm able to walk, I'll do everything within my power to turn you over to the authorities," Pernell said.

North absorbed the warning thoughtfully, then said, "At the scaffold . . . you were trying to kill yourself."

Pernell frowned. "Meg shouldn't have told you that."

"She merely explained the reasoning behind what we all saw."

"You should have left me there to die."

"I know."

Pernell glared at him. "You mock me, sir? I wouldn't expect a man of lawlessness like yourself to understand."

"I understand enough," North insisted. "A life for a life. In a way it's noble. Do not the Scriptures say, 'Greater love than this hath no man, than that a man bestow his life for his friends'? However, in this instance I fear the sacrifice is misguided."

The quoting of Scripture caught Pernell by surprise. It angered him. "You will hold your tongue in my presence, sir," he barked. "What right do you have to quote Scripture? Have you been schooled in theology? Trained in the languages of Scripture? I warn you to be careful lest you—"

"Lest I what? Lest I draw closer to God through the reading of his Word? Lest I hide his words in my heart as a daily guide? Lest I become inspired by them? Lest I allow them to lead me to think of things that are true, honest, just, and pure? If you're warning me not to do these things, sir, you are too late."

North was on his feet and at the door.

Before leaving, he turned and said, "If I'm a heretic for loving God's Word, then let me say I'm proud to be a heretic. And if it's a crime to read the Bible in my own language, in my own country, then I stand readily condemned."

He slammed the door behind him.

Meg jumped at the sound of the door.

Nicholas stood still for a moment, collecting himself. After a time he motioned her to join him outside. That was where they all went whenever they didn't want Pernell to hear what they were saying.

"That didn't go well," he said.

"I heard."

Nicholas clasped his hands in contrition. "I shouldn't let him get to me like that," he said. "We're on opposite sides of this issue, pure and simple."

"Maybe someone should change sides," Meg said.

Nicholas stared at her in disbelief. "After all this, you think he's right? You believe I'm wrong for wanting to read the Bible in English?"

"I said one of you. It doesn't have to be you."

His eyes crinkled in thoughtful surprise. "He'd never . . . would he?"

Meg shrugged. "You knew it was illegal to read Master Tyndale's New Testament, yet you read it anyway. And after reading it, you fell in love with it. Am I right?"

Nicholas was beginning to see her point. He said, "At first I thought my sister and brother-in-law were insane for taking so great a risk."

"Yet once you started reading it . . ."

"I couldn't get enough, regardless of the risk."

"That's the way it was with me too," Meg said. "Even the queen of England found consolation in the pages of that condemned little book."

Nicholas leaned back, grinning from ear to ear. He said, "You are a remarkable woman, Meg Foxe."

She said, "The only question is how can we get Pernell to discover what all of us have discovered?"

The next day North bolted into Pernell's room, his arms loaded with books.

"What's this?" Pernell groused.

"A challenge," North replied.

Pernell turned his head to the wall.

North wasn't about to let a little thing like Pernell's inattention stop him.

"This," North said, "is a copy of Tyndale's English translation of the New Testament. Its corner is damaged and its edges are charred. Your wife cared for it enough to rescue it from the flames. At the moment it's the only one we have available to us . . ."

Pernell heard a thud, the sound of a book hitting the floor.

"This," North continued, "is a Greek New Testament. The work of Erasmus. I'm sure you're familiar with it."

Another thud as another book hit the floor.

"And this," North said, "is a Greek lexicon. You're familiar with it too."

A third thud.

"You're the professor," North said. "So teach me. I challenge you to prove to me that William Tyndale's translation of the New Testament is in error, that it is dangerous and heretical."

Pernell kept his face to the wall. He said, "I have no interest in playing tutor to an uneducated baker."

"If you succeed," North continued, "and you prove to me that Master Tyndale's translation is dangerous to England, as soon as you're able, I'll personally take you to Lambeth Palace, where I will turn myself over to Bishop Stokesley. As for you and Meg, you can do whatever your conscience dictates."

Pernell turned to face him.

"I have your word on that?"

"You have my word."

Pernell studied the man's face. He saw no hint of trickery in it.

"Where did you get the Greek New Testament and lexicon?" he asked.

"They belonged to my brother-in-law."

"He's a student?"

"He was one of your students."

"At Oxford? What was his name?"

"James."

"Such a common name . . ."

"I'm sure you remember him. Dr. More and you had his house burned to the ground. Then you locked him, my sister, and four others in the fish cellar."

"Your sister . . . she died."

"You remember," North said.

Chapter 37

On the day Pernell was well enough to take his first steps, Raedmund installed a lock on his door. Pernell didn't blame the man for doing it. If their positions had been reversed, he would have done the same thing.

He'd been able to sit up—with assistance—for nearly a week now. Yesterday he'd taken his first step, with North under one arm and Raedmund under the other. Last night the lock was installed.

As best as Pernell could determine, he'd been on his back for the better part of three weeks. During that time he'd thumbed through the books North had dropped next to his cot, but found it difficult to concentrate for any length of time. Mostly he listened to what was being said outside his room. The men and Meg seemed frank enough in their conversations. They'd be fools to think he wasn't listening.

Pernell learned that Raedmund and Bink would soon be leaving, resettling in farm country outside of York. Raedmund had a brother there. A fishmonger all his adult life, Raedmund didn't know if he'd like being a farmer.

On one day Raedmund's wife came to the warehouse. Pernell listened to an emotional scene as the woman heaped apologies on North for the way she had treated him. It was never clear to Pernell what North had done. But it was clear to him that North and Raedmund were close. Pernell understood now why North risked his life rescuing the fishmonger and his son.

Pernell also overheard sketchy plans about North's future. Nothing definite was discussed. One thing was certain, though. North could no longer stay in London and practice his trade.

A mud lark scratched in the low-tide silt. Gulls chattered overhead. The historic Thames paid them no mind as it dutifully flowed seaward, just as it had for thousands of years. The river had etched its mark on the life of every London resident since Julius Caesar had crossed it in 54 B.C. Constant. Unfaltering. Irreversible. Like time, it moved ever forward, never looking back.

Meg walked casually along the river's edge. She envied the river. Its course was set, its existence uncomplicated. Her life, on the other hand, seemed to grow more complicated every day.

Her former life stretched before her on the far side of the river. She could see Saint Paul's spire and the hustle and bustle of the market all along Cheapside. It seemed so much farther away than it actually was. Maybe because, as with the past, she knew she could never go back there. Hidden away among the tightly packed structures was a house to which she could never return, a kitchen in which she'd never again prepare food, a bed in which she'd never again sleep.

She thought of all the things she was leaving behind. None of them irreplaceable, but all convenient for living, she realized now that she didn't have them.

There was her mother's tulip bulb, though. She'd like to have that if she could.

Yet she couldn't complain. She'd been given back her life for the second time by the same man. A man she loved dearly. A man she would always love dearly. At the moment, though, they were enemies. His choice. But then, he would say it was her choice, since she was the one who brought the New Testament into the house.

Maybe he was right.

As she said . . . complicated. Why must life be so complicated?

Meg closed her eyes. She let the breeze from the river caress her face. She wished it would simply blow all the fog from her mind so she could think clearly.

"Want some company?"

Nicholas ambled up beside her.

One of her complications.

She liked him. He was Pernell's enemy. And he liked her, perhaps too much and in the wrong way. At least that's what she sensed when she caught him looking at her, which was often.

She'd be lying if she told herself she didn't feel an attraction to him. He was an exuberant man, full of life and spirit. A man who felt deeply about his beliefs. A bold man who took great risks for the things he believed in. But he also had a melancholy side. He bore deep wounds. And he was lonely. She could see it in his eyes.

He respected her contemplative mood and did not begin talking right away. Instead he bent down and picked up some pebbles and tossed them into the river, one at a time.

"How do you think he's doing?" he finally asked. Before she could reply, he added, "I ask because you've known him for years. And I imagine he acts differently when you're in there with him. I've only seen one side of him. Grumpy."

Meg smiled. She knew Nicholas well enough to recognize his style. His inquiry was sincere enough yet he felt it necessary to mask his sincerity with humor, lest anyone get the wrong idea and think he was actually concerned for Pernell.

"Physically, he's healing well enough," she replied, stating the obvious.

"And other than physically?"

"He's still Pernell, if that's what you're asking."

Nicholas winced. "I was afraid of that."

"You expected differently?"

"I was praying my challenge would change him."

"Change him?"

"Soften him. Smooth the hard edges. Blunt his desire to kill me."

The sun was descending rapidly now. It was dusk and the breeze kicked up. Meg folded her arms to ward off the chill.

"Are you certain he's reading the New Testament?" she asked.

"I think he is. Either that or he rearranges the order of the books to pass the time. But do you think it will make a difference?"

"It changed me," she said. "And it had to make a significant difference in your life; otherwise you wouldn't be doing the things you do."

Nicholas was out of pebbles. He picked up some more and resumed tossing.

"You never told me how you first came upon the New Testament," Meg said. "Did your sister introduce you to it?"

Nicholas threw a pebble and watched the ripples it produced. His face saddened. He seemed reluctant to tell her. The memory was obviously painful to him. "I was the one who showed it to her and James," he said. "So in a way I'm responsible for her death."

"I'm sorry," Meg said. "I didn't—"

"A band of players," he interrupted. "It was a band of players who first showed me the New Testament."

"Players? You were involved in theater?"

"Does that surprise you?"

"I've always thought of you as a baker."

Nicholas laughed. "Starvation forced me to reconsider the bohemian life."

"What sort of acting did you do?"

Nicholas's face came alive in such a way that Meg wondered why she hadn't seen it before. There was a presence about the man, a confidence in dealing with people, that she had always associated with players.

"As a youth, I was captivated when bands of strolling players came to town," he said. "They would present plays on the tops of wagons at inn yards. I would stand atop a barrel to see them, often neglecting my duties, for which I paid dearly later."

He rubbed his backside, causing Meg to laugh.

"I watched every performance. And not only the players but the audience as well. The commoners would gather around the stage, while the well-to-do watched from their balconies. Rich man or poor, every one of them was enraptured by the play. And I thought, here is a form of communication that can reach every man." He turned to her, his face bright. "Have you ever seen one?"

"No, my father thought players were disreputable rabble . . ."

"They are!" Nicholas cried joyfully. "Most of them anyway."

". . . and Pernell—"

Nicholas stopped her with an upraised hand. "No more explanation is necessary."

"What were you?" Meg asked.

"What was I?"

"I mean, what kind of plays did you perform? What roles did you play?"

"Brome's *Abraham and Isaac,*" he said. "A powerful presentation of the biblical event. True to the original source, at least so I'm told. I was Isaac."

Even in the dimming light she could see in his eyes that he was reliving the performance. Maybe it was the time of day, but the lighting on his face made him look dramatic.

"And Wakefield's *Second Shepherd's Play.* It was a retelling of the birth of Christ, with certain liberties ... For example, there was a racy subplot about the stealing of a sheep and its concealment in the manger."

"I'd call that a liberty," Meg said, laughing. "Did you play the role of the stolen sheep?"

Nicholas howled. It made her feel good that she was able to make him laugh.

"Then there was Chester's *Deluge,* a witty retelling of Noah and the ark. And then there was—"

"Tell me about that one," Meg said. "The Noah play."

A pleased look crossed Nicholas's face. "Noah's wife," he began playfully, "didn't want to get into the ark unless she could take her gossiping friends with her. She tells Noah that if she can't take the gossips, he can row forth where he pleases and get himself a new wife!"

"What does he do?"

"He forces her into the ark, and for saving her life he is rewarded with a slap!"

Meg laughed. "I think I know that woman!"

"The best thing"—Nicholas sobered a bit now—"the best thing about the plays is that they mix domestic situations with sacred subjects. People see themselves in the plays, and then we try to show them God. We call them miracle plays."

"And what has this to do with being introduced to the New Testament?" Meg asked.

"Well, your father was right about one thing. For the most part players are disreputable companions, and declaring something illegal attracts them to it. One lad got his hands on a New Testament and began passing it around. Like the others, I was drawn to it because of its forbidden nature. But then ... oh, the beauty of some of the passages ... the power ... I began memorizing long sections and quoting them onstage before performances."

"I'd think that would get you in trouble."

"What did the audience know? They'd never heard these words. They thought I wrote it!"

Meg laughed. "Do one for me," she said.

All of a sudden Nicholas became shy; either that or he pretended to be shy so she'd beg him to do it. If that was his plan, it worked.

"Please," Meg said. "Please ..."

"Just one," he said.

He set his gaze in the distance, staring across the Thames to prepare himself. When he spoke, his entire demeanor changed. His voice was rich, his presence commanding. His entire being became the words he spoke.

"'Though I spake with the tongues of men and angels, and yet had no love, I were even as sounding brass, or as a tinkling cymbal. And though I could prophesy, and understood all secret, and all knowledge: yea, if I had all faith so that I could move mountains out of their places, and yet had no love, I were nothing. And though I bestowed all my goods to feed the poor, and though I gave my body even that I burned, and yet had no love, it profiteth me nothing.'"

Never before had spoken words moved her as these words did. They penetrated her, resounded within her, saturating her soul and charging her emotions. By the time he finished, her cheeks were tracked with tears.

"Have you been crying?"

Pernell tried to sit up. Meg moved to help him. He waved her off.

"It's time for me to start taking care of myself," he said.

With a few moans and a lot of wincing, he managed to swing his legs over the edge of the makeshift bed and sit up. Two large hands gripped the edge of the boards as, with lowered head, he caught his breath and waited for the pain to subside. After several moments he took one final deep breath and looked up at her.

"Your eyelids are red and puffy," he said. "You've been crying."

Instinctively Meg's hand rose to her eyes, dabbing them with the side of her index finger. "Nicholas . . . ," she said.

"He hurt you?"

Pernell's anger was swift.

"No," Meg cried. "He would never hurt me. We were out by the river and he was telling me about when he was a player . . ."

"A player?" Pernell said. "That explains a lot."

"He quoted a passage to me. It was emotional. That's all."

"Players manipulate people's emotions," Pernell said. "These are the tools of convicts, sycophants, and players."

"Why must you always be so mule-headed? It was a passage from the Bible!"

Meg regretted the outburst even as she said it. But he'd angered her.

His reaction was physical. As though she'd slapped him. He said nothing.

"It was a beautiful passage," she said more softly.

Several moments of silence passed.

"Let me read it to you," she said.

A tense jaw and a hard look was his reply.

With a sigh Meg stood. Walking to the corner, she picked up a pile of blankets and arranged them on the floor beside his bed.

Aiming her voice over the walls, she said to those on the other side, "We're retiring for the night."

A moment later the door was latched and locked from the outside. Pernell reclined, pulling a blanket over his shoulders. Meg extinguished the sole candle in the room.

She fumbled in the dark, finding, then climbing beneath, the top blanket. "Good night, Pernell," she said.

There was no reply, only darkness.

Meg closed her eyes. If she thought about Pernell, she'd only get angry and wouldn't fall asleep for hours. So instead she thought about the passage Nicholas had quoted to her. It comforted her all over again.

In the darkness Pernell listened to the rhythmic breathing of his wife's slumber. He couldn't get over how much she'd changed. And though it vexed him, the change added a dimension to her character that wasn't there before. And he felt something for her he'd never felt in the past. Admiration. He'd always loved her. But he'd never admired her. This new facet of her character only made her more alluring.

Some men needed a weak woman to make them feel strong. He wasn't one of them. From the first he'd been attracted to Meg not only because of her physical beauty but because of her intelligence, her wit, and her sparkling disposition. It was the combination that made her beautiful. More than beautiful, stunning, even as the years rolled by. Meg was the kind of woman who grew more beautiful as she aged.

Yet for all her beauty, it was the person he adored.

He lived for her laughter.

He was desperate to please her.

He enjoyed life with her so much, the very thought of living without her was hell on earth. He would sooner live without arms or legs than face the daily torture of life without her. He would sooner die.

Her newfound strength only made her more attractive. Like her mother's prized tulip, she was blossoming.

As far as he knew, she hadn't had an episode since the night of the queen's execution. The woman he saw standing on the execution platform, under a barrage of abuse, minutes from a painful death, stood there with grace and dignity and personal resolve.

She was amazing.

The thing he found unsettling was that she credited the New Testament for the change. He couldn't accept that. There had to be another reason.

Chapter 38

Pernell held the New Testament with bandaged hands, intent on reading it. The act itself was illegal. When Thomas More was commissioned by the crown to refute the German heretic Martin Luther, he was granted royal dispensation allowing him to read the heretic's writings. Pernell had no such dispensation. If he opened the book to read it, under the law he would be as guilty as those who smuggled the book into England.

He ran a bandaged thumb along the charred edge of the book. It smelled of executioner's smoke.

He reasoned that should he open the book, he would be doing it for righteous motives. His intent was identical to that of Dr. More. To refute error, to prove that the translation was misleading and dangerous, and by proving this, to win back those who had been led astray by it due to their ignorance.

In this way he would finally defeat North. By convincing the man of his error—thus taking North at his word—Pernell would persuade him to cease his smuggling operation. Reason and argument were Pernell's weapons. With them he would prevail where ecclesiastical and secular authority failed.

Pernell was confident in his success, even though he knew that lawbreakers who make grandiose promises rarely keep them. When confronted, they always manage to find some rationalization to wriggle out of their oath. But what other course of action did he have, hobbled as he was?

And so it was decided.

Pernell Foxe lifted the cover of the Tyndale New Testament, and for the cause of righteousness he became himself a heretic.

"Ever since I met you, you've looked at me with a familiarity that is unsettling," Meg said.

She and Nicholas stood outside the abandoned warehouse. The morning sun glistened off the river with a brightness that promised a hot day.

He wanted to say to her, "Don't you know I would never intentionally do anything to cause you the slightest discomfort? If I have offended you in any way, my only defense is that from the day I first saw you, you awoke feelings within me that have animated and inspired my dreams."

Instead he said, "Didn't mean to unsettle you."

Meg lowered her gaze. She pulled at stray hairs in an embarrassed fashion. "I'm sure you meant nothing by it," she said.

"You're correct about one thing," he said.

She looked up.

"The familiarity."

"Then we have met before!" she cried.

"No, no . . . ," he said. "We've not met."

"Then what?"

"I've . . . ," he stammered. He thought a moment, then started again. "I've watched you from a distance. . . . No, wait, that didn't come out right."

Meg's eyes quickened.

Nicholas felt instant regret; he had to say something quickly to set things right.

"Not in a bad way," he insisted.

He wanted to say, "Dearest Meg, if only you knew how I felt about you, you'd know that I would banish myself to the netherworld before ever causing you a moment's pain."

Instead he said, "I'm making a mess of this."

Meg wasn't making it any easier for him. She folded her arms and waited. She wasn't smiling.

"My parents were Lord Culpepper's cooks," he blurted.

"The Culpeppers? You knew my first husband, Robert?" A nervous hand raised to her throat.

Nicholas nodded. "I was raised on Lord Culpepper's estate."

"You knew Robert. . . ," she repeated.

"I knew him in the way a servant knows his master."

"Then you knew of his—"

"Unstable nature?" With a grimace he nodded. "Wild, disturbing things began happening around the estate about the time he was twelve years old. The groundskeepers would find small animals that had been mutilated, not as if they'd been killed by another animal but as if they'd been killed in disturbingly twisted ways."

Meg had retreated to those horrible days. She was seeing them again in her mind. This wasn't going the way he'd planned.

"The Culpeppers?" she asked.

"Yes, they knew. The madness would come over him at certain times. Other times he was charming, witty, a gentleman. When the madness came, his parents would have the groundskeepers wrestle him into the closet. They'd lock him away until his mind returned. I once saw the inside of the closet door. He'd shredded it attempting to claw his way out."

Meg was becoming despondent before his eyes. It hurt him to see her like this. He wanted to do something to ease her pain.

"I shouldn't have told you this," he said.

"No! I'm glad you did," she said, with a voice that wasn't convincing. She placed a hand on his forearm. "I'd always wondered how much his parents knew."

Nicholas felt he'd said too much already, but now that he'd gone this far, he had to say one thing more.

"When the marriage was announced, my father spoke to Lord Culpepper; he urged him to inform your family about Robert's violent nature. He said to do any less would be cowardly and wicked."

Meg recognized the implications immediately. "He took a great risk."

"Lord Culpepper rebuked him severely but at the same time assured him that everything had been discussed openly between the families."

"But they never—"

"I know. My father learned the truth while working at the wedding. He confronted Lord Culpepper again, right there at the celebration. He threatened to tell your parents the truth about Robert himself."

Meg was aghast. "Oh, my. He dared to speak to Lord Culpepper in that manner?"

"He was a man of high principle, my father," Nicholas said. "Watching you grow up from infancy when the families got together, well . . . he took a shine to you."

"All this was going on during my wedding?"

"Quietly. Lord Culpepper summoned a few of his groundsmen. They took my father away. Whipped him. Beat him. Carted him, my mother, and me off to London and dumped us in the streets. My father never fully recovered from the blows. He was never right in the head after that. He died a year later."

"Nicholas . . ." Again she placed her hand on his arm. "I never knew . . ."

"You couldn't know."

A softness filled Meg's eyes. "I wish I could have thanked him."

Nicholas wanted to say, "It was my father's obvious love for you that made me first notice you. And it was at the wedding that, in a way, I fell in love with you too. From that day on you've been the perfect woman to me. All these years I've searched and failed to find a woman like you."

Instead he said, "So that explains the familiarity."

As best he could despite the pain, Pernell hunkered over the open New Testament. In the book's frontmatter William Tyndale had composed a foreword titled "W. T. Unto The Reader." In part it read,

> For the nature of God's word is, that whosoever read it or hear it reasoned and disputed before him it will begin immediately to make

> him every day better and better, till he be grown into a perfect man in the knowledge of Christ and love of the law of God: or else make him worse and worse, till he be hardened that he openly resist the spirit of God, and then blaspheme.

Pernell looked up from the book. It was a point he couldn't argue. Had he not lectured the very same at Oxford? That the diligent study of the biblical text would bring change in a man, whether good or ill? Had his lecture somehow contributed to the thought behind this paragraph? The difference, of course, being that he was referring to the approved Latin text and study by qualified scholars.

Yet how could he account for the change in Meg? Was she not a different person—stronger, more confident—for having read this pernicious translation? Yes, but instead of arguing for the value of a rogue translation, didn't that merely prove the power of God's Spirit? That he could take a defective translation and use it for good? Pernell grunted. That argument gave any illicit translation a value it didn't deserve. In other hands what could it do? More ill than good, he surmised.

Still, Pernell couldn't shake the thought. He leaned back, the memory of a Scripture passage rising to mind. Wasn't this equally true of the verbal proclamation of the gospel? Didn't the Apostle write, "For after that in the wisdom of God the world by wisdom knew not God, it pleased God by the foolishness of preaching to save them that believe"?

Did the same hold true for the foolishness of a language translation?

"Ah!" Pernell sat forward, struck by another thought. He winced. While the thought struck his mind, the sudden movement struck his wound. However, the pain was not sufficient to cause him to lose his thought.

But what if the translation is in such great error that it distorts the truth? Therein lies the danger! Does it not?

He returned to the text. Another thought from Tyndale's personal comments garnered his attention.

> Wherefore I beseech all who would to translate the scripture for themselves, whether out of Greek, Latin, or Hebrew.

"'Translate the Scriptures for themselves . . .'" Pernell slapped the bed. "Yes! Translate the Scriptures for themselves. Challenge accepted," he said. Raising his voice, he shouted over the walls of the room.

"North! North, get in here!"

There was a sound of approaching steps, then the door swung open. The smuggler's eyes grew wide when he saw the open New Testament. He made no attempt to hide his grin.

"I'll need a Latin and Hebrew text," Pernell said. "Also pen, ink, and paper. And a Hebrew lexicon, if possible."

An insufferable smirk formed. "I'll see what I can do," North replied.

The door closed and locked.

"Give me a day or two and I'll remove that smirk," Pernell shouted over the walls.

Three days later Pernell had a Hebrew text, a Latin text, and writing instruments. He set to work, determined to destroy the work of his former student.

He was well into the study when the sound of hushed voices interrupted him. Male voices. One was North; the other he didn't recognize. The voice was deep, scratchy, and the man spoke with a breathy pause between sentences, which themselves were abrupt.

Pernell strained to hear what was being said.

"With the tide the *King William* sails. Loading today."

"Tomorrow morning, then," North said.

"Aye. That be the time."

"I don't know. . . . It's sooner than I anticipated."

"Your decisions are your decisions. Come morning we sail."

"Understood."

"How many?" the man asked.

"Three," North said. "Possibly two."

The two men moved outside and Pernell heard no more. He set his things aside and walked quietly to the door. He tested it. It was locked.

The conversation was ominous. It might not have anything to do with him and Meg. Then again, it might have everything to do with them.

There was little he could do at the moment. But somehow he might be able to use this information to his advantage. He'd just have to remain alert.

Pernell returned to the bed. Over the last twenty-four hours he'd done little else besides study. His approach was to examine the text with an academic eye. He compared it with the Greek, then when the other books were made available to him, to the Latin and Hebrew, where applicable.

He recalled that William Tyndale had displayed a remarkable talent for languages at Oxford. The boy was skilled in seven of them—Hebrew, Greek, Latin, Italian, Spanish, German, and English. But what Pernell wasn't prepared for was Tyndale's lyrical ear for English. The rhythm of the sentences, the patterns, the weight, the stresses ... they were remarkable.

Pernell started a page of phrases that particularly impressed him, and before he knew it, he had more than two pages full of examples, with phrases such as:

the powers that be are ordained by God

signs of the times

fight the good fight

They ate, they drank, they married wives and were married, even unto the same day that Noah went into the ark.

ye of little faith

The spirit is willing, but the flesh is weak.

Eat, drink, and be merry.

A prophet has no honor in his own country.

a law unto themselves

Pernell marveled at the beauty, directness, and at times everyday immediacy of the language in the translation. How many times had he heard scholars insist that the Bible could not be translated into English, that the language was too rude to convey such lofty truths.

The work he held in his hands proved them wrong. Some of the passages were so musical that in comparison they made the Latin translation sound like stuttering.

To his chagrin, after a time Pernell found himself studying less and simply getting lost in page after page of English text. The linguistic aids lay neglected beside him as he was swept away by the clarity and the sheer power of the written Word.

CHAPTER 39

Pernell found himself squinting at the text. The light was fading. The afternoon was waning soon after it had begun.

As he rose to light a candle, it occurred to him that he hadn't heard any sound in the warehouse beyond the room for several hours. Even now it was strangely quiet.

He walked to the door and tested it. As usual it was locked. He'd checked it periodically. It wouldn't have been the first time a lapse in attention to detail had proved to be a criminal's undoing.

His hands on his hips, he assessed the walls, then stretched his midsection to determine his physical capabilities. He'd thought that once he was healed sufficiently, he might be able to use the crates and boards from his bedding to fashion an escape. The walls were high. And physically he wasn't quite there yet.

Soon. But time was running out. Would it be soon enough?

Easing himself back onto the bed, he took up the New Testament, holding the page to the candle.

A commotion arose from beyond the outside doors. Indistinct and distant at first. It caught Pernell's attention but not enough to pull him away from his reading. In the back of his mind he thought that North and Meg were returning from somewhere, possibly bringing others with them.

But the indistinct sounds grew into a definite din and then the crashing sound of wood slamming against wood, followed by shouts and pounding and chaos.

In the midst of overlapping voices came "What's this?" The next thing Pernell knew, the entire wall in which the door was placed shook convulsively with heavy blows.

The door flew open.

Guards fought each other in their rush to squeeze through the opening. The wall quivered but held.

Pernell found himself staring at the points of three lances. He recognized who the men were by their uniforms and wasn't surprised to see . . .

"Thorndyke," he said.

The young man stood in the doorway. Unlike Pernell, he was surprised. Yet pleased.

"A little pond," he said. "But a big fish."

"Talk to him," Nicholas said. "He has no future here."

In the twilight the docks were growing quiet. When they'd arrived, the place was a beehive of carts and workers and towering cranes hoisting cargo from and to the bellies of several merchant ships. Among them the *King William.*

Meg gazed at the fading pink ribbon of sky that adorned the western horizon.

"Antwerp . . . ," she mused aloud.

"Simply the destination of the ship. From there you can resettle anywhere on the continent."

"We could go north. Manchester. Edinburgh."

"But you would never be able to rest easy," Nicholas said. "You'd always live in fear that someone will discover your past and then you'd have to move again."

"William Tyndale wasn't safe in Antwerp."

North hung his head. He didn't have a response.

"Are you settling in Antwerp?" she asked.

"Germany. Worms," he replied.

"Why Germany?"

"I have an uncle there, on my mother's side. He's a printer." He glanced around. Seeing that no one was within earshot, he said, "He prints New Testaments and occasionally needs someone to make the river run, though now that I think of it, my cousin Gunther may be old enough to do that now."

"I would have thought that by now you'd have had your fill of dangerous work."

He shrugged. "Baking is boring." Then, glancing at the warehouse, he said, "Talk to your husband. Convince him that Antwerp will give him time to sort things out. We can't stay here much longer. It isn't safe."

"How do you know that once you unlock that door, Pernell won't go straight to the authorities and turn you in?"

"I don't," Nicholas replied.

"Think, Kyrk, think!" Pernell cried.

He was on his feet. The guards had backed off with their lances but remained vigilant.

"I'm being held against my will. There was a lock on the door."

"But you were in league with him at the scaffold. Working in concert to rescue three heretics."

"I was rescuing my wife. For that I'm guilty. But I was never in league with North. He just happened to show up."

"Unconvincing, Professor," Thorndyke said. "I came for North. At least now I won't return empty-handed. And won't the bishop be pleased to see you again."

"And how will the bishop feel when you tell him you've let North slip through your fingers? How many times has it been now? Three, if I'm not mistaken."

A cloud of anger passed over Thorndyke's face. He clearly did not relish the scene as Pernell described it.

"I can give you North . . ."

"In exchange for your freedom. No, Professor, you're far too valuable for me to—"

"In exchange for my wife's safety only," Pernell said. "You get North and me. Meg goes free. Think, Thorndyke. You know I want to capture North as badly as you do."

Thorndyke leaned against the doorjamb. His eyes squinted in thought.

"This is your last chance to get him," Pernell said.

Thorndyke grinned confidently. "I have my sources," he said. "He can't run from me forever."

"After tomorrow the task becomes that much harder."

Thorndyke stared at him, trying to assess if this was true.

"He's leaving England. I overheard his plans. I know where and when."

Thorndyke bit his lower lip.

"All I ask is that Meg be allowed to go free. That was my intention on the scaffold. You let her go and in return you get Nicholas North and Pernell Foxe."

Thorndyke was teetering.

"Won't the bishop be pleased," Pernell said. "And Lyssa too."

—

North was the first to notice something was wrong. Meg walked two steps forward before realizing he'd stopped and was staring open-mouthed at the riverfront warehouse.

The huge front doors were demolished. Reduced to kindling.

Meg gasped.

Running to the cavernous maw, Nicholas stared inside. It was black as pitch. Meg started to rush past him. He stopped her.

"It's too dark," he said. "Too dangerous. We don't know who or what is in there."

He searched the rubble that littered the doorway for something to use as a lantern or torch.

She shouted, "Pernell! Pernell!"

Her voice was swallowed by the darkness.

Nicholas managed to make a torch. He held it high and prepared to go in.

"Stay behind me and step where I step," he said.

She grabbed the back of his shirt and followed him in.

The place was in shambles. The floor was cluttered with smashed items—crates, chairs, desks—everything reduced to splinters. Huge holes had been punched in the side walls.

"Pernell?" Meg cried with a shaky voice.

She listened between each attempt, hoping to hear a muffled voice or moaning or groaning or something. A sound, any sound, would mean he was alive. With destruction this extensive, silence meant death.

They reached what was left of the door to Pernell's room. It had been ripped from its bottom hinge and hung at a crazy angle. It bore jagged cracks and scars from the assault.

"Dear God . . . ," Meg said.

The torch went in first, then Nicholas, then Meg.

The room was obliterated.

Meg kept an unbreakable grip on Nicholas's shirt as he explored every inch of the room by scooting the debris around with his foot.

There was no sign that Pernell had ever been there.

For over two hours they searched the inside of the warehouse. Pernell simply wasn't there.

"What do you think happened?" Meg asked.

"From the destruction, I would guess . . ." He shrugged. "I don't know."

"Do you think he's alive?"

"I don't know."

"Do you think someone has him?"

Nicholas looked at her sadly. "I don't know."

"We've got to find him!" Meg cried. "Where do we go from here?"

Nicholas wanted to say, "Meg, we don't know if he was taken or if he went willingly. We don't know if the people who took him did this or if he did this as a warning to me. We don't know if Pernell managed somehow to communicate with someone who came to free him or if they surprised him. But one thing I know. Whether we find him or not, I will give my life before I let anyone harm you."

Instead what he said was "We start by getting out of here."

Chapter 40

The day of Kyrk Thorndyke's ascension had come. On this day he would make a name for himself, and a fortune as well. In the predawn hours, he peered from his hiding place at the dark forms on the dock. A shiver of excitement ran up his spine. Like ants in a line, men were moving barrels on their shoulders from the ship's hold to waiting wagons. They did so without benefit of light.

Smugglers didn't use lights.

He scanned the docks. Somewhere, concealed in the dark shadows, Nicholas North waited to board the ship and make good his escape. Only, unknown to him, his trip would be delayed . . . for a lifetime. And he would have Kyrk Thorndyke to thank for it.

A figure caught his eye. He moved among the wagons with authority. Though his words could not be heard, men's courses changed after they encountered him.

"That would be North," Pernell whispered from behind him.

Thorndyke nodded. The guards awaited his signal as the eastern horizon grew light. This was the dawning of the day that would make Kyrk Thorndyke famous.

"My wife goes free," Pernell reminded him.

Kyrk nodded his head.

The nod was a lie. He did it to placate Pernell Foxe. Kyrk had no intention of letting anyone go free. Within days the entire city would once again assemble in front of Saint Paul's Cathedral to witness the burning of heretics. Only this time there would be no rescue. For the former rescuers would themselves be prisoners.

In his mind's eye Kyrk could see the day. There would be three poles: one for Nicholas North, one for Pernell Foxe, and one for Foxe's wife. Kyrk would sit on the cleric's platform next to Bishop Stokesley, where he would receive the congratulations of the bishop and bask in the adulation of the crowd. No doubt the king himself would reward him as defender of the faith and servant of the crown.

Naturally, Lyssa would be at his side, looking ever so lovely on his arm. He would be the envy of every man in London.

The only thing separating him from his dream was a hand signal to the guards, a signal that would set in motion the events that would change the course of his life.

Meg braced herself against the morning chill as she paced the stern of the *King William.* The crew was preparing to set sail. An impatient captain barked orders to men on the deck, belowdecks, and perched like birds in the masts.

Both captain and crew were testy. Loading cargo had taken longer than expected. A commotion had erupted farther up the dock, throwing the entire port into confusion for over an hour. If the ship didn't sail soon, it would miss the tide.

Ascending a set of steps, Nicholas approached her. "We set sail within the half hour," he said.

"I can't go. I can't leave Pernell."

Nicholas looked at her sadly. He started to argue with her, then thought better of it. "I'll debark with you," he said.

"No, you must go."

"Meg . . ."

"No, you *must,*" she insisted. "You've risked too much already. If something were to happen to you now, I wouldn't be able to bear it."

"But where will you stay? And how will you search for him? You're a fugitive. You can't just walk the streets asking questions."

Meg bit her lower lip. "I wish I knew what I was going to do but I don't. All I know is that Pernell is my husband. Twice in my life he has rescued me from death. How can I leave not knowing whether he needs me? Even if the worst happens and I'm captured again, I have to make the attempt. How can I do otherwise?"

Nicholas wanted to say, "Knowing the danger that awaits you, how can I let you go?"

Instead he said, "I understand."

Placing a hand on his shoulder, Meg leaned into him and kissed him on the cheek. "How can I ever thank you?" she said. "God placed first your father and now you as my protector, and until recently I never knew it. Now that I do, I find it hard to leave you. Will I ever see you again?"

"Our futures are in God's hands."

Meg stepped around him to leave.

What she saw made her catch her breath.

The first mate was approaching them. Beside him was . . .

"Pernell!"

"Says he's your third," the first mate said to North. "That true?"

North looked at Pernell suspiciously. He wanted to say, "I've never seen this man before. He looks dangerous, if you ask me. If I were captain, I wouldn't let him board my ship."

Instead he said, "Yes, he's our third."

Meg ran to him and encircled Pernell's neck with her arms. He winced when she bumped against his wound.

"Pernell, what happened? When we saw the warehouse, we feared the worst."

Pernell kissed his wife on the cheek. "Forgive me for the anguish I must have caused you. It couldn't be helped. Last night, after you'd gone, we had a visit from Kyrk Thorndyke."

North nodded. "That explains the destruction. And you escaped how?"

Pernell nodded toward the commotion on the docks.

"I remembered Bishop Stokesley telling me about Lord Northrup's late-night tax-evading activities. Spices and the like. I took a chance."

"Judging by the commotion, Lord Northrup was none too pleased to see your young charge again," said North.

"But how did you know about the *King William*?" Meg asked.

"I overheard the plans."

Despite the pain he felt, Pernell held Meg tightly. "There was no way to forewarn you."

The *King William* shuddered beneath their feet, then slowly began to move out into the river. The tide caught her hull and ushered her seaward.

North looked uncertainly at Pernell. "Your plans?" he asked.

"At the moment, Antwerp. After that, 'Take therefore no thought for the morrow: for the morrow shall take thought for the things of itself.'"

North's eyebrows raised. He recognized the reference as scriptural. He started to say something, then seemed to think better of it.

"Good enough for now," he said. He excused himself and went to the railing.

On the docks Kyrk Thorndyke could be seen standing opposite Lord Northrup. Both men were red-faced, shouting, their arms waving wildly. A carriage arrived, bearing Bishop Stokesley. Thorndyke and Lord Northrup rushed to the side of the carriage, both talking at the same time, looking like children in trouble pleading their case to the schoolmaster.

The *King William* slipped by unnoticed, leaving the bishop to sort through the mess.

Pernell gazed longingly in the direction of the city. In the distance Saint Paul's spire stood tall and unwavering.

"Are you going to be all right?" Meg asked.

"As long as you're by my side."

Meg smiled. "Sweet talk. You haven't talked sweet to me in a long time."

"Too long a time," he said.

Reaching into his overcoat pocket, he said, "I have something for you."

When his hand reappeared, dirt fell between his fingers onto the deck. A splash of red dangled atop a delicate green stem.

"My mother's tulip!" Meg cried.

"When chaos erupted on the docks, I was able to slip away. I went back to the house for the tulip. I figured you'd want it. It seems the two of you are destined to be together."

Meg kissed him. "I could say the same about us," she said.

He reached into another pocket. "This too belongs to you." He pulled out a hand-sized New Testament with charred edges and a damaged corner.

"Pernell . . . really?"

"I want you to keep it," he said.

She looked up at him in disbelief. "You're serious?"

"I can't say that I don't have reservations about it. But I've found it to be a faithful translation, worthy of further study. Besides, how could I deprive you of something that makes you more beautiful every day?"

Meg threw herself into his arms. The pain from Pernell's wound flashed and burned. He didn't notice it.

A Note from the Author

This is the second novel I've written that features an English translation of the Bible. The first, *Glimpses of Truth,* told the story of the impact the Wycliffe English translation had on the people who first received it in A.D. 1388. For nearly two hundred years these Bibles were used by traveling preachers called Lollards to preach God's Word to the people of England while the authorities tried unsuccessfully to stop them. This set the stage for William Tyndale's translation of the New Testament.

And what a translation it is! The Tyndale New Testament, and the portion of the Old Testament he was able to translate before he was imprisoned, became the unquestioned foundation for translations to come. Eighty-five percent of the Tyndale translation was used by the translators of both the Geneva Bible (the Bible loved by the Puritans) and the Authorized Version of 1611 (more commonly known as the King James Version).

Moreover, Tyndale's English is universally recognized for its excellence. According to a recent exhibit cosponsored by the British Library and the Library of Congress, "Contrary to what history teaches about Chaucer being the father of the English language, this mantle belongs to William Tyndale, whose work was read by ten thousand times as many people as Chaucer." The British Library described Tyndale's New Testament as "the most important printed book in the English language."

Only two complete copies of the Tyndale New Testament are known to have survived. Most were burned or used until they fell apart.

As for the story contained in these pages, here are a few historical notes.

Pernell and Meg Foxe are fictional. However, many of the people in this story, and the events in which the couple are involved, are not.

The scenes in which William Tyndale appears, the shipwreck and his capture, are historical. The events that led to his capture in Antwerp at the home of Thomas Poyntz are historical, as is the role and person of Henry Philips, who befriended Tyndale before betraying him.

The description of the New Testament, its printing in Germany, and the smuggling operation is based on reality.

King Henry VIII and the dramatic events surrounding his reign are historical, as is Whitehall, the palace in which these events occurred. Queen Anne Boleyn's relationship with her husband, her desperate desire to provide him with a male heir, her miscarriage, and the events surrounding her arrest, trial, imprisonment at the Tower, and execution are based on historical documents. Of course, Meg's relationship with the queen is fictional, though I have done my best to portray the queen in keeping with her personality. The queen's final words are a matter of record.

As surprising at it seems, Queen Anne's possession of a Tyndale New Testament and his book *Obedience of a Christian Man* are based on historical finding. That she gave the books to her husband the king is also historical.

As for the king himself, his athleticism, his love of masques, his being knocked unconscious during a jousting tournament, and his open courtship with Lady Jane Seymour even while Anne was being tried and executed is drawn from historical records. The tale the storyteller recounts in chapter 7 is an actual story that was told in Henry VIII's day.

Other historical characters involved in the story include Sir Thomas More, the great lord chancellor of England who opposed Henry VIII's marriage to Anne Boleyn and who was executed for his stand. More opposed vehemently the works of Martin Luther and William Tyndale and wrote public letters against them and their language translations.

Bishop John Stokesley and his background are historical, though his brother-in-law Lord Northrup is fictional.

Nicholas North is fictional, though his love of theater is based on the popular morality plays of the sixteenth century. Historically speaking, at the time in which this story is set, Shakespeare is standing in the wings awaiting his entrance cue.

The incident North described about the student heretics at Oxford who were locked in the fish cellar is based on an actual event.

One of the frequent tools of a writer of historical fiction is truncating time for the sake of the story. I did this in the early chapters. In reality there is a six-year gap between Tyndale's shipwreck (early 1529), during which he loses all of his Old Testament pages, and his capture (May 1535). The one notable event to occur during that gap was the crowning of Anne Boleyn as queen (1533). For the convenience of the story, I telescoped those six years.

As I researched the events surrounding the printing of Tyndale's New Testament, I was humbled and inspired by the nameless men and women who risked their lives to smuggle English-language New Testaments into their country. God knows who they are and someday their identities and stories will be revealed. Until that day this story is told in their memory.

JACK CAVANAUGH
CHULA VISTA, DECEMBER 2001